ONE HAND KILLING

Also by Nancy O'Hara

Find a Quiet Corner – A Simple Guide to Self-Peace

Just Listen – A Guide to Finding Your Own True Voice

Work From the Inside Out – 7 Steps to Loving What You Do

3 Bowls – Vegetarian Recipes from an American Zen Buddhist Monastery

Serenity in Motion – Inner Peace: Anytime, Anywhere

Zen by the Brush – A Japanese Painting and Meditation Set

An excerpt from the opening pages of *Killing Sacred*, the second book in the Alex Sullivan Zen Mystery series, follows the conclusion of this novel.

ONE HAND KILLING

An Alex Sullivan Zen Mystery

Nancy O'Hara

Published by NOH Books, New York, New York

Cover Art by Carl Graves

Book Design by Cheryl Perez, www.yourepublished.com

ISBN: 978-0-9848938-5-0

*"Nothing is as it seems,
Nor is it otherwise."*
Zen Proverb

Prologue

The uniforms had already strung the yellow tape. Alex couldn't go past the shoe room into the basement, which included the lounge. *Where is everyone? Where the hell is the dead body? And who the fuck is it?*

She spotted Muin beyond the barrier and a sigh of relief that it wasn't him swept through her. Their eyes locked. Muin spoke to the guy in blue with a Smith & Wesson 357 strapped to his hips. She was given access. *He must have played my detective card. I have to see the body before Wolfe gets here, and he's right on my tail. He'll kick me out, as he should. But this is my place and I have to see it for myself, damn it.*

Muin pointed to the boiler room. She made her way through the narrow door and into the small dark space. There the body was elegantly laid out on the floor next to the furnace. In his robes, hands clasped and resting on his belly. With a tree branch between his teeth, as if he'd been hanging on for dear life.

Her detective's mind clicked into high gear. She remembered a koan about a man in a tree. Then she noticed his freshly shaved head. He hadn't been a monk, but everyone knew it had been everything to him. *Had Roshi denied him that path forever? Did that have something to do with the returned rakusu and the line from the heart sutra? Didn't Sonja say Roshi had reconsidered? Did he kill himself?* The questions came fast and furious, and with them Wolfe.

"Who let you in here?" Wolfe growled.

Alex said nothing as she walked past him and out the door lost in thought. *How long has he been there? Was he there this morning when I stood next door in the lounge drinking coffee? Did the noise in the hall last night have anything to do with it? What's with the tree branch?*

Alex hadn't had time in the boiler room for her turning-in-place crime scene ritual, so she did it on the other side of the tape. At the end of it she was willing to bet that the basement wasn't the scene of the crime. And that it was murder, not suicide.

1

October 6, 8:37 AM–New York City

Alex stared at the lifeless form on the bed and wondered if it might be the last dead stranger she would set eyes upon. *Possible, if I actually sign on the dotted and retire from the force this year.* But that was a question for another day. Right now she had to process the scene. First things first: She needed to feel the space that now carried death. Her bones, her flesh, her heart and gut had to take in what happened. She knew her eyes were at times unreliable witnesses, filled with history and expectations, so she'd fully engage her hazel greens only when she felt ready.

The other cops on the scene allowed Alex to perform her sensing ritual. What they really wanted to do was barge right in and get started with the details: Cause of death, murder weapon, stuff like that. But with a grisly homicide and no perp in sight they were open to any quirky idea that might help them catch a break. So they waited and watched as she did her thing.

Her *thing* had evolved over twenty years as a cop into a three-hundred-and-sixty-degree turning-in-place ritual. It began as a sixth-sense cop thing when she pounded the pavement in uniform. She thought she was like every other cop who *knew* which guys were selling drugs, who was carrying a weapon, who beat their girlfriends.

But she happened to be right more often than anyone else. Uncle Charlie said she had a nose for evil since she was a little girl.

Her sixth sense and nose for bad guys put her on the fast track to detective, providing crime scenes to process and real criminals to find and catch. She would always walk slowly through a crime scene, imagine what had gone down, and come up with a theory that sometimes led to the perp.

Since she started visiting a Zen Buddhist monastery in the Catskills eight years ago—after yet another relationship blew up and she was beginning to acknowledge burnout as a cop—and she had developed a meditation practice, she began to incorporate the stillness that she'd found there into her police work. The stillness helped her dive deep inside her own psyche and enter criminals' minds. Some monks she knew claimed they could see behind them while meditating. Alex never quite believed them, and she never acquired that skill, so her new practice of standing still in a crime scene to suss out the who-what-when-why eventually turned into a slow-turning habit.

She would drop into a state not unlike deep meditation. It wasn't that exactly, but just as in meditation, all the outside noises and distractions would settle into a soft murmur and leave her feeling alone and fully immersed in the surroundings, with all its history and story and love and hate.

Lately, she would start her ritual with eyes closed and recite in her mind a verse from the diamond sutra:

> All composite things
> Are like a dream, a fantasy, a bubble and a
> shadow,
> Are like a dewdrop and a flash of lightning.
> They are thus to be regarded.

Then she'd open her eyes halfway and softly focus them out in front of her as if she were sitting in meditation. And at a snail's pace, she'd turn around in a complete circle listening with her nose, seeing with her ears, and smelling with her eyes, letting the story of what happened to the dead seep into her skin and into her bones.

Not that she could actually see anything that wasn't there or know exactly what had taken place, but certain details would stand out and she'd be left with a hunch or theory about what happened. Her impressions would never hold up in court, but the tangible evidence always supported her findings ... eventually. Her Zen teacher's favorite saying came alive in the real world of crime: "When time is ready, the truth will reveal itself."

It wasn't a paranormal or hocus-pocus technique that Alex employed, it was more of a right-brain activity, where she tapped into the same gray matter in her skull that helped her solve puzzles, which she's loved doing ever since she was a kid. And except on days like this one when she was called out for a case halfway through her bowl of oatmeal—lately more the rule than the exception—her breakfast dessert was usually the *New York Times* crossword puzzle.

The puzzling aspects of a homicide case helped her to keep some distance from the actual fact of death, from the actual fact that someone's life had been extinguished by the hand of someone else. The puzzle of it kept it in her brain right where she wanted it— ordered and out of chaos.

But on this day, October 8, on West 90th Street in a sixth-floor Manhattan apartment with sun streaming in the southfacing living room windows, Alex felt twisted up inside, her senses clouded by something she couldn't figure. It wasn't that it was 8:30 Sunday morning and her breakfast had been interrupted and her plan to run the eighteen-mile marathon tune-up in the park had been quashed.

It was something else. Her right brain was on lock down and the only organ that seemed to be operating was her heart. With it, as she spun in place, eyes softly opened, ears and nose wide open, she felt an overwhelming sense of sadness.

When she finished her three-sixty, opened her eyes wide, and let the scene enter her field of vision, the story of what happened in that room began to write itself. The framed wedding photo on the bureau began the story. The dead woman sprawled on the bed and the one in the photo were the same, ten or fifteen years separating them, but one and the same. The wife was dead on the bed, the daughter was dead on the bed across the hall, the young son's body was still alive in the third bedroom. The husband was nowhere in sight, except in the one photo left standing, a spatter of blood on the white wedding dress, the rest of the collection face down on the bureau top, folded away from the scene of the crime.

With a slight nod at the photo, Alex said to the detective waiting for her to finish, "Hey, Manny, that make you think this was personal?"

Manny looked over at the bureau top. "Even without that I'd bet on it."

One photo peering out, watching. A sad smile on the wife, her new husband beaming, his arm around her shoulders drawing her into him. Mementos such as these, of lives cut short, were poignant reminders that the dead bodies had once pulsed with life. Trips had been taken, rites had been celebrated, disappointments had been suffered, and joy had been shared. In death, in stillness, it all ended and skidded into nothing. Locked forever in photos that would hang on no one's wall.

"Where the hell you think the husband is?" Alex said over her shoulder.

"All's I know is he ain't here," said Manny.

Alex didn't know if her deep sadness emanated from yet more dead bodies, or if her spirit just couldn't absorb one more gruesome ending, her quota for the macabre long ago used up. All she knew was that she was tired of all the dead bodies and even more tired of those who made them dead. But she never imagined that her faculties would malfunction and betray her like this. Try as she might to wake up her brain, nothing worked. Today she was all heart.

Alex struggled to push this heart energy a little lower, into her gut, her belly, her supposed second brain—a label her Zen teacher used when referring to that part of her anatomy just below the navel. He'd always encourage her to "think from here," slapping his own round belly for emphasis as he said it, "breathe from here," slap, "be from here," slap. She'd been moderately successful at dropping her breath into her gut since first hearing this exhortation eight years ago, but the thinking function still emanated from her skull, especially when she was working a case. Today, it felt like her Zen brain wanted to engage, but it was getting stuck on the way down, smack dab in the center of her chest—a surefire liability for a homicide detective, an awakened heart.

When Alex began to move around the room, her fellow cops sprang into action. They conducted the first sweep in silence.

2

Six Months Later

Friday, March 30, 7:11 PM

*W*AAAaaaaa WAAAaaaaa WAAAaaaaa. The insistent, incessant, infuriating wail of the siren raced up Amsterdam and assaulted Alex's every nerve. It felt like thousands of razor blades had been flung into her nervous system by a gale force wind. She tried to steel herself against the sound.

It didn't work.

She tried to embrace it, let it in, in the Zen way of letting everything in and resisting nothing.

That didn't work.

Her coping skills were shot. The siren eventually faded, but a delivery bicycle sped by her on the sidewalk and almost ran over the Maltese barking at its wheels. A cab door slammed behind her. Some jerk was shouting at someone on his phone, blind to everything and everyone around him. Horns blared, jackhammers blasted into cement, and brakes on every M104 bus screeched—it seemed like on every corner. If she hadn't made plans to retreat to the monastery next day, she would have done it that instant.

She stopped outside the diner window to see if Charlie was already inside waiting for her. Of course he was. She was a few minutes late and he was early, both as usual. If he looked up from the paper in front of him, he'd be looking straight at her. But he was absorbed, so it gave her a minute to watch him. Most likely working that day's *New York Times* crossword puzzle.

With his salt-and-pepper, slicked-back hair, his ruddy outdoors complexion and cheerful demeanor, he was the kind of guy you'd stop in the street and ask directions, or for the use of his phone, without a moment's hesitation. He didn't look like a typical city type, but he was clearly comfortable in his own skin and would not look out of place anywhere. If she hadn't known him so well and saw him as a stranger sitting there, she'd decide that he was a handsome, slightly older gent who liked people. *I know he's in his sixties, but he sure doesn't look it.* Her breathing slowed down a tad just watching him.

Charlie was more a father to Alex than an uncle even though they shared no blood. Leon, his friend, her father, had died when she was ten, killed by a drunken teen at the age of thirty-five. Charlie stepped in and took on the role without hesitation. Good thing too, since someone had to take care of Alex's mother, who never completely recovered and was often the child herself. The event transformed Alex into a ten-year-old adult and Charlie into an instant parent at thirty. She started calling her mother by her first name, Marissa, rather than Mom, because her mother basically stopped being a mom, and calling her Marissa made it easier for Alex to feel more like the adult circumstances required her to be, and less like hating her mother. It also helped her to set aside her need for comfort from anyone else and to rely on herself. She became a cop so that she could catch real bad guys like the one who'd killed her father, throw them into jail and have a place to vent her anger. Her father had been one and Uncle Charlie was one, and they were the only two people in the world she ever truly trusted.

As she began to move toward the door, she caught a glimpse of herself in the darkened window. In contrast to Charlie, she looked almost bald. Her thick, auburn hair was pulled tight off her face into a long ponytail down the back of her neck. She hadn't had a second these past six months to even think about styling her hair or getting it cut into any kind of shape. Her face looked clear in the dark reflection, but she knew it carried a smile and frown lines from forty-three years of living and worry lines from twenty years of policing and six months of the worst stress ever. *I should be relieved today, we got the guy, he's going to prison for a long time. What the hell do I have to worry about right here, right now? I'm on vacation. Muin, it's got to be about Muin. Seeing him after all this time won't be easy.*

Alex ripped the elastic band from her hair. *Ouch!* She had run out of coated bands and hadn't had a minute to buy new ones so she used anything she could find and they were doing a number on her scalp. She shook her head and let her hair spread to both shoulders. *Probably looks like shit, but I don't care, it feels better.*

As Alex opened the door, Uncle Charlie lifted his eyes and waved her in. A broad smile lit up his face. He stood and wrapped his arms around her. Alex relaxed into his embrace.

"I want to hear all about everything," Charlie said. "I just figured out that I haven't seen you in over a month—"

"But..." Alex interrupted.

"I know, I know, sweetheart, I don't take it personal, you've been on a tough case. But this ol' guy needs to catch up with your life... and, yes, I know you call me all the time but it just isn't the same as sitting across from that beautiful face and breaking bread with you. Are you hungry?"

"I'm starving. And I'll be eating rice and tofu all week, so right now I'll be a little sinful and have a tuna melt with crispy fries and a vanilla shake."

"Let's order then. It's on me. I think I'll have the vegetable couscous." It was the same thing he always ordered, but with his perusal of the menu and his delight in the choice, it seemed like a new culinary discovery.

After they placed their order, Uncle Charlie stretched his arms across the table and took Alex's hands into his.

With a loving look of concern he said, "Alex, are you okay?"

"Yeah. It's just this case I've been on has been a killer. Turns out it was the husband, no surprise there, but I can't stop thinking about the traumatized son. His dad not only killed his mom and sister but will be behind bars for life. Kid'll never recover from all that.

"I'm wiped out. I feel ancient, maybe I'm getting too old for this shit."

"Hardly. But anytime you're ready to throw in the towel with the police department just let me know. Come to think of it,"—he stroked his chin and looked as if he just had a brainstorm of an idea—"why not retire? You're close to the twenty-year mark on the force. You can come work with me, become a PI—lots of cops make that transition—plus, you'd have a freer rein and get to see me more often."

Uncle Charlie lived an hour and a half out on Long Island— distance in New York being measured in time rather than miles—in a small blue-collar community on the ocean. He had a private detective business that dealt mostly with cheating spouses and crooked business partners. Mostly it was about money—lost, stolen or hidden. It was his job to find it and put it in the hands of his clients. Sometimes he found things he wasn't looking for—like contraband or dead bodies.

"And the bonus is you'll get to spend more time at the beach, which I know you love."

"Hmmm, there is that," she said, pretending along with him that it was the first time he'd proposed such a thing. She still didn't know how she felt about it. Leaving the force, becoming a private investigator, spending all her time with Charlie. It was too much to think about right now.

"And, let me add, you're only forty-three,"—Charlie raised his palm to fend off Alex's objection— "soon to be forty-four, I know, I know. But you got lots more years in those legs to chase down bad guys."

As if reading her mind, Uncle Charlie said, just as their meal arrived, "Let's have a nice dinner together, no more shop talk allowed. Deal?"

"Deal," said Alex as she relaxed into the leatherette booth seat and picked up a hot fry.

As they ate and chatted about nothing much, Alex kept floating off into thinking about being at the monastery. She was looking forward to being in the mountains and catching up with Sonja, a woman she befriended and kept in sporadic touch with after they'd roomed together six years earlier for their first ever sesshin, an intensive, seven-day silent retreat. Sonja was Jacqueline back then, a new student, just like Alex. Since then, Jacqueline became Sonja when she took her Buddhist vows, then became a nun. It bothered Alex that they'd grown apart and had less and less in common as the years passed.

That and pangs of worry about seeing Muin kept interrupting her thoughts and distracting her from paying attention to anything Charlie was saying.

After their dishes were cleared and they were sipping tea, Charlie said, "You've been someplace else all evening, Alex, what's going on with you? Care to unburden yourself to this ol' guy who loves you?"

Alex did not want to confide in Charlie about her mixed up love life so she avoided the subject of Muin.

"It's nothing really. I'm just so stressed out, and worried about Sonja."

"That the Swiss girl I met a couple times, the one who decided to live at the monastery after your first retreat together?"

"Yup. She's caught in some weird triangle with a couple guys up there and, well, I don't think she's very happy. I don't know, maybe it's me. I haven't really talked to her much. I'm sure it's all fine. I'll know more soon as I see her. You know me and how I like to worry about everyone else."

"That it?"

"Well, there is one more thing."

"Do tell," said Uncle Charlie.

"It's been such a long time since I've been to the monastery and my meditation practice is about nil right now so I'm not sure I'll even be able to sit on a meditation cushion. Plus, there's the matter of my koan. I've told you about Zen koans, right?"

"And I've done some reading. If I understand the concept, isn't a koan an old nonsensical story that a teacher gives a student to meditate on and come up with an answer?"

"Yeah, and if you meditate on one long enough it's possible to solve the puzzle and gain some insight into the nature of reality. Or so they say."

"You have a koan you're working on?"

Alex nodded. *Maybe this'll keep us away from the Muin topic.*

"That's cool," Charlie said. "I'm impressed. You never told me that."

"Well, it's sort of private, you know, between me and Roshi. Besides, I don't tell you everything. A girl's got to have some secrets," teased Alex.

"Anyway," she added, as she slumped back into her seat, "I've been sitting with the same koan for years now. I don't think I'll ever solve it. I wish I could go up there and just do nothing, which is what this business of meditation and Zen is supposed to be all about.

"I don't know, Uncle C, I'm just confused right now. And in need of some silence." Alex closed her eyes and hoped that was the end of the conversation.

"Right," said Charlie, who was well trained not to pry. "Well, since you're on your way there tomorrow, be a dear and bring me back some of that matsu-no-tomo incense, would you?" Charlie loved saying this foreign word almost as much as he enjoyed the pine scent of it.

"You sure do love that stuff, don't you?"

"Yeah, it's like a campfire in a bowl with some spices and flower petals thrown in. And I can light up a stick anytime, indoors, year round. It really does relax me, almost as much as being in the middle of the woods with a real campfire."

"Careful you don't get addicted to it."

"I think I already am!"

"Tell you what, I'll bring you some of that incense and one that's Roshi's favorite. It'll be a surprise, I know you'll love it. But don't get too addicted to that one, it's not the cheapest flavor.

"Hey, I've got an idea," Alex added. "Since you're so curious about this Zen stuff and love the incense and all, why don't you come with me?"

"I thought you liked going up there alone?"

"I do, but I also resist it. I want to be alone, I don't want to be alone. It's like Mara, the Buddhist demon, is in my brain, trying to seduce me into not going. I know if I go, I won't regret it, but ..."

"How about I take a rain check on your invite?" Charlie said. "Seems like it'll be good for you to go up by yourself."

"I'm sure you're right. As usual," Alex said with a weak smile. "Just to be around people struggling to find a better way—even if most of them are loons."

"Will the big kahuna be there?"

"Yup. I sure wish you'd come up with me one of these times so you could meet Roshi. He's a unique guy—just like you."

"He's like me, is he?"

"Oh no, no one's like you. What I meant was you're both unique individuals, in similar and yet different ways."

"Hmmmm," said Charlie as he stroked his chin.

Alex laughed. "It does sound crazy, right? Here's where you're alike: Now don't let this go to your head"—Alex knew he wouldn't—"you're both kind, generous, patient, unconditional with love, stern when it's called for, charismatic ..."

"He sounds like a nice guy," Charlie said with mock seriousness.

"And here's where you're different: He's bald, he's Japanese, and he loves ping pong. You garden, love cats—he hates them—you like opera—Frank Sinatra's his favorite—and you're a head taller than him, although he probably wouldn't mind that, unlike most men."

"So, is that it?"

"In a nutshell. I'm sure I missed plenty of things, but for now it'll do. Oh yeah, and you both are baseball nuts—maybe the most boring sport in the world."

"Ah, Grasshopper," Uncle Charlie said with his palms together in front of his chest. "The day you enjoy baseball will be the day you have reached enlightenment."

"Ah, so, Master. I will keep trying," Alex said with her hands in prayer and her head bowed.

By the time they hugged goodbye in front of her apartment building at 9, she felt lighter. She had no clue about her future or what to say to Muin. But she had nine days, two hundred and sixteen hours, stretching out in front of her where the worst thing that could happen would be some leg pain from sitting on a meditation cushion for too long. *At this point, that will feel like a state of bliss.*

3

Saturday, March 31, 1:27 PM

A lex slid behind the wheel of her new Subaru Outback (an early
birthday gift to herself with help from Uncle Charlie) later than
she'd planned. Esmerelda had been able to squeeze her in at ten for
a shearing so she was running late. Her new gently layered bob with
bangs would have normally had her feeling glamorous, but all she
felt was weary. Turning the ignition shot a wave of guilt through her
brain for driving such an expensive vehicle to a place where
residents had few possessions. Kido, her first monk friend, who was
dead five years, would have said, *"It's not such a crime to have
things, the crime is in being attached to them. If you can let them
go in a moment's notice without suffering ... then, no problem."*

She was happy to be getting out of Dodge. As she eased into
Broadway traffic in front of a blue and white patrol car, her busy mind
landed on the subject of uniforms. Behind her cops in blue, and ahead
of her monks in black. If Uncle Charlie were sitting next to her he'd
posit some theory about Catholic school nuns and their persisting
influence. He'd make her laugh.

She turned on the radio, which was just talk, talk, talk or music,
music, music. She turned it off. She flipped through her CDs.

Nothing appealed to her. She drove with the hum of her new car as background music.

Her cell phone lay silent in the passenger seat next to her Glock 19, her department-issued sidearm. She wouldn't need them while on the mountain, but couldn't imagine leaving either one at home.

The cell phone would be useless once she hit the mountain, but the signal was strong still and would be for two more hours, yet it refused to ring. No one had called all morning. *Can the world really do without me all of a sudden?*

She slipped onto the West Side Highway and headed north toward the George Washington Bridge. There was no turning back even if Mara the tempter had her toying with the idea all along the way. On and on her mind rolled. On and on her new wheels carried her north and west toward the Catskill Mountains and Nekoji Monastery.

***

Once Alex was out on the open road her mind began to slow down and turned to thoughts of Muin. They'd had an affair a few years back after Kido had died, but when it became clear that Muin was a monk through and through and would never live in the civilian world, and Alex would never reside full or part-time at any monastery, they agreed to resume a platonic relationship. The love word had been whispered and the sex was sublime, so it wasn't easy to go cold turkey. During her subsequent visits they'd slip out to Kido's cabin at least once to feed that hungry ghost.

But last time, Alex told Muin the sex would have to end. If she were going to hook up with another guy—and she did want to before she got too old—keeping the pilot light on with Muin interfered with that.

He took it in his monk's stride at first, but next day flirted and tried to cajole her into a late night tryst after a day of meditation, when her defenses were down, her heart open and all her senses awakened. A day on the cushion heightened lovemaking into the sensuous and deeply satisfying act that sexy magazines and movies promised it would be. Better even. It took all her willpower to stand firm and say no.

Muin avoided her the next day and they never even said goodbye. He hadn't tried to reach her since.

She missed him, not just the sex, but him. He'd become a good friend. She hadn't had a date in months and there was no other guy on the horizon. *What the fuck should I do? I don't trust myself to keep saying no. But that's a fucking rabbit hole. I really have to stop using that word, much as I love it. Fuck, fuck, fuck!*

Halfway through the three-hour trip on Route 17, she rubbernecked along with everyone else to gawk at a station wagon that was parked on the shoulder with engine trouble and a flat tire. It was chock full of Hasidic Jews, men covered up in black suits, black beards and black hats, with a small swatch of white at their throats.

They'd all been born into that culture of religion. For them there was no question of what to believe in, what to do with their lives, or how to dress. *Was there? What are their dreams like? Are they content? What do they talk about with each other? They seem so out of place and of another time.*

Maybe they're just another tribe in a different uniform. By choice or by birth, it doesn't matter, it's the cloth that binds each tribe together, makes them feel connected, like they belong to someone, some place, some thing. Her self-assigned koan question right now was, "Where do I belong?"

***

When Alex took the exit off the highway and began the mountain climb, she slowed down for the family of deer crossing the road, took a deep breath and let her brain relax. The ascent to the monastery would take an hour. Alex rolled down the window and sucked in the cool mountain air.

This part of the trip was her private purification ceremony. The higher she climbed the "cleaner" she got. The air cleared her lungs, the rush of the river alongside the road washed off the city grit, and the thickening forest pushed open her heart. Everything began to relax—her skin, her bones, her legs, her guts, even her lips. It was as if all the tension she carried with her flew out the window, some of it taken by the wind and some of it by the downstream flow of the river back toward the city where it belonged.

She was different when at the monastery. Maybe it was the mountain itself—the lore was that it was once a sacred Native American healing ground that had magical curative powers. Maybe it was the monastery and the cumulative energy of meditation. Maybe it was the Roshi effect. Zen wasn't a cult and Roshi didn't cast spells and force his followers to commit acts against their own will. But his charismatic influence was potent and Alex was not immune to it. Whatever it was, she didn't need to figure it out.

Down mountain she could hold her own with any man, no matter how tough or powerful. But when in the presence of Roshi she became shy and, while not intimidated, certainly deferential— and to a greater degree than his Zen Master status demanded. It had something to do with her cop mind being relaxed and something to do with his Zen Master charisma.

Whatever it was, it was a confusing mixture for Alex and turned her worldview topsy-turvy. Roshi was always talking about upside-down views and how Zen can set things right, but this confused Alex even more. She didn't know up from down or right from wrong when under Roshi's spell. Still, she always left him feeling better and stronger and safer. She wanted to know what force made this so, but every time this thought flared, she remembered something Kido had said to her:

"You mustn't think so hard, don't worry about answers just yet. You must learn to radically accept what is—and just be in the question."

Now that he was gone she couldn't ask him at what point in her Zen practice she'd be allowed to seek an answer.

When the monastery was in sight Alex took notice of her gun as if it were shouting to her: "I shouldn't be here!"

"Yeah, yeah, yeah," she said out loud, and quickly covered it with her sweatshirt. *No need to freak anyone out.*

***

Less than three hours after leaving the city, Alex was at the basement door of the monastery. She'd made good time. When she turned off the ignition and stepped out of the car, a profound and pervading stillness embraced her.

The monastery sat near the summit. There was more height behind the buildings and dense forest on all sides, but it all belonged to the monastery, 1,900 acres as far as the eye could see. Pine, evergreen, fir, birch, ash, maple and red oak trees mostly. All donated by the Rockefellers or some such wealthy philanthropist almost fifty years ago. So there was no danger of a high-rise or freeway popping up anywhere or anytime soon, not in her lifetime and certainly not during this trip. No threat of planes flying over either. No sirens or machine or human sounds that didn't belong there.

It was remote. Just what Alex's inner doctor ordered.

She'd found the occasional Bud can on her hikes through the woods in the past, a few signs of old campfires, and animal droppings for sure, but nothing else.

Not a soul was in sight, and only nature was breathing alongside her. Before going inside, she walked around the monastery to treat herself to the raw magnificence of nature, that included a half-mile-long lake that sat about 200 yards down a slight incline off to the east. Tall trees and thick woods bounded three sides of the monastery.

The Japanese-style monastery was a three-story brown and white wood structure with sloping roofs at different levels, and an outside walking deck that wrapped around the back. There sat the meditation hall, or zendo, as it was known by those who used it; large, sliding glass doors on the front end, and windows, some with closed shoji screens, on the sides, a raked circular rock garden along the eastern side, small cairns here and there, and stone sculptures in the western courtyard and at the majestic southern front entrance. It was eternally the same and forever different. There was always some new tastefully placed bell or gong or sculpture or small garden that hadn't been there last she looked, but fit in as if it had always belonged. Today, she noticed a small statue of Jizo, a protective deity and savior of souls, in the woods just opposite the door to the kitchen that she had never seen before. By the end of her circumnavigation, Alex felt like she was back home. She took a deep breath of the cold, late winter air, and slowly exhaled until she was completely empty. Her breathing was now considerably deeper than it had been just twelve hours ago. *The cure's working already!*

More familiar scents and sights greeted her as she removed her shoes in the entry hall and ventured farther into the bosom of the monastery. Twenty people resided there and you wouldn't know it, the common halls and rooms were so still and soundless. The main corridor leading to the chanting and meditation halls was narrow, dark, and long, night-lights near the gleaming cherry wood floor being the only illumination. At the end of the long hall, glowing from the late afternoon light that filtered through shoji screens at the windows, an enormous golden Buddha on the altar beckoned her forward. Flickering candles, the sweet-spicy-woody fragrance of burning incense, and the sleek wooden floors radiated calm. Eight years ago, the first time she walked down this corridor, a bald monk in flowing robes, his face hidden in shadows, had spooked her.

An unsettled feeling caught the edge of her mind today, but she brushed it away and attended to more pleasant sensations. Throbbing silence. Soothing energy. Aromatic incense. With palms together she bowed at the dharma hall entrance, far now from the madness of the city.

***

When she raised her head, a robed figure was standing smack in front of her just inside the dharma hall. Reflexively, and with a sharp intake of breath, she drew away. It took her a moment to realize who it was.

"Damn, Kosen, you scared the shit out of me. Where the hell did you come from?"

Kosen had a penchant for creeping up on visitors. No sound, no warning, no nothing. The sleek but sometimes creaky wooden floors posed a challenge to anyone wanting to move around the halls soundlessly, even in bare feet, not to mention the yards of fabric worn by the monks. Somehow Kosen could silently step on the old wood.

With his thick, black wavy hair and pale, brown eyes, he stood there for a few seconds with a wide grin on his chiseled, innocent face. "Hi Alex, when did you get here?"

"I just walked in."

"Me, too."

"Very funny. You know you ought not do that to people, sneak up on them like that. Give somebody a heart attack."

"Nah. Most people get a kick out of it. Wakes them up, you know, it is a Zen monastery for Pete's sake."

"I suppose so. Woke me up, that's for sure, so thanks, I guess."

Alex met Kosen about five years ago when he'd first arrived. His story was that he'd been drawn there after reading Kido's obituary in the paper. Because of that connection she decided to like him right away even if he was a little odd. She fancied him as Kido's reincarnation, even though they were nothing alike.

And Sonja, who'd come the year before that for a retreat and decided to stay for a while to think about getting ordained, had taken Kosen under her wing. He was a bit of a lost soul and she liked to take care of such creatures, be they animal or human, and so they became dharma buddies. Lately, according to Sonja, he'd developed a crush and she was attracted to someone else there, though she hadn't said who yet, and it was causing some discord between them.

"What's happening around here these days?" Alex said, ignoring Kosen's weirdness and sidestepping the subject of Sonja. She'd check in on her next.

As soon as this came out of her mouth she wanted to take it back. Kosen was not the one to ask. Kosen, not yet a monk though yearning to be, was the monastery prankster and troublemaker who didn't mind getting caught and thrived on the attention. Once, when Alex was visiting he'd placed a fart cushion under Roshi's seat in the meeting room. He was in the doghouse for a week, but everyone else thought it daring and funny, and that was enough for him.

"Oh, big things, big things," Kosen said mischievously.

"Like what?"

"I can't really say. It's a surprise. Roshi would kill me if I told anyone."

Alex knew he and Roshi were the last to share a secret. *What must it be like to be inside Kosen's head?*

"Well then, I guess I'll just have to wait," said Alex. "Can you tell me when this big surprise will be taking place? I want to be sure I'm here for it."

Kosen looked around checking for interlopers, leaned close to Alex, and whispered, "Next Sunday, Buddha's birthday, but you can't tell anyone."

"Good. I'll still be here. And this will be our secret." *Hmmm, I wonder what imaginative scheme he's dreamt up this time.*

"Promise?"

"I promise."

"I always liked you, Alex. That's why I'm telling you this. Roshi doesn't even know."

"Oh? Didn't you ... oh, never mind." She didn't have the energy to try to make sense out of nonsense. It never worked even when she was at the top of her form.

More of Kido's wisdom ran through her mind: *"Be especially compassionate toward the fool."*

Easier said than done.

Kosen stood there, smugly. Waiting for what?

She moved to safer terrain. "When does the evening schedule start?"

"The usual time, six-thirty."

"Why then the robe? And where's your rakusu?"

Robes were worn for zendo activities, chanting and meditation, not during work or rest periods, and never without the rakusu if you had one. So it was strange that he was dressed in his robe this time of day. The rakusu dated back centuries when Buddhists were persecuted and wore this miniature version of their robe under their lay garments. A rakusu, or Buddhist bib as Alex had nicknamed it, was given to all students, along with a new dharma name, when they officially became Buddhists and vowed to uphold the precepts, during the yearly jukai ceremony. She wondered if she'd ever make that vow. The rakusu was made of black cloth on the front side and white cotton or silk on the back side, on which was written the student's new name and the date of the ceremony, with some calligraphy by the Zen Master who assigned the name. It draped around the neck and hung down over the torso. It was a very cool Buddhist accessory. Kosen looked naked without his.

"Shhh," said Kosen, leaning close to Alex, his finger over his lips. "Don't tell anyone. I'm looking for it. Thought if I had my robe on it would act like a magnet and I'd find it faster. Have you seen it anywhere?"

"You lost it?"

"Don't say that! It's here somewhere, it has to be. Roshi will be pissed, won't he?"

Alex shrugged.

Kosen walked away down the hall, mumbling to himself and fretting about the missing rakusu.

"See you later, Kosen," said Alex, though she knew he didn't hear her. *Why is he so upset? The missing rakusu was probably just a prank, some monk turning Kosen's devilishness back onto him. It's something Kosen would do to annoy a monk.*

With her back to Kosen's receding figure she heard the rustle of his robes and wondered again how he could move so silently when he wanted to.

4

Jito, the head cook, or tenzo, of the monastery, was in his kitchen, also called the tenzo, pacing. Kosen, monk wannabe, continued the hunt for his rakusu. Zenji, the current jisha of the monastery, rather like a den mother who arranges the cleaning schedule and takes care of guests, was taking a shit in the resident's wing bathroom. Hokan, general manager of the monastery and the jikijitsu, the monk who leads the meditation sessions in the zendo and is the spiritual control unit when they were all sitting, was in his office balancing the accounts. And Muin, the Zen Master's inji, or personal attendant, was with Setsu Roshi in his quarters writing letters. All the others were in their rooms doing whatever they were doing—napping, reading, sitting, daydreaming.

All the names seemed strange to Alex at first, but she quickly realized they were just names to call them by. Names that were given to them by Roshi when they became Buddhists. Names that when translated carried the poetic beauty of indigenous cultures: Great Vehicle, Morning Wisdom, Thunderous Heart, Snow Cloud. Names that they were to use when at the monastery, and in the case of the monks and nuns, always and forever. Some of their heads were shaved, but if they were put on the streets of New York City they could have been mistaken for fashion victims rather than renouncers of vanity and ego.

Alex had been to a few ordination ceremonies over the years and loved witnessing the transformation of a person from ordinary citizen to monk. They would shave all but a small section of their head the night before, leaving that last little bit for Roshi to shave off during the ritual, in front of the sangha, the community of Zen practitioners. It symbolized their entrance into monkhood and their willingness to leave vanity, fashion and all other worldly attachments behind. It didn't always stick. Some monks, once they shaved their head and donned the black robe, began at once to feel superior and saintlier than everyone who wasn't a monk. It took some of them a while to become right-sized. Some eventually got there, some never did.

In a couple of hours all the monks and students in the Nekoji Sangha would be sitting on their cushions in the zendo. Till then they had two precious hours of private time—something hard to come by in this monastery community.

Alex walked to the office to check on her room assignment and say hi to Sonja, who was there manning the phones and doing whatever else needed doing. Sonja was the only nun in residency. It irked Alex that Buddhism was as patriarchal as most religions, including Catholicism, the religion she'd been born into. Buddhism wasn't a religion, but it used some religious nomenclature and called ordained women nuns rather than monks. That pissed her off. She thought she was done with nuns when she refused to attend church after her father died.

Sonja was light years different from the nuns she'd known as a child. Stubbornly, Alex thought of her as a monk, not a nun. When they were roommates and sat through their first seven-day retreat together, Alex couldn't believe how still her new friend could be on the cushion next to her. In contrast, Alex suffered tremendous physical pain, could hardly sit still and felt like she was constantly squirming and disturbing her neighbors. Although Sonja, Jacqueline back then, had never sat on a meditation cushion before in her life, she was like a rock, as if she'd been born to sit. By the end of the week she knew without a doubt that she'd found her calling. Alex was more confused than ever. Go figure.

The night before Sonja's ordination ceremony four years ago, Alex helped her prepare. They had their own little ceremony when they cut off her foot-long black braid and shaved all but a silver dollar circle of hair with a six-inch braid. When Roshi cut and then shaved the last bit off the next day, Alex cried. She'd never witnessed anything so beautiful. Her friend's transformation from regular woman to Zen monk was complete and it fitted her like a glove. Alex knew it was selfish of her, but she prayed in that moment that she wouldn't lose her new friend now that her commitment to practice had deepened so thoroughly.

When Alex got to the office, Sonja was on the phone. She gestured that she'd be a while, and slipped Alex a note with her room number and message: WE'LL CATCH UP LATER, OKAY?

Alex kissed the top of Sonja's bald head and went to get her bag from the car. Her room was on the main floor where transient guests stayed. Alex dropped her bags and went to see who else was around. Unpacking could wait. Before she left she made sure her gun was buried in her bag, the chamber cleared of bullets, and the magazine safely tucked away in the inside zippered pocket of her denim jacket.

She wanted to take a walk while the sun was still up. The phase of the moon was nearly full, and she'd be able to see well enough after twilight, but she yearned to see more of the lake, the forest, the sky—the raw nature surrounding the monastery—before dark. She was desperate to breathe in more of the mountain air, take in the visual perfection, continue the renewal process that the drive up had begun, and put all the stress of the city in the back of her mind. Her job now was to relax and renew. Just that.

As Kido would say, *"There's nothing to do, nowhere to go. Just BE!"*

She'd been in high gear for so long that the sudden screeching stop had her spinning so fast she wasn't sure she could just be. In fact, she wasn't sure she'd ever learned how to just be.

But she did know how to do, so she went to find Jito to catch up on things. She found him where he always was, dependable as a ticking clock, in his kitchen sanctum.

Alex approached him as he leaned on a counter, his back to her, studying what looked like a recipe. Wrapping her arms around his waist she nestled her face into his back for the few seconds it took him to react.

He swiftly turned and wrapped her close to him.

"Dahling! I didn't know you were coming. When did you arrive? Naughty girl, sneaking up on me like that."

"Ah, Jito, it's good to see you, too."

Jito, dear, sweet Jito, who, despite his big nose and enormous feet, moved around his tenzo domain as graceful as a ballet dancer. He would have even looked a bit like Baryshnikov if he'd been six-feet tall with no hair on his head. At least he cooked up meals that would challenge any master chef. Not only was he the best cook Alex knew, he was the best hugger. Because he was flamboyantly gay—the cherry on top of his unique personality—it was all innocent, good fun with him.

"Everything okay?" asked Jito as he hugged her tight.

"Yeah. Bushed is all. It's been a little crazy down there in cop town."

"God, tell me about it. Some of that insanity has made its way up here."

"What do you mean?"

"Oh, it's nothing. Never mind. Nothing to worry your pretty head about, a wee bit of monk-ey politics. You know how that goes."

Usually chafing to spread any little bit of gossip, Jito's restraint surprised her.

"How are you? How've you been?" Jito asked as he fiddled behind his back with the papers he'd been poring over.

"What have you got there? A new creation?"

Jito was always concocting new uses for tofu. Calling his experiments an obsession wouldn't be far off the mark.

Alex playfully reached behind him to have a look. Jito tensed up.

"Aw, c'mon. Let me see. I'll bet it's great, like all the rest."

"Not yet. It's not ready. Maybe later."

She had the thought that it wasn't a recipe they were tugging with, but didn't have the energy for their usual good-natured fooling around. Funny thing, the good nature on Jito's side was missing, too.

"Okay, okay." Alex raised her arms in mock surrender.

"I'm sorry, I'm just a little stressed out," Jito said as he shoved the papers deep into his apron pocket.

"It's okay. It seems we're both a little tense."

Jito moved to another counter. Alex intuited that he wanted to put some space between them.

"Are you sure you're okay?" Alex said.

"Yeah. I have a lot on my mind with next Sunday's festivities and all those people that'll be descending upon us. And I didn't get much sleep last night. We'll talk later, okay?" Jito said as he escorted Alex out of his kitchen.

"Okay, later then."

Sunday was Buddha's birthday celebration with a ceremony and an afternoon feast planned for one hundred people. These were hit-or-miss affairs in her experience. Alex had witnessed the whole community fall apart as they prepared for some big event. She'd always thought Zen was about keeping your cool under any and all circumstances, no matter what. It was one main reason she'd sought it out in the first place.

She recalled the allegorical story of Buddha or some other Zen patriarch who sat in meditation while his arms and legs were severed and still he hardly noticed. Maybe that was true enlightenment, but at times Alex thought it was denial.

***

Alex bumped smack into Clark as she left the kitchen, neither of them paying attention.

"Sorry, Miss Alex, so clumsy of me," said Clark. "I didn't know you were up here." He held open the swinging door for her with the stump of his right hand and bowed with exaggeration. "Please, allow me."

"Thanks, Clark." Alex moved quickly past him and out into the hall. She had no interest in chatting him up.

One story on Clark was that he'd lost his fingers in some jailhouse brawl and had come up to the monastery to serve out the balance of his prison sentence. His incarceration had been drug related and it was his idea to contact Roshi, who had taken in other criminals over the years. By now, Clark had lived at the monastery longer than any other resident except Muin, but he rarely participated in any of the meditation or chanting activities. He mostly helped Jito in the kitchen, which was a feat given his one-handedness. Alex chalked it up to Roshi's compassion, taking in convicts like Clark, but she didn't have to like him.

Alex walked down to the lake. A daily visit to Kido's grave for a chat with his spirit was an established routine of hers while up there. But never on the first day. The emotional jolt was too much for her so soon after leaving the city; she'd end up weeping and missing Kido and her father more than she could possibly bear. So she always waited twenty-four hours for her first conversation with Kido.

Paying attention to each footfall, to how many steps she took on each inhale and each exhale, she began to prepare her body for the sitting-still meditation she'd be doing later. Her body and breath fell into a rhythm that allowed her to be in the abundant beauty, without being distracted by it.

The undulating mass of forest reaching up to the mountaintop spread across the sky. The view through the still-bare trees revealed the white and brown Japanese structure of the monastery, a slow, steady stream of smoke rising from the furnace chimney the only sign of human life.

Then she heard shouting, Beaver Lake water acting as a megaphone. She couldn't be sure where the sound was coming from, or what the voices were saying. All she heard was elevated, angry tones. Two of them, both male.

Alex hurried back toward the monastery. She spied a monk through the trees storming up the hill path from the guesthouse on the lakeshore . The baldhead and blue samugi or work clothes, told her it was a monk.

"A day of no work is a day of no eating," is one of the first rules of monastery life. And work practice, or samu, was a principal element in a monk's training at Nekoji Monastery, and as vital as meditation practice. All monks wore black robes for meditation and dark blue or grey samugi for work. A two-piece loose fitting outfit generally made of cotton, the top was styled like a kimono, the trousers like sweat pants. Elastic cinched the sleeves at the wrist and the pants at the ankles, all for ease of movement and comfort.

It was unusual for Alex to hear such anger at the monastery. On the streets of New York for sure, but not up here. *Did one of the shouting voices belong to the monk racing up the hill?*

As she got closer, with only one hundred feet of bare trees separating her from this angry monk, she saw that it was Zenji, and knew that he was one of the shouters. His pock-marked face, which must have been hell to live with as a teenager, was beet red and set in a gritted-teeth scowl. She pitied whomever he had been screaming at.

Zenji had a reputation for being Mr. Know-It-All, especially when it came to Zen practice and tradition—so maybe he'd been engaged in a dharma battle with someone and setting them straight about some universal truth. Dharma was the teaching of Buddha and he fancied himself the expert. She rejected that notion when she saw his face; the clash had something to do with more unwholesome matters.

As Alex approached the lakeside house—an old sprawling structure that the monastery rented to outside groups for spiritual retreats—she saw Kosen and Sonja in verbal embrace and knew at once that Zenji was the subject.

He must be the one Sonja had hinted about being attracted to. She never would have guessed it was him. *Guess there's no accounting for one's sexual attractions.* Zenji might have been okay to look at if he had hair, which his eyebrows indicated would be blonde and would soften his face a bit. But his shaved head and face left his lumpy, pasty skin exposed and his pale blue eyes, rather than soft and inviting, were often piercing and off putting. He couldn't hide anywhere, under anything.

Kosen was wearing his samugi, no longer in his robe. Maybe he'd found his rakusu. Or maybe that was what the argument was about. From a distance, with his dark, wavy hair, chiseled features and smooth skin, he and Sonja made a handsome couple, even if they were fighting.

As she approached, Kosen stomped off toward the monastery. Sonja slumped into one of the wooden chairs. Alex joined her.

Alex saw immediately that Sonja was not in a sharing mood. She decided to leave it alone. Whatever was going on wasn't her business, and she simply didn't have the energy to pry and deal with someone else's problems. Sonja would talk when she was ready, that much she knew about her. They sat there in silence, a distant thunderclap and the wind as company.

"Rain's on its way," said Sonja.

"I hope it holds off till we're sitting tonight," Alex said.

"Yeah, it's always special when it starts while we're all sitting. But there's no predicting the weather."

"Difference up here is that there's no getting away from it, especially when it rains," Alex said. "It's about the same inside as out. A little drier under a roof, but other than that I feel it deep down in my bones. It's not like that in the city."

Alex thought Sonja might start to open up, talk about the emotional weather.

"Full moon in two days," was all she said.

5

When Alex walked back into her room she felt grateful to have no roommate. She both wanted and didn't want to live with others. Very Zen, she amused herself with this idea as she made up the futon bed and unpacked her few things.

She tucked her gun in the now empty bag in the back of the closet. On her first visit when she'd worn her piece hidden underneath her jacket—it had become an appendage that she took little notice of—everyone who got wind of its presence flipped out. She'd been asked, very politely and adamantly, not to carry it on monastery grounds. This had been almost enough reason to keep her away forever. Or maybe it's why she'd stayed.

She was hooked on Zen after her first weekend and could no more stay away than she could do without air. Once, she left her gun at home but the separation anxiety nearly killed her so she buried it in her bag and no one was the wiser.

'I will not be violent, nor will I kill,' was the first and most precious of the Ten Precepts of Buddhism. Casting their eyes on a weapon that could take a life left the monks uneasy. They never saw her gun after that first visit and they never asked about it. So she didn't tell. If only the doors had locks.

The simplicity, some might say starkness, of her room, pleased her—a futon on a tatami mat, a small table and lamp, one hanging calligraphy, beige walls, wood floors, gray wool blankets, and a closet with a few plastic hangers for her things. The austerity made her feel safe, and free to disencumber herself, unpack her internal baggage, air it out, and see what was there. She looked forward to that. In the meantime, she'd practice being in the present moment, not in any past or future one.

Everyone would be catching a few quiet minutes alone before the evening sit. Alex decided to take advantage of the hour that remained to rest her eyes, take a catnap. She wasn't much good at napping except on the mountain where time seemed to pass so much slower.

Forty-five minutes later she was jolted awake by the shinrei bell, a small handheld bell that some monk or other would ring as he walked the corridors to alert everyone to the sit that would be commencing in ten minutes. No one, except the monk in charge of keeping the schedule, had to wear a watch or know what time it was. In fact, during sesshins, the silent retreat periods that happened monthly, watches were prohibited in the zendo. There was always a bell or gong or clapper being struck somewhere in the vicinity of all ears to announce the next thing.

Alex quickly donned her robe and felt a slight queasiness in her stomach. She hadn't eaten a thing in hours, but the feeling had less to do with hunger and more to do with knowing she'd see Muin soon. She didn't feel ready. *It's time, I have to do this!*

She quietly opened her door and stepped out into the hall, which was alive with robed monks and students gliding their way to the zendo. The five-foot wide hallway was lined on each side by guest rooms, and flanked by the dharma hall on one end and the sangha meeting room on the other. The night lights along the baseboard and the light emanating from the two gathering spaces cast enough light on the gleaming wood floor and the white walls to see where one was going, but often not enough to distinguish one monk or student from another until they were quite close. Monks wore black and were bald. Students usually had hair and wore blue or gray or brown robes. Other than that, the robes served to give comfort while sitting, offer an anonymous and consistent color palette in the zendo to keep outside distractions to a minimum, mute the separation between each person and help everyone to easily settle into their purpose for being there and support one another in the endeavor.

Alex's room was six doors away from the dharma hall entrance to the right. Four doors down to the left on the opposite end of the long hallway was the meeting room, where she knew Roshi would be waiting till all students were in the zendo, to make his entrance. And Muin, the ever-attendant inji, would be standing sentry outside the room. As always.

Despite her effort not to look toward Muin, she couldn't help herself. Sure enough, he was standing there, in shadow except for the right side of his head, which was dimly illuminated by candles behind him. There was no mistaking him for any other monk. His ears stuck out from his head almost at right angles. He was wearing his glasses. His six-foot, lean frame stood soldier erect, his hands cupped together at his belly. She couldn't see if his eyes were open or closed, but she knew he saw her as he cocked his head ever-so-slightly in greeting. The small movement sent a shiver down her spine. She smiled a smile that he couldn't see so she simply turned and bowed to him.

What she wanted to do was go right up to him, throw her arms around his neck and whisper in his ear. But a determination to stick to her vow to not get physical kept her in place, along with Roshi's figure sitting in the doorway. *Thank you, Roshi.* The faint sound of the warning bell ringing down a distant corridor snapped her back. She turned and walked toward the zendo, her heart in her throat.

When she got to the zendo entrance, her head was spinning. She stood there a moment to collect herself and drink in the beauty before she made her way to her seat. To do zazen—sitting meditation—in the zendo it helped to untangle the mind's web. She would see Muin later after her lust had a chance to adjust to the environment.

This zendo was singular in its beauty, its aesthetic helping to soothe the painful experience of meditation. Alex had visited a few zendos around the country and this one was by far the most exquisite she'd seen. It had deep brown oak floors, black cushions atop tawny tatami mats lining two sides of the eighty-foot long room, and the altar at the front with the essentials—a Buddha statue, an incense burner, a candle, a bowl of water, and a vase of flowers. It was a visual field of simple elegance. The room held a spiritual weight that compounded when it was packed with robed students.

She bowed at the entrance, padded her bare feet to her spot, bowed to the altar, bowed to Kosen who was sitting across from her and sat down on her cushion. She folded her legs under her, erected her spine, cupped her palms, rested them on her lap, took a few deep breaths, softly focused her gaze out and down in front of her, and began to count her exhalations, preparing herself for the next forty-five minutes when she wouldn't be allowed to shift her body or emit any sounds whatsoever that might be heard by anyone in the room.

Zazen was meditation pure and simple, even if Roshi hated the word meditation.

"Too lofty," he would say. "Too complicated. What we do here is sit. We do zazen. We are zazen. Meditation only confuses things, and you're all confused enough already."

No scratching of itches, no blowing of noses, no wiping away tears, no coughing, sneezing or sobbing allowed. Many times Alex had to fight hard to suppress a compulsion to scream, to stand up and run out, to throw something at the jikijitsu, the monk in charge of the bell that would release them from the hell of sitting, and allow them to walk for ten minutes, to stretch the cramps in their legs only to sit back down again at the end of the walking kinhin for another forty-five minutes of torture. There were times when she thought she'd internally combust from the pressure, and maybe then she'd know Buddha, or her Buddha nature, and be enlightened.

It wasn't always so painful. If Alex stayed concentrated on her breath, on her koan, in the present moment, and didn't wander into the future to ask when it all might end, the zazen seemed like no time at all and she would sometimes sit straight through two periods back-to-back. *Don't think that's going to happen tonight, I'm too out of practice.*

One by one, the monks in black robes and the lay students in blue and brown ones floated into the zendo. How peaceful and centered they all looked, pious and reverent as they made their way to their cushions. How many years would she have to sit to feel the calm that they radiated?

Along with everything else that was on her mind, Kosen's lost rakusu was still a mystery. She'd noticed tonight that he was wearing a rakusu but it wasn't his. It was too short and too stiff to be his. It was probably the extra one that was always hanging in the jisha's closet for anyone unlucky enough to forget or lose their rakusu. The jisha, a position currently held by Zenji, was the zendo housekeeper and the closet held all the necessary supplies to keep the zendo running smoothly: Extra cushions, first aid supplies, instruments that were used only occasionally, a small sink and stove for making tea, a stash of sweets for special occasions. All these were in the control of the jisha. Zenji was an odd choice for that service, given his gruff and not very hospitable manner. Roshi probably assigned him to that job so he could cultivate those qualities. *I wonder if that's possible. Either you're born to be generous or you're not.*

And after what she witnessed at the lake, she wondered if Zenji had given Kosen a hard time about lending him the spare rakusu. But this wasn't her problem, she had enough to occupy her chaotic mind.

After everyone was seated Roshi made his entrance. Tonight he was late. No one, not even the boss man, was ever late. This surprised Alex since she'd just seen him sitting serenely and ready to come to the zendo. The evening sit never started behind schedule. Alex noticed Muin and Hokan, the jikijitsu, who was in charge of timing the sit and maintaining the atmosphere in the zendo, exchanging a few words.

With her peripheral vision Alex watched Roshi as he walked to the front of the zendo. She'd never seen him so ruffled. His face was set in a frown, his gait was stiff and lacking its usual grace. There was so little light in the zendo that even if she dared try to get someone's attention to confirm her intuition no one would see her. Maybe it was leftover cop suspicion on her part and nothing to worry about. Maybe.

What the hell could have happened in the few minutes since I saw him and now?

Finally, the bell was struck to announce the official start of the evening. Alex wasn't the only one who desperately needed the upcoming zazen. Everyone around her sunk into their cushions and deepened their breath.

By the end of the first hour the rain came. What light there was had faded. Darkness darker than dark settled in around the monastery, the moon not yet risen above the high trees. There was heaviness in the air all night, which she blamed on the mountain rain. She hoped she was right.

As soon as that word passed over the transverse in her mind, one of Kido's dictums chased right after it, practically screaming in her brain: *"Give up all hope!"*

6

Instinctively, Alex knew something was wrong. She was always right when this feeling of dread came upon her—maybe it was her cop training or that nose of hers, but she knew immediately that things were not right as soon as she saw Kosen was absent from the zendo. Her worry about him during the sit last night was a premonition. Zazen sometimes caused certain synapses to cross—it tapped into a different stream of intuition altogether, firing off impulses that competed with her cop instincts—and created confusion. But the signal this morning came through loud and clear. Kosen hadn't just skipped the morning activities, he was gone from the monastery.

After breakfast, Alex pulled Muin aside on their way to the morning tea and coffee session to see what he knew. A private moment with him before the day started was in order. He'd been locked up with Roshi till the wee hours last night so they hadn't had a chance to connect and she needed to see if he'd forgiven her or if his six months of silence meant their friendship was over.

The previous evening's sit, the bit of sleep that she got, and the morning service had helped to settle a few things. If she let herself get distracted with Muin, she knew she wouldn't be open to any other man. And she wanted to hook up with someone before she became an old lady. The chapter with Muin as possible mate had closed. They were now just friends, end of story. Today she'd find some time to visit Kido's grave and have a "chat" with him about Muin, her future and her sad love life.

"Mornin', Muin," Alex said, linking her arm with his.

"Mornin', Alex," Muin said, kissing her gently on the cheek she offered. The electric charge that shot down to her groin was mixed with relief that all was well with her and Muin.

"What's going on?" asked Alex. They slowed down and let a group pass, bringing up the rear, as they moved en masse to the meeting room.

"We don't have time before the meeting," Muin whispered.

"I figured something was up, but nothing as bad as all that.".

"Oh, don't fret. It's not a cop alarm thing, just some monkey business."

"Is that why Kosen's not around this morning?"

"No doubt."

"What's he up to this time? Is he okay?"

"I'm sure he's fine, and just being a pain in the ass."

"Aw, c'mon Muin, you can tell me."

"Oh, okay. Seeing as how you're so persuasive."

Normally Muin would have dragged out the telling of it, had a little fun with Alex, knowing how it tortured her not to know everything in less time than it took to tell it. But he wasn't in the mood and used time as his excuse, because the meeting was about to start.

"You know how Icky won't abide lateness? And not showing your face at all, especially if your head is shaved, can put you in the dharma doghouse for months?" Muin said.

Alex nodded, thinking of Roshi's own tardiness the night before. The Icky appellation for Roshi, a reference to Roshi's namesake Ikkyu Roshi, probably meant that Muin had logged some doghouse time himself since she last saw him. As Roshi's assistant, Muin had to be at his beck and call every waking hour and then some, and being on Roshi's bad side really sucked.

"Well, Kosen's in deep shit. He's been acting out worse than usual lately, no one has a clue why. Knowing him, it could be the misalignment of the planets or something equally bizarre, but even Roshi noticed. So Roshi assigned him some interminable Sanskrit chant to memorize. He was supposed to recite it to all of us this morning in the meeting. And now he's gone AWOL. I can't say I blame him this time. Those chants are killers."

"Better be prepared. Roshi will be fit to be tied. He's liable to drag the rest of us into the thing, make us all learn the whole damn chant this morning, and then everyone will be pissed at Kosen if they're not already.".

"I guess that explains Kosen's behavior yesterday," Alex said. "I ran into him, literally, when I first got here. He went on about some secret or other between him and Roshi and some big surprise for Sunday. None of it made sense. He was being weird."

"He's always weird, or hadn't you noticed?" Muin laughed under his breath as they entered the meeting room.

Not only did Kosen, the wannabe monk, have a penchant for silent stalking, but he loved pissing off the real monks. If Muin were right they'd all be itching to get their paws on him.

Every resident knew that this morning was to be Kosen's solo chanting debut. Most of them figured he had spent the morning practicing and would show up at any moment, make a dramatic entrance, like the time he wore a bald skullcap the day after Roshi denied him his plea to become a monk.

Tea and coffee were served. No one spoke, waiting for Roshi's cue. He sat with closed eyes, unmoving, the patient rock.

"Gyozan!" Roshi said.

"Hai!" said Gyozan, one of two Japanese monks in residence.

"Go find Kosen. Bring him here."

"Hai!"

No one but Zenji would take much pleasure in watching Roshi make an example of Kosen. Another mood, another day, it could be any one of them. Accustomed as they all were to sitting together peacefully, the tension now was palpable. They waited in silence.

***

Alex had a few moments to surreptitiously study Roshi. The mood she saw in him last night was either gone or well hidden. *Did I imagine that?* This morning he displayed only a mild peevishness at Kosen's bad behavior and lack of respect.

Here in this small room, surrounded by devoted students, there was no question who was in charge. Roshi set the tone, called the shots. He never abused his power as far as Alex knew, but she'd known him only a short while. There were stories.

Gyozan returned quicker than expected, and alone, which signaled that bad news was coming. If he had been American and not Japanese, he would have burst back into the meeting room and loudly proclaimed his discovery. Instead, he returned quietly, sat down, and waited for Roshi to ask.

Even though Roshi sat with his eyes closed, he knew when Gyozan returned, and kept still until the point of Gyozan's good manners had been made. It was a cultural thing. Roshi had chosen to live in America, and loved Americans, but often harped on how rude they were. In his monastery he insisted that his monks and committed students learn some Japanese etiquette. Probably no American in that room could have displayed Gyozan's restraint, burdened as he was with shocking news.

***

Roshi opened his eyes and set them on Gyozan. Had the floor not been carpeted, a dropped pin would have resounded as loudly as a Zen bell.

"He is gone, Roshi," said Gyozan.

"Gone where?"

"His room is empty. There is no trace of him. All his belongings, gone."

Gyozan might as well have been telling Roshi what they were having for lunch. There was no visible or verbal reaction.

"I checked zendo. I not notice this morning, but his name tag and cushions also gone."

Alex had noticed that Kosen's cushions were missing that morning. She was trained to notice such things. But she had chalked it up to one of Kosen's idiosyncrasies. *Damn, I really do enter another zone when I'm up here. I should have put it together, trusted my instinct that he was gone, told someone.*

Kosen had left during the night, or early morning, when the monastery slept. It was hardly a surprise that no one had heard a sound, given Kosen's affinity for moving soundlessly. Very Zen of him, Alex thought. Kosen leaving behind no Kosen. Maybe he'd gotten tired of waiting for Roshi to deem him fit for monkdom.

"He left one thing, Roshi." Gyozan got up and presented this item to Roshi, placing it on the table in front of him.

Roshi glanced at it, anger flashed behind his eyes. Everyone was stunned.

It was his rakusu. On top lay a piece of paper with something written on it. No one but Roshi could see what it said.

"Sonja, did you know about this?" Roshi asked.

"No, Roshi." Being Kosen's only close friend, the question had to be asked of Sonja. Everyone believed her. She sat in obvious shock and bewilderment.

"Anyone else know about this plan of Kosen's?" Roshi scanned the room looking directly into each pair of eyes. Heads shook all around. No one had a clue, or wasn't ready to give it up if they had.

Roshi read the note silently and handed it back to Gyozan to read aloud to the group. "Ga te ga te pa ra ga te para sam ga te bo dhi sva ha." Everyone knew the syllables by heart. They were the final words to the heart sutra that they chanted daily.

And everyone knew the translation. It was about going to another shore. *Typical Kosen, this gesture.*

Roshi stared at the rakusu. Anger passed over his face like a cloud. Then he closed his eyes and tilted his head toward the ceiling as if lost in thought. No one moved. He looked back down at the rakusu. His eyes were barely open, the anger was back. He unfolded the rakusu to view the side he had written on. In black ink calligraphy it held Kosen's name and its meaning: 'Ancient Fighting Spirit.'

Roshi refolded the ten-by-fifteen-inch square of fabric. The silence was now so big that it pushed at the walls of the small room.

Not one more word was spoken. Roshi rang his bell to end the meeting that never turned into a meeting. No beginning, no chanting, no end.

In giving back the name Roshi had so carefully chosen for him, a name that was meant to last a lifetime, Kosen was saying more than good-bye, and Roshi was pissed.

7

Alex was assigned to work with Jito in the kitchen. He gave her permission to go snooping around. Something was bugging her about Kosen's abrupt departure and the business with his rakusu.

"I can let you have a half hour, that's it," Jito said. "We have to start prepping things for next Sunday. I was hoping I'd have both you and Clark to help me this week. With Kosen out of the picture there's one less pair of hands around here, and too much to do. Kosen's still making trouble—and he's not even here anymore."

Alex slipped out of the kitchen through the back door and took the outside stairway to the long-term resident's wing. No one would be there this time of day. She was confident she'd be alone and undisturbed. How simple it was to move around the place without a soul noticing—in broad daylight. How much more so it would be in the darkness of mountain night.

As soon as she stepped inside the hallway and the outer door closed behind her, delivering her into near blackness, she felt like an intruder betraying her monk friends. But she had a mission and Jito had given his blessing. That was as good as a search warrant. She wasted no time.

Kosen's room was the second door on the right, Jito's the third. Sure enough, Kosen's room was empty of all personal effects. Only the futon, a pillow, blankets and a small, empty bookshelf remained.

The search wouldn't take anywhere near her allotted half hour. She found nothing, not even in the corners of the closet.

The monks shared a bath and shower room in the hall but a few of the rooms had private bathrooms shared with just one other room. Kosen's was one of those. How did he get so lucky? As soon as she opened the bathroom door Alex knew it wasn't Kosen's good karma that had got him the private bathroom, it was Jito's position as head cook and the privileges that came with it that afforded Kosen this luxury. It had probably been the only room available when he arrived. Kosen and Jito shared the bathroom.

This could explain why Jito had heard nothing, the bathroom helped to insulate sound. There were no sleeping pills in the medicine cabinet. *That's a relief.* Maybe Jito had been telling the truth when he'd said, "I was so pooped last night I passed out at ten. I slept the sleep of the dead. I can't believe it, but I heard nothing."

If Jito had a stash of pills they'd be well hidden in his room. Her license to snoop didn't include his room but she couldn't help herself. A cop's curiosity. She was confident that Jito was in his kitchen and no one would be on the other side of his bedroom door, but she took care to open it as she would any closed door during the course of an investigation. Her hand automatically reached for her gun that wasn't there.

Because there were no locks on any of the doors in the monastery, she wasn't surprised when Jito's door opened readily, but when a chain lock prevented it from opening more than four inches, suspicion shot through her.

Why would Jito need such a lock? What is he afraid of? Who is he keeping out? Why didn't he share his concerns with me? Granted, Jito had become more distant this past year, but still, she was a cop and he'd told her many times how much he respected that.

His favorite uncle had been a cop back home. Some of this hero worship fell onto her. Well, she'd be that cop right now and check his other door on her way out, all propriety blown to hell by that out-of-place lock.

The few inches of Jito's room she could see revealed little, except that he wasn't as neat in his private space as he was in his kitchen. Alex recalled the first time she visited him in his room, before she knew the rules, he had needed ten minutes to straighten up before she was allowed in, and wasn't happy about the intrusion. On subsequent visits Alex always gave him plenty of warning. Her trained cop's eyes would have noticed the lock had it been there previously.

Before leaving the bathroom, Alex closed her eyes and began her usual crime scene ritual. It wasn't a crime scene, she wasn't on duty, but something called to her to perform her routine. At the completion of her turning-in-place Alex opened her eyes and knew immediately what was weird. Two things. One was the lingering smell of incense. This was not so unusual, incense permeated every square inch of the monastery till the walls and floors throbbed with scent. Every resident had a favorite flavor that they burned privately, adding to the many competing fragrances. But here in this bathroom Alex's nose detected an incense flavor that didn't belong.

It took a few seconds to place it, but she recognized the scent as Shun-yo, Beckoning Spring, one of Roshi's favorites, one that at almost two dollars a stick was too expensive for a monk. It was the one she wanted to buy for Uncle Charlie as a treat. She knew it was made from agarwood, like most premium incense, but it was different from the everyday incense that was usually burned around there. Maybe it was the clove and patchouli spices in it. Whatever it was, it had a soft, subtle and lingering aroma that smelled expensive and what she imagined a deep mountain glen in Japan would smell like. *What's it doing here? What's Kosen or Jito doing with some of Roshi's private stash? And how and why did they get their hands on it? Only Roshi and Muin had access to it. If they'd bought some, where'd they get that kind of money?*

The second thing that stood out as strange was that the bathroom hadn't been cleaned in a while—boys will sometimes be boys no matter what the calling—yet the small straw wastebasket under the sink was empty. Not a tissue, not a Q-tip, not a string of used dental floss.

Do two nothings—an empty wastebasket and a scent in the air—add up to something? In Zen parlance, maybe not. In cop-speak, maybe so. Everything, including nothing, meant something until a case was done. As if she wasn't confused enough, the concept of emptiness or nothingness was too enigmatic for her brain to digest. But there it was, nothing, taking up space in her brain.

Alex used a washcloth to pick up the basket to get a closer look inside. There were a few stains, but one of them looked fresher than the others. What she wouldn't give for a forensic kit to test for blood. But even if there was blood, and it was Kosen's or Jito's, it would prove nothing. They both shaved and a nick here and there was inevitable. No crime had been committed as far as she knew, so she returned the basket and cloth to their proper place and moved out into the hall.

Jito's hall door was like all the others, with no lock of any kind. Satisfied, Alex turned to leave. Instantly she turned back and opened wide the door. The anomaly of the bathroom door lock stirred her innate need to know, but friendship with Jito kept her at the threshold. Resisting the urge to search his room was almost as hard as stifling the lust she felt around Muin.

She began to rationalize. *This isn't life threatening, no one will know, Jito will understand eventually, I'll be out of there in a jiff.* She let the door close. She wasn't on the job, so she chose to respect the unspoken rules of friendship.

Jito sure is a slob. She had clearly seen that the trash basket in his room was full. Why then was the bathroom's empty?

Alex moved down the hall to the empty room on the other side of Kosen's. This room mirrored Kosen's exactly, except for the bookshelf. Not expecting to find anything, Alex opened the closet door anyway.

There, the first tangible clue. Of what she didn't know, but she treated it as evidence. A roll of duct tape. Tucked away on the back of the closet shelf. Her cop instinct warned her not to touch it, to keep it free of her fingerprints. Latex gloves and plastic bags were in plentiful supply in the pantry—she'd come back later for the evidence, seal it up for possible dusting for clues later. *One can never be too careful.*

Before returning to the kitchen, Alex checked out the communal bathroom. Maybe someone had been assigned to collect all the trash from all the bathrooms that morning, which would explain the empty one in Kosen's and Jito's bathroom. The wastebaskets in the large bathroom had trash, though nothing she wouldn't expect to find—and no sign of fresh blood. Whatever had happened to Kosen, she was sure that the communal bathroom hadn't been involved. She made her way back to the kitchen.

***

In mid-morning Alex took a break from her cutting, chopping, slicing and dicing work in the kitchen to get a warmer pair of socks. On her way she slipped back upstairs to collect the duct tape. It was now swathed in plastic and safely hidden in her bag in the closet right next to her gun.

When she wrapped her hand around her bedroom doorknob and was about to pull on it, she heard loud whispering outside the door. She froze in place.

One of the two voices sounded distinctly female. The only word she could make out was Kosen. It was probably Sonja fretting over his disappearance. But who belonged to the other voice? Alex didn't want to surprise them so she waited until the whispers died down and she heard retreating footsteps.

As Alex turned the corner on her way back to the kitchen, she crashed smack into Sonja who was leaning against the wall, head in hands, weeping silently.

"Sonja, I'm so sorry, I didn't see you. Are you okay?"

Sonja shook her head.

"What's wrong?"

"I have no idea where Kosen is. I'm so worried. He would have told me something. I know most everyone here couldn't stand him, but no one knew him like I did."

"He'll probably be in touch with you when he gets to wherever he's going," Alex said, even if she had her misgivings.

Sonja pulled herself off the wall and straightened her shoulders. She drew a tissue out of her sleeve, wiped her tears and blew her nose gently.

"Sorry for you to see me like this. It's not good."

"Oh, please, it's me here, Sonja, I understand. You're just upset. You're allowed to have feelings. Who was that you were talking to?"

"Zenji, he called his cousin. Even he doesn't know where he went, or why." Sonja immediately regretted saying so much.

"Zenji?" Alex was unable to stifle her incredulity.

"He was trying to help. I asked him to. He's not so bad, you know."

"Yeah, well," Alex said, letting go of that one. *Shit, he is definitely the one she's got a thing with now. Damn, I never would've guessed him. I'll ask about that later.* "What's Zenji's cousin got to do with this?"

"Kosen's cousin, not Zenji's. Zenji called Kosen's cousin. I wasn't up to it. It was nice of him to help."

Alex thought back to the scene at the lake with the three of them.

"People come and go from here all the time. Maybe Kosen felt it was finally time for him to leave," Alex said.

Sonja shook her head. A tear slid down her cheek. Staring straight into Alex's eyes she said, "He would have told me. We were close, as you know. He loved me, told me everything."

She cast her eyes to the floor. "Plus, Roshi was finally talking to him about ordination. Kosen wanted that more than anything. He wouldn't just leave"—she looked back up at Alex— "without saying one word, at least to me."

"What were Kosen and Zenji arguing about at the lake yesterday?"

"Me probably, but Kosen wouldn't say. I got down there as Zenji was leaving. Kosen and I had a fight. Angry words were our last exchange." Sonja blew her nose. "He wouldn't just leave like that. Something's wrong—I know it."

In her gut, Alex concurred. "It'll turn out fine, you'll see." She hugged Sonja.

"I hope you're right. Thanks. You know, Kosen always liked you," Sonja said as they parted.

When Kosen conveyed this news to her yesterday, she thought it just part of his usual ramblings. Now, with Sonja telling her that Kosen liked her, Alex wondered about her own people skills. *Am I so out of touch that I don't even know or care if someone likes me? Why did I never bother to get to know Kosen?* She took it on faith, from what Muin and Jito had told her about him that he wasn't worth her time. *Since when do I let others determine such things for me?* This was worth thinking about at some point.

***

Routine settled things down throughout the monastery. By lunch a normal rhythm, minus one, had been restored. No one had forgotten about Kosen's disappearance, and Sonja's worry had spread to the rest of the sangha. There was little anyone was thinking about but how and why and when. If they did know, they weren't sharing it. Kosen was enigmatic, but this dramatic act seemed out of character for him. The reality of "No Kosen" was beginning to become integrated into the is-ness of the place.

Work continued after the post-lunch break. Normally Sunday afternoon and all day Monday were designated rest days. But with so much to do before Buddha's birthday celebration, the normal routine was disrupted and the rest period sacrificed. A late wake-up was planned for the next morning, along with an informal breakfast and the morning off from chores for most of them—this was as far as Roshi was willing to bend.

Everyone else knew he wouldn't be resting. And even though they had his blessing to rest in the morning, very few would. They weren't there to rest, as Roshi so often reminded them. It wasn't a spa they were at, it was a Zen monastery!

Thoughts of Kosen flitted in and out as the afternoon progressed, but no one except Sonja and Alex obsessed. Life ticked on. No big deal. Kosen was gone. That was that. Until Roshi made his announcement seconds before the evening sit, everyone seemed ready to move on, even Alex.

"Kosen has decided to leave Zen and return his rakusu. We will not speak of it again. He is Robert once more—there is no Kosen," Roshi pronounced. "The Kosen name is dead, not to be bestowed again. You will not speak it."

Ever the charismatic leader, Roshi took a lengthy pause. Alex pictured a big blackboard in the sky with Zen students' names written on it and Kosen's name being erased for all eternity.

Roshi could be pretty severe and uncompromising when he wanted to be. This was one of those times.

"There will be no gossip concerning this! This is it!" Roshi bellowed.

His usual emphatic tone resounded through the zendo. Tonight the pitch was tinged with an angry righteousness that Alex had never heard before.

"Now, let us do zazen!" Roshi declared.

8

Sunday, about midnight

No one felt like retiring early, and since Monday was rest day there was no morning zazen scheduled and wake-up was later than usual at 7:30, with informal, optional breakfast at 8:00—not sleeping in by most people's standards, but for monks and Zen students it was downright lazy time. They all hung out in the basement lounge, gaining some comfort in each other's company.

Unlike the rest of the monastery, where there was order, symmetry, and beauty everywhere, the lounge was an eclectic mix of flea market kitsch and college dorm grunge. The only thing that the extraordinary assortment of characters had in common was their meditation practice. And Roshi.

All Roshi's students felt special, and uniquely close to him. Robert/Kosen had been no exception. If Alex were honest with herself, neither was she. No one else could have brought together such disparate characters as were collected in the lounge. *What is it about Roshi that makes him a magnet for so many loonies? And why are so many emotionally unstable people drawn to a spiritual life? I know what this says about the Kosen and Zenji types, but what does it say about me? And Muin?*

"He just couldn't stand the idea of living with Zenji. And he knew Roshi was planning to make him Zenji's assistant next week—to teach him some bullshit lesson about tolerance or some such thing—so he split," Clark pontificated, waving his stump around because he knew it annoyed most of them. He rarely mingled with other students in formal or informal sessions. But whenever he did he made his presence known

"Robert felt betrayed by Roshi and couldn't stomach the idea of having to work for Zenji," Clark shouted. "I can't believe you guys can't get that. And Roshi didn't even like Robert. Why wouldn't he let him be a monk? What was up with that? Roshi lets anyone who wants to become a monk, become a monk—Zenji being the perfect example—he'd probably even make me a monk if I wanted it."

He can be such a jerk sometimes. She was on one of the two overstuffed chairs, legs draped over the arm, with notebook and pencil in hand. She drew Clark's tiny black eyes, bushy eyebrows, and frizzy head of brown-turning-to-gray hair as if it were an art project. She tried to ignore the stump of his hand.

"What the hell did Roshi have against Robert anyway?" Clark ranted. "I think Robert just had enough of the bullshit. He's probably with some other teacher right now who will ordain him. And good for him. He's better off out of this place."

He left in a huff as if he'd just made the decision for himself to disappear from their lives just like Robert had.

"Kosen ... oops, I mean Robert, really hated Zenji, or maybe he couldn't handle how much Zenji hated him. But I can't believe that would send him packing," said Gyozan, who was always working on his English idioms. He'd been the one to discover Kosen's empty room and was more animated than usual.

Alex amused herself. She sketched Gyozan in caricature, exaggerating his pointy ears and wide grin. Like all monks his head was shaved, but she gave him spiked, jet black hair in her drawing and made his eyes smile more than usual. If he let his hair grow it would most definitely be black.

"He's been on his way out of here ever since he got here. It makes sense he'd do it the way he did. He was always looking for attention and right now he's probably having a good laugh about it as we all sit here worrying about him," Muin said.

Alex knew he couldn't abide ambivalence, especially when it came to Roshi and Zen practice.

"Who's worried? I for one am glad he's gone. And good riddance to him," Zenji said. "And Gyozan, you're wrong. I didn't hate him, I just didn't think he fit in here. I don't know why we're all still up. What do we think, he's gonna walk back in any minute? I don't know about the rest of you, but I'm ready to call it a night." Zenji stayed put and didn't even pretend to make an exit.

Alex drew Robert/Kosen from memory as Zenji spoke. Made him look like a movie star with his thick, black hair and dreamy eyes. Then she sketched him without hair. *Hmmm, he'd look good as a monk.*

Sonja sat on the couch, curled into a ball, chin resting on her knees. Her grieving was palpable. "Robert loved Roshi more than he hated Zenji—you all know that. I can't believe he left willingly, knowing how much it would upset Roshi. Something just isn't right about this."

Alex noticed that Sonja and Zenji were taking pains to keep their distance from each other. Sonja would steal a glance at Zenji, but he was a cool customer and ignored her all night long. It was as if he'd put up a wall to keep Sonja out. *What is going on between them? What had gone on with them and Robert?*

"He hate to clean toilet, maybe more than he hate Zenji, and Zenji would have him clean toilet, and his hate for Zenji would be more. Wow, it is confusing. Maybe he couldn't stand to hate so much, that was why he leave."

Over the course of the night, Zenji spewed forth more than the others. Redundancy personified. Even with Robert out of the picture Zenji was competing with him, trying to get everyone to see his side. *Blowhard is what he is. What the hell does Sonja see in him? No accounting for attraction, I suppose.*

Listening to and sketching her Zen friends, Alex came to the realization that she didn't know much about any of them, except Muin. And since Sonja had been ordained, Alex felt like she didn't know her anymore.

She decided to have Uncle Charlie check backgrounds on Robert aka Kosen, the missing wannabe monk, Zenji, his nemesis, and Sonja's paramour, Gyozan, the only Japanese monk there and the one who'd discovered Robert's disappearance. And, Buddha forgive her, Jito, whose locked room kept nagging at her, and who was way too silent all night. It didn't even cross her mind to include Muin. She hated putting Jito on the list, but what did she know about him really? Or any of them? *What can it hurt? Worst case scenario, at the end of the week I'll know a little more about my Zen friends.*

At about 12:00 when everyone had run out of things to say, they remained put and sank into a silent mood worthy of the zendo upstairs. It was as if they were all waiting "for the truth to reveal itself."

Alex thought of the Zen adage: "Before enlightenment, chop wood, carry water, after enlightenment, chop wood, carry water."

No difference, enlightenment and non-enlightenment. So what were they waiting for in the lounge that night or on their cushions day after day? If Zen had it right and pre- and post- enlightenment were one and the same, then maybe they were all just wasting their time and falling into the human trap of hoping that something better lies ahead.

Sonja was the first to leave the lounge. Zenji followed five minutes later. By 12:30, one by one, the rest of the group began to drift away. Ten minutes later, Alex and Muin were the only two left.

***

"Looks like it's you and me, kid. Just like the old days," Muin said.

"It's so good to see you, Muin, I've missed you," Alex said as she moved to join him on the sofa.

She plopped down, brought her feet up to the cushion and let her knees fall to the side, her new favorite sitting position. A whiff of woody incense mixed with a tint of body odor, Muin's body odor, wafted over to her as she turned to face him. His blue eyes were bloodshot, his head and face had a few days' growth. He was twelve years older than her and if he let his hair grow out she would see he'd have some gray now mixed in with the early stages of salt and pepper. With hair, without hair, unshaven, didn't matter, he had a dark charm about him she found hard to resist. She wanted to reach out and hold him. She crossed her arms against her chest to squelch that urge and then dropped her hands into her lap. She couldn't sit still.

"Like my new haircut?" she said, with a toss of her head and a smile. *What the hell am I doing? Flirting with him? What is wrong with me?*

"Oh yeah," he said as he gave her 'do a quick glance. "It looks great, you always look great."

"What's up? You seem tense," said Alex.

"Exhausted is all." He turned away from her, laid his head on the sofa back and stared at the ceiling. "With Kosen's shenanigans and Buddha's day coming up, all the planning that's gone into it ... I just can't wait till it's over. I'd love to stay up with you and talk, but I'm pooped, I really do need some shuteye. I'll be good for nothing if I don't get some rest soon."

Alex knew there was something he wasn't saying. "Turned down by a monk." Alex poked his side. "You know what that can do to a girl's ego?"

He turned his head toward her and raised his right eyebrow, the one with a scar just above it, the one she'd kissed many a time in the past, as if to say, "What the hell are you doing, Alex? What game are we playing here?" *What the hell am I doing? Cut it out!*

Alex shifted, tucked her feet under her. Muin sat up.

"You know it's not about you," he said. "I—"

"Only kidding," said Alex. "I'm just being selfish. I'm wiped out too. We'll catch up tomorrow or later this week."

"Thanks for understanding," said Muin, looking relieved.

"Don't thank me yet. Time for one question?"

"Sure."

"Why are so many people coming up for Buddha's birthday? I don't remember it being such a huge deal in the past."

Muin let out a long sigh. "It's a long story, Alex, and quite a guest list. Can we do this another time?"

"Sure thing." Alex bolted upright to the edge of the sofa, and shot both feet to the floor. "Wait, did you hear that?"

They sat still, held their breath and listened.

"I don't hear anything," Muin said.

"Shh, there it is again."

They both heard it this time. A rustling, like something big moving through space. The floor was basement concrete so there was no sound of feet.

Without a sound, Alex got up and made her way to the door, Muin right with her. By the time they reached the hall and peered left and right, whatever had been lurking was gone.

"Probably just a chipmunk or mouse," Muin said.

"It sounded a lot bigger than that." If Kosen wasn't already gone, I'd place odds that it was him."

"Look, someone left the outside door open," Muin said. It was freezing in the corridor. He walked over to the door and closed it. "It could've been a porcupine. They can get quite brazen this time of year, end of winter and all, especially if there are no car brake lines for them to gnaw on."

Alex worried about her new Outback, but remembered that it was parked with all the other cars in the porcupine-proof, fenced-in area down by the woodshed. She also thought the rustling noise they'd heard had come from something larger than a porcupine.

"Let's call it a night, Alex, shall we?" Muin held out his arms.

"Of course," Alex said as she walked into his hug. He released her almost before they'd touched and kissed her on the cheek. He didn't exactly push her away, but it sure felt like it.

They said goodnight and retired to their rooms, putting a distance between them that was a more accurate reflection of the emotional remoteness Alex had sensed all night.

9

Monday, April 2, 6:30 AM

Alex was up early despite her exhaustion. Something had her on the alert when she planted her bare feet on the cold floor. It was the anniversary of Daddy's death but with each passing year that was a gentler tremor. She was reminded of the first day the tidal wave of that news hit her, it was not a memory she cared to surf today.

It would take longer than usual to settle into the mountain rhythm. This morning, a good long run was in order. There was no zazen and there'd be plenty of food left when she returned.

Her running routine and discipline had been compromised the past few months and if she intended to run the NYC Marathon in the fall she needed to ratchet up the training. Ten miles would be a good start—ten high, hilly miles. Her legs and lungs perked up at the thought. A Luna food bar, a shot of coffee from the lounge, a bathroom stop and she was on the road in a half hour. Not bad for a weary old lady, she thought.

Her first mile was downhill to the monastery gatehouse where she took a left on the main mountain road and ran uphill from there. With only a few houses set back from the road, a small campground, and a state park with a lookout tower at the very top, it was less traveled than the lower road. It was almost five miles to the top of that section of road, so there and back would do it.

The day was gray and drizzly, the terrain unpaved, rutted and lonely. Her body absorbed the effect and turned sluggish. She felt every step and never hit a groove. Before the end of the first uphill mile she wanted it over. Wishing away time always spelled disaster, yet nothing could shake her from projecting ahead. So she pushed on and accepted that her usual runner's high might come later than usual, or not at all.

At the third mile mark Alex noticed a red pickup truck parked in the woods. There was no house or driver in sight. It wasn't unusual to see vehicles parked alongside the road, as the river was a favorite spot for trout fishermen, and some men hunted nearby, flouting the NO TRESPASSING NO HUNTING signs in plain sight. Alex figured it was one of them and was glad to have worn her orange sweatshirt. The last thing she wanted was to be mistaken for a deer by some cocky guy with a rifle.

How safe was it to be running alone on a deserted road near men with guns? This question came from the blue; she'd never entertained such a suspicion before while on the mountain. She quickened her pace and let the red truck and its mystery driver be. It was not her business whatever he was doing at that hour alone in the woods.

***

Less than two hours later she was back at the gatehouse, but had no energy left to run the last mile section uphill to the monastery, so she chose to walk, cool down, take her time, maybe stop and stretch along the way, and visit Kido's grave. Halfway up, a patrol car's siren blast and flashing lights startled her off to the side of the road. She stood stock still as one, two, three patrol cars passed, lights flashing, drivers intent on the curvy, rocky incline, traveling as fast as they could, but slow as molasses given the urgency expressed by the sheer volume of wheels. Two unmarked cars, lights spinning on dashboards, took up the rear—detectives for sure.

The second-to-last car stopped, its passenger door flew open, and the driver barked: "Get in." Alex got in.

"You stayin' up there?" the detective said, his broad chin and black eyes darting uphill. He was bulging out of his tweed sport coat, his face flushed as if he'd just run up the hill.

"Yes. What the hell happened?" Alex asked.

"Out jogging were you?"

"Yeah."

"So, what the hell happened?" Alex asked again. *This has to have something to do with Kosen, of course, damn it.*

"How long've you been out?"

"About an hour and a half," Alex said. Knowing that she would have asked the same didn't make her like being on this side of that question.

"Everything okay when you left?"

"Of course. Please, tell me, is someone dead?"

"What makes you think that?"

Understanding turned to exasperation. "Look, Detective ..."

"Wolfe."

"Detective Wolfe. I don't live here, I'm just visiting. I'm a detective from the city."

"Is that so?" Wolfe said as he gave her a sideways glance that spoke volumes about his mistrust of city cops, particularly if they were of the female persuasion. She'd met the likes of him before.

"Please, let me in on whatever is going on." Alex didn't bother adding, "As a professional courtesy."

"I've a right to know what happened. I know these people," Alex said.

Wolfe sat there, stubborn, concentrating on his driving. Then he spit out: "Someone is dead."

"Oh my god. It's Kosen, isn't it?"

"Who's that?"

"One of the residents who left yesterday morning without telling a soul. He just vanished. It was like he disappeared into thin air. No one knew where he went or why ... shit." Alex plopped her skull back onto the headrest. This car was taking much too long to reach the top.

"People in the habit of disappearing from up there and then turning up dead?"

Alex did not like this guy. The feeling was mutual. She would hold her tongue till she knew more.

"D'you notice anything weird this morning? Weirder than usual, that is?"

"Nope."

Again, the sideways glance from Wolfe.

Alex had her hand on the door handle before the car came to a halt. Wolfe reached out and grabbed her left wrist.

"Keep your nose where it belongs, detective. I'm in charge up here, not you. Until I say otherwise, everyone is a suspect, including you. Got it?"

"I got it." Alex jerked her arm from his grasp and flew out of the car and into the monastery.

***

Muin waited for Alex to finish her turning-in-place crime scene ritual. Then they walked upstairs together to join the others in the dining room.

Poor Kosen. He might've been a pain in the ass, but he didn't deserve to be killed. No one deserved that. Her once resolute stance on capital punishment was yielding to the Buddhist precept not to kill. But if Kosen's murderer were standing in front of her right now she had no clue how she'd feel.

She did know what Kido's advice would be. It was as if he were sitting on her shoulder whisper-shouting in her ear.

"Don't be a breathing corpse! Quick! Act! Don't think!" If he were really there in front of her he'd be snapping his fingers as he said it, grinning demonically.

She was pissed that some bad guy had invaded and polluted her hallowed space, Roshi's and Muin's and everyone else's holy temple. There'd be no rest for her this week. At that moment she didn't care. All she wanted was to find the guy—intuitively she knew one person was responsible—the guy who took a life, the most sacred of sacreds, and despoiled the monastery.

"I can't believe I was out running. Who found him?" Alex asked.

"Clark. It was his turn to feed the furnace," Muin said. "Damn, this is horrible."

"How's Roshi taking it?"

"As you'd expect."

Alex wasn't sure what that was. "Do you think the noise we heard outside the lounge last night could've had something to do with this?"

"I've been thinking the same thing. I wish I hadn't been so tired. I wish I'd investigated that open door. I wish—" Muin stopped mid-thought. He was holding something back, Alex was sure of it.

"What?"

"Nothing. Of all weeks for this to happen, the timing couldn't be worse."

"There's no good time for this sort of thing, is there?" *What had he been about to say, what was going on with him, why is he acting so odd? This is not just about us.*

"No, I guess you're right. I don't know what I'm saying."

They were at the door to the dining room. They peered in, expecting to see no one, the room was so silent. But there they all were sitting on the floor at the long, low, wooden tables over their uneaten cold breakfast.

Alex surmised that most had never seen a dead body outside of a casket in a funeral home. And now they sat, stunned, rather like breathing corpses.

To see one of their own, dead, without warning, in their spiritual space, was just too much. It unraveled the group close to the brink. Alex was right there with them, furious that her precious monastery was no longer a safe harbor, that the evil that plagued the rest of the world had found its way in. Alex didn't know about the before and after enlightenment sameness, but what she did know was that before and after dead were nowhere near the same.

Alex joined the group, and Muin left to check on Roshi. Keenly scrutinizing the gathering, Alex noticed the students who had the most years of consistent practice under their butts seemed the least disturbed. There was a new student sitting by himself, unmoving, and Alex decided it was shock.

Gyozan, just as still, embodied equanimity. A striking contrast, maybe cultural, probably not. The degree of calmness or anxiety in each of them was proportionate to the length of time spent on the cushion. Alex had no time to dwell on this fascination.

Her composure came not from her eight short years of sporadic sitting practice, but from twenty years of being a cop and dealing with dead bodies. Her anxiety came from the fact that she had no authority as a cop to do much of anything, and that each person there, including her, was a suspect.

Then came the waiting, something they were all practiced at, at least on the meditation cushion, waiting for the Kensho or enlightenment experience. Waiting for the light, the spark of recognition, the awareness. When the truth reveals itself. Or a corner of the truth, a slight glimpse of what's really going on.

In this case, for the mystery of Kosen's death to become clear, for their questions to be answered. They knew how to wait. And they knew how to fake it if necessary, as they sat enveloped in one form of pain or another.

Alex was afraid that her detachment would be compromised by her connection to the players. She'd never been so personally related to a killing. She ought to let go of any involvement on a professional level. She took the whole thing personally. Someone had fucked up her asylum. There'd be no relief until she found the fucker. A blast of bourbon right about now would help, but she settled for cold scrambled eggs. Sitting and chewing, she reviewed in her mind the details of the previous day and evening.

She then took a closer look at her Zen friends to see which of them was a cold-blooded killer.

10

Detective Wolfe swaggered into the dining room with Muin at his side and spoke to the group. Roshi was still tucked away somewhere out of sight. For an event of this magnitude Roshi would normally take charge—but as far as Alex knew this was the first dead, maybe murdered, student in Roshi's long career as Zen teacher-monk and maybe he was having a hard time coping and did not want his students to see him unnerved.

"We'll be meeting with each of you soon. It goes without saying, but I'll say it anyways, none of you are to leave the premises," Wolfe said.

"The detectives will be working in the library," Muin said. "I'll post a list of names with interview times on the bulletin board in about an hour. Please check it and report to the library when it's your turn."

"And what do you expect us to do till then?" Zenji asked.

"I got this," said Wolfe. "Muin tells me this was supposed to be your morning off. But due to the possible murder of one of your people we can't have you roaming about, so you can sit here in this room and wait or do some chores in this building ... in twos, I don't want anyone alone."

"I have work assignments for those who want to work," Muin said, waving a sheaf of papers. "You can check with Zenji," he added as he handed the pages to Zenji, "until I'm available."

"So we're prisoners then," Zenji said, shooting daggers at Wolfe and Muin and looking at the pieces of paper in his hand as if he didn't know how they got there.

"Till we sort this out and talk to each of you there's no going anywhere without my say so—if that means prison to you, so be it. It's my job to find some answers here." Wolfe threw back to Zenji his angry eyes. "Till then, you're all just suspects."

The meaning of these two sentences riveted them into silence.

A sob from Sonja pierced the air. No one spoke, they hardly breathed.

Gyozan raised his hand. "What?" Wolfe barked.

"I hate to say this about a fellow student, but is it not obvious that he killed himself?" Gyozan asked.

Wolfe softened his voice a tad. "Nothing is obvious when someone dies, especially when it's in such a weir- ... an unusual manner. If it's suicide, you're all off the hook, but till we know for sure, everyone stays put. Got it?"

There were no more questions.

After Wolfe and Muin left, Alex couldn't just sit there and she wasn't ready to get to work. She still hadn't showered since her run. She assumed she'd be working with Jito in the kitchen again—they would continue to prepare and serve meals even if no one wanted to eat—but from the look of Jito, he was nowhere near ready to cook.

Sitting up against a wall, knees drawn up to his face, arms wrapped around his legs with his chin sunk deep into his chest, Jito was the picture of inner torment. Alex figured that most of the room's occupants shared his grief, they just weren't as physically expressive. If there was a killer and he was among them, there was no outward or emotional sign of who that was.

Alex's Zen mind went to suicide—if it was Clark or Zenji, even Muin, dead in the basement, she would believe it, but as crazy as Kosen was, suicide seemed way out of character. She saw him more as a killer of others, not of himself. Then her cop's mind settled on murder and she knew her initial instinct had been the right one.

She needed to talk to someone about this. As soon as this thought entered, Muin poked his head back in the room and called out, "Alex."

She sprung up off the floor and was at his side in a flash. "Yeah?"

"The cops want to talk to you first. They're up in the library."

"Good." She headed off and then stopped when she realized Muin wasn't with her. "You coming?"

"Nope, they want you alone. I'm sure you can handle it."

"Okay, see you later." She was all business.

***

Alex took a deep breath outside the library door and braced herself for some unpleasantness. She pushed the door open and walked in for her interview with the detectives. She knew she hadn't killed Kosen but they didn't. She also knew the job they had in front of them, but still she hated being on this side of the interrogation table. Out of respect for their badges she'd try to be civil. Besides, it wasn't definitively murder yet.

Alex walked into the library and was greeted with a pacing Wolfe, and another guy, sitting awkwardly on a folding chair that had been set up at a card table, makeshift office furniture. It was so obvious who was good cop and who was bad that she almost laughed. The good cop got up to greet her, extending his hand in welcome. He was about her age, maybe a couple years younger and had a youthful and at the same time confident, experienced air about him. His hair was dirty blond, thick and long on top, clipped short around the edges, wavy and slicked back with some sort of hair product. He was in good shape under the boxy sport coat and just the sort of guy Alex would be drawn to over a mug of beer. Like many handsome men, he didn't think much about how he looked, leaving room for a friendly demeanor.

"Hi, I'm Detective Tom Kluny. And he's Howard, er, Detective Wolfe." Kluny nodded toward his partner. *I wonder if they chose each other? Beauty and the beast.* "I'm state, he's local, we partner up when anything big happens around here."

"Hi," said Alex, shaking his hand. "Detective Wolfe and I met earlier, sort of ..." She wasn't sure whether to introduce herself as a detective or a Zen student.

Wolfe solved that dilemma for her. "So, Alex Sullivan ... it might be Detective Sullivan in the city but that means nothing up here, understand?"

"Sure thing, detective." She couldn't control her sarcastic tone.

"Detective Wolfe told me you were out jogging this morning. Is that right?" said Kluny, a good-cop lilt to his voice.

"Yeah, I left about 7:00 and got back just when you guys arrived."

"And you heard and saw nothing before you left?" said Kluny.

Wolfe was tapping a pen against the top of the table he was standing next to, glaring at Alex, visibly impatient with his partner. He was the Alpha cop, with the chip on his shoulder. His obvious anger could be due to current circumstances, but most likely stretched back to some past hurt that was lost in a stomach ulcer or some such physical ailment. Or it could just be attached to the unopened pack of Marlboros sticking out of his shirt pocket. Maybe he just needed a nicotine fix.

"Look, detectives, I know you have to ask these questions, but I didn't kill Kosen ... if he was killed. So let's not waste time, okay? There's a dead Zen student downstairs and I'm sure we all want to know why. Maybe I can help."

"We don't need your help, but you can go. For now ..."

Alex tried to object. "Bu—"

"Now! You can go now. Watch your Ps and Qs and stay out of our way. You got that?" Wolfe said more as a statement than as a question.

"I got it," Alex said, but she didn't like it. What she did get was that she had been first on their list so Wolfe could give her the message to stay out of his business.

She extended her hand to Kluny. She needed to check her own anger and there was no need right now to provoke Wolfe.

"Thanks detective," she said, shaking his hand. "If I can be of any help please let me know."

"Will do—"

Wolfe interrupted their pleasantries. "If you see or hear anything about what happened, don't do anything stupid. Report it to us and let us do our job."

"No problem, detective," Alex said in the sweetest voice she could muster as she looked squarely into Wolfe's eyes. She would not be cowed by any angry cop, even if he was wearing a sports coat and jonesing for a cigarette.

"Glad to be of service if I can. Nice to meet you, Detective Kluny."

She turned and walked out. Halfway down the stairs the library door opened again and Kluny came bounding down.

Alex blocked his way. "Detective, can I have a word with you?"

"Sure thing, but let's go somewhere else. Wolfe'll have a fit if he sees us—he can't stand anyone pissing on his territory, especially a girl ... sorry about that."

"Not a problem, I'm familiar with the type. Let's go out on the deck around back. He won't see us there."

Alex started whispering before they got around the first corner. "I know this is your terrain as cops, but if you ask me, we should treat this as a homicide right away. If it comes back as suicide, fine, though I don't think it will, but it's best to get a head start. There are three important things to look at. One, the—"

"Whoa, missy, whoa, slow down. Wolfe doesn't want you involved ... and at this point I have to agree with him."

"I get that, but look, I'm not saying that you need me because of my homicide experience, I'm sure you can handle that part of the crime if it comes to that. But it'll take you guys forever to wrap your minds around the foreignness of the culture here. Sure, this place is in the Catskills, your home turf, but it might as well be on the other side of the planet. It's taken me years to even begin to understand the Zen mentality. Plus I know how cops think. So I can only be an asset to you, interpreting both ways. If I could at least be in the room when you guys question everyone ..."

"Geez Louise ..." Kluny said, scratching his head. "For the time being, this is Wolfe's case, and I really don't think he'd allow—"

"Look, first, Kosen's head was shaved. It wasn't when he was alive the day before yesterday. That's gotta mean something. And he left behind, or his killer did, his Buddhist bib, which he had supposedly lost and was searching for when I arrived on Saturday.

Thirdly, the branch in his mouth might refer to a koan—I'm sure it means something ... something that you guys will never fathom. Sorry, no offense, but this is a mysterious practice and no one other than maybe Roshi fully understands koans."

"What the hell is a koh-on?"

"Exactly what I'm talking about—I don't have time to get into detail now, but a koan is something Roshi gives us to meditate on, it's an enigmatic story that has no easy answer. You guys need me at this point and you can't trust anyone else here."

"Okay, you might be right, and if it were up to me I'd consult with you. But Wolfe's another story."

"Can't you talk to him?"

"I'll try. I'm sure you noticed he's a little edgy and trying to quit smoking, so he's not always in the best mood."

"I gathered that. But if he's trying to quit, why the hell is he carrying around a pack of smokes?"

"Says it helps, knowing he can have one if he wants."

"I quit once and having a pack so close would've been torture."

"Yeah, well, Wolfe is a rare bird."

"Seems like it."

"I'll talk to him, but in the meantime why don't you get me some info on that koh-on about the branch, would you?"

"Sure thing. Thanks, Kluny. I'll catch up with you later."

Alex had to find a way to be in the room with Wolfe and Kluny as they interviewed, or in Wolfe's case, interrogated, her friends. She might be too close to the community to have a healthy perspective, but then again, maybe her attachment would usher in perfect clarity.

She knew one thing for sure, that it would be difficult, just like a certain koan promised.

Kido's voice filled her brain, *"Just be yourself, Alex, know what your duty is ... and just do it!"*

But what is my duty here? And what am I, Zen student or cop? Can I be both at the same time?

11

Alex returned to the dining room to find it empty of people and food. *Did something else happen? Zen students don't just sit around unless they're in the zendo. Where the hell did they all go?* She rushed into the kitchen to check on Jito. Her intuition told her that everyone was simply doing something useful, and sure enough, Jito was there huddled together with Clark, whispering in a corner. Her presence didn't startle them. Jito waved her over to hear the latest.

It surprised her to see him so animated after the shock of Kosen's death had had him in a fetal position in the dining room just before she'd left to talk with the cops.

"What did I miss?" Alex said.

"We all think it was murder," Jito said.

"Let's not jump to conclusions," Alex said, even though she agreed.

"Oh, don't be such a cop. Kosen might've been unstable, but he wasn't the slit-the-wrist type. Not that he slit his wrists, but you know what I mean."

"And what's the general consensus on why. And what about how?"

"Word is that Sonja dumped Kosen for Zenji, though for the life of me I can't imagine why ... and we figure with that and then with

Roshi on his case, well, let's just say he was never going to be Roshi's dharma heir, not to mention ever becoming a monk under Roshi. And maybe Kosen felt like he didn't have much to live for, which is why the cops will probably be misled into thinking suicide. And whoever killed him knew all this, which made it easy for him."

"Wow! You've really thought about this. And the how?"

"Drugs," Jito said.

"Where's all his stuff? Where'd he get the drugs?"

"We're still working on the theory."

"Well, you might want to leave that to the cops." As soon as it was out of her mouth, Alex regretted saying it.

Kido in her ear: *"You must discipline your mind and watch what you say. You can never take back words. An undisciplined mind causes greater harm than those who hate you."*

Sure enough, Jito was offended. "I can't envisage you as one of them."

Maybe that's why he never fully trusted me. Respect maybe, as with his cop uncle, but trust is another story. She understood the aversion.

"Yeah, well, I never did fit in. At first it was all like make believe, like I was still a kid playing cops and robbers. Now it's just something I do." Alex shrugged.

"So what's your cop instinct telling you?" Jito asked.

"I'm reserving judgment for now. If I knew why, it'd be a lot easier to get to who, if there is a who." .

"A lot of us wished him gone."

"Yeah, but only because he was a pain in the ass. Hard to believe someone would have killed him for being a jerk."

"If he was killed ... some of us think it was Zenji, since it had to be one of us, no? And he had the perfect motive, to get rid of his competition. Both he and Kosen were in love with Sonja, and with Kosen gone it would be much easier for Sonja to walk away. Some say she couldn't make up her mind between them."

"I thought she chose Zenji?"

"That's just a rumor."

"Hard for me to wrap my mind around a monk killing a rival out of jealousy. What about you, Clark? What's your theory?" Alex asked.

"There are a few people in this place I'd put my money on, but I'm done talking about it. No one listens to me anyway," Clark said. "Like when I suggested we put locks on all our doors, but no, no one cared. Now maybe ..." He moved off mumbling under his breath over to the sink to wash lettuce for a salad he was preparing. He spun the salad spinner and sliced tomatoes like a normal two-handed person. Alex marveled at his dexterity.

"If Zenji wasn't a monk, I'd tend to agree with you," Alex said. "He's not the nicest person alive and he hated Kosen with a passion, but he does take his monkhood seriously. Maybe he harbored some resentment and imagined life without Kosen would be easier, but I doubt he'd ever kill anyone."

"I don't know about that. You're not here enough," Jito said. "Didn't you hear about the time he almost ran Kosen down with the truck? If he hadn't jumped out of the way, I'm not convinced Zenji would have stopped. Then there was the time that they nearly came to blows. The group stopped it, but Kosen showed up the next morning with a shiner. He wouldn't say how it happened, but we were all convinced he got in the way of Zenji's fist.

"If I'da known before I got here that monks behaved so recklessly I might've thought twice about becoming one myself. I still can't believe some of what they do, and, girlfriend, I've seen just about everything.

"And here's something else I bet you don't know." Jito loved being the first to relate provocative details. "We think they knew each other in California."

"Zenji and Kosen? Who did you hear it from?"

"Clark, tell her."

"I overheard Zenji and Sonja talking yesterday, something about Kosen's cousin, California, the people they knew ..."

"Sonja, too?"

"No, I don't think so, just Zenji and Kosen," Clark said.

"In what context?"

"That wasn't clear, I only heard bits and pieces."

"So you're not really sure then?"

"I'll bet they knew each other," Jito said. "The bitterness between them wasn't born up here. And if it's true, you can be certain they didn't meet in charm school or the boy scouts. Probably juvenile court, or detention, knowing them. That's my guess, anyway. They were probably locked up together some place and cooked up a scheme there. Then they came here pretending to be devoted Zen students. Humph!

"They were bad boys and I for one never thought it was a coincidence that they both ended up here. I'd be willing to bet they were in on something together, their animosity toward each other just a cover. Maybe things went wrong and Zenji had to get rid of Kosen before he exposed them."

"And according to your theory, what were they here to do?" Alex humored him.

"I dunno. Maybe get rid of Roshi."

"Jito, I think you've been up in the thin mountain air too long. Or reading too many of those mystery novels. That's a bit far-fetched, don't you think?"

"You haven't been here Alex. You haven't witnessed their idiotic, bordering-on-violent behavior day after day. It's been more than outlandish. We all knew something was brewing. But we never figured murder. And now no theory seems too off the wall."

"They were both wacky. But you know how it is with Roshi, drawn to crazies. And they were both devoted to Roshi," Alex said, not quite believing it, surface appearances rarely revealing the truth. "What other theories have you heard?"

"Clark thinks it might've been Sonja, or Zenji and Sonja together, but I told him he's nuts. Sonja was the only one who liked Kosen—though that was bizarre in its own way—and everyone knows she wouldn't hurt a spider. I don't buy it. After the two of them, Zenji and Sonja, the theories dry up."

In a whisper to Alex, his hand cupped around his mouth, he said, "Clark has ideas about everyone here and how and why they would have done it but that's just his zaniness."

In a normal voice he continued, "Realistically, after considering Zenji and Sonja, there's no one else. I'm betting on Zenji."

"Clark might be on to something," Alex said, glancing over at Clark, who seemed absorbed in his task and uninterested in her opinion. *I'd like to hear all his theories at some point.* "I ran into Sonja and Zenji whispering in the hall yesterday. Sonja said she asked him to call Kosen's cousin. This was before Kosen turned up dead."

"The three of them, all eccentric, though I still can't figure how Sonja got involved with those creeps. And the cousin! He's a piece of work."

"You know him?"

"Nah, not really. I saw him a few times when he came here to pick Kosen up, but I wasn't ever interested in meeting him. I figured if he was anything like Kosen I should steer clear. One of them was enough to deal with. He was too scary looking. He actually has a rifle hanging up behind him in his truck. No-o-o-o-o thank yew. He gave me the willies." Jito shivered.

Clark moseyed over to them. "I overheard Sonja on the phone with this guy. He's coming up here today."

So he was listening. "Does anyone know this guy's name?" Alex asked.

"Lawrence, I think," Jito said. "But we've never exchanged even one word."

"By the way, Jito, what was your beef with Kosen anyway? Aside from his being an asshole? You never did tell me. Was there something else?"

"Never mind. It was nothing. And now that he's gone we can just forget about it. It's over and done."

But Jito couldn't hide his nervousness. *Maybe Clark knows something about that. I'll pull him aside later.*

Alex changed the subject. "What would you like me to do today?"

"Nothing, dahling. You've been reassigned to Zenji. I know, I know, you poor dear. So sorry. But I really need Clark this week. He's my bread expert, kneads dough better than a machine." Jito clenched his hand into a fist and pointed his thumb at Clark's back. "And we need to bake lots of it. For next Sunday, you know—"

"Roshi's still planning to have the big event on Sunday?" Alex interrupted. She was shocked, but on second thought knew she ought not to be. Sunday was six days away; plenty of time to process

Kosen's death, get rid of the cops, and prepare for the celebration. Roshi never allowed anything to interfere with his schedule. *But this is a murdered student*, argued her rational mind.

Kido, who directed theater before becoming a monk, roared sarcastically inside her brain: *"The Zen show must go on ... no matter what!"*

"Yup, Sunday's still happening. And with Kosen now gone, they couldn't spare both of you to work here," Jito said, matter-of-factly.

She had the distinct impression that Jito would rather not have her around. And yet, just yesterday he was happy to have her in the kitchen and not Clark. For the moment she chalked it up to the whims of a chef and hoped that's all it was.

He shooed her out of his kitchen. When she glanced back over her shoulder through the window in the door, she saw him pirouette over to the counter where Clark was chopping vegetables, the salad done. It amazed her how such a big man could be so graceful, and that monks carried on the way they did. *Why is he so chummy with Clark all of a sudden?*

12

After a long, hot, guilty shower, trying to work out in her mind how she was going to insert herself in the investigation if it turned out to be murder, Alex looked up the tree branch koan in her book of koans to check her memory of the details of it. And then went off in search of Muin to see if there was anything he could do to get her into the library with the cops.

Along the way, it felt as if Kido had taken up permanent residence on her shoulder and was whispering sweet Zen things in her ear. He'd never before been such a persistent presence, but she did love his company. She tried not to entertain the idea that she was losing her marbles. Whatever was going on, she'd keep it to herself.

Now Kido was saying: *"Remember Nansen's advice, 'Knowing is delusion. Not knowing is confusion.'"*

Did Kido ever say this to me? Do I actually know all this stuff? Or am I just deluded or confused, or both? Is Kido pointing to someone else? Is he trying to tell me not to get involved?

Distracted, she nearly walked right into Muin, who was standing at the dharma hall entrance.

"Hey ... just who I was looking for. You got a minute?" Alex asked.

"Yeah, matter of fact I was looking for you."

"No kidding, what for?"

"You first."

"Okay. You know how all of us have to go talk to the cops? Well, I just saw them, and boy, that Wolfe sure is a piece of work, isn't he?"

"Harsh words, Alex, will come back to haunt you if you're not careful."

She swatted at her shoulder as if this could dislodge Kido. Advice like this she didn't need right now.

"You okay, Alex?"

"Yeah ... anyway ... I think I should be present for all the interviews. I can't imagine some of you guys being alone with them. Do you think you could arrange that?"

"Funny you should ask. Practically everyone here has already come to me asking if you could sit in on their interviews with the cops. They trust you. They wonder if they need a lawyer. They'd feel better if you were there. I was coming to find you to ask if you'd do it."

"That's perfect. Have you spoken to the detectives? Are they okay with this?"

"As you might expect, the gruff one, Wolfe, hates the idea. The other one's fine with it. Wolfe said, and I quote, 'Only if she keeps her trap shut.' Think you can do that?"

"I doubt it. You know me."

"Will you at least try?"

"Ye-e-e-s, but only because I really do think I need to be there. Should I let Zenji know that I won't be helping him today?"

"I think he's next up with the cops, why don't you escort him?"

"Gladly."

She found him sitting on the floor alone in the large, dark jisha's closet between the dharma hall and zendo.

"Knock, knock," Alex said. "I'm told you have an appointment with the cops. I'm here to help you find your way." She tried to lighten things up. She expected a sarcastic comeback from him at the very least. Figured he'd offer her his wrists for handcuffing, but he slowly unfolded himself from the floor, hardly glanced at her, and walked out the door toward the library.

She was surprised he was taking Kosen's death so hard. For someone he blatantly and publicly detested, he sure was displaying a lot of upset and grief.

Nothing like a suspicious death to reveal someone's true nature. It worked a lot faster than zazen. Everyone she ran into was acting outside their usual behavior. *Does this display their true self? Does Kosen's dead body skew reality or clarify it?* Alex wasn't sure yet. Things had changed, her sanctuary was no longer safe, there might be a murderer walking amongst them and he might be the monk in front of her.

***

"So, what did you have against your dharma brother, Robert Leetes, or Koh-sen?" said Wolfe, the foreign word uncomfortable in his mouth.

"Nothing," said Zenji, sitting rigidly in a folding chair, arms tightly crossed on his sunken chest.

Alex wondered how Wolfe knew about dharma brothers. Probably from Muin, but weird he'd use the term.

"Isn't it true that you and Robert hated each other, loved the same woman, and often came to blows? Didn't you once nearly run him over with a truck? You gave him a black eye on one or more occasion," Wolfe said, getting louder and more in Zenji's face with each question.

"You don't know anything about it," Zenji said, not rising to the bait.

Alex figured that Jito must have been in to see the detectives while she was showering. Maybe that had pulled him out of his funk.

"Well, we know that you knew him in California, before you ended up here," Wolfe said.

"Who told you that?" Zenji sat up straighter.

"It doesn't matter. You knew him, didn't you?"

"No. I never saw his face before he came to pollute this place."

"Yeah, well, we'll see about that ... did you kill him because you hated him? Because you guys were enemies before you even got here? Or did you kill him so that you could have the girl all to yourself?"

"I thought he killed himself." Surprise and fear filled Zenji's eyes. He looked over at Alex, questioning. She didn't respond.

"We don't know that for sure yet, and I'm betting you had something to do with it."

"Well, ha! Ha! You lose." Zenji slunk down into his seat and crossed his legs out in front of him.

"Look, why don't you tell us about your relationship with the deceased," good-cop Kluny piped in, "so that we can go home and you can go back to your life here. Ask your friend, Alex, she'll tell you it's the thing to do."

Zenji looked over at Alex, who nodded.

"Okay, I hated him, and why is none of your business ... but I didn't kill him. And as far as Sonja goes, she and I were planning to go away some place together. We were going to tell Kosen, and everyone else, after Buddha's birthday on Sunday. I had no reason to kill him."

"Well, aren't you the little lovebird monk," Wolfe said.

Zenji's body tensed, his eyes shot bullets of anger at Wolfe, but he said nothing. Alex was impressed with his restraint, a quality he wasn't famous for. *What's he holding on to?*

"We're seeing your girlfriend next, so if we find out that you're lying and Robert's death was not self-induced, you'll be at the top of my list and behind bars so fast, this place you live in here will look like a five-star hotel in comparison. Now go, get out of here," Wolfe said. He turned his back and walked over to the window that looked down onto the lake.

Zenji left, and Sonja was due in ten minutes. "Want me to go find her, speed up this whole thing?" Alex asked.

"Nah, you'll waste that much time trying to find her," Wolfe said, still with his back to the room. "But since you're here, I have a few questions for you." He turned around and leaned against the sill.

"One, do you think Zenji's being straight with us? Two, Kluny told me about what you told him, so what the hell is a koan? And three, what's the significance of the tree branch in Robert's mouth?"

Alex could tell he hated consulting her, but what choice did he have?

"First, I think Zenji's holding something back, but I don't think he killed Robert. Especially if Sonja backs him up on their plan to run off together.

"And koans, well, that's a bit more complicated. I'm no authority, that's for damn sure. So I'll keep it simple. Or maybe I should get Muin or Roshi in here to explain it to you, they're the real experts."

"Let's hear your version."

"Yeah," Kluny said. "Those guys will only confuse us. You speak our language."

"Okay. First, there are different kinds of Buddhists, sorta like there are different kinds of Christians ... Catholics and Protestants for instance, and then sects like Lutherans and Methodists, etc.

"Setsu Roshi, here in this monastery, is a Rinzai Zen Buddhist and his lineage as teacher can be traced all the way back to Buddha. So, a sort of baton is passed down from teacher to teacher—when a student is so-called enlightened and the teacher deems him fit to carry on his lineage, he is proclaimed a dharma heir, and then given the title of roshi. Any Zen teacher who can't claim to be an heir of someone in the lineage is considered a fraud by many.

"Roshi means true master and they are rare in this day and age, at least in Japan and in the Rinzai lineage, which is where Setsu Roshi is from. Some Zen teachers want to join this elite group and pass themselves off as roshis, but it's sort of like doctoring your resume and claiming you're a PhD without ever have gone through the whole process. I'm not even sure what that is, but it's intense. All I know is it's not easy to become an authentic roshi."

"What's this got to do with koans?" Wolfe said impatiently. He began pacing. He was like an animal in a too-small cage.

"I'm getting to that. Rinzai, a Zen Master who lived in the ninth century in China, began a tradition of using shouts and sticks to awaken monks. From that came the use of enigmatic stories to help with the goal of enlightenment. All of these techniques are still used today. The stories accumulated over the years and were collected and written about by various Zen Masters. There are a handful of koan collections today that contain hundreds of these stories, many of which have been translated into English."

"I'm impressed that you know so much of the history, being a cop and all," Kluny said.

"I'm a little surprised myself. I guess I paid some attention these past few years. ... So, when a Zen teacher assigns a koan to one of his students, the student is supposed to sit with it and then go to the teacher with an answer, or his understanding of what it means."

"So, what the hell does a tree branch in a dead person's mouth mean?" Wolfe was exasperated. Or maybe he just needed a cigarette. Alex noticed the pack remained unopened.

"I can only tell you the story and what I think it means, not what it truly means. See, the answer might be different from one person to the next—though they might both be right."

"What the hell does that mean?" Wolfe finally sat down.

"I'm pretty much out of my depth here, but if you, Kluny and I were to describe the taste of water to someone ... I mean, we all know what water tastes like, right? But to tell someone who has never tasted water what it tastes like wouldn't be so easy. And we might choose to describe it without words. Anyway, we would each communicate the taste of water in a different way, but we'd all be right." Alex waited for Wolfe to pipe in but he was just staring at her.

"As for the tree branch ... there's an old Zen story about a man hanging from a branch of a tree by his mouth. His hands and feet can't touch any part of the tree, or the ground, he's so high up. Someone comes along and asks him a question—the question is too Zen specific and might only confuse things here, so let's just say he was asked a question. If he doesn't answer he fails to respond to the question. If he answers he falls to his death. So, the teacher might ask the student, 'How would you answer?'"

"So what's it mean in this case?"

"I can only guess, but if Kosen did kill himself, maybe it means he found out about Zenji and Sonja and hated losing Sonja, hated himself for not having the right words to keep her, and so killed himself. Or maybe he said something to Sonja that he regretted. Maybe it was the thing that had her reject him for Zenji and he couldn't go on living. I don't think we'll ever know the truth."

"And what if Zenji or someone else killed him, what then would it mean?" Kluny asked.

"I haven't a clue. I guess we'll all have to sit and contemplate that when the time comes."

They heard a soft knocking at the door.

"That must be their Jezebel now," Wolfe said.

With raised eyebrows and a grimace, Alex asked Kluny what the hell was wrong with his partner.

"Don't mind him. This is Wolfe-lite. If this turns into murder, then watch out—you'll get Wolfe-mean then," Kluny said as he got up to open the door. Wolfe sat still with a sour grin on his face.

***

Sonja was reduced to tears and confused uttering throughout the session. She admitted to caring about Zenji and Kosen, though she did not use the word love, and they never got a coherent answer from her about plans to run away with Zenji.

It seemed to Alex that she was just sorting through her grief. Alex felt sorry for her and though Wolfe seemed to be a bit of an asshole, he was still a good cop, so he cut her loose quickly. All three felt that Sonja had no part in Kosen's death.

As Jito had said, "She wouldn't hurt a spider."

The few others they met with that morning revealed nothing new. When it was close to lunchtime, Wolfe said, "Let's all take a break. I'm starving and beginning to think that maybe the dead guy did himself. We'll see what the autopsy says, but that's how I'm leaning."

"I'm thinking the same thing. What about you Alex?" Kluny asked.

Before she could respond, Wolfe said, "But we'll wait for the test and forensic results before we sign the dotted line to that effect. 'Cause with that tree branch and the neat placement of the body, even if he did kill himself, with drugs or whatever else, he easily could have had some assistance. It ain't over yet. But I don't think we'll be needing your help anymore today, Ms. Sullivan."

"Aren't you talking to people this afternoon?"

"Just the deceased's cousin, who hasn't requested your presence, and Roshi, who asked to see us alone, without you or anyone else from his flock."

"No kidding?"

"No kidding ... but if you hear anything ..."

"Yeah, I got it, you'll be the first one I call. See ya. Bye, Kluny."

"So long, Alex, thanks for the help."

***

Alex headed toward the dining room. On her way, she stepped out onto the rear deck to bathe in the afternoon sunlight for a few moments. As usual, spring would be coming late to the mountain but the sun on her face told her it was near. Closing her eyes as she sat on the edge of the deck and lifted her face skyward, Alex felt the sound of the woods: The harbinger birds, chipmunks scampering on the forest floor, deer traipsing through, hungry at winter's end, hoping to be fed by a sympathetic monk. A forest symphony.

Suddenly, there was a noise that didn't fit the aural landscape. Not recognizing it with eyes closed she opened them and quickly stepped back inside. It had to be human and she didn't want to get caught loafing. A blue-plaid flannel shirt emerged from the woods and headed toward the kitchen. She recognized it as Clark's shirt.

Wonder what he was doing out there. It was probably an innocent excursion but she'd ask Jito later. Maybe they were planning a garden and he was working on it. They spoke of it every year. Maybe this was it finally happening. *But wasn't he supposed to be baking bread?* She turned to go. More rustling. She kept herself hidden.

Zenji was now coming from the same path as Clark. He was carrying a spade. It could be a coincidence. Maybe they were working together to prepare a garden area. She'd ask around.

Clark had been so adamant that morning about Zenji being the perpetrator and the two of them never got along, so they couldn't be in on anything together. Or could they? Anything was possible, but what could explain what she just saw? If Kosen weren't dead and she saw the same thing, would she still be suspicious? Only time would tell if it meant something—maybe. Maybe not.

13

Alex was pissed that Wolfe excluded her from the interview with the cousin and slightly peeved that Roshi wanted to talk to the cops alone. She understood, but still wasn't happy about it. She'd corner Muin later, see what he could tell her about both sessions. Being Roshi's eyes and ears, he always knew before anyone what was really going on. If Muin wasn't available, maybe Kluny would divulge the goings-on to her.

In the meantime, she checked in with Zenji to see what she could do, and was given the task to wash floors. She wanted to remind him that the floors had been cleaned yesterday, but that wasn't the point.

She said, "Thanks, it's my favorite job," as he handed her a rag and a bucket.

She was not satisfied that Kosen's death was suicide and had so many questions swimming around in her brain that she couldn't think straight. The exertion of labor might settle things down. Appropriately enough, as she filled the bucket with water and a splash of Murphy's Oil Soap and set out to do the job asked of her, a passage from the *Tao te Ching* came to her mind, in Kido's voice, of course.

Do you have the patience to wait
till your mud settles and the water is clear?
Can you remain unmoving
till the right action arises by itself?

She knew the answers she was seeking would come in time. But patience was not her strong suit. Treating the nagging questions as she would a baffling koan, Alex concentrated on washing the floors and the movement of her body and breath.

After a while, the physical exertion helped her brain settle down and for the most part she was able to attain a modicum of quietude. The afternoon passed without major incident or answer.

The only thing of note was Kosen's cousin's appearance. Alex had worked her way around the halls, washing floors, and by late afternoon had made it to the front entrance. By the time she got there he was leaving, stepping into his red pickup truck, no rifle in sight though he looked the type to use one, even from the quick glimpse she got of a lot of hair, camouflage pants and jacket.

Alex watched him drive away down the long, rocky road.

A minute later another red truck was coming toward the monastery. *What the hell? Had there been a sale on them this month? First, the one in the woods that morning, then the cousin's and now this one, newer and cleaner than the first two, but still.*

Alex waited to see who it was, maybe he belonged to the cops. She saw that he was athletic as he bounced to the ground and took the wide entry steps two at a time to the front door. Good shape, about her age, moved like a cop, like he was carrying a piece.

Alex snuck around to the front and saw Muin usher this guy into Roshi's meeting room. She only got a glimpse; sandy brown hair, thick and slicked on top, shorter around the edges. *Could be ex-military, looks like he hasn't shaved in a few days so it'd hurt to kiss him. Fuck! Get a grip!*

Muin left red truck number three with Roshi and then went up to the library. As soon as she could get him alone she'd learn about red truck's business with Roshi. Till then she'd bide her time.

She needed to talk to someone about all of this, and get her hormones under control. Muin was plainly indisposed. The instincts that made her good at her job took over. She got up, walked to the office where there was a phone that the residents were allowed to use, and put in a call to Uncle Charlie.

***

Uncle Charlie was good at what he did and famous on the east end of Long Island, in a quiet sort of way. He wasn't flashy, but he knew lots of people and how to get to the truth—or at least to the answer to whatever he was working on. And he was adept at gaining people's trust. He was much like Roshi that way with his charismatic personality, charming people into telling him things that they didn't even know they knew.

"Petal, how are you?" Charlie said when he answered on the second ring. "Is something wrong? Are you okay? Aren't you at the monastery? Did something happen?"

Charlie knew something was wrong. Alex never called him when she was at the monastery. And Alex knew, when Petal slipped from his tongue, that she had interrupted his concentration and he was worried to hear from her.

Petal was a childhood endearment. While watching *It's A Wonderful Life* one night, Uncle Charlie had put his arm around her and, as she nestled in beside him, gently kissed the top of her head during ZuZu's petals scene and softly said, "You're my petal."

Alex couldn't recall if it was the movie or Uncle Charlie's tenderness that made her cry that night, but it became her habit to cry at movies, beginning with *The Wizard of Oz* and *Lassie Come Home*. There were years, however, when she didn't watch movies, and years when she'd only go alone—her angry, self-righteous years—years when she wouldn't allow Uncle Charlie to call her Petal anymore. So she was surprised to hear it from him, and even more surprised how it soothed rather than aggravated her. Maybe she was changing.

"Yeah, I'm at the monastery. And something did happen, but not to me. One of the residents is dead.".

"Oh dear."

"We don't know yet what the story is. Could be suicide, but there's something strange about it ... thought I'd call and run it by you."

"Of course ... shoot."

"Robert, or Kosen, as we knew him up here, the dead guy, was laid out in his robes in the boiler room. No one knows how or why. He left during the night on Saturday. We thought he'd just moved out. His room was cleared of all his belongings and only his Buddhist bib was left behind with a note. His body was found this morning with his robes on and his head shaved. Plus, the weirdest thing ... he had a tree branch between his teeth."

"Hmmm. What did the note say?"

"It was the last line of one of our chants. It means 'gone to another shore.' The tree branch could refer to a Zen story about a guy in a tree who would fall to his death if he answered a question being asked of him. I can't figure it out yet. I'm not convinced he killed himself, I guess I think someone else did. I don't know what to think. Which is why I wanted to talk out loud to someone."

"Anything I can do other than listen?"

"Check out his past for me, would you?"

"Anything for my girl."

Alex rolled her eyes, but refrained from comment. The magnitude of Uncle Charlie's love was stunning. Taking a deep breath she moved on.

"His name is Robert Leetes. L-e-e-t-e-s. In his mid-thirties. Word is he was born in California or someplace out West. I don't know much about him, except that he was an only child. He had some relatives and was known to visit a cousin on his days off who lives some place close by here. The cousin was called after Robert had gone missing but apparently knew nothing about it. He was just here talking to the cops."

"How long had Robert lived up there?"

"He came up a few years after me. You remember me talking about Kido? The first monk I met? The one who helped me see what a mess my life was back then?"

"Died soon after, didn't he?"

"Yeah, less than three years." In a half-pause, half-breath, Alex's death-aftermath relationship with Muin flashed through her mind. Their desperate clinging to each other after Kido died. Their mostly secret trysts. Their infrequent forays together into the mainstream.

"Robert's story was that Kido's obituary had caught his attention and drew him to the monastery," she continued. "At first I was drawn to Robert because of it. I thought he was some sort of replacement for Kido. I entertained the idea of reincarnation for about a split second. But I found out soon enough I was wrong— Robert was a little too childish, sort of like an overgrown kid, and not someone Kido would have hung around with, although he probably would have taken him under his wing, since no one else up here did. He was too much of a pain in the ass.

"I think he was just socially awkward and over compensated by playing games and pulling pranks. At times I felt he just needed a mentor but nobody stepped up for some reason. Frankly, I haven't paid all that much attention to him since he arrived."

"When exactly was that?"

"I can tell you almost to the day. Let's see now. I first came up in the spring eight years ago, Kido died January three years later, and Robert arrived at the beginning of the spring season that year, at the end of March sometime."

"I'll get on it as soon as I clear up a few loose ends here."

"Thanks, Uncle C."

"You bet. Call me later this evening. I'll call you if I don't hear."

"Okay."

"Any idea who the cousin is?"

"Not yet. I'll know more later or tomorrow about him. And this may all be for naught when the autopsy comes back."

"Anything else?"

"Guess you could check on Zenji, aka Jason Smart, at the same time. They were mortal enemies up here, claimed to not know each other from the past, but rumor has it that they grew up together in California. Not sure what the truth is, but it's worth checking out ... if you don't mind."

"Course I don't mind, sweetie, you know that."

"You're right, I do. Thanks Uncle C. I'll call you tomorrow sometime."

"Goodnight, Petal, and get some of that rest you went up there to get."

"I promise."

"Bye for now. Don't forget who loves you."

"Bye, Uncle C, I love you too."

***

Alex looked forward to the evening: A few hours of zazen and hopefully some time with Muin. Roshi had reinstated the usual evening meditation schedule, there was nothing more they could do.

His answer to everything was: "Just sit, no matter what." So that's what they were all going to do.

Ten minutes into the sit she knew that everyone else wanted to sit as much as she did. The collective, determined energy was palpable. The unity of the group felt in every breath. Alex knew it would be a powerful evening. And it was.

Little work had gotten done and the talk that day had moved from "Who do you think did it?" to "Why do you think he killed himself?" Suicide was the consensus of most everyone there, and the easiest end to embrace.

During the walking period between sits, no one left to use the bathroom and some of the students sat straight through, the sort of intensity usually reserved for weeklong silent retreats.

To Alex it felt as if they were breathing as one and all the hungry ghosts of those who'd died were sitting there with them. Kosen was there. Kido and her father were there. They were of one mind, and for those few precious hours there was no mystery and nothing to solve.

During the second sit, memories of her father floated up. Right on cue, her internal slide projector focused on the last photo taken of him, with her mother, locked in place and time. Red lipstick showed off Mother's smile, Daddy's eyes were squinting, trying to wink, his mouth set in a huge crooked grin. They were holding hands. Their yellow Dodge Dart gleamed in the driveway behind them.

Alex pictured the two of them wrapped in each other's arms, happy forever, frozen in time. Her heart responded and struck a chord of deep sadness. The tears came, catching her off guard. She let them come.

Tired, sad, missing her father, Alex settled in for the ride and gave herself over to her old grief. Maybe this is what old Zen Master Dogen meant when he talked about 'the heart as practice hall.' Maybe not. All Alex knew was that the hole in her heart that was Daddy still hurt and might never stop hurting.

14

After zazen, Alex was amped up and not sleepy. She wanted to talk to Muin but couldn't find him. She looked for Kluny. He was already gone. He and Wolfe were planning to return in the morning to wrap things up unless the autopsy results came back as murder.

"They did know each other in California," Uncle Charlie said.

"That's not good for Zenji," Alex said.

"It seems they went to the same high school in Long Beach. I don't know if they ran with the same crowd or not, but both had clashes with the law. Petty stuff mostly. Nothing dangerous. Shoplifting, marijuana possession, a couple of fights. Kid stuff, really.

"There's nothing in the record to indicate that either would grow up to be a murderer, but you're not a murderer till you kill someone, are you? Sometimes there's no predicting. I've rarely known a killer who didn't have fingerprints or mug shots already on record. And these two boys had both." Uncle Charlie paused, Alex knew he wasn't quite finished.

"Killer or victim. Sometimes I wonder which is the worst destiny," Uncle Charlie said, a little plaintively she thought.

She waited a long moment.

"So I guess the rumor that Zenji was white trash from Tennessee is just a rumor then? That's a long way from California," Alex said.

"Well, yes and no."

Alex bit her tongue so as not to groan or say a word. *Here he goes with all that Zen Master stuff again.*

"It sort of makes sense. Zenji, or Jason Smart, as he was known back then, came to Long Beach his junior year. I don't know where he transferred from. Could've been Tennessee. Could've been Alaska. Didn't think it so important. Do you care? Do you want to know?"

"No, not really. Not at the moment, anyhow. Do their records show that there were clashes between them in high school?"

"Nope, but high school was a long time ago. I'm betting if something happened it happened after that. A Los Angeles buddy of mine is doing some more checking. To see how deep their connection was. See if it went beyond high school.

"Jason, or Zenji as you call him, doesn't seem to have any family. He was living with foster parents in high school. Probably doesn't even know who his parents were. Robert's parents are still alive."

"And then there's the cousin," Alex said. "And, um, another thing I forgot to mention" —she hated her lack of focus— "his name is Lawrence. That's all I know."

"That'll help. I'll do more checking."

"Oh, yeah. I got a glimpse of his license plate earlier. It's L-T-nine something. I couldn't see the whole thing. Looked like a vanity plate. It should be fairly easy to check. He's driving a red pickup, Ford."

"I'll check into it."

"Thanks, Uncle C." Alex said nothing more. Neither did Charlie. She knew that he knew it was her turn and that she had something to say. It was now or never.

"This might all be a waste of your time, Uncle C, especially if it comes back that Kosen did commit suicide, but with Zenji lying about knowing him in the past, I'm curious as hell about a couple other people up here."

"Not to worry, my dear, it'll give this poor guy something to do. It's pretty quiet right now and you know me, I love to keep busy."

"Okay, if you're sure. It feels bad to even ask, but would you check out two more of the residents here?"

"Of course."

"Who knows, before this is over you may have to check out everyone up here. But if it comes to that, I'll leave some of it for the locals, let them do their job." Now that the door had been opened, she wanted to check into the past of all her Zen friends. And then again, she didn't.

What was that thing that Kido had said to me?... Where is he anyway?... 'Knowing is delusion. Not knowing is confusion.'

Knowing about their past could change how she related to them. *Do I want that? Will I be content not knowing?*

"Who do you want me to check out?"

"A Japanese resident, name of Gyozan Tanzaki. Gyozan is his Buddhist name, I don't know his real first name. I think he hails from Hirosaki."

"Given that he's living here now it should be easy enough. Who else?"

"Jito." She put Gyozan on the list just so Jito would be in good company. It also made her feel less disloyal.

"Your friend, the fellow I once met?"

"Yeah, I hate doing it, but truthfully I don't know much about him, not really."

"Don't feel too bad, Alex. Someone's dead. You're doing what you're trained to do. In the end you'll be glad you did. And you may learn something about your friend. There's every reason to believe he's not involved and it won't hurt to confirm that."

"I guess." Uncle Charlie's words weren't helping.

"What's his birth name? Where was he born?"

"Steve Carter. Michigan, I think. Yeah, Michigan. Detroit."

"Okay. Don't worry, Alex, I'll bet nothing pops up on him."

"I hope you're right. How's everything else?"

"Like I said, slow."

In the past, slow would have been a complaint. But for Uncle Charlie, who'd become an avid gardener when he turned sixty, slow was an opportunity to spend time digging up his backyard, or making plans to dig up his backyard.

"By the way, who's in charge up there?"

Uncle Charlie knew a lot of people. She'd be surprised if he knew these guys. On second thought, nothing about what Uncle Charlie knew would astonish her.

"Tom Kluny, the good cop. State detective who partners up with the one local detective on something big like this, name of Howard Wolfe. It's his case since it happened in his jurisdiction and unless he fucks up bad it'll be his case to the end. He's like every other cop you've ever met, only more so. Not stupid, but might as well be, for all the imagination he's got. You know the type."

"Yeah. Not only that, I know him."

Alex's raised eyebrows and shake of her head filtered into her voice. "Really?"

"Well, not him exactly, but his father. Howard Sr. I can't imagine there'd be more than one Howard Wolfe working as a cop in the Catskills. Must be the same. His father and I were on the force together. I never liked him much. Mean son-of-a-bitch. Everyone was amazed when Howard Jr. became a cop. He'd been in lots of trouble as a youth, his father constantly bailing him out of scrapes. He hated his father. But I guess blood is thicker. You know how that goes."

"Yeah, 'fraid so. Anyway, is he a good cop under all that bravado?"

"I don't know really. When his father got shot and went out on disability, Howard Jr. moved to the mountains where he'd hunted all his life. I guess he couldn't stand to be around his father anymore. I heard that the father grew more bitter and angry as the years passed. I think his wife finally left him, too."

"The father drink a lot?" Alex could spot an alcoholic a mile away or a generation removed.

"To put it mildly. What I know about Howard Jr. comes from the guys talking in the locker room. You know how nosy they are about everyone else's business. No boundaries and all."

"Boy, do I."

"In any case, I don't remember any talk about Howard Jr. drinking. He witnessed first hand the damage it can do and swore off it for good after his first drunk—or so I heard. His father was merciless—making fun of him all the time."

"I sensed his rage. As soon as words came out of his mouth I thought: 'This guy needs a drink.' A guy like that, repressing so much, can be more dangerous than someone who drinks a quart a day."

"If he gives you any trouble let me know. I could give him a call. Put in a good word for you."

"Thanks, Uncle C, but no thanks." Sometimes his concern infuriated her. "And they'll be out of here tomorrow if there are no surprises."

"Okay. What else?"

"There's something that's bugging me and I can't tell if it's personal or professional, you know, if my feelings are hurt or if some people up here are trying to hide something from me. It may be nothing ..."

"Maybe I can help."

"Well, all the residents here who went in to talk to the cops wanted me in the room—you know, they know me and wanted a friendly face ... they were a little freaked out about the whole thing,"

"Of course, I can't blame them."

"But the two I'm closest to, Jito and Muin, went in alone, didn't ask to have me there. In their defense, they were the first two to be interviewed and the idea of my being in the room only came up after, I think, but I guess I worry that they're hiding something."

"Maybe you're being sensitive ... I know you find that hard to believe, but ... or it could be you're used to knowing every detail of a case and you don't here."

"Maybe you're right."

"Or maybe they've got something to hide."

"Damn ... and then there was Roshi. He actually requested that I not be there. What should I make of that?"

"Could be that he just needs to keep certain boundaries between him and his students, and if some delicate issue came up with the cops he'd want to keep it private and confidential. I'm sure he'd trust you as a cop, but you're not that to him, you're his student."

"I guess you're right again. But damn, I wanted to be there for all of them. I want to know what they know."

"Well, in the case of your friends, you can just ask them. As for Roshi, maybe it's best that you don't know everything."

"Only problem with that is then you begin to believe the rumors."

"Rumors?"

"Yeah, I never thought too much about them, not really, but now. ... Roshi came to California in the late sixties, or early seventies, straight from Japan, set up a zendo, and as the story goes, got involved with drugs and women. One really crazy story was that there was drug money being laundered through the temple."

"Do you believe it?"

"No, not really. At least I didn't, and I suppose I still don't, but if this was a case and I were on it, I'd definitely check it out. What I do know about and believe is that more than once Roshi has upset his students enough to break up the sangha—"

"Sorry, but what's that?"

"Sangha?"

"Yeah."

"It's the Zen community, students, teachers, etc."

"And there were times when the community split up?"

"Yeah, but I'm not even sure of the reasons now ... but at some point in the eighties, or maybe later than that, one of the monks left with many of the students to form his own zendo. Name was Enji I think. Story is that they had a huge fight—over drugs, money or women, or maybe just a difference in philosophy, there are lots of stories but the truth is unclear—so I don't think anyone but the two of them know what that is. I never paid much attention, figured it was just people being people, dissatisfied, always wanting more. You know how that goes."

"I do. Why don't you try to get some sleep now and see how you think of it in the light of day?"

"Yeah, I will. I feel better just having said it all out loud."

"Now go to bed ... and call me tomorrow."

"I will. Thanks. And, in case I forget, when you see Marissa tomorrow night give her a big hug for me, would you?" Uncle Charlie had dinner with Alex's mother every Tuesday night without fail.

"I will. I always do."

About to hang up, Alex shouted, "Uncle C, hold on, are you still there?"

"Still here."

Uncle Charlie had a habit of waiting for her to hang up before he did. She almost always had something to add.

"I almost forgot. One more name for the list. Okay?"

"Of course."

"Clark, Clark Winston. He grew up not far from here. I don't think he's ever left the northeast. He's about thirty-five. He went to SUNY Rochester, I'm almost sure. Got involved with drugs, went to prison upstate for a couple years. Somehow, he was able to serve the last few years of his sentence up here under Roshi's wardenship. He was free to leave long ago and doesn't."

"That's not so strange, is it?"

"No, except that he doesn't sit or chant or participate in any of the normal monastery functions."

"Maybe he's just institutionalized and knows he can't make it out there in the world."

"Maybe."

"Roshi make a habit of taking in criminals?"

"As a matter of fact, I've known a couple of them. Nice guys really. And both cleaned up their act after their stay here, became normal citizens. Seems Roshi's been doing this sort of thing for a long time."

"That's interesting. Okay then, no problem. He's on the list. We'll talk tomorrow."

***

She was exhausted by the time she got to bed, and it wasn't till she was falling off to sleep that Muin came to mind. *Is he avoiding me? Or me, him? I have to make him a priority tomorrow even if ...*

15

She was on a stained mattress on a floor, no sheets, in a dingy room with no windows. She was naked. She was sweating blood. It wouldn't stop. Tossing and turning and moaning in agony. The next thing she knew she was swimming away from someone then remembered she couldn't swim. Two people were kissing passionately. Where was she?

Alex woke with a start, for a moment confused. *Right, at the monastery. Kosen is dead.* She hadn't slept much and woke with the sense that Muin was going to great lengths to avoid being alone with her. Before the shinrei bell roused those who were still sleeping she went in search of him to prove herself wrong.

For anyone who asked why Muin's room was on the main floor and not in the resident's wing, his answer was that it put him closer to Roshi. But Alex knew the truth to be different—he preferred to be separate from the other monks. She never asked why, never questioned it. Now she wanted to. *Why the hell does he insist on being split off from the rest of the monks and students?*

She knocked lightly on his door. No answer. *That's odd. Muin's always the first to rise, and spend the first hour of his day alone in his room reading.* She eased open his door a crack and saw that his bed had already been made up. Or never slept in.

Alex roamed the halls in search of him and checked all the common areas. No trace of him. She turned a corner and nearly collided with Roshi.

"Sorry, Roshi, good morning," Alex whispered and bowed to her teacher.

"Good morning, Alex." Roshi bowed back. "Getting an early start on zazen this morning?"

"Um, sort of. And I'm looking for Muin. Have you seen him?"

"Not yet this morning. He'll turn up. He's probably sitting." Roshi's voice faded down the hall as he continued on his way.

Muin was pissed at her for something, some unknown faux pas on her part. Maybe he was more upset about her ending their relationship than he'd ever let on. She could understand that, but if it were true it would break her heart.

Alex made her way to the zendo. The usual morning schedule, an hour of chanting, an hour of sitting, was back in place beginning at 5:00. Roshi was right, Muin was already there sitting—she'd bypassed the zendo on her search. *Not superb detective work.* About half the residents were also there, sitting through their grief and worry. *I should have known.* She heard the rustle of robes and bare feet moving toward the zendo. The others were on their way. Zazen would help them cope.

Breakfast at 7:00 was informal—no robes or chanting, talking was allowed so that the two detectives who had just arrived could be included. Alex figured they'd be gone for good by day's end. With Kosen's body at the morgue and none of his personal effects to sift through, there wasn't much to keep them around.

***

After breakfast Alex was in the basement sewing room, happily stuffing meditation cushions, a refreshing respite from washing floors. The monastery did a brisk trade over the Internet, selling meditation supplies—incense, bells, cushions, etc.—to other monasteries, small stores and individuals, and the orders were piling up.

The focused work absorbed her enough to take her mind off the Kosen/Zenji connection, Muin's remoteness, Roshi's secretiveness. She kept telling herself there was no case, as her mind automatically went into high-detective gear. Slowing it down and turning to a Zen channel would give her some practice at minding her own business.

Okay, she had placed a few phone calls to Uncle Charlie and had him doing some research, but she could call him off at any time. She hadn't been close to Kosen and she hardly missed him. The cops on the case would figure it out sooner or later. They didn't need her. Dead was dead, that couldn't be disputed. Just as in the koan about fire being fire, no need to even comment on it. She'd have Uncle Charlie stop his background checks. She looked forward to a peaceful day.

No such luck. Almost as soon as her brain relaxed and began to settle down, the quiet of her basement chamber was disturbed by frantic voices and hurried footsteps all around her—upstairs and in the halls of the basement.

She put aside her work and went out to investigate, crashing into Roshi as she ran out the door. Something was up, he never visited the basement area except for a game of ping-pong. No match was scheduled, not at this time of day. But there he was, along with everyone else. Including the two cops whom she figured were long gone.

***

"Is Sonja down here with you? Have you seen her? When did you see her last?"

The questions came at her rapid fire from Roshi, Zenji and Wolfe. She looked from one to the other and said, "I haven't seen her. Don't tell me she's disappeared now!"

She knew this was stating the obvious but said it anyway. It sliced into the collective anxiety the way only a simple truth can, stopping the salvo for a moment to give Wolfe a chance to establish order.

"Stay calm people!" Wolfe said. Twenty pairs of eyes locked onto him as if his saying so could make it happen. But the hope disappeared before it had a chance to settle in.

"I've got more people on the way. In the meantime we can all start looking for her," he added. "Let's move up to the dining room so's we can get search parties set up. Quickly, quickly, people, move!"

On the way Alex caught up to Zenji, who was beyond distraught. "What happened?"

"She was cleaning the guest house. I brought down some linen. She wasn't there. I looked everywhere. It's not like her to wander off and she knew I was coming ..."

Probably one of their little assignations. Maybe Kosen had caught them at it the other day.

The group entered the dining room as if they were attending a funeral.

Wolfe didn't have to get their attention. "Detective Kluny along with Hokan here have divided up this place into sections to be searched. I want you all to choose a partner and check in with them." He pointed to Hokan and Kluny sitting with blueprints and pages spread out on a table. "Then go to your assigned area and look for Sonja. Don't let your partner out of your sight! Come back here in an hour and not a minute more. If you find anything at all before that, come back at once and report to me. I'll be in the library. Got it?"

Heads nodded, the room buzzed with voices and movement. They chose partners. Roshi and Muin were not in the room, maybe they were already searching out their assigned space.

While they were getting organized Alex made her way over to Kluny and whispered, "Any results yet on Kosen's cause of death?"

"Drug OD and probably not self-administered. At least not all of what he had in his body," Kluny said.

"Shit."

"Exactly. Keep it to yourself for now."

"Right."

Alex paired up with Jito, who rarely joined in on group projects, busy as he was with feeding everyone. But food was the last thing anyone was thinking about now. Still, it was odd, he had a lot to prepare for Sunday.

Alex had never seen him so unstrung, but dead bodies and disappearing nuns will test anyone's pluck, monk or no.

The two of them were assigned to the retreat house. They were told to check out all the closets, rooms, and storage areas—any space big enough for a body, as if she had to be told where and how to look.

"You don't really think whoever killed Kosen has come back for Sonja, do you?" Jito asked.

"We don't even know that Kosen was killed."

"Do you believe that?"

"It doesn't matter what I believe, we have to wait for the science—tox screen, forensics, stuff like that—to know for sure."

"That's bullshit," Jito said. "He was killed sure as my head is shaved."

"Let's just look for Sonja so we can get back to the group. Maybe the cops know more now."

"Why would anyone want to hurt her? She is such an innocent. Just because she and Kosen had a thing going? It doesn't make any sense. Oh my god, do you think it could be Zenji? No, he loved her too." Jito was animated with anxiety.

Alex was used to his histrionics, but this was a decidedly new pitch. His extreme reaction boded well for his innocence—but there was that short career as an actor, pre-monkhood. She hated being so suspicious of her friend. She couldn't wait till the whole thing was over.

"We don't know anything yet, Jito. Let's not jump to conclusions. Maybe she didn't feel well and is taking a nap some place. It's not like her, but she was pretty shaken up by Kosen's death, and no one knows until something like that happens how they might react." Alex accepted his feverishness as real, for the moment.

"I know, I know. But something just doesn't feel right. I'm scared something bad's happened to Sonja."

"You might be right. But all we can do now is help look for her." Alex knew in her gut that he was right.

"Oh my god! Do you think she killed herself? Maybe she was so distraught over Kosen she did herself in ... maybe ... oh my god ...who will be next? We don't even have locks on our doors! How will we be able to sleep if something has happened to Sonja? Or if we don't find her? It was bad enough with Kosen, but now Sonja ...."

He's not making any sense. Or is he?

"Let's just make sure we cover every inch of this place," Alex said, visualizing Jito's door lock. Alone with him she'd snatch the opportunity to broach the subject.

The Japanese custom of not wearing shoes indoors was extended to the non-monastery living spaces. It was a good thing too, since most of those rooms were carpeted in off-white wall-to-wall.

The sparseness of the monastery was carried through to the retreat house and the carpet gave it a feeling of Western luxuriousness and comfort that the monastery lacked. The groups that rented this space returned year after year, and even if they never stepped foot in the monastery they always left feeling as if they had, so powerful was the spiritual energy of the whole place. She feared that Kosen's murder, and now Sonja's disappearance, would forever change the atmosphere. If today was any indication, it was gone, gone, gone.

The vacuum cleaner in the center of the large common room on the ground floor was one sign that Sonja had been there. From the looks of things she had been interrupted in her chores.

Her shoes and jacket were in the shoe room by the side entrance, a clear sign that her departure hadn't been by choice. Extra sandals were always lying around the entrances for anyone to wear. Sonja could have used a pair of those to take a walk outside and then lost track of time as grief engulfed her. Maybe it was a simple case of a nun having a nervous breakdown. She was human after all.

Damn, I wish I'd paid more attention to her yesterday. Maybe she didn't want the space I was giving her. I was so focused on Muin I forgot about her. I wish she had come to me. I wish we hadn't grown so far apart.

Alex saw through a window that Gyozan and Zenji were searching the grounds around the house. The ground was still wet from the morning rain. Alex felt moisture under her bare feet before she saw it—tracked-in dirt, just inside the sliding glass doors that led out to the lakeside patio where she and Sonja had sat together her first day there.

Someone had been in this room with shoes on. Alex knew it hadn't been Sonja or any other resident, as they were all used to removing their shoes.

This slight bit of evidence had her Zen mind clearing all the residents from suspicion. Her cop brain said, *forget that! It would be just like Zenji, or any insider, to wear shoes inside to divert attention from them.*

The cops needed forensics up there pronto to analyze the source of the dirt, and dust for hand and footprints. She slipped out the side door to warn Gyozan away from the area around the patio. There would be shoeprints for sure.

Alex and Jito systematically went through the rest of the house, but she knew they'd find nothing more. There was no doubt in her mind that Sonja had vanished, and not of her own free will. Alex wasn't jumping to conclusions, she trusted her instincts. Jito seemed to know it, too. He got paler and more panicky as the minutes ticked by.

"I don't know how you can be so cool about this. Clearly Sonja's been kidnapped. Things are out of control." Jito sat on the floor, put his back against the couch, his face in his hands, and wept.

Alex gingerly slung her arm around him as she sat down by his side.

"There's something else, isn't there? What is it? You can tell me. Maybe I can help."

Jito's tears eased up, but he could only whisper. His drone seemed self-reflective, as if he were alone.

"I heard them this morning ... the preliminary finding ... drug overdose ... sleeping pills ... oh my, oh, oh, oh ... and now Sonja ... what have I done ... I can't bear it ... it is out of control ... I never expected ..."

"What're you talking about? What did you do? You've got to tell me, Jito. Did you hear about the drugs from the cops?"

Jito nodded. And then turned his head to look directly at Alex, tears gone.

"There's something I have to tell you." He put on a stoic face. "I don't want to, but there's nothing else to do now." He was back in full control of his voice, perhaps all those years of acting and voice lessons paying off.

"What is it?"

"I gave Kosen some Xanax last week. I know, I know. I shouldn't have had it in the first place. But I did. And he found out. The creep went through my things. We shared a bathroom..."

"Hence the lock?"

Jito nodded. "He threatened to tell Roshi. I'da been thrown out. He'd given me one last chance." Alex didn't know it had been as dire as all that. "I have nowhere to go. He took my whole stash. My god, I never expected him to kill himself."

"You'll have to tell them." Alex would save the lecture on drugs for later.

"I know, I know. Does Roshi have to know?"

"Maybe not. I can't say yet. We have to see what happens,"

"Oh my god, what have I done? Poor Sonja." Jito covered his face again.

"C'mon, we have to get back."

"Will you tell them for me?"

"Of course, but I'm sure they'll want to talk to you."

"Can you be there with me?"

"Maybe. Do you need a lawyer?"

"No ... no ... No ... No ... I don't think so, do I?"

"I'll arrange to be there when they question you. If it comes to that I'll let you know."

"Thanks. I'm so sorry. I just can't absorb what's happening," Jito said. "Do you think Sonja's planning to kill herself? Do you think they had a pact or something?"

That's a stretch of imagination even for Jito. "No, of course not. Not based on how upset she's been. C'mon, let's go."

Is Jito telling the truth? Is Jito intentionally misleading me? Did Kosen confiscate his drugs?

One thing was for sure, she could never trust drug addicts or alcoholics, monk or not. She was pissed at Jito for relapsing—she didn't believe for a minute that he was taking the Xanax as prescribed.

The image of the hungry ghost in Buddhist mythology helped Alex to make sense of an addict's insatiable appetite, even her own when it came to booze. It helped her to turn down the third drink knowing that even one was too many and a thousand never enough.

For a hungry ghost there's never enough, its huge belly can never be filled up and the thirst for more is unquenchable. Never enough booze, drugs, sex, money, you name it. Even the craving for good can turn into bad when the hungry ghost is stimulated. It lives in a constant state of greed, envy, and jealousy. The torment of such hunger causes otherwise sane people to act insanely. Jito's hungry ghost was alive and well and screaming for more.

On their way back to the dining room Alex said, "I've been thinking. Don't say anything to anyone yet. I'll handle it. I'll tell them when I think the time is right. You just stay out of the way for now. Keep your head down. We'll tell them what we found down here and let it go at that. For now."

Alex's intuition told her that Jito was in no way involved, and while the drugs might have helped the killer with his plans, Kosen would have been killed with or without them. The cops would just waste their time looking at Jito if they knew about the drugs. She had to do her part now and try to steer this investigation onto the right path.

"Okay. I trust you know what's best," Jito said, relieved to have unburdened himself.

Do I? Will I later be accused and maybe convicted of aiding and abetting, withholding evidence? Am I an accomplice after the fact?

Her instinct told her to keep her trap shut for now. So that she would do.

16

Alex and Jito gathered with the others in the dining room.
It was unusual for Roshi to attend a meeting he wasn't presiding over. But he was sitting regally at the head of his table, relaxed and ready to pounce, the eyelash-sized opening in his eyes seeing everything.

The two detectives held court and took each report in turn. Detective Wolfe asked the questions. Kluny took notes. So did Alex. There wasn't much to write down. The dirt tracks in the retreat house and Sonja's shoes and jacket left behind were the only obvious clues. Her room was as it always was. There wasn't a trace of her anyplace else. No one had seen or heard a thing that morning. Nada, zilch, a big fat empty nothing.

"Okay, folks. Things have changed around here. Looks like your friend Robert was not a suicide, which means that Sonja's disappearance could be connected—or maybe she was the killer ..." Wolfe let that idea sink in.

"But I doubt that that's the case so we're looking for someone else. Hopefully, we'll be in time to prevent another death. Goes without saying we need your cooperation here. And none of you are off the hook yet, so like yesterday everyone remains put."

Zenji couldn't help himself. He spit out at Wolfe, "Seems to me, since the whereabouts of everyone in this room can be accounted for this morning, that you need to start looking elsewhere for a suspect."

"Maybe. Maybe. But no one saw you during the half hour you claim you waited for Sonja, did they?" Wolfe stared straight at Zenji with clear intention to intimidate. "Seems to me."

He was in charge and Zenji was under suspicion. With a Robert De Niro-like tilt of his head, Wolfe continued. "Seems to me, also, that your whereabouts can't be accounted for before that half hour either. So you'd better be careful what you admit to."

"I'm not admitting to anything except that I didn't do it. I loved her." This was the first time he admitted that to the community, but it looked like he didn't give a damn who knew now. "I'd start to consider that maybe, just maybe, we have an interloper on the property. Someone besides one of us. Maybe that cousin, Lawrence, or LT, or whatever his name is. If I was you I'd focus on him."

Wolfe at that moment would have been interpreted by a fly on the wall as man-with-blood-boiling. Alex was surprised that it took so little to rile him. Maybe this trait accounted for his being in a sleepy mountain town where not much happened. Or it could be his quit smoking campaign—the unopened pack still in his pocket.

"It also seems to me that given the way you work around here, spread out all over the place, and the break after breakfast when you're all hard to find and when Sonja might have disappeared, that all of you are suspects till I say different." Wolfe scanned the room. "Sorry about that but I have a job to do, and while I'd like to consider that no one here is involved, until we find the perpetrator ..." He trailed off, no need to repeat himself. They got the message.

"Detective Wolfe. May I say something?" Alex turned on her polite, let's-keep-this-civil-and-get-along tone.

"What is it, Detective Sullivan?" This appellation meant to send a message to Zenji that even Alex carried more weight than he did. Clever. Zenji's black robes didn't impress Wolfe, Alex's badge did.

Before she had a chance to answer, Wolfe scowled at Zenji. "And if I was you, I'd sit there and shut up." Just like Zenji, he couldn't help himself.

Alex realized that the tension between Wolfe and Zenji went beyond Wolfe being a cop and Zenji being a possible suspect. Their temperaments had a similar cadence. They could have been separated at birth, twin brothers from different mothers, and the only things separating them now were a badge, a gun, and a shaved head.

"Let's just say it's not one of us," Alex said. "Can we for just a moment consider that there might be an outsider lurking in the vicinity?"

This was a nod to Zenji—she wanted him on her side. He might have been capable of killing Kosen, but she knew he wouldn't have harmed Sonja. "Is this even a possibility?"

She needed Wolfe's cooperation and wanted to get him off Zenji and into more productive thinking. *Me, the self-appointed diplomat. Ha!*

"Could be." He paused, took his time. Alex and the rest waited, all eyes on the detective.

"I've been thinking about that potentiality." Anyone with the slightest power of observation could see that he hated admitting this in front of Zenji, thus the big word. He wanted to solve this case and Zenji was his boy.

"Surely if there was someone," Wolfe continued, "he'd need a vehicle of some sort to get up here. Someone would have heard him coming. I hear every car and truck that comes within a mile of this place." Despite his limitations and rushes to conclusions he was a good cop. Alex got that.

"Maybe they parked far away. And then walked the rest of the way," Gyozan suggested.

"Whoever it was would still have to drive past the gatehouse entrance. And we've seen no cars or trucks that don't belong," Peter the gatekeeper added. He'd tied back his long hair into a ponytail for the occasion. "I would have heard something. This morning or on Saturday."

"And since that's the only way in or out ..." Wolfe paused. "But it's still a possibility, especially considering that all of Robert's stuff was removed and doesn't seem to be anyplace in or around the monastery. We've already thought about this and are exploring this theory. I'll get forensics back up here to have a look around the retreat house. In the meantime that place is off limits to everyone." Wolfe took a last glance in Zenji's direction, just to underline his authority. Zenji glared back at him, unwilling to bow.

Kluny whispered something to Wolfe.

"Oh, yeah. Just so you all know. We'll be doing room searches beginning this afternoon. We have a warrant coming but Roshi has given his permission. Anyone who wants to wait for the warrant to get here see Detective Kluny, he'll be coordinating the searches.

"And all private rooms are off limits for the time being. Any questions, you know where to find us."

They all nodded or murmured their assent. Clark raised his hand.

"What is it?" Wolfe asked.

"When can we leave here? I don't know about the rest of you"— Clark looked around—"but I'd like to get outta here soon as possible. No way I'll be able to sleep tonight without a lock on my door."

"Nobody's allowed to leave till I say so. Until we get all your rooms searched no one's going anywhere. And no one's allowed to be alone. You'll all partner up and get attached to each other by the hip or wherever else suits you, even when you use the facilities. Don't let your buddy outta your sight.

"Better yet, make it threesomes. By my count there are sixteen of you, not counting Roshi, Muin, and Detective Sullivan, so that's four groups of three and one of four. And let Kluny know who's in what group. It's the only way we can ensure your safety for now, before we get more bodies up here. And unless you got some urgent business elsewhere stay right here in this room for the rest of the day.

"If we find nothing in your room and you're dying to get out of here we'll have a van up here at the end of the day to take you into town if you don't have your own car. But till then, stay close. We'll be talking to some of you again.

"Zenji, you're up first—report to the library right after lunch, and make sure your two partners escort you. Then Clark. We'll let you know who's next soon as you need to know."

No one but Zenji had a word to say. Under his breath and for all, especially Wolfe, to hear, he said, "This is bullshit, wasting time, with Sonja out there. Shit, man."

No one got up to leave except Roshi, who had sat stock still throughout the meeting reacting to nothing. Alex wished she could crawl inside his brain. No one was sure what to do next.

Muin crept over to Alex and whispered that Roshi would like to see her in the meeting room in ten minutes. She nodded, checked her watch, and waited for the time to pass.

***

When Alex walked into the meeting room, Roshi was sitting in his usual place, on the floor at one end of the large rectangular table that filled up the center of the room. It had taken Alex a long while to get used to conducting serious matters sitting on the floor, but now the foreignness of it barely registered. She pulled a cushion out from under the table and sat down across from Muin, who was also there, as he always was.

It was the first chance she had to talk with Roshi this trip and it wouldn't be about her meditation practice and how she was doing with her koan. On the one hand that was fine with her. On the other, well, she was too pissed and consumed with death and abduction to dwell on it.

"Hello, Alex. Welcome back," Roshi said.

"Hello, Roshi. Thank you. Good to be here ... well, that is, you know, except for ... well, you know." Being in Roshi's company with no clear agenda unsettled Alex.

"Yes. And what do you think about this matter? As a professional. You are still the detective for police, yes?"

"Yes, Roshi." Alex's nervousness disappeared as she moved into familiar territory. "I have a strong hunch that it's not one of the residents, although I was leaning that way before Sonja disappeared. Don't worry, we'll get whoever did this soon enough."

Did she really believe that, or was she trying to console Roshi the way she would any victim's family? It was tricky with Roshi, striking a balance between wanting to please and being honest. He could see right through any fabrication.

Roshi waited a beat just to be sure Alex was finished. He was a master at listening. And he wanted to believe her.

"Do you know these two detectives, Tom Kluny and Howard Wolfe?" Roshi read the names from the piece of paper in front of him.

"Not before this week."

"I would like for you to help them."

"I'd be glad to Roshi, but I have no official jurisdiction up here. They may not want help from me."

"It has already been arranged. They are amenable. For you to be involved. For you to inform me of all developments." This was Roshi's bent toward relying on those he knew, preferably his own students, when it came to matters dealing with the outside world.

Being a traditional Japanese man from a certain generation, Setsu Roshi preferred dealing with men when it came to important matters. But he'd been in America long enough to be influenced by the feminist movement and many, many female students. He had become open to women in authority. No doubt, at this moment he would have preferred Alex to be a man, but being his student trumped any male outside the sangha.

"What did they say, exactly?" Alex could imagine their feelings of relief at not having to deal directly with Roshi, mixed with being ticked off about having to communicate through her.

"As long as they are in charge, is okay," Roshi said.

Alex smiled. *Typical.* "That's fair."

The Detective Sullivan designation then had been Wolfe's first gesture toward including her, not simply a means of putting Zenji in his place. Maybe it could work out, her working with them. She'd try to be nice—amenable, as Roshi would have it.

"Anything you need to ask of, anytime, just let Muin know. I will make myself available for you," Roshi said.

Alex looked over at Muin. They silently acknowledged the arrangement.

"There is something I must tell you. It may be of some pertinence," Roshi said.

Alex nodded almost imperceptibly.

"Maybe only Muin and I know about it. There is old logging road on other side of lake. More than ten years it has been out of use. If it can still be used, maybe someone else knows. This could account for no noise on main road. If person responsible is from some other place."

"Do the detectives know about this?" Alex said.

"No. I wish for you to tell them."

Alex wasn't sure if she'd be a hero or if the news would set them off against Roshi for not telling them sooner. She didn't care.

"Okay. Anything else you can tell me that might be helpful? Where does the road lead?"

"There are three or four letouts—all lead to main road—all above our road."

Alex's mind flashed to the red truck she had seen yesterday morning. "Anything else?"

"Also there are here, on the monastery property, some paths to walk on, trails not big enough for vehicles. They too lead to other roads. Some long neglected, not well marked, easy to get lost. But if someone knows how to travel such paths, they could go and come with no one to see them."

"How many people know about these paths?" Alex asked.

Roshi closed his eyes for a few moments. Alex knew it came from his sincere desire to answer accurately. She could see his mind working, translating as thoughts arose. *I wonder if he dreams in English. Or are his dreams beyond language?*

"All I can say is many monks and students walked these trails much in the past. There were many who were intimate with these hills. Intimate—it is proper to say this?"

Roshi's grasp of the English language was impressive. After more than thirty years in America he had a deep and often subtle understanding of its nuances. But he sometimes got confused with the idiomatic grammar. He was always learning new forms of expression and asking about proper usage. Or was that a convenient ploy to put others off guard? A wave of anger rushed through her, its heat reddening her cheeks. This whole mess was sowing distrust everywhere. *If I can't trust Roshi who can I trust?*

"Remember Buddha's final words Alex, 'Be a lamp unto yourself.'" Was Kido telling her not to trust Roshi?

"Perfect choice," Alex replied. *Though it isn't perfect that there are so many ways in and out of this place. The detectives won't be thrilled either.*

17

Alex left Roshi and went to see what was going on in the dining room before checking in with the cops. Normal duties and evening zazen were cancelled. Jito, Clark and Gyozan were in the kitchen preparing lunch. Zen students not doing zazen or chores were at loose ends, so the afternoon and evening were planned as work sessions, with everyone chipping in to prepare a catalog mailing.

Not business as usual exactly, but sitting around idle was never an option in a Buddhist monastery. They were all happy to be doing something. Alex usually enjoyed these impromptu group work sessions when Jito fed them and work took the place of zazen. But this would not be a happy occasion.

She made her way to the library. She had a lot to tell the boys. She'd call Uncle Charlie after lunch. And she'd find some way to get Muin alone.

***

Wolfe wasn't exactly cordial in welcoming her, but he wasn't as hostile as he had been. Roshi had either charmed or intimidated him into including her. Knowing Roshi and Wolfe, she bet it was the former. As for Kluny, he went along graciously.

"Welcome to the team, Detective Sullivan," Kluny said, getting up from his chair and extending his hand.

"Please, call me Alex. Or Sully."

"Sully?" Kluny asked.

"Yeah, short for Sullivan."

"Detective Wolfe here is better known as Wolfey, to those of us who like him." Kluny laughed. "Lucky for me my name already had the y ending. What is it about us cops and nicknames anyway?"

"Sorta like one big school yard. It's all right with me." Alex laughed. Kluny laughed with her, and Wolfey, well, he smiled, sort of.

"You do know that you can only be involved in the informational aspect of this case, right?" This from Wolfe. "Nothing we can do about that. Our hands are tied. You are here in an unofficial capacity only. That okay with you?"

"That's okay with me," Alex said.

"Good. Now, what have you got for us?" Wolfe asked, avoiding calling her anything at all. The detective label might be fine around the likes of Zenji but privately she sensed that his using it would confer too much authority onto her.

Alex told them about the logging roads, the hiking trails, and the large number of people from the old days who knew about these pathways in and out.

"So, are you saying that it could be someone from the past, with no connection to Robert or Sonja, who's back to perpetrate murder?" Wolfe asked.

"Maybe. And Robert and Sonja could be distractions. I don't think we should exclude the possibility that the real target is Roshi. He's upset a lot of people over the years," Alex said. This admission surprised even her. She hadn't been consciously aware that this idea had been lurking.

"What do you mean by upset? Enough to kill him? Or others connected to him?"

"Maybe, yeah." She was working this through as they went.

"What could he have done, being a monk and all, that could be so bad someone would want him dead?"

Alex didn't want to air Roshi's dirty laundry in front of these guys, and was unclear herself how much Roshi's past would figure into the case. Truth was she didn't know much about his past, not really. She had to consider that there might be some truth to some of the rumors she'd heard about Roshi's past transgressions, and that they might have something to do with Kosen's death and Sonja's disappearance. But she wasn't ready to share what she knew just yet.

I'll give him the one everyone knows about, start there.

"You may have heard this already from some of the students, but some time back one of Roshi's monks, name of Enji, like Zenji only without the z, left on bad terms to start his own zendo. Took some of Roshi's students with him."

"Yeah, yeah. We heard about him. So far from what we gather, he doesn't seem like much of a threat. We're looking at him again, just in case. What else you got?"

Alex strained to keep her emotional lid on as she responded to Detective Howard Wolfe. She didn't want to let her personal feelings and protective instincts toward Roshi cloud her thinking and color her judgment on the one hand, or betray her teacher because of some ugly rumors on the other hand.

"Look, monk or not, Roshi is still human. And some of the people who become his students are not always the picture of sound mental health. I'm sure you already know about people like Clark, who come to the monastery to complete their prison sentence. Well, he's not the first ... I don't know how long the list is, but it's been going on for years.

"A few times in the past some of his students, the non-criminals, have been angered by his behavior, to the point where they've written and published bad things about him, and ditched him as their teacher, or so I've been told. I'm not saying that my theory has any validity, but if it does, Robert and Sonja probably figure in someplace. I'm just thinking that it may not be over, and that Roshi might be a target. Call it intuition. If you want my opinion, when your guys get here, put one of them on Roshi full-time. Better safe than sorry is how I like to play it. None of us wants a dead Roshi on our hands."

"I already have that covered," Wolfe said. He clearly didn't want her strategy advice.

Alex wouldn't second-guess him. A battle of egos was not one she wanted to enter into. "Good," she said. "I know that you've talked already to Robert's cousin, and I have no doubt you were thorough, but you might want to look at him again. I saw a truck that looked like his yesterday morning on my run. In the woods where it didn't belong."

"He was an odd duck, that's for sure. Said he was in these parts to watch over his cousin, not to hurt him," Kluny said. Detective Wolfe scowled.

"Zenji brought his name up earlier, and I know he phoned him yesterday before we found Robert. Maybe he knows something about this cousin, or vice versa," Alex said.

"Cousin said he didn't know Zenji. We had no reason to doubt him, but it won't hurt to take another look, especially if something does happen to Sonja," Kluny said.

"Zenji! I'd slap his ass in jail before the cousin's, but we got nothin' on either of 'em," Wolfe said. "There are lots of red trucks in these parts, it could've been anyone. Meantime, why not see what you can dig up in the way of names and addresses on Roshi's old students. Anyone who might have had a beef with him. And pray that Sonja shows up. Or light some incense or bow to Buddha or whatever it is you all do up here."

If that attitude weren't so typical of cops she might be pissed. But she was inured to such an asshole way of thinking that she just let it slide.

"And what about the other red truck that visited Roshi yesterday? You guys know about him?"

"Course we know, but you don't have to know everything ... if it's important for you to know we'll tell you," Wolfe said.

"Well, look, since I'm on your team now," Alex said just to get under his skin, "I'll have to move around here solo, not be paired up with one of the residents."

Wolfe closed his eyes and squared his jaw digging for a comeback. She beat him to it. "And I might as well tell you now, I have a gun with me, and you know I know how to protect myself if it comes to that, so you don't have to worry about me."

"Don't you go off being Miss Brave City Cop and doing something stupid," Wolfe growled. Much as he hated agreeing, he knew he had no choice. "And check in every couple hours here or, Roshi's wishes or not, you're done here. Got it?"

"Got it."

"Don't mind him. Under all that gruffness he's an okay guy," Kluny said after Wolfe left to make some phone calls in the main office.

"I'll take your word for it."

An awkward silence fell on them. It being her turf but not her case muddied the waters on how she was to operate. This confusion lasted less than the moment it took to notice it.

"So, what were the autopsy results on Robert? Can't imagine why I shouldn't know that." She noticed that she referred to Kosen as Robert in the company of the detectives and as Kosen when talking to her Zen friends. It took no effort at all. She seemed to be slipping easily from cop mind to Zen mind and back again depending on circumstances and was not stressed about it. That was a good thing.

Kluny shrugged. "Don't know why you can't know what we know, Wolfe will come around at some point.... Tox screen showed high levels of Xanax and heroin. Enough to kill him. The asphyxiation was overkill. Whoever killed Robert knew his drug chemistry."

"Xanax and heroin? Shit." Right about now was when she should spill the beans on Jito and his drugs. She decided to hold on to that secret for a bit. "How were they administered?"

"Injected directly into the bloodstream. Needle in the arm. It didn't take long. Painless way to go, really."

"Want some help with the room searches?" Alex really wanted to get into Jito's room. He'd said nothing about heroin. Had his hungry ghost gotten the better of him?

"No thanks, we've got a team on their way up. Best you not get that close."

"Right.Anything else on the scene? Fingerprints? Shoeprints? Anything?"

"It's the cleanest crime scene I've ever seen. And in a boiler room. Impossible, but true. He wasn't killed there is all we know," Kluny said. "There was one thing, though. A coupla hairs on

Robert's robe that were definitely not human. Animal of some sort. Probably cat. Is there a resident cat here?"

"No. Not that I know of, but I'm not here all the time. Roshi doesn't much like cats, but these monks do a lot of things that Roshi wouldn't approve of. And one or two might have a cat somewhere just to break a rule. But if no one has a cat, won't that take suspicion off the residents?" Alex knew the answer but maybe here in the country they'd be a little lax.

"Not yet. If someone here is involved they could be in collusion with someone outside. We can't rule out anyone just yet."

Doesn't hurt to ask.

Or does it? What's going on with me? Someone's dead, someone's missing, and here I am trying to protect Roshi's flock. I'd better watch out or I'll never be able to spot the perp even if he shows up radiating guilt. Is this awareness enough to keep me and those I care about out of harm's way? Already I'm holding back information that might help the investigation. Fuck.

***

Lunch was informal, they were allowed to talk but ate in near silence. Butternut squash soup with chunks of sweet potato and pumpkin, spinach salad with mushrooms, cherry tomatoes, and red onions with honey-Dijon dressing, and crusty whole grain bread served with a beet-tofu spread. Sonja was still missing. Cops, local and state, were being gathered to comb the surrounding woods for her.

Muin served Roshi in his room. Two cops were posted at the gatehouse entrance. Other than that, they were all there, along with the two detectives, and the three CSIs who'd arrived to search through the residents' personal stuff. The visitors were all knees and elbows as they tried to get comfortable eating on the floor. Alex ate more than she was hungry for, trying to satisfy her need for comfort. It never worked. Her hungry ghost was restless.

Everyone wanted to leave, but most of those who were in the clear once their room was searched chose to stay with the group, displaying sangha togetherness and Rinzai Zen toughness—the warrior ancestry taking hold.

Alex needed to talk with Muin about his history. Yes, she had slept with him for a time and they had shared confidences, but Muin held his past very close. He was much of a mystery to her.

Before Alex walked out the door to head for the library, Clark came rushing out of the kitchen, white as a ghost. "Go get the cops! Don't go in there! Fuck! This is nuts!"

Someone asked, "Is it Sonja?"

"No, no, no, thank Buddha," Clark said as he paced to and fro along the windowed wall still holding his dirty dishes in his one hand.

"Calm down, everyone," Alex said. "I'll go take a look. Zenji, you go get the detectives and bring someone with you."

"I'll go with you," Clark said. "I gotta move." He put his plate on a table and ran out of the dining room on Zenji's tail.

I don't like the two of them going off together, but what the hell ...

"The rest of you please sit down, wait for the detectives," Alex said.

She couldn't wait. She needed to witness Clark's discovery before whatever was in there changed.

On the counter, a cat, dead, in two pieces. There wasn't much blood. The sawing in half had been done elsewhere. The cops would be there in a minute.

It made sense to Alex that no one had heard a thing from the kitchen while they all ate. The doors and walls were built to contain the clanging of pots and other meal-making sounds. But the intruder, and there had been an intruder, had taken a huge risk entering the kitchen and depositing his "gift" while five cops, six including her, and the whole sangha minus Muin and Roshi, sat eating in the next room.

She executed her spinning-in-place ritual. The butcher was long gone. It was broad daylight.

What the hell is going on? What the hell does a cat have to do with anything? Where is Muin? And Roshi? They were the only two absent from lunch.

Her cop mind put them both on her list of suspects. Her Zen mind wanted to scratch them off.

18

The cops took over, four students volunteered to take the dirty dishes down to the lounge to wash, and the rest of the sangha stayed in the dining room wondering what the hell was going on in the kitchen. Alex met with Roshi and Muin. Zenji was scheduled to meet with the detectives at 2:00. She wouldn't miss that interview for the world.

"Alex, do you know of the koan, Nansen Cuts the Cat in Two?" Roshi asked.

"Vaguely."

"Muin, please tell her."

"Hmmm, let's see ..." Muin cast his eyes to the ceiling, avoiding eye contact with her. "'Nansen Osho saw the monks in the Eastern and Western halls arguing over a cat. He held up the cat and said: 'If you can say a word of Zen, I will spare the cat. If not, I will kill it.' The monks gave no answer. He cut the cat in two.'"

The three of them sat there and let the words of the koan and the reality of the dead cat in the kitchen coalesce.

"So you think whoever killed the cat is sending a message that involves this koan?" Alex asked.

"Perhaps," Roshi said.

"Do you know what that message is?"

"I will have to spend some time sitting with this before I know for certain."

"You have some idea?"

"I cannot say for sure."

Damn it!

"Roshi, excuse me, but if you think you know something, anything, even if it's supposition, you must let us know. It could help us discover whoever is doing these things. And Sonja is still out there somewhere." Alex couldn't keep the irritation out of her tone.

"I have not forgotten that. It is all I now think about. But I can't say a thing right now to save her. If I could I would. This is not a koan. Those are simple matters compared to this. I'm afraid a Zen word cannot save her."

I wonder if there's a deeper meaning here, damn it.

"Did anyone here have a cat? Does that cat belong to the monastery?"

"No, of that I am certain. I do not know where that cat is from. I have never seen it before today. Which says to me that whoever is doing these things is not of this sangha, he is an outsider, and you must find him. Soon, you must find him soon."

All three sat in silence. Alex sensed that Roshi wasn't done with her. She was not yet dismissed. He sat with closed eyes, still as a mountain peak. There was something he wasn't sharing, she was convinced of it. A few agonizing minutes passed. Alex could hear breathing, her mind was on warp speed. Sure enough, as Roshi always predicted, "when time is ready ..." he was ready to speak.

"I hesitate to tell you this Alex." Roshi turned his body slightly toward her. "And unless you think it has merit, please do not say it to other detectives. Keep it to yourself, because it may not be of pertinence."

Fuck, secrets even from him ...

"An old student of mine, name of Enji—I have not seen him in more than thirty years—will be attending the Sunday celebrations. This Nansen and cat koan was one he was stuck on—no ... that is too strong. He was working on this koan when we parted. Muin will fill you in on our history. It may mean nothing. I hope that to be true.

"Alex, I will trust you to tell police if you think it must be so. And if you feel you must communicate this, let Muin know first so I will be informed."

"Hai!" *The one word of Japanese I know. Yes, okay, hai! There's nothing else to say. Now at least I'll have a chance to meet with Muin. Roshi dictated it and Muin will obey.*

"Roshi, I noticed that you had a visitor yesterday who showed up in a red truck. Can you tell me about him and his business with you?"

"I have told the detectives about that matter. Please ask them."

"Hai! Thank you, Roshi." Her brain was screaming: *But they wouldn't tell me.*

Alex and Muin agreed to meet that evening in her room, right after supper, if that was happening. There was so much chaos, food might be the last thing on everyone's mind, especially with the dead cat in the kitchen. Either way, around that time worked for Muin. As much as she wanted to talk with him right then and there, she couldn't risk missing the interrogations of Zenji and Clark. And she'd wait to see what Muin had to say before she told the cops about Enji being stuck on the cat koan. The dead cat was too literal an interpretation of the koan for it to be significant. *Koans don't quite work that way. Do they? How will Wolfey integrate such a thing?*

When she peeked into the kitchen she could see he was much too engrossed to bother with koan theories. Telling him could wait. She decided to use the found time to phone Uncle Charlie.

***

Alex brought Uncle Charlie up to speed on the dead cat, the animal hairs found on Robert that were probably connected, and her meeting with Roshi.

"Things are getting weirder and weirder up here Uncle C and whoever's doing it isn't done yet, I feel it in my bones. But I haven't a clue what's next or even what connection Robert and Sonja have to the cat and what it has to do with anything. I have a bad feeling about Sonja and the fact that she hasn't shown up yet."

"Is the autopsy report in on Robert yet?"

"Yeah, drugs. Xanax and heroin. With asphyxiation, just to make sure the job was done."

Charlie exhaled a long, soft whistle through his teeth.

"Yeah, it's wild." Alex lowered her voice, "What they don't know is that some of the drugs came from Jito."

"I'm listening."

"Jito's had a hell of a time kicking pills. I thought he was done with them. Turns out I was wrong, he had some Xanax and who knows what else. He copped to the Xanax. He told me Robert found out and threatened to tell Roshi if Jito didn't hand some over. Jito felt he had no choice. This is his story, of course I never had a chance to question Robert. Jito was so beside himself I'm leaning towards believing him. I haven't told the cops yet but I plan to soon."

"Good idea." Uncle Charlie paused. "It doesn't look good for Jito either way."

"I'm worried about him, and I vacillate about his involvement. Rooms are being searched as we speak, though the cat's been a distraction in that endeavor. We'll see if they come up with anything. I might hold off telling Kluny and Wolfe what I know about Jito till tomorrow. There's nothing they can do today anyway and they've got their hands full. It'll give Jito a chance to get some rest." Alex didn't know what she was saying.

"And what about Zenji? How's he behaving?"

"Well, I don't think he's the one doing the killing, I really think he loves Sonja so whatever's happened to her he couldn't be involved—he's out of his mind with worry. I can't help thinking he's mixed up in it some other way. Cops'll be talking to both him and Clark soon—and they've agreed to let me sit in."

"That's big of them."

"Roshi had something to do with that, but whatever, it works for me. Any more news on Zenji and Robert's relationship?"

"Nothing yet. Robert's parents are on their way east. Maybe they'll be able to enlighten you, if you ever get to have a chat with them. And, of course, there's the cousin. I can't tell where he was when Robert and Zenji were in high school. All I know now is his last name is Bowden and both his parents are dead. The mother was Robert's aunt, his father's sister. Married name of Bowden."

"How'd the parents die?"

"Mother died of an overdose. Father killed himself a few months later, gun to the head. This cousin Lawrence left home years before that, fifteen at the time. No record of him anywhere, at least not under that name."

"Right. He could be our guy. Most homicides being family related I wouldn't be surprised," Alex said. "And if Zenji knew

Robert in California, maybe he knew the cousin. Or maybe they're all cousins."

"If there's something to get, guaranteed you'll get it, Alex." Uncle Charlie never stopped encouraging or praising her. She often wondered if she would have done anything with her life without him.

"I hope so. Like I said, I have a weird feeling that it ain't over yet. I can't figure out who's next, but as I told the detectives, I think we should assume the ultimate target is Roshi."

"You could be right. Any thoughts on why the killer didn't go straight for him then, if that's the case?"

"Nope. I just hope we get to this guy before he gets to Roshi, if that's his plan."

"It sounds like you could use some help up there. Want me to come up?" Uncle Charlie knew that Alex liked to work alone and did not like to mix the personal with the professional. But he also knew that she valued his advice. With her so close to the community, he thought it could only help to have a more objective pair of eyes.

"Hmmm. That's a thought, let me think on it. I'll let you know later tonight."

"Okay. On the other hand, maybe I can do more good staying put and helping with the background stuff. By the looks of things I'll have more than enough to keep me busy. In the meantime, I'll check out Sonja's history. What did you say her name was?"

"I don't think I said. It's Jacqueline Simonet. She's from Switzerland. French and German parents I think. Some say she comes from money, but I've never noticed any. I think she liked Robert because no one else did. I don't know why she and Zenji were screwing around though, and I can't believe she'd run off with him.

Roshi is heartsick about her. He seemed to take Robert's death in stride, but Sonja vanishing into thin air has him really shook up."

More to herself than to Uncle Charlie she added, "I can't help but wonder what he knows. Poor Sonja."

"My guess is she's only involved because of her association with Robert," Uncle Charlie said with a trace of sadness. He had an unlimited capacity for compassion.

"I think you're right."

"I guess this is a case of it not paying to be too nice."

"Most of us don't have to worry about that."

"There's another someone up there who's on the wrong side of nice. That place oughtta bill itself as a halfway house or training ground for wannabe and ex-criminals," Charlie said.

"Whaddya mean? Was Jito in trouble before he got here?"

"I'm not sure about him yet. So far he looks clean."

"Thank God."

"But drug addicts can't be trusted."

"Don't I know it. So then, you mean Clark?"

"Yeah. He was a badass down here. Like you said he spent his life in this state, most of it upstate on the SUNY campus selling drugs and a long stint in Greenhaven for it. He either got interested in Zen or found out about Roshi's policy of helping out convicts. He got in touch and Roshi agreed to have him. Maybe he got used to life in an institution, three squares a day, the monastery the closest thing he could get to it and be free."

"Not to mention it'd put him below everyone's radar. Think he's still dealing?"

"He could be. The monastery would be a great cover."

"Come to think of it, he's the designated errand boy up here. He goes to town at least once a week to shop, run errands. Maybe he conducts his drug business while he's there. Maybe he's Jito's drug connection. Maybe this whole place is a bevy of drug addicts. Maybe it's all about drugs and Roshi's not in danger, or maybe he's on drugs. Shit, I don't know what to think anymore." Alex pushed her bangs off her face. *What was I thinking with this fucking haircut?*

"Maybe Robert and Zenji were in cahoots with Clark and running drugs for him. Zenji and Clark returned from being out in the same patch of woods yesterday at the same time, which made no sense at all given how vocal Clark has been about implicating Zenji first in Robert's disappearance, then in his death, and they never got along far as anyone here could tell. Or so I've been told. But maybe it's all a big pack of lies. And the way he lost his hand was gruesome."

"How's that?"

"Clark lost all his fingers on one hand. One story is that he was drunk or high, camping in the woods with a friend. They were chopping wood for a fire with an ax that didn't belong on a camping trip. Clark was holding the wood, his friend missed and cut off all his fingers and most of his thumb in one stroke."

"Sweet Jesus."

"Or maybe it was some drug deal gone bad. Or maybe he lost it behind bars. No one but he knows the real truth and far as I can tell no one here ever asked. He gets by okay though, except for his temper. I guess I've given people up here more slack than I would most civilians. Maybe we ought to arrest them all? As much as I'd like to, I think we can't leave anyone shy of suspicion. I'll send you a complete list of everyone here. State cops are doing background checks on the group but it wouldn't hurt to do our own."

"I'm at your service," Uncle Charlie said. "But let's not convict before all the evidence is in." He never rushed to judgment and never put anything aside until every last t was crossed. Monks selling drugs and killing each other didn't go down easily.

They said their good-byes. Neither hung up. Charlie reflected on his youth as an altar boy and his once-upon-a-time belief that a priest could do no wrong. When the overwhelming evidence of priests molesting young boys had come to light over the past few years, Charlie's faith had been shattered and he stopped going to church for a while. Even so, he wouldn't condemn anyone without due process.

The sadness in each of their hearts traveled heavily between the phone lines and settled in their lungs. Their breath was now in sync and the only sound passing between them.

"Uncle C I've gotta go. I don't want to miss the Zenji and Clark show upstairs ... but let's talk later tonight ... I'm due to meet with Muin at some point and he's going to fill me in on Roshi's history and on one of his old students who's coming up on Sunday. They haven't seen each other in over thirty years. It's hard to believe that he'd be involved, holding a grudge for that long would take more than not passing a koan."

"What's that?"

"Oh, nothing ... just some Zen bullshit."

"Who is Muin, Alex? How do you keep the names straight?"

Alex laughed. "It takes a while, but once you begin using someone's Buddhist name it sinks in and seems normal. I often forget the birth names. By the end of this you won't think any of the names odd."

"I doubt that."

"Well then, maybe by October, if I get a new name, if I decide to go through with becoming a Buddhist after this week, it'll start to get easier for you."

"Maybe ..."

"Anyway, Muin is one of my closest friends up here. You met him as James. I brought him with me to your backyard barbeque a few years back. He beat everyone in bocce ball, remember? That pissed off all your cronies, the regular players, 'cause he'd never played before."

"Ah yes, now I remember. The guys dubbed him 'Beginner's Luck.' I liked him, he was a good sport."

"He's a terrific guy. Up here he's Roshi's assistant, or inji. All Zen Masters have one. Sort of a chief of staff or right-hand-man. He handles Roshi's correspondence, schedules, meetings. He's a liaison between Roshi and the rest of the sangha, and between Roshi and the outside world.

"Muin's been with Roshi forever. Way before I got here. He's a fixture in this place. Knows everything, sees everything, blends in with the woodwork. Fascinating personality, once you get him away from Roshi. Quite funny, really. A few nervous tics, but a nice guy.

"He knows a lot, and he's so used to keeping secrets, not talking out of school, that he wouldn't offer any information unless pressed to. Roshi practically ordered him to talk to me, which is a good thing because I've hardly had two words with him alone since I arrived. He usually makes time for me when I'm here." Alex had never confided in Charlie the sexual nature of her relationship with Muin and now wasn't the time.

"It has been a rather unusual week, Alex."

"Yeah, I know, but it still feels like he's avoiding me. I hope he keeps our date."

"I've forgotten, what is Muin's birth name?"

Alex felt her insides bunch up into a ball the size of her fist, smack in the middle of her solar plexus. Her tough-girl-cop bravado was swiftly cracking. "It's James Fagan. He's from the Bronx. He can't have anything to do with this."

"I'm sure you're right. But you know me, thorough as a summer day is long."

"Right. I'll call you later or tomorrow, and I'll fax or email you a complete list of residents when I get a chance," Alex said, annoyed that Charlie was taking liberties with her friends before she offered them up.

"That's great. We'll talk later then."

She was irritated with Charlie when she hung up, and knew that it was irrational. She did not want him to investigate her former lover and friend. It felt like an invasion. But she also knew that it had to be done. *Maybe this is what's making my stomach queasy.*

19

The students were still assembled in the dining room, the CSIs were in the kitchen, Kluny and Wolfe were in the library making phone calls and tending to other cop business. Landlines had been hooked up; they figured they'd be there awhile. When she walked in Kluny asked her to go retrieve Zenji.

"Maybe being his 'dharma sister' and all," Wolfe said as he held a phone between his shoulder and ear, and punctuated the air with quotation marks, "you'll be able to get something out of him on the way. I'm convinced he knows something."

It bugged her, Wolfe's use of the monastery lingo. "Did Zenji tell you I was his dharma sister?"

"Nah. Zenji told me squat. I picked that up from Muin. Told me some about the life up here. A little off the wall, but hey, to each his own. I sort of get the brother/sister thing. Kind of like the fraternity among cops."

"Yeah, kinda," Bursts of anger and jealousy exploded into her field of focus. *Muin's talking to him and not me?*

"Cops and monks, people in uniform ... in either case you don't get to choose who the members are," Alex went on, smoldering inside, trying to tamp it down. "Sorta like your birth family—you can love 'em, but you sure as hell don't have to like 'em.

"The sangha is important to Zenji, probably 'cause he never had a family of his own, so I'll play to that."

"Yeah, but don't get carried away with the questions. Bring him straight here." Whomever he'd been waiting for on the other end of the line was back. Wolfe turned his broad back to Alex and returned his attention to his phone call.

***

Alex found Zenji alone in the laundry room.

"Hey, Zenji."

No hello back. Not even a turn of his head. This didn't bode well.

A little louder she said, "Sleeping standing up again, Zenji?" This was a joke among residents after Muin's and Gyozan's stint in one of the strictest monasteries in Japan. The monks and nuns were on such a rigid schedule that time for sleep was hard to come by, so they caught a few winks whenever and wherever they could. Many developed the knack of sleeping perfectly still while sitting on their meditation cushions. The hardcore were even able to sleep standing up.

"Aren't you all remanded to the dining room and not allowed to be alone?"

"Fuck that." Zenji continued sorting and folding.

"Yeah, well ... look, the cops sent me to get you. They're ready for you upstairs."

"So, what're you, their gofer?"

"No" —Alex was getting pissed— "it's just that we have to talk to you again—you're the closest link to Kosen and Sonja."

"We, huh? Whose side are you on here?"

"I wasn't aware there were sides. I'm only interested in helping however I can to find Kosen's murderer and Sonja's abductor ... if there is one. And whoever cut up that cat."

"Yeah, well, I guess I don't trust cops. Never have. And I never got it that you were one till now. Bit of a shock really."

"Some of us are not so bad," Alex said, softening her tone.

Zenji's shoulders softened a little.

"Maybe. I just want this to be over. Sorry. It wasn't meant to be personal."

"It's okay, we're all a bit testy. Let's just go upstairs before they send out a posse for us, shall we?"

Wolfe was off the phone and pacing again by the time they got to the library. *He should just light up already.*

"Sit down—" Wolfe pointed to a chair— "and no more lying!"

Zenji sat and just stared at the floor, the fight gone out of him. Sonja's disappearance was taking its toll.

"You knew Robert in California, before you both got here, why'd you lie?"

"So I knew him, so what? We were never really friends, we went to the same high school and we wound up at the same Zen center. But I never liked him, and when he got here I didn't want anyone to know about the history and now none of it matters," Zenji said in a quiet monotone. His hands were clasped, one thumbnail digging into the flesh of the other thumb. Looked like it hurt.

"Maybe you think it doesn't matter, but everything matters," Kluny said. "Who was your teacher out there?"

"Guy named Enji." Zenji was looking at the floor when he said it, so didn't notice Wolfe and Kluny exchanging a surprised look. But Alex noticed.

"Is that right?" Wolfe asked.

"Yeah, so?"

"And why'd you both leave him and come here to Roshi?"

"I haven't a clue what Kosen's reasons were. Mine ... I was just looking for another teacher, felt Enji wasn't enlightened enough."

"Don't lie to us!"

"Look, Zenji," Alex butted in, "maybe you don't care what happened to Kosen, but don't you want to find Sonja? Nothing matters now but finding her before it's too late. Tell us what you know. You may not think it'll help, but the truth always does."

"You're right that nothing matters now ..." He raised his head and looked at Alex, releasing the pressure on his thumb and dropping his hands into his lap. "Okay." Zenji closed his eyes. "Enji sent me here years ago to check out Roshi and report back to him—about what I was never really clear. After a while I realized that Enji deserved to be an outcast and that Roshi was the true teacher. Besides, I didn't get along with Enji's head monk, and knew I'd never get the chance to be that with him there, so I stayed here. Being head monk here didn't matter, I like Muin and, well, Roshi was the real deal it seemed. I never even contacted Enji once I got here. Then when Kosen showed up, I figured he was sent to spy on me and Roshi so I steered clear of him."

"And did Roshi know any of this?"

"When Kosen arrived, I told Roshi that I'd once been a student of Enji's—I didn't want him finding out from someone else. I also told him that Kosen had also been Enji's student. I didn't tell him that I was sent to spy, but I warned him about Kosen."

"I bet you were vying to be Roshi's successor, his whaddya call it? Oh yeah, dharma heir," Wolfe said. "You were hoping to be the favored monk here, weren't you?"

"You don't know what you're even talking about." Zenji's hands were back in their grip. *Maybe the self-inflicted pain helps him keep his temper in check.*

"Did you kill Kosen?" Wolfe asked, now using Robert's dharma name.

"No, I didn't kill him. I didn't like him, but I didn't kill him."

"And what about the cat? Did you kill it?"

"Of course not," Zenji said, casting a disgusted look at Wolfe.

"Do you know where the cat came from? I thought Roshi hated having cats around. Was it one of the resident's?" Alex asked.

"Why don't you ask your boyfriend?"

"What do you mean?"

"Muin. Your boyfriend, ask him."

Talk about a ton of bricks. Alex could hardly breathe. *I thought we'd done such a good job keeping our affair secret. We'd been so discreet. Damn it! Maybe secrets are impossible in a closed community. I wonder if Roshi knows. Will this transparency get them to the killer sooner?* Her head was spinning.

"What's Muin got to do with the cat?"

"Didn't he tell you? I thought he told you everything. It was his. He kept it down at Kido's cabin."

Alex's mind was reeling. *Is this why Muin's been avoiding me?*

Kluny jumped in to save her. She couldn't even look over at Wolfe, she knew he was furious. She also knew he had every right to be, her keeping this secret from them. And Muin, too. If Muin was the one they were getting all the Zen info from, he hadn't told them about his cat, if it was his, or their affair.

"Did Roshi know about the cat?" Kluny asked Zenji.

"Nah. He hates cats. Muin didn't seem to care. He loved that cat more than Roshi. Well, maybe not quite, but close. ... Most of us feel like Muin's cat belonged to all of us. It actually helped us get along better. We all pitched in taking care of it. Having this little secret made us closer, established a bond of sorts, I guess you could say." His hands were once again relaxed.

"Except for Kosen," he added, almost as an afterthought. His thumbs were back at it with the mention of Kosen.

"What do you mean?"

"Kosen never helped with the cat, who we named Joshu, we all voted on it. I think Kosen held it against Muin that he wasn't included, although he was invited to be part of it. I overheard them arguing recently; Kosen threatened to tell Roshi about the cat."

"When was that exactly?" Kluny asked.

"I don't know, last week some time I think."

"How long has the cat been here?" Kluny was doing all the questioning. Wolfe and Alex slipped to the background.

"Only about a month. I think most of us are more bummed out about the cat than about Kosen." Zenji sat up as if he only just heard what he'd said and mumbled, "I don't mean that, really I don't, I don't know what I'm saying. It is a shame about Kosen even if I didn't like or trust him."

"What about Clark? Was he part-owner of the cat, too?"

"Ah, I forgot about him ... no, he wasn't. And being that he found Kosen's body and the dead cat you might want to question him—"

"Leave us to do our job, wise guy," Wolfe jumped back in. He didn't like Zenji, but Alex could tell that he was coming around to believing he wasn't Kosen's killer.

"I'm just saying, being an ex-con and all ..."

All three cops got it. Alex got it that the list of Roshi's students who had spent time behind bars was too long for her liking—maybe they'd have to look at those guys if their perp turned out to be someone not currently residing at the monastery.

"And the cousin? You knew him too, didn't you?" Wolfe asked, the pack of cigarettes now clutched in his hand.

"Since it's true confessions here, yeah, I did. Sorta. From California days ... he used to buy us booze when we were in high school. He was a jolly drunk, war vet as I recall. But I never really knew him."

"That's just great ... now get out of here. But stay close," Wolfe said.

"Where would I go? Jeez, you guys are unbelievable," Zenji said as he practically ran out of the library.

Alex followed him before Wolfe could grill her about Muin. "Wait up, Zenji, I'll escort you. You're not supposed to be alone, remember?"

To the cops she said, "I'll bring Clark back with me."

***

When Clark sat down for his interview he straddled the folding chair he was offered, rolled up his sleeves and placed his tattooed, muscular forearms on the back of the chair, his fingerless hand hanging down as if it were a trophy he was showing off, transforming himself from reluctant Zen student into recalcitrant convict.

Before they could ask question one, he said, "Look, I know my rights, maybe more than most people up here. I didn't do anything but discover Kosen dead and the cat cut in half. And that's all I'll say. I'm not your guy. If you have any questions I want a lawyer present. I know too well how things can get twisted up and go against the innocent."

"So that's it?" Wolfe asked.

"That's it ... but if you're gonna keep us here longer I suggest you get someone up here to put locks on the doors. I've been asking for that since I got here, no one's listened. Maybe you will. If you're smart–"

"That's it ... now get out of here. We'll have a lawyer up here soon as we can, just for you," Wolfe said.

"I can hardly wait."

Alex didn't want to be alone with Kluny and Wolfe just yet so she escorted Clark back to the dining room.

She told Wolfe and Kluny, "I'll be back in a jiff. I want to stop in my room, pick up a book of koans, show you the one that I think whoever killed the cat was referring to."

"Isn't this room a fucking library?" Wolfe asked as he looked around. "Surely that book is here."

"It'll be quicker if I get the one in my room. I'll be back in no time."

Before the door closed Alex heard Wolfe say, "We gotta get that cousin back up here pronto, damn liar, see what else he didn't tell us ..."

20

After retrieving her book of koans, Alex swung by the dining room to see what was going on. No one was inside. They were all on the outside deck gathered like statues in a long row, gazing out toward the lake. The mountain wasn't pitch dark yet, but close. They stared spellbound through the bare trees to the lake. All they could see from that distance was one of the aluminum canoes floating in the middle of the lake with a pyramid pile of branches ablaze. It reminded Alex of the early stages of the traditional bonfire that was lit during O-Bon, the ceremony every August that commemorated the dead, but this was in the middle of the lake not on dry land. And there was nothing going on here to celebrate.

Flames licked up toward the sky. Orange and yellow flashing bright, reflecting itself in the mirror of the lake and growing brighter and taller with each rising spark. Alex knew there had to be sound effects to this surreal light show, the twitching, crackling and rustling of wood burning and spreading and settling, but they were too far away to hear it. The gigantic Buddha statue on the distant shore sparkled in the firelight. The dancing flames set against a backdrop of deep blue sky peeking through and above the tall black trees on the opposite shore was a portrait in primary colors.

For a few moments the group was mesmerized by the light show. The hot glow of the fire didn't reach up to them, and watching the blaze made the cool mountain evening air feel even chillier. They wrapped their garments tighter around them and hugged themselves against the cold, transfixed.

Zenji broke the spell with a gasp, "Oh my god!" and a dash toward the floating fire. This woke the group the way a clapper or bell or strike of the kesaku, 'encouragement' stick, against their aching shoulders during meditation would. They moved into action and ran to the lake.

By the time they all got there, the collective insight was clear. It was Sonja in the boat even if they couldn't see her body.

Some residents crumbled in place into disbelief and shock. Some wanted to help, but had no clue what to do, so they stood hugging themselves to control the nervous shaking. Clark and Gyozan sprinted into action. They put the second boat into the lake and rowed out with flashlights and fire extinguishers.

Moments later, Detective Wolfe arrived on the scene and stood on the dock directing the recovery of the errant boat. Zenji ran back to the monastery to alert Roshi and Muin. Kluny and Alex dealt with everyone else. If it was Sonja burning out there they needed to keep people from viewing the result.

One murdered dead body and a butchered cat was enough to set eyes on. There was no reason they should be subjected to a third body, charred at that. They got everyone else back to the dining room and put Jito in charge. Giving him something to do would help his nerves.

By the time the fire was out and both boats tied up, it was clear that Sonja was in the boat, but they couldn't see how bad it was right away. Clark and Gyozan were sent back to be with the other students, leaving the CSIs to deal with the remains. The extra cops who had been in the woods looking for Sonja were also there. They'd had no luck finding Sonja, but maybe the arsonist would be easier prey. They spread out while some light remained in the sky. The full moon would be up soon to assist them.

They would have to wait for morning to effectively search the area. Whoever killed Sonja was most likely long gone, so by morning the trail would be cold. One of the state troopers made arrangements to have lights transported up the mountain to illuminate the woods and search for clues, but there weren't enough lights in the whole state to penetrate the thick forest.

The monastery property stretched out in all directions, consuming 4,000 acres, and State Forest extended far beyond that. It was improbable that they'd find a trace of Sonja's arsonist even in broad daylight.

Zen might tell Alex to let events take their course and not interfere with the natural order of things. But there was a dead body, a friend of hers, and this was her sanctum. She felt nausea, despair and frustration in equal measure swirling in her gut. Zen patience was not an option.

While everyone was busy, Alex slipped away to retrieve her gun. With the heel of her hand she clicked the magazine into its chamber. The familiar sound satisfied her. She strapped on her gun belt, which felt both wrong and perfectly right given the circumstances, slid the Glock into its holster and returned to the dining room.

Like a magnet to metal, every last pair of eyes was drawn to it as soon as she entered. No one said a word. Wolfe hardly reacted. She figured he was happy to have all the help he could get at this point.

All the residents harbored hope that she wouldn't have to use it. So did she, but that wouldn't stop her if it became necessary.

Most of them felt safer knowing she was trained to protect, and guilty for feeling that way. With her gun holstered and strapped on, the detective-on-scene clicked neatly into place.

***

"Meet us in the library in half an hour," Wolfe said to Alex. It was 8:00. No one mentioned eating, which was fine with her. "And bring that cat koh-on with you."

"Right." Alex's meeting with Muin was now postponed indefinitely. Maybe she could catch up with him later. She wouldn't be getting much sleep and figured he'd be up most of the night, too.

When Alex got to the library Kluny was alone. "Where's your partner?"

"He'll be here any minute. Did you bring that koan stuff?"

"Yeah, I wrote it out for you, the cat one and the tree branch one. Figured you might like to have it in front of you. But before we get to that, okay if I ask you a couple questions?" She was glad Wolfe was late.

"Sure."

"Roshi said that he told you guys about the red truck guy and his business here. Care to clue me in?"

"Yeah, but I got a feeling you're really not gonna like it, given that this is your place of worship—or whatever ..."

"Yeah, well, I don't like anything that's going on here, but having half the story doesn't work either."

"The red-truck guy, as you call him, is an FBI agent and Roshi is being blackmailed."

"Oh man ..."

"Yeah, it's bad. We're not sure yet if Kosen and Sonja were connected to that, but after what Zenji told us, they probably were in some way."

"What does the blackmailer want?"

"For Roshi to make Enji his dharma heir."

"And what did he threaten Roshi with if he didn't do it?"

"Note said he'd make public some old transgression—didn't specify. The language was rambling and filled with Zen jargon."

"You saw the letters?"

"A couple of them. Apparently there are many."

"Well, this sucks ... and puts everything that's happened in a different light. I wonder where the hell Enji is now? Think he's still planning to come here on Sunday? Will there even be an event on Sunday now with what's happened?"

Kluny shrugged. "Who the hell knows?"

Wolfe walked in as they were both thinking about this. Alex noticed that he still hadn't opened the pack of cigarettes—she was rooting for him to conquer that beast but would never let on about it. Something had changed in his demeanor.

Alex had witnessed this shift in cops before when some innocent witness or suspect that they've questioned in a case shows up dead. And in this case, it was in such a gruesome way. Even Wolfe had tender feelings.

"You got that stuff we can look at? Do you think the cat and Sonja are connected?" He was asking Kluny and Alex.

"I wrote out both koans, the one pertaining to Kosen, and the cat one, which may point to Sonja. I have a theory, but read this first. Here." Alex handed each of them a piece of paper. As cops she knew they'd take the stories literally.

They weren't Zen students and maybe in this case that was the way to a solution. They all studied the piece of paper in front of them.

Kyogen's Man up a Tree

Master Kyogen said, "It is like a man up a tree hanging from a branch by his mouth, his hands cannot grasp a bough, his feet cannot touch the tree. A man appears under the tree and asks him, 'What is the meaning of Bodhidharma's coming from the West?' If he does not answer, he fails to respond to the question. If he answers, he will lose his life. What do you think he should do? How would you answer?"

Nansen Cuts the Cat in Two

Nansen saw the monks in the Eastern and Western halls quarreling over a cat. Nansen held up the cat and said, "If you can give one word of Zen, I will not kill it." The monks said nothing, Nansen cut the cat in half. Later, when Joshu returned, Nansen told him about the incident. Joshu put his sandal on his head and walked off. Nansen said, "If you had been here, you would have saved the cat."

"So, do you think the East/West quarrel pertains here?" Wolfe asked. He continued thinking out loud. "Roshi's originally from Japan, the East, and now he's here in the West. Enji was Roshi's student on the West Coast and now Roshi's on the East Coast. They had some sort of quarrel ...

"And Kosen and Zenji were Enji's students on the West Coast and then Roshi's on the East. And Kosen and Zenji were always fighting with each other ... Any theories? Anyone?"

Alex put in her two cents. "I'll have to sit with all of this longer, but my first reaction is that the cat refers to Sonja, that somehow she got in the way of something. I don't think whoever is doing this planned to kill her. And I think whoever's doing this is not in residence here."

"And he just slipped by all the cops out there, set Sonja on fire, and then afloat and left without anyone noticing?" Wolfe asked.

"But we were all here, the residents were all in the dining room, so that leaves Roshi and Muin, which is preposterous to even consider ... so it's got to be someone from the outside," Alex said. Even as she said it she knew her Zen allegiance was interfering with sound judgment.

"Well, first, I'm not going to rule out Roshi and Muin as suspects, not just yet. And second, since we weren't downstairs keeping an eye on things, we have no idea if someone slipped out and back to light a match to Sonja. Third, if you weren't so close to the pool of suspects here—and if you've got any more secrets you're holding about any other relationships you've had up here, tell me now ..."

Alex shook her head.

Wolfe continued. "If you had more objectivity you wouldn't automatically proclaim Muin and Roshi innocent. We have to talk to both of them again ... and we have to widen our scope, look at old students who had a beef, especially the criminally minded ones."

"If Kosen weren't already dead, with what Zenji told us today I'd point to him as the primary suspect," Alex said. It would take her a while to wrap her mind around Muin or Roshi as suspects. Wolfe looked at her like she was crazy.

"Tsk, tsk Alex. You know attachment to anything or anyone creates suffering. And now your mind is like a glass of muddy water. Detach with love, my dear, detach with love." Kido was back on her shoulder.

Kluny broke the silence, all of them sitting there trying to figure it out. "Maybe the guy we're looking for thinks he's Joshu—the monk who put the sandal on his head—who thinks he knows more than all of them. Maybe Enji and Roshi are both targets."

"Shit," Wolfe said. A sentiment that captured how they all felt.

Two phones rang, breaking up the conversation.

Room searches hadn't been completed, so alternate sleeping arrangements were made. Under escort, the residents were able to retrieve a few necessary items from their rooms such as toothbrushes and robes.

Ten residents were bunking in the dorm room on the first floor—normally only used when there was an overflow of students during retreat weeks, and futons were laid out in the laundry room for the rest of them. A cop guarded each room. No one complained. It was cozy, and with the extra protection made them feel safe. Alex was allowed to sleep in her room with her gun as roommate.

***

Alex wanted to talk to Muin alone as a friend before she talked to him as a cop. There wasn't much she could do with Wolfe and Kluny so she bided her time with the other students in the dining room until Muin became available. She knew there was something they were missing. Like a word on the tip of her tongue refusing to budge. She wanted to bite it off, but concentrating on it made it more elusive.

She pushed the mystery down into her second brain, into her belly. The answer would come. She just needed some time. But all her years as a cop told her that when it came to catching a murderer, time was a luxury, and there was never enough of it.

She put in another call to Uncle Charlie.

"When we finally got to her she was nearly unrecognizable, but there's no doubt that it's Sonja. We don't know how she died. I hope she was dead before she was torched," Alex said. Only a few hours had passed since they last spoke and much had happened.

"Do you think the burning of the body holds any significance?"

"Well, Buddhists do opt for cremation. Other than that I don't know. I'll check with Muin. He's the expert on such things."

***

Alex was determined to have a talk with Muin before she got any shuteye. She would find him and nail him down, there was only so far he could go. It wasn't like he could jump on a subway, head for the Bronx, and get lost in his old neighborhood. After checking every conceivable location, Alex concluded that Muin was ensconced in Roshi's quarters, so she staked out at the bottom of Roshi's stairs. Muin would have to leave Roshi at some point and she blocked the only way down. He couldn't avoid her.

To make good use of the time Alex got a cushion from the zendo to sit in meditation as she waited. She was not surprised to find that Cheetah, the name she gave to her monkey mind, was jumping around in her brain, but she did manage to get a few minutes of peace.

She must have dozed off during zazen. Startled awake at 2:00 A.M., Alex drew her gun and pointed it at the empty darkness that carried no one. Whatever woke her wasn't a moving body and it wasn't Muin. Either he'd slipped by her as she slept and was nestled in his own bed, or he was still up with Roshi doing whatever Zen monks and their masters do to cope with a double murder, triple if the cat counted, under the roof of their monastery.

Alex gave up the wait. Again, she made a vow to confront Muin in the morning. He'd be there. So would she. Tomorrow would be the day. That and her chilled bones convinced her to slip back to her room and into bed. By the time she turned off the light it was 2:15. She'd get a few precious hours. She'd need them.

21

Alex slept through her alarm and woke with a jolt at the shinrei wake-up bell. She bolted out of bed, strapped on her gun, ran down the hall to pee and brush her teeth, and returned to her room. She quickly donned her robe and walked briskly to the zendo. All the residents were already there, Roshi's teaching in action: "Do zazen, no matter what."

After zazen, the cops on site were served breakfast in the lounge, giving the residents an opportunity to eat in the manner they were accustomed to: In robes using their jihatsu bowls and chopsticks, mostly in silence except for a little chanting at the beginning and end of the half hour. Everyone was exhausted, and the return to ritual reminded them that life goes on.

They ate their usual morning fare, Alex's favorite: Rice gruel with spicy Kimchee, nori seaweed, toasted sesame seeds, soy sauce, scallions, and a hard-boiled egg, orange juice and fruit. After eating, Alex wasn't completely renewed, but she was ready for the day.

A meeting with Muin was on her agenda. He promised to find her in the library within the hour.

Alex walked the halls to see what was going on, before joining Kluny in the library to help with the lists of ex-students including ex-cons.

Wolfe was coordinating the room searches and dealing with some disgruntled cops. "What if I have to chase a suspect and have no shoes on? It's stupid and I will not take them off. It's downright dangerous."

"It's okay, Dwayne, you don't have to remove your shoes. Only if you want to. Tell everyone that, will you?" Wolfe said. *He's being awful nice.*

All of the doors along the corridor were opened wide to give the cops free access to search all rooms. The place was transformed, everyone's private sanctum and personal habits exposed to the public. Alex felt embarrassed for some of the residents who weren't very neat. It was as if they'd been caught with their pants down, in dirty underwear, for all the world to see.

When she opened the kitchen door, it was so still inside Alex presumed it was vacant. Stepping out of the darkened entrance and further into the spacious working area she saw Jito at the stove, his back to her, and Clark at the double sinks under the window. Both were absorbed in their respective tasks.

Alex was struck with the sanctity of this chamber and how it was Jito's place of worship much more than the zendo. There was an industrious yet church-like quality in the air, with no trace of yesterday's cat carcass and its aftermath. Alex also understood at that moment why no one was allowed in there unless invited, and felt as though she'd barged into a private and sacred ceremony.

As she was about to back out, Jito saw her and beckoned her in.

"Clark and I were just about to have tea. Care to join us?" Jito said.

"Love to, if you're sure ..."

"Of course, dahling. We'd be delighted. Wouldn't we Clark?"

"Miss Alex is always welcome," Clark said. She was surprised at his warmth.

"Brava, Alex. How very Zen of you."

Kido's words and the atmosphere in the kitchen seduced her into believing that Clark had been a victim of New York State's harsh drug laws. She now saw the prison time behind his eyes and wanted to feel sympathy, but that would have to wait.

"See? C'mon. Let's sit down," Jito said.

Jito added a third cup to his tea tray and carried it to the table. He was passionate about his tea, and Alex looked forward to whatever he served. A few times he had treated her to a green tea bursting with so much flavor that it galvanized more taste buds than she knew she had, and lingered in her mouth long after the last sip. It was a pricey and rare tea from one of Japan's southern islands, reserved for special occasions, special guests.

Jito always had on hand many other teas that weren't as dear, but had their own unique characteristics and were more appropriate for daily consumption. Today he poured the monastery's staple green tea, Gold Sen-Cha—distinctive in its own way. She savored the taste.

Alex learned nothing new from Jito or Clark, except that Sonja's body and the dead cat had been transported down the mountain before daybreak. After changing the unpleasant subject, Alex enjoyed being in their company, in their private temple. Being with them, drinking tea, and chatting about nothing, made death, suspects, and the real world seem light years away.

***

A workstation had been set up in the library for Alex, complete with phone, paper and pens. No computer. That would have been asking too much. But she didn't need one. A stack of old folders, brown with age, sat at Alex's place.

"What are these?"

"Welcome to the stone age," Kluny said. "These are old student records, about five years' worth, since Roshi came to the East Coast and before the monastery got their state-of-the-art computer system going. Let's hope we don't have to go any further back, if any records even exist from those earlier years.

"You and I are supposed to call each student and find out what we can."

"You must be kidding," Alex said.

"Nope. But first we got to wade through them, put a list of names together and fax it to State Police headquarters. They got resources we don't. Someone will run the names through a computer and fax back current information to us. Then we can start making calls."

"Jeez, this'll take all day. Are we sure it's worth the time?"

"It's not as bad as it looks. I already made my way through that pile over there and faxed a sheet of names to some computer geek who probably lives for this kind of mission, peering into people's private lives. They can probably tell us how many times a month someone gets a pedicure, or what drugs they take, legal or illicit. They'll get back to us in no time."

Alex sat down with a sigh. Combing through these ancient lists was most likely a waste of time, but maybe such a daunting task would keep her from obsessing over which of her friends could be capable of murder. On the other hand, if any of Roshi's old students were involved, there had to be a more direct way to get to them.

Deskwork had never been her favorite activity. It was usually anathema to her and one of the particulars that would influence her decision to retire or not. She hated that she so neatly fit the cop stereotype: Loved the field detective work, hated sitting at a desk. Slick technology and fancy computers only added to the piles of paper and number of variables in a case, most of which usually led nowhere.

Alex sorted through the pile hoping something would jump out at her. A hint of something, any clue she could follow up on. Instead, all she got were names with no meaning, not even with a face attached. *The question was like the others, The answer was the same.*

She noticed that the records only went back to 1981, to the year the monastery was built, it got her wondering about all the students that came before, the ones on the West Coast. She wished Muin would hurry up so they could talk. Forget computers—he was the memory bank that she had to tap into.

The blank page of her note pad stared up at her. She hated empty spaces. She wrote a note.

The Questions:

1. Ask Muin/Roshi about W. Coast student list

It was a start. That first notation often spurred other thoughts. She continued to write.

2. talk to Muin re: HIS CAT!

3. talk to Muin re: Enji, did he know him?

4. talk to Muin re: fire and Buddhism

5. meet with Roshi—known enemies? past threats?
*   disgruntled/unstable students?*

6. explore hiking/logging trails—maybe today with Kluny?

7. Kosen — Sonja — Zenji: connection?

8. West Coast — Kosen + Zenji + Roshi + Enji

9. Did Muin know Kosen & Zenji before they got here?

Alex flipped to a clean page and started a second list.

The Suspects:

a. Zenji—his past with Kosen, their acrimony, his past with Enji

b. Clark—his criminal past, any connection to Zenji? Jito?

c. Gyozan—not a likely suspect, how well did he know Roshi in Japan?

d. Jito—who did he know at the monastery before he arrived?

e. the cousin, Lawrence—why was he in the vicinity?

f. Enji?

g. everyone else

h. should Muin be on this list?

i. what about Roshi? How innocent is he?

I know the answer to h is yes, but I'm not ready to admit it. Damn. I really thought I knew him as well as any friend or lover can be known, but I don't even know if he'd been with Roshi in the early days on the West Coast. Fuck.

And a third list.

The Facts:

I. Kosen missing Sunday and then dead—Monday

II. Cat cut in half—Tuesday

III. Sonja missing then dead—Tuesday

(note: will there be another dead body today, Wednesday?)

IV. Robert + Zenji—high school together, both students of Enji

V. Xanax (from Jito?), Heroin (source unknown)

VI. The cousin knew Zenji, lied about it the first time (from Kluny)

Alex stared at her lists and at the stack of folders. If Alex were on Wolfe's payroll she'd have to do his bidding, but being the unwanted interloper she could defy his command and do as she pleased.

What she had to do now was wait for Muin.

She got up and moved slowly around the room, walking, perusing the books on the walls, looking out the window. She felt as if she were sleepwalking. She found a deck of playing cards on a shelf. She picked them up and moved back to her desk. She shuffled and laid out the deck for a game of solitaire.

Kluny raised an eyebrow and then returned to his task. Solitaire sent her mind to the left side of her brain while the right relaxed with the items from her list. It would make some intuitive sense of them in time. Trying to force a solution with the left, logical side of her gray matter never worked.

As the cards randomly and neatly fell into place, creating a mathematical dance of beauty and natural rhythm, Alex ruminated about her history with Muin.

She had never thought much about his past in this life, nor about his trustworthiness. He was simply Muin, Kido's confidante. Good enough for her, it put him beyond reproach. But two murders in his domicile flipped everything upside down. She had no choice but to treat him as she would any suspect.

It was after 10:00. Muin was late. She brought the card game to a close, tucked the deck in her pocket, and told the detectives she was going to hunt down Muin.

Stephen, a very polite resident, with a mellifluous phone voice, was working at a computer in the main office. He was sorry but didn't know where Muin was. In the corridor, another student told her he had seen Muin in the laundry room about ten minutes earlier. So it was back to the laundry room for Alex, where she'd found Zenji yesterday.

22

"Muin, what the hell's going on with you? Did you forget about our meeting?" She felt like a spurned lover and knew her anger was over the top.

"*Alex! Become the master of your emotions! Don't be a slave to them!*" She didn't need Kido to remind her of this. She had to pull herself together, dig deep and find some objectivity in her heart. *Am I even capable of that with him?*

"Sorry Al, you're right, I lost track of time. Guess I'm preoccupied," he said as he turned to face her.

"Yeah, well, aren't we all, but—" When she saw his face she stopped. They stared at each other, an ocean of sadness between them. She resumed walking toward him and didn't stop until she had her arms wrapped around him in a warm embrace. Their bodies remembered each other and warmed to the touch.

Alex's anger subsided. The old attraction recalled itself. This was good and bad news. Alex stepped back and gently brought her palm up to caress his cheek.

"I know that everything that's going on here really sucks ... and boy, do you look like shit. But really, I do have to talk to you." She didn't even want to say his name. With the heat between them she couldn't trust herself to keep lust from misbehaving. She had to defuse the chemistry and get back to work.

Muin laughed. "You always say the sweetest things. That's what I love about you."

"Seriously ... can we talk? Roshi isn't desperate for clean underwear, is he?"

"Nah, tasks like this calm me down. Let's go to the lounge. There won't be anyone in there."

***

Once they were settled and sitting across from each other with a table between them to keep it from getting too personal, Alex pulled out her notebook.

"Okay, Ms. Policeman, ask away. I can't believe I finally get to see you in action," Muin said. "It's very sexy. And if it weren't for the circumstances, I could really enjoy this."

"Muin ... please, don't make this harder than it is."

"Okay, okay. So whaddya wanna know?" Muin said, calling up his long-faded Bronx accent.

Alex placed her notebook in front of her and glanced at her lists. She wanted to appeal to him as a friend, ask why he'd been dodging her, commiserate with him about the goings-on, lean on his shoulder. She took a deep breath and shifted into cop gear.

"First thing I have to ask you about is the cat. Had you seen it before?"

"Very clever, Ms. Detective. I ran into Zenji earlier and he fessed up that he told you about the cat. Joshu was loved by all of us. We're devastated. He was such a gentle soul. I can't imagine any one of us killing him. It had to be an outsider who knows their way around here and wants to destroy the place."

Alex made a mental note that he didn't claim ownership of the cat.

"Did Roshi know about the cat?"

"He knew. He pretended not to know, but he knew."

That's funny, Roshi claimed he knew nothing about the cat. Who was he protecting? Muin? Or is Muin lying? He was there when Roshi denied knowledge of the cat. Why isn't he covering for Roshi now? Damn it, I hate being suspicious of the sangha.

"I thought he hated cats," Alex said.

"He doesn't hate cats—it's just that they remind him of the Nansen koan and the rift he had with Enji, so he'd rather not have them around. He was fine with us having Joshu, as long as he didn't have to see him."

"And how did it happen that Enji is coming up here on Sunday, all of a sudden, out of the blue, after all this time? Who got in touch with who?"

"Enji started writing to Roshi about two years ago. The ice seems to have melted, there's forgiveness on both sides and now they plan to reunite on Sunday. Roshi's idea, the time and place. Big crowd, big party, Enji will be just one of many old students coming to celebrate Buddha's birthday. Roshi didn't want to make a special deal out of Enji's visit."

"Do you think Enji means to hurt Roshi? Could he be behind the murders here?"

"From what I know about Enji, he's capable of anything. Roshi doesn't think so though."

Muin's holding something back, goddamn it. There's more to this story. And I know him well enough to know that a direct attack now would have him clam up. I'll leave this topic for a while, come back to it.

"I need more history lessons," Alex said.

And then almost under her breath she said, "Hard to fathom I don't already know some of this," which Muin chose to ignore.

Alex checked the first item on her list. Was that the most important question? Might as well start somewhere.

"Okay, when did you first meet Roshi? Were you with him in San Francisco?"

Muin stretched his legs out in front of him, rested the back of his head in his hands and looked up at the ceiling as he went down memory lane. His relaxed posture, his neck, the spread of his legs, his two-day growth of hair on his face and head. The sum of it was a beacon shining straight into her groin. She crossed her legs and bit her lip to listen.

"I knew Roshi in San Francisco, but not from the very beginning. I didn't become his student till eight or ten years after Enji, who was one of the first and Roshi's first ordained monk in America. I went to San Francisco when I was a teenager and pretty heavy into drugs and politics. I was a lost soul. Every Thursday I'd go sit at Roshi's zendo, listen to his talks. He was quite popular back then. A lot of us were stoned. We thought that was part of the spiritual experience, a carryover from the sixties I suppose when Zen first came to this country." Muin closed his eyes.

"Yeah, I always regretted being born too late to be a hippie," Alex said.

Muin sat up straight and looked at Alex. "Yeah, well, it was the best of times, it was the worst of times ... I finally realized at some point that I was burning out and it wasn't 'better' as Neil Young promised. So I started going to the zendo without being stoned.

"I began to think of Roshi as my teacher after we had a few one-on-ones. Then I became active in zendo life and before I knew it I had moved in and was taking care of the place and of Roshi. I stopped questioning my place in life and knew I was meant to be a monk. I was the first monk to be ordained here at the monastery. I suppose I'll die here."

"So was it all peace and love back then, or did Roshi have enemies?"

"No. And I don't know. Maybe."

"Can you get me a list of his students from that time? All we have is lists from when this place opened."

"Possibly. I'll have to dig through some old boxes in Roshi's closets. He might know where those files are. We weren't too good about keeping records back then. Whatever we had, I think Roshi kept. I'll check," Muin said, crossing his legs and arms.

"Think you can do it soon?" Alex was leaning forward on the edge of her seat, elbows on knees.

"I'll run it by Roshi after lunch, see what works."

"Thanks. As soon as you come up with that list let me know. If you can think of anyone who might have it in for Roshi, from that time or since—even if it seems farfetched—let me know that, too. Okay?"

"Sure thing. You think Roshi's the target, don't you?"

"Can't say for sure yet. Possibly. It can't be ruled out." She wasn't ready to tell him that both he and Roshi were potential suspects.

All Muin's reflective energy went toward Roshi. Alex didn't understand that kind of devotion. She envied him a little. *Is he as devoted as everyone thought? What happened back in the era of drugs and rock 'n roll?*

"We'd better get going." Muin pushed his chair back and they stood up.

"Yep. Thanks again."

They hugged. The lonely hole in her heart that was Kido throbbed with sorrow. The fire between her and Muin had been tamed. They were hugging as friends in the dharma.

"Do you have a few more minutes? There's something else I'd like to say that has nothing to do with any of this, but who knows when we'll get another chance?" Muin said.

"Sure, of course."

They moved over to the couch. Too close for Alex's comfort, but her cop brain was engaged, her suspicious nature activated, she wouldn't let it get into a treacherous neighborhood.

"I know you think I've been avoiding you," Muin said, "and, well, I guess I have been. It's been, what, six months since you dumped me? And—"

"I didn't dump you. I just couldn't keep the long distance thing going. I thought we talked this through. I'm just not good in relationships, never have been. It's not you, I told you that, it's me …"

"I know. And I believe you. But … well, I'm not very good at this either—makes us the perfect pair don't you think? At first it was no big deal … I have my life here, it satisfies me … but when I saw you on Saturday I realized how much I've missed you and I just wanted to be close again. Especially with our clothes off," he added with a smile.

Alex laughed.

"It's not funny to me," Muin said. "It's troublesome. I might be a monk, but I knew I couldn't handle rejection again so I figured it was best to keep my distance."

"Wow …" Alex said. "I sure wish Kido were still around. Wouldn't it be great to go and talk to him about this, get his advice?"

"Yes. He'd probably tell us to run away from everything, get married, have a bunch of kids and enjoy."

"He would, wouldn't he?" Alex laughed. "God, I do miss him."

"I'll bet not nearly as much as I do. Sorry, that's not really fair, maybe it's close. Shit. But I've got no one up here to talk to. At least you've got Uncle Charlie. He's pretty cool. I liked him a lot."

"I sure got lucky with him. If I ever told him about us he'd probably say the same as Kido. But I don't have a clue what to do ..." Alex thought about retirement and how that would give her more time to be with Muin if she wanted. She still couldn't see herself making that huge a leap in lifestyle.

"I feel like a teenager," she said. "I still have feelings for you too but you live here. I live in the city. I'm not ready to live here and you'd be miserable down there. Seeing each other even once or twice a month, which is what would happen under the best of circumstances with my schedule, isn't fair to either of us."

"I know all that, it runs through my head like a chant ... and I think we made the right decision, but I had to clear the air. I don't want to keep avoiding you."

Does this confession take him off the suspect list? Experience won out and he stayed on the list.

"I love you," Muin said.

Awkwardness saturated the space between them. Neither of them moved. Alex held her breath.

Muin broke the uneasy silence. "Kido always told me that if he wasn't gay, you'd be the woman he would marry. He didn't think the monk thing would get in the way."

"Yeah, he told me that once," Alex said.

"I feel something akin to that. I'm a monk and married to that. Even though Roshi would be fine with it, I can't marry anyone. If I could it would be you—or, I guess I shouldn't be so presumptuous— I'd want it to be you. I'd ask you anyway. I'd—"

Alex put her hand on his. "That is so sweet. I don't even know what to say. I'm not sure I can ever marry either. I hope you know that you are special to me, I treasure our time together. I don't know what else to say."

"Well, goddamn, Alex Sullivan at a loss for words. Kido's spirit is sure to be laughing at that."

"Oh shit, look at the time, we missed lunch, everybody's got to be wondering where the hell we are. I'm sure they're worried. We gotta go," Alex said as she sprang up off the couch.

Muin held onto her hand. "One last hug?"

As they wrapped their arms around each other, the door opened to Wolfe followed by Hokan and Zenji.

23

"What the fuck were you two lovebirds thinking?" Wolfe asked, his fury written in the red of his face and the clench of his fists. "Think no one would notice your absence?"

"Yeah," Zenji said. "Just like the old days when you'd sneak off and—"

"You" —Wolfe pivoted and pointed his finger at Zenji — "out!"

"Wha—"

"Now! I want to talk to these two alone. Hokan, you can leave, too. Let everyone know we've found them," Wolfe said, his temper tamped down a tad by Hokan's presence. "And close that door behind you."

"Look," Alex said, raising her arms in surrender, as if that could ward off his wrath. "I'm sorry, we lost track of time." She dropped her arm as a peace offering. "We—"

"We nothing, What about you? As a professional? How could you be so reckless and inconsiderate? Not to mention keeping the relationship a secret in the first place?" Wolfe stared through Alex and got so close she thought she smelled tobacco. She refused to look away to check his pocket.

"Detective," Muin said. Wolfe's eyes darted to Muin and then back to Alex. "It's not her fault, it's mine. She was doing her job."

"Yeah?" Wolfe looked back at Muin. "She embrace all her suspects?"

"Wolfe!" Alex said. "Look, we both fucked up. We're sorry." She looked over at Muin to get him on this track. "We should have kept our eyes on the time, known you and Kluny would worry. Sorry, really. We won't do it again. Right, Muin?"

"Right."

Before Wolfe could say more, Alex said, "Look, Wolfe, we're not the enemy here. Why don't we pretend this never happened and concentrate on getting the real monster?"

"Pretend?" Wolfe's face had settled down to its normal pinkish white, the worst of his temper subdued. "Oh, what the fuck, don't ever waste my time like this again. And him" —he cocked his head toward Muin —"he's still a suspect no matter how many times you fuck him. Now, both of you, get upstairs, show your face. Like it or not people are worried."

***

After scarfing down some lunch, Muin returned to Roshi, and Alex joined the detectives in the library.

"Any news from forensics?" Alex asked as she walked through the door. She didn't want to give Wolfe a chance to scold her again.

"Yeah, some," he said, and took his time getting to the details. She didn't push it.

"The dirt tracks on the carpet in the retreat house were made by a size ten male boot. We haven't found the boot among the residents' shoes, but that doesn't rule out anyone yet. They got a fairly good imprint in the flowerbed just outside the door and they're working on the make and model et cetera."

"Any fingerprints?"

"None that don't belong to one of the residents. None in the house or on the boat. But there was something that was found at both scenes confirming what we suspected all along—it's the same guy did both victims and killed the cat. Cat hairs from that cat were at all three scenes. So all we got is a guy with size ten feet who hates cats. Not much, but more than we had yesterday."

"Cause of death the same?" Alex said.

"Yeah, drugs, combination of Xanax and heroin. No asphyxiation with Sonja, just the drugs. Guess she was weaker than Robert, didn't put up a fight. Traces of chloroform. Probably used to knock her out, enough to carry her off and administer the drugs. She never woke up. Probably never knew what hit her. And our perp was strong. Able to lift and transport bodies. Has us thinking there could be more than one."

They sat silently absorbing the facts. There was a shared relief that Sonja hadn't burned to death. Small comfort.

Alex broke the silence. She couldn't keep her secret a second longer. "I've got some news you guys aren't gonna like. But try not to shoot the messenger."

"Shit," Wolfe said. "What is it?"

"Some of the drugs, the Xanax at least, could have come from Jito."

"What the fuck!" Wolfe blurted.

Alex raised her arm and pushed her palm toward Wolfe as if that could stop the onslaught of anger. "Let me finish ... Jito's story, and I believe him" —Alex harbored doubts —"is that Kosen discovered Jito's Xanax—he's had a prescription for years to help with his anxiety—and threatened to tell Roshi. Jito didn't want Roshi to know—he thinks everything can be solved with meditation—so he gave some to Kosen. Xanax only, no heroin far as I know."

"What the hell is a monk doing with tranquilizers?" Wolfe couldn't help himself. "And blackmail? Jesus, it's as bad up here as anywhere."

Alex let it slide. "And there's one other thing. Roshi told me yesterday, said to keep it out of the investigation if I thought it irrelevant, but nothing is now ... Enji, his old student, who's coming up here on Sunday, the same one who the blackmailer wants to see become the next Zen Master ... well, when he and Roshi split, and we don't even know the why of that yet, he was working on a koan. Guess which one that was?"

Wolfe said nothing, just sat, looking impatient.

"Nansen's Cat Koan. It's weird to me that Roshi remembered the koan Enji was on. Makes me think it had something to do with their breakup."

"Great, just great! Goddamn it," Wolfe said. "Got anything else you'd like to share with us? Please, don't hold back. Just let 'er rip."

"There's nothing more. That's it. That's all I know."

"Kluny, find out where this guy Enji is ... what's today?"

"Wednesday."

"He's probably still in California, if he's not the one here killing people. Call someone up out there, have them go talk to him ... or get him on the phone, better yet.

"And get that cousin, Lawrence, back up here today ... he's got some explaining to do. I wonder if he knows this guy Enji."

"What about the logging roads? Have they been used recently?" Alex said. All eyes were on Wolfe. Alex could see that he liked being in charge, the center of attention—the only-child syndrome she was all too familiar with.

"Yeah," Wolfe said. Tire tracks indicate that only one vehicle has recently used those roads. It could be our guy. We're working on eliminating the cars and trucks belonging to the monastery."

"Any of these roads come out on the main road above the monastery? Where I was running Monday morning and spotted that red truck?" Alex asked.

"Right about where you said, that's the inroad we think was used. We'll compare tread marks to the cousin's truck, whenever we locate him. He doesn't answer his phone, and either he lied about his address or has the worst handwriting in the world. In the meantime, we're posting men at the entrances, to make sure no one has access," Wolfe said.

"What about the foot trails?" Alex said.

"We've hired a few locals who know their way through these woods. Probably a waste of resources." Wolfe shrugged. "He had to have used a vehicle, which means he traveled on a logging road. For all we know he's long gone by now. Came and did here what he wanted, and now he's off to Canada or Europe—or wherever nuts like him run off to."

Alex didn't think Wolfe really meant this, probably just blowing smoke, but she didn't agree. She held her tongue for now.

"Okay if I take a drive and have a look at the roads this afternoon?" Alex asked.

Detective Wolfe communicated his displeasure in body language.

"I guess it couldn't hurt. If you notice anything unusual or suspicious I want to know about it right away. Do not take any action on your own," he said.

"Fine."

Alex spent a few more minutes with Kluny before she left. No leads from the lists yet. Alex told him about Muin's project of checking with Roshi about the lists of student names from the San Francisco days, if there even were any. Out loud they shared the hope that a break would be forthcoming. Silently they conveyed despair.

***

Alex passed the afternoon in her Outback exploring the logging roads and the section of the main road where they connected. Nothing noteworthy. No people, no cars, no trucks. For long moments at a time Alex forgot that she was on the lookout for a murderer. It felt like a day in the country spent just as she'd planned five days ago.

After a couple hours there was nothing more to see or learn, but she loathed the idea of going back to face the stack of brown folders on her desk. She delayed her return by paying a visit to Kido's grave.

When she first started visiting Kido's grave, she would sit there and weep. The chats, or monologues, didn't begin until a few years after the grief moved into a less painful stage.

At first she felt silly talking out loud to a statue of Kuan-yin, the Bodhisattva of Compassion, which marked where his ashes were buried. After a while the self-consciousness wore off and she enjoyed the chat, and knew that Kido did, too. Saying things out loud always helped her to make better sense of things.

Alex filled Kido in on all the details of the week including all her suspicions and fears.

"There's something about it all that I'm just not getting," Alex said. "I'm afraid by the time I do, it'll be too late. I wish you were here. And Muin says he loves me and I haven't a clue what to do with that." Alex was sitting cross-legged on the cold ground. It was drier than she expected and the cold hardly bothered her.

"Anyway, one thing he said seemed really strange. I asked him for a list of students from the San Francisco days and he said that Roshi kept those files. But Roshi never gets involved in those details, does he? It seems to me Muin would've been the one to keep the records and transport them here when they moved. I think he's hiding something and you're about the only one I feel safe telling that to, and you're dead! Funny, eh?

"I suppose things could have been different in the early days. Roshi was a lot younger. I suppose he could have taken a more active role back then. But I doubt it. I'll just have to see what Muin comes up with. I can go straight to Roshi if I have to, though I'd rather not. No need to stir up something that doesn't need stirring. Muin'll come through.

"What do you make of all this, Kido?"

"The real answer is not difficult. Keep away from choice and attachment and you will know. Stay out of your own way. Pay attention! Things are not as they seem ... nor are they otherwise. You know this, Alex. Trust yourself."

"Right! Easier said than done, I think, except I don't have a clue what you've said. Nice chatting with you. God, how I wish you were here in the flesh."

***

When Alex got back to the monastery, two red trucks were parked in front. *What did I miss?* There was no sign of the Feeb guy, owner of the clean red truck, but by the time she walked into the library, Lawrence, the cousin, owner of the muddy red truck, was just sitting down. Kluny saw her peek through the door and waved her in. Things had changed since yesterday.

"Okay, Lawrence ... or is it LT?" Wolfe began.

"Either works, but I prefer Lawrence."

"Why'd you lie to us?"

"What're you talking about?" He looked nervous, his eyes darting from Wolfe to Kluny to Alex, searching for some clue, or an ally, or something else he wasn't finding.

"Zenji, you said you didn't know Zenji. And unless he's lying, you knew him in California."

"Dumb kid," Lawrence said under his breath.

"What did you say?"

"Nothing. It's just ... ah, never mind ... okay, I knew him, knew him as Jason. He used to hang out with my cousin Robert. They were always getting into it with each other. Maybe you should be talking to him about killing Robert. I had no reason to. I loved the kid." His eyes continued searching for the one who'd believe him.

"That why you're in these parts? To look after your cousin?"

"Sort of like that, yeah. He's the only family I got and I guess I'm getting sentimental in my old age." He gave a half smile and looked down at the floor as if embarrassed.

"How old are you anyway?" snapped Wolfe.

"What's that got to do with anything?" His head shot up and his eyes challenged Wolfe's.

"Just an innocent question, how old?" Wolfe softened a tad.

"Yeah, right, innocent ...ha!. I'll be fifty soon. Bet you couldn't have guessed."

"Which war were you in?" This session Wolfe was the main interrogator.

"What're you talking about? You guys ever ask direct questions, stuff you want to know?" He looked behind Wolfe at Alex and Kluny, saw they weren't going to be of help, and settled back on Wolfe.

"Heard you were a vet, that's all."

"Who the hell told you that? I ain't never been near a war, except the one going on up here." He pointed to his head. "Ha!"

"Why would Zenji, that is Jason, say that out of the blue then? Where d'you think he got the idea that you were a soldier?"

"I might've misled him and others 'bout my past. It was harmless." He was almost whispering now.

"Then tell me again about your harmless association with Zenji and Robert and the Zen center they went to, the people there." Wolfe got up close, leaned right into his face.

Lawrence leaned his head back and raised his voice. "Do you mind? You don't have to suffocate me, I'll tell you what you want to know."

Wolfe sat back. "All right then, tell us."

"All I know is they, Jason and Robert, used to hang out at my house when they were teens. They started going to Enji's Zen place when they got a little older. Kept coming to my place for a while, but then they lost interest in me, followed Enji around like little puppy dogs."

"Hear any weird stories about Enji or others there?"

"The whole thing was bizarre if you ask me, and you are asking me, aren't you?" He smirked at Wolfe. "Anyway, they all loved Enji. No one could stand the head monk and a few others there, but I figured that was normal people stuff. Never heard anything criminal if that's what you mean to be asking."

"How'd you and your cousin get along?" Kluny asked.

"I really loved the kid. He was a little mixed up, but he never meant anyone any harm. And he really loved that bald gal, that nun, Sonja. I can't believe they're both dead. Who would want to kill them?" Lawrence shook his head.

"That's what we're going to find out. You can go, but stay close to the phone. If you haven't heard from us in two days, you call us to find out why. You got it?" Wolfe said.

"I got it. Don't worry, I want to know more than you do who killed them. I'll even become a deputy if you want, help you out."

"You watch too many movies," Wolfe said. "Get the fuck out of here."

"I'd talk to Zenji again if I were you ..." Lawrence said as he was walking out the door.

Wolfe shot him a steely just-shut-up look and stared after him till he was gone.

***

"Say, Alex, what's so special about Buddha's birthday?" Kluny asked. He, Wolfe and Alex were sitting idle after Lawrence left the library, not yet ready to dig back in to the task of calling ex-students.

The late afternoon light through the windows was rapidly fading. No one got up to turn on a light. They sat and talked in the half-darkness.

"Why do you ask?" Alex said.

"Well, Wolfe's been talking to Roshi, trying to get him to leave this place, and call off the party that's planned for Sunday, but Roshi won't budge."

So they'd been talking to Roshi again without her. "Roshi's saying he won't leave because he's got a party planned?" Alex knew there was more to it than that.

"Not just that," Wolfe chimed in, "he says,'This is where I live, detective. Would you empty a small town, or an apartment building, if someone was murdered? No, you would not. This is my home. I will not leave. You cannot make me. We will stay and face whatever our karma is, no matter how painful.'"

"Sounds like Roshi," Alex said, though she was ticked that she hadn't been there to hear it herself.

"Buddha's birthday is sort of like Christmas for Buddhists without the tree and the gifts. It's always celebrated on April 8. It's a big day worldwide. It hasn't become commercial like Christmas—it's just a time to give thanks and to celebrate."

"Clue us in a little on Buddha, will you Alex? Is he the same as God or Jesus to Buddhists? If we're supposed to figure out the koans, the cat and the tree branch, it might help to know something about the guy who started all this. Was he a real guy?" Kluny asked.

"Yeah, Buddha ... he's not the first and only Buddha, but that's too complicated to go into now and it won't help this case ... the Buddha that you want to know about was born over twenty-five hundred years ago in India. He was the son of a rich prince who wanted for nothing. You may have heard the name Siddhartha—also a book by Hermann Hesse—that was his birth name before he became Buddha. His mother died seven days after he was born. He was raised in wealth and his father tried to protect him from experiencing any pain or misery. He eventually married and had a son. But, as the story goes, he was not content.

"One day he left the walls of the palace and ventured off on his own without his protectors. For the first time he witnessed people suffering from old age, sickness and death. He also saw a monk. All of this had such a profound effect on him that he decided to leave his family and go in search of a way to relieve human suffering. For years he roamed about and followed various religious teachers and tried many forms of asceticism that were in currency at that time. But nothing satisfied him."

It had gotten darker and darker in the room. Still, no one moved. It felt a little weird to her, telling these two detectives this story. *Wonder if this is how Scheherazade felt.*

"Then one day he decided to sit down under a tree, a tree which hence became known as the Bodhi-tree and has become very famous, and not get up until he had the answer. For forty-nine days he just sat there—why we all sit on those black cushions day after day—at the end of which he was awakened to the truth of suffering."

"Eventually his teachings were set down as *The Four Noble Truths*, which essentially lays out a path to follow for liberation from suffering. That's a bit much to go into now but in a nutshell that's Buddha. Simple, really."

"And what about cats cut in half and such? I always thought that Buddhists didn't believe in killing," Kluny said.

Wolfe wasn't asking the questions but Alex could tell he was paying attention even though his face was in shadow.

"You're right, they don't. And as far as I know no war has ever been waged in the name of Buddha."

"So then, whoever's doing the killing and butchering isn't a Buddhist?" Wolfe asked.

"I'm not so sure about that. A wayward Buddhist maybe. Certainly a confused one. Maybe lapsed? Maybe a fundamentalist? Even Buddhism has its share of those, not so many, but some."

"Well, Buddhist or not, it's not safe here. And since Roshi won't leave, and his students seem intent on staying with him, and we can't force them to leave, we're taking Clark's advice," Kluny said.

"Come again?" Alex asked.

"We're having locks installed on all the doors soon as a locksmith can get here. If he can't get to all the doors before lights out we'll have to get through another night as best we can."

24

Evening zazen went on as usual and though Alex could have excused herself to attend to "police business," she didn't. The sitting would do her good. Muin wasn't in the zendo, but she'd expected that—and hopefully he'd have the student lists from San Francisco for her by the end of the evening. Zenji was likewise missing but he often had so much to do as the jisha that he'd skip a sit or two now and then to catch up.

Work was also a part of a monk's meditation practice so Roshi allowed it. With all the extra guests, cops and CSIs to take care of she figured he was up to his eyeballs in it—and if the locksmith had arrived he was probably overseeing that. Plus, Zenji had no official assistant now that Kosen was dead. But Alex was worried, she couldn't help herself.

Fear wandered in during the sit. No matter how hard she tried there was no sense to be made of all the killing. As jaded as she was after working twenty years for the NYPD, Alex still held on to the notion, albeit tentatively, that people in spiritual communities behaved holier than the rest of the world, but after all that had happened over the past few days, this belief was slipping dangerously out of her reach.

Is a deeper commitment to Zen in my future? Last week I was close to yes, this week no seems to be winning. Why the hell would I expect Buddhists or religiously minded people to be different from the rest of us? Maybe deepening my practice could give me some insight into this?

Going the Zen nun route she knew wasn't her style, but becoming an official Buddhist could be a possibility. She didn't know if she could go forward and take that vow, but she did know that she could never again be the cop she used to be.

Stepping out of that tribe might be the only solution and the first step into the unknown future. It scared her and she didn't know why. On and on her thoughts rolled.

During a break, she bowed out and went in search of Zenji, just to ease her mind. She had about ten minutes. He wasn't in the basement, office, or kitchen area. The last Jito had seen him was at supper, helping with the cleanup. Maybe he was with Muin. She doubted it. She had never been to Roshi's quarters before as it was strictly off limits. She had no solid case for defying that rule just now.

Roshi was sitting with the rest of his students in the zendo and she couldn't go blithely snooping around in his rooms. Maybe Muin was there. She'd have to sit with the not knowing for a while longer. She was used to that. She never liked it, but now someone's life might be at stake.

By the time she got back to the zendo everyone was already back on the cushions with one strike of the bell left before she had to be sitting still. At the very least, she wanted to alert Hokan, the jikijitsu, to Zenji's absence. But he was sitting way at the front of the zendo and, from habit drilled into her, she couldn't disturb the silence that filled the room.

These were exceptional times, extraordinary circumstances. *Am I the only one who's worried about Zenji's nonattendance?*

Since no one else was doing anything about it she supposed they knew his whereabouts, that his absence could be explained. *He must be working somewhere in the building.*

The seconds ticked by. Now, a few minutes into the sit, it really was too late to cause a ruckus. She should have done it before. The silence got bigger. She forced herself to concentrate. She felt her gun strapped to her body and couldn't get comfortable. *It's okay. No it isn't. What should I do?*

When the bell rang to end the session Alex was so preoccupied that she was downstairs on her way to search for Zenji before she remembered that she had an appointment to meet with Roshi and Muin, so she turned around, climbed the stairs and rushed to the meeting room. She wouldn't keep Roshi waiting. Muin wasn't present. Alex could tell Roshi was eager to get down to business. She got straight to it.

"I noticed Zenji was missing from the sit tonight. Do you have any idea why?"

"He mentioned something about some unfinished work at the guest house and thought he'd do it tonight. I approved, of course."

Damn it. He's too cavalier about all this.

"He planned to go there alone?"

"He said he would check with detectives, and if they thought it wise he'd bring someone with him."

This brought no relief. She moved on to other matters.

"I explored the logging roads today, Roshi."

"Yes?"

"It's clear that they've been used recently. Other than that I learned nothing."

"I see."

"There is evidence that a man wearing boots was in the retreat house. The prints couldn't be matched to any of the residents. The cops have hired some locals to help with the foot trails." Alex didn't want to bring up the subject of the lists till Muin got there. *Where is he?*

How much does Roshi know? I'd feel a whole lot better if Muin were here. Has Muin told him that he might be the ultimate target? I don't want to bring it up, worry him unnecessarily. I'd never think this on the job, why am I being so stupid now? Sitting in front of Roshi, all I can think is it's fine, he'll know what he needs to know in good time. I just have to protect him from the worst while I can. Damn it Cheetah, shut up!

"Muin tells me that you think I might be the target."

So there it is.

"It's possible."

"If I am the target, why would Kosen and Sonja be dead?"

"We don't know yet, Roshi. And we may be wrong about you. Just in case, the detectives would like to post someone outside your door tonight. Will that be okay?"

"Yes. Fine. Is anyone else in danger?"

"At this point we all are, since we haven't even figured out why Kosen and Sonja were killed, which is why Detective Wolfe wants you to leave for a while. There is a chance that the murders were random acts, perpetrated by a lunatic, though we all figure it's someone who knew them. Either way we're all at risk. I know you don't want to leave so there should be enough cops around to keep us safe for now, and arrangements have been made to install locks on the doors."

After a long pause that she knew Roshi wouldn't fill, she said, "Roshi, can you think of anyone, anyone at all, who might want to kill you?"

"I, of course, have been considering just this question since yesterday. There were some decisions and some actions I made in the past that confused many. As you may know some students left the sangha. I cannot think of anyone who would kill Kosen and Sonja. There were many bruised egos. Some had pride hurt. Many never forgave. Some of those who left are back, willing to put past behind. I am sorry. I wish I could be more helpful. Maybe the list Muin is gathering will help you."

"Do you have any idea how many names might be on that list?"

"Hundreds, I suppose. That's Muin's department. I never got involved in the keeping of records."

"But you still have those records?"

"Well, Muin has them somewhere. I don't know where, he said he had them."

What the fuck? Now I know I can't trust Muin or anything he tells me. This is definitely an unexpected thorn.

"Good. I'll see if I can find him when I leave here."

"He wanted me to tell you to meet him in the lounge."

"Thank you. I guess I'll do that now then."

"Good. And thank you, Alex."

"Thank you, Roshi." Alex put her palms together and bowed slightly. She got up and left quickly to find Muin and then locate the whereabouts of Zenji for her own peace of mind.

Before she was even out of the room, Roshi had turned his attention to some papers in front of him. He didn't seem worried.

She quickly changed out of her robe, donned her jeans and a sweatshirt. Usually when not in her robe she wore baggy sweat pants, but they weren't conducive to wearing a gun. She made her way to the lounge, cogitating along the way.

Muin told me that Roshi had the files. Why would he lie? Who is he trying to protect? It doesn't compute that he would be involved in this, could I be that wrong? Am I allowing my personal attachment here to cloud my vision? Am I missing something that's right in front of my face?

And what the hell did Roshi do to piss off so many people? I know the gossip—sexual improprieties, maybe drugs, maybe money involved. Those are just rumors, aren't they? No one seems to know the truth, or they haven't divulged it to me.

Forget the creed of innocent till proven. Because someone said it out loud, it had to be true, right? And then they jumped on the self-righteous bandwagon and split to find another, more perfect, teacher. I never expected Roshi to be perfect, but I didn't expect this either.

***

Muin was alone in the lounge when Alex walked in. He was poring over a batch of papers spread out in front of him.

"Hi, Muin," Alex called out as she approached the table.

Muin raised his head. "Hey."

"I thought you'd be in my meeting with Roshi."

"I figured that you didn't need me, this was more important." Muin gestured toward the pages on the table.

"So you found the files?"

"You might say that."

"You've got a list of names, then?" Alex controlled her impatience, trying like hell to be the master of her emotions.

"As complete as it'll ever be."

Alex's mind skipped over to Zenji. "Have you seen Zenji since supper?"

"Wasn't he in the zendo?"

"No, that's why I'm asking. Roshi said he skipped the sit to work at the guest house, but no one else was missing, which means if he went he's down there alone. I'm worried." Alex stood up as she spoke. "I meant to check with Hokan. I'm going to do that now, see if he knows Zenji's whereabouts."

As Alex turned to leave, Hokan entered the lounge in an agitated and worried state.

"Have you folks seen Zenji?"

"No, I was just about to come and see you about that. No one knows where he is?" Alex asked, not really wanting to know the answer.

"No. Darn it. How can it be possible that we've got another person missing?" Hokan was as furious as he could get, underneath the worry.

"Have you alerted the detectives yet?"

"Not yet. I wanted to check the obvious places first. I guess I'll head up there right now," Hokan said.

"We'll be right behind you." Alex turned back to Muin. "What do you make of this, Muin?"

Muin was lost in thought, staring at the papers in front of him.

"Muin. Are you okay?" Alex snapped him out of his reverie.

"D'ya think Zenji could be gone, too?" he asked almost as a whisper.

"Could be." Alex was irritated. At Muin, at Zenji, at whoever was responsible for Sonja and Kosen.

"Can I have these?" Alex reached out to take the papers Muin had been working on.

"I'm not finished. I was just going through and starring the names of those who left the sangha. Double starring the ones who were especially angry, as I recall."

"That's great. And what about the criminal types, you know, the ones that completed their prison sentence with Roshi as warden?"

"Oh yeah, I forgot about them. That won't take too much longer. I'll highlight those guys."

"Muin, I am really trying to be patient here and give you the benefit of the doubt all the way around. But why the hell haven't you been upfront with me? What is going on?"

"What do you mean?"

"You said Roshi had the lists, he knew nothing about it. You forgot about the ex-cons—"

"I'm sorry, Al, I'm not myself, you have every right to be pissed. I don't know why I'm being such a jerk. I'll get this stuff to you soon as I can, I promise."

"Can you give me anything to get started on?" Alex wasn't satisfied with his lame excuse, but she let it go for now.

Muin shuffled through the stack. "Just give me a sec..." He highlighted a few names. "Here." He handed Alex a sheaf. "It's about half. It'll take an hour or so to go through the rest."

"Thanks." Alex pushed her chair back and stood to leave, papers in hand. "You know where to find me."

When she got to the door, she turned and said, "Any idea why Enji's not reachable? Cops have been trying to call him and there's no one picking up at his zendo, just a message to leave a message. His home phone just rings, no voice mail."

"What? Who?" Muin had been lost in thought.

"Enji ... cops can't get in touch with him ... his zendo is closed ... any idea why?"

"Roshi said something about him driving across the country, visiting other Zen centers on the way. I have no idea where he is now, doubt Roshi does either."

"Think he has a cell phone?"

"Maybe, he always went in for stuff like that—the modern monk, you know ..."

Wolfe had probably already checked on that, but she'd mention it anyway.

In a near panic about Zenji, she spent a frantic hour helping in the search for Zenji and came up with nothing. She figured her time might be better spent trying to find some answers so she returned to the library, which was empty of other souls.

By the time she sat down to sort through the names Muin had given her, she had only one thing on her mind—they had to find the killer, and soon. The names in front of her were their only resource right now. As she took a closer look her frustration soared, and any optimism she might have held about these names supplying the answer took a fast and steep nosedive. The starred names outnumbered the others three to one. There were hundreds of them. She knew that students had left Roshi, but she never realized it had been such a mass exodus. And these were only half the names! *What the hell did Roshi do to upset so many people?*

She was not prepared for that answer.

As she flipped through the pages, the task before her seemed daunting. Needle-in-a-haystack-daunting, and this might even be the wrong haystack. If the name of the killer was on the list, what difference could it make knowing his name? By the time they got to it, who knows how many more corpses there'd be, and if Roshi would be among them? Was Roshi orchestrating the whole mess? Or if not Roshi, maybe whoever it was planned to kill off everyone, one by one until only he and Roshi were left. Then what? A battle to the death?

There was no time to sort through all those names. There had to be another way. Times like this she missed having a partner to use as a sounding board. Talking out loud, alone, wasn't nearly as effective.

Uncle Charlie, her secret weapon. He might have some news for her that would obviate the need to get in touch with all these people. And he'd listen to whatever she needed to say.

25

"Zenji's gone missing." Alex didn't even bother with hello, how are you. They'd get to that.

"No kidding?" Charlie replied. "Jeez. Sounds like you've got a one-man army up there."

"Think there's only one?" Alex was convinced that there was more than one person involved in this and one or more resided inside the walls of the monastery.

"It's possible," Uncle Charlie said, as if reading her mind. "But my instincts say it's not likely."

Alex sat with that for a moment. "Yeah. I think that whatever lunatic is doing the killing, he's had some help."

"What's the current plan?"

Alex let out a long, exasperated sigh. "Well, right now I'm staring at a list of hundreds of names. I was hoping it would lead us to the guy, but now I don't know. It's overwhelming that so many people abandoned Roshi. Muin put this list together ... which reminds me, did you find out anything about him that could be helpful?" Alex crossed her fingers, held her breath and slammed shut her eyes, a custom from childhood that had long been dormant.

"He seems to be totally devoted to Roshi. If his behavior looks suspect it could be because he's trying to protect Roshi from something. Exposure, perhaps?"

"Uncle C, the cat belonged to Muin! All the residents thought of it as theirs—except Kosen and Clark, or so Zenji said. And Muin and Kosen nearly came to blows over something and Kosen threatened to tell Roshi about the cat. The worst part is Roshi told me he didn't know about the cat and Muin said just the opposite. Someone's lying. Why ever they are, it's beyond me at the moment. All this lying and deception among people I trusted with my heart, it rattles me, Uncle C. I can't imagine that Muin or anyone else would kill over a cat."

"People have been known to kill for less."

"In the civilian world, yeah, but up here? And Muin has become a complete mystery to me. I'm trying to stay as detached as possible, pretend we were never ..."

What the hell is the right word to describe my relationship with Muin? Uncle Charlie doesn't know we were lovers, and I'd like to keep it that way. Can I be impartial with Muin? Even I'm messing with the truth now. All this in a nanosecond of brain activity.

Anyone else wouldn't have noticed the hesitant groping for a word. Uncle Charlie missed nothing. She went on. "... friends. Maybe pretending will give me some sort of objectivity. Muin gave me half a list—he's still working on the other half—names of people who were Roshi's students in San Francisco, before he came here. He highlighted the ones that left, most in anger. They outnumber the ones who stayed, three or four to one. And then there are the few ex-cons that Roshi took in. It's impossible. Even if you help, we don't have time to do this—especially with the body count already at two. Any suggestions?"

Alex let out a big exhale, then closed her eyes and held her breath hoping against hope that Uncle Charlie would offer a solution. She didn't think there was one—not a simple one anyway. Zen koans claim that the answer is always right in front of our noses. *Before a step is taken, the goal is reached.*

Maybe true in the search for Nirvana, but not always in a murder investigation.

"Can you fax me what you've got?" Charlie asked.

"Yep. But don't waste your time investigating these names. I don't think it'll lead anyplace, and we'll get some of the locals to do that work if we have to," Alex said peevishly.

"Right. I'd just like to get a sense of what we're looking at here. Having the list in my hands will help me think better."

"I'll fax it soon as we hang up. Or better yet, let me go stick it in the fax machine right now. Hold on a sec." Alex pressed the hold button, walked over to the fax machine and dialed Uncle Charlie's fax number. "There, you should begin getting them any minute now. I've only sent half of what I've got. It'll give you an idea of what we're up against. I'll send the rest later if you want them.

"Whaddya think about checking out those who chose not to desert Roshi? They might be cooperative. And they might know something." Alex knew she was reaching, but wanted Uncle Charlie to agree.

"Good idea. Let's run all the names through the system first, see if there are any criminals in the bunch. And then we'll split up the loyal students—start making phone calls. If we can get a couple bodies up there to help, it shouldn't take too long."

"I'll run it by Wolfe and Kluny. Get them on board. Unless they have another idea, it seems like the only choice we have at this point." Alex was relieved to have some plan of action, anemic as it was.

"Your fax is here. I'll go have a look. Why don't we check in with each other first thing in the morning? Call me when Zenji reappears, no matter the time."

"Okay." Alex paused. "How's Marissa? Did you see her last night?"

"She's doing pretty well. Understands how busy you are, but she would really like to see you. Can I tell her you'll be by to see her soon?"

"I've been thinking about that. How about Mother's Day next month? This will surely be over by then."

"That will make her happy, knowing you're coming. And Mother's Day to boot."

"If you think it'll be too much for her—you know how excitable she can get on holidays—I'll come another time. I just thought Mother's Day would be, well, appropriate." *Or maybe ironic. Maybe by arriving for a visit on Mother's Day, Marissa will be reminded of their relationship and her expected role in it. Nah, it's probably too late to count on my own mother to act like one, though I do keep wishing for it, don't I?*

Once again Alex was grateful for Uncle Charlie and didn't even want to think where she would have ended up with him missing from the scene. Probably not on this side of the law.

"Mother's Day will be perfect. I'll cook dinner. We'll have a nice time," Uncle Charlie said.

"Don't go overboard, Uncle C. Let's keep it simple, okay?"

"Sure, honey, sure thing. Let's talk in the morning. I'd like to spend a little time with this list."

After hanging up, Alex allowed herself a few minutes to play the "what if" game, knowing that circumstances would keep her from dwelling.

What if Uncle Charlie hadn't been a part of my life? I'd probably be behind bars or dead, maybe not by my own hand, but by taking crazy risks with bad guys carrying guns.

What if I hadn't started sitting? I'd undoubtedly be stewing in some self-righteous hellhole someplace.

It was dangerous to play this game. Today she had some compassion for herself and it extended to others. Today she knew she could kill but hoped she never would again. The one time one of her bullets had stopped a heart from beating, it took her months and many quarts of bourbon to forgive herself. It had been a "good" shooting, according to the department. Never felt like that for her. Today she didn't know where she stood on the issue of capital punishment, though it once had been so clear: Criminals needed to be punished and everyone was better off if they were dead.

Maybe it would be a good thing if I retired. With this wishy-washy attitude I'll be a danger to myself and everyone around me.

What if Daddy hadn't been killed?

This thought called up a blank screen in her mind. She couldn't afford the fantasy of filling it in.

***

Charlie perused the list of names and wondered how it could possibly help them find their man. Slowly he read down the pages, repeating each name in his mind as his eyes passed over it. He wondered how many lists his own name was on and if there was anyone studying his name at this moment. The common denominator on this list was Roshi, and not one person on it, or maybe just one, had the vaguest clue that he or she was a suspect in a multiple murder investigation.

As his brain recorded each name he tried to imagine what they might be doing right now. A useless exercise perhaps, but it helped to take his mind off the problem just enough so that when he returned to it he'd be clearer and sharper.

Who the hell was this guy? What was he after? Why? With not a hint of an answer, Charlie thought it quite likely that revenge could be part of it.

Distracted by these thoughts, he pulled himself back to the names and continued down the list, creating a simple scenario for each one. He placed them all in California since that was their last known address. It was about 7:30 P.M. there.

In his mind's eye he had some of them just coming home from work, others picking up kids or preparing dinner. One guy was cleaning his garage, another his car. A few were in a yoga class together (it was, after all, California), and some were at a zendo with their new teacher.

Charlie fell into a rhythm as he perused the names, forgetting for a few moments that he was searching for clues to two murders.

As his eyes locked onto the next name, his mind paused and re-read it. Mark Bowden. What was it about this name? He glanced at the next name. Linda T. Bowden. Same address. Who were they? He'd seen these names recently.

Sitting perfectly still he coaxed his mind to summon up their origin, and got to it in no time. Gratified that his mind was still agile, he got up and moved over to his desk. Before his mind ran away with this coincidence he wanted to confirm his discovery. There it was. He was right. Robert's aunt and uncle, his cousin Lawrence's parents. They had been Roshi's students. No shock in that, but he was mystified as to why their names weren't starred. He figured they would have left Roshi. They were dead, he reminded himself, but that was another way of leaving, not the kind that was significant in this case. Or was it? Not believing in coincidences, he knew there had to be a connection.

***

Midnight

There was no sign of Zenji anywhere. No one wanted to sleep, but there was nothing else to do. All possible places had been thoroughly searched including Kido's cabin, which was deep in the woods. He'd built it as a remote retreat house for himself with money his mother had left him, and willed it to the monastery when he died. More cops and the lights that they'd just brought back down the mountain were on their way back up to resume the search, this time for Zenji.

Alex was on her way to her room from the hall bathroom, looking forward to lying down at least for a catnap, toothbrush in hand, towel on her shoulder, when she saw Roshi about to enter his Dokusan room. This small eight-foot-square space was sacrosanct and off limits to the sangha except during retreats when Roshi would meet one-on-one with his students to hear their solution to whatever koan they were meditating on.

It seemed to Alex in her limited experience that his job was to tell each of them, "Not yet, try harder, you're almost there!" Sometimes, especially when she was exhausted, like now, the whole weird practice seemed arcane and ridiculous.

Roshi's nightly ritual before retiring was to pay a visit to this room where photos of his teachers and their teachers and their teachers hung, and chant a few sutras. It was the traditional way— one that had been passed down over the centuries—of saying good night and thank you to the ancestors. And with Buddha's birthday coming up in a few days, that sacred ritual this week surely held special significance.

It flashed into Alex's mind as she saw Roshi turning the doorknob that no one had searched that room. It was so sacred, no one dared.

"Roshi! Wait!" Alex whispered and screamed at the same time. She didn't want to needlessly scare anyone but she did want Roshi's attention. She got it.

"I don't think we cleared this room earlier. Please let me check it out before you go in, just to be sure."

"Of course. Please be careful." He backed off.

She pushed her towel and toothbrush into Roshi's arms, feeling rude and silly for a split second, and then drew her gun and morphed from doting acolyte into auto-cop. There could be someone waiting inside, maybe even Zenji, to kill Roshi.

Alex swung the door open and scanned the room, gun out in front of her. No one there. But someone had been there, her cop's nose relaying that truth. A candle was flickering on the altar. An unattended candle in a mostly wooden structure spelled hazard.

"Is that candle always burning?"

"No, only when I'm in the room," Roshi said.

Just as I thought. So there had been someone. Roshi wasn't likely to forget to snuff out this candle when he left. Not with all those artifacts that he so cherished.

She switched on the light.

"What the fuck! Roshi don't come in here."

"What is it? You must tell me."

"It's a hand. On your cushion. It's someone's hand."

Roshi said something in Japanese that Alex couldn't understand. She closed the door.

"I'm going down the hall to get word to the detectives. Please stay here, don't let anyone in, and don't say a word. I won't let you out of my sight."

"Is it Zenji's?"

"I don't know. It seems likely, but we won't know right away."

"Which hand is it?"

"What do you mean?"

"The left or the right hand?"

Alex thought for a moment. "The left."

"Please, before you go, check to see if there is a yin/yang tattoo on the thumb."

She checked. There was, it was Zenji's.

Kluny and Wolfe were still there, planning to sack out for a few hours on futons in the library. They weren't happy for more than one reason. Zenji had been Wolfey's boy and now he was most likely dead.

"Okay, that's it, we're all out of here tomorrow," proclaimed Wolfe as soon as he saw Zenji's hand.

There wasn't much blood but the tan cushion it sat on was ruined. The sanctity of the room was defiled. The whole place was slipping ever more rapidly into the gutter of human resentment and revenge. It would never be the same again.

No one got any sleep that night. Wolfe stationed one cop at the retreat house, one outside Roshi's quarters, and two to patrol the perimeter of the monastery building. The rest of the cops were out searching the forest for Zenji's probably, by now, dead body.

Alex knew the residents were safe enough. The room searches had been completed and some locks had been installed. The eight residents who were still unlocked camped out in the dorm room with two cops at the door and two sleeping inside with them.

She lay on her bed, trying to recoup some energy, and fell into a dreamless slumber.

26

Alex was startled awake by noise in the corridor and sprung out of bed. The clock read 5:00. She slept some, but didn't feel it. The haze of sleep confused her for a moment as she stood stock-still, orienting herself. The noise in the hall is not the usual patter of morning feet. She thought of Zenji, strapped on her holster and pulled on her bulky cardigan.

She hated that her habit at home of strapping on a gun first thing was becoming routine under the monastery roof. As she opened the door she was wide awake and ready for business.

Before entering the hall her cop instincts clicked in. She put her ear to the door and listened. Then she drew her gun and held it out in front of her as she walked out into the corridor. The overhead lights in the hall were on, illuminating the darkness. She saw Wolfe, some of his men and a few residents in robes in the dharma hall at the end of the corridor. She tucked her gun back under her sweater and joined the group.

Zenji was laid out on the altar, dead. All the mortuary tablets commemorating long dead teachers and special sangha members had been shoved aside to make room. The incense burner had been overturned, the water bowl broken.

Alex's brain took in all the details. Such disregard for the sacred—flowers, statues and books strewn everywhere. Only the candle remained, placed above Zenji's head as he lay there with his arms placed neatly across his chest, his right hand covering the stump of his left. Dead.

In the short while it took Alex to walk down the hall, Wolfe had moved everyone away from the altar. They needed to safeguard the area, leave it as found, dust for prints. Alex was certain there'd be none, but she wouldn't advise foregoing this procedure. Sometimes they got lucky, sometimes the perp got stupid or lazy. Maybe they'd catch a break.

The residents, escorted by a cop, made their way to the lounge to commiserate in their grief and fear, leaving Alex with the detectives and a few of their people. The forensic guys were still there, a break of sorts. At least they'd know sooner rather than later what they did and didn't know. Alex was guessing there'd be more in the "don't know" column than in the "know" one.

"Not knowing is the beginning of waking up, remember that, Alex. 'I don't know' allows the mystery of life in. Stay in the present with the not knowing and you'll know."

Damn, Kido, now is not the time for this Zen stuff. This is now way out of control.

"What better time than now?"

"How the hell did he get by your guys, Wolfe? I thought you had the entrances covered," Alex said in as calm a voice as she could muster. Her tone belied her mounting frustration and anger.

"I had two guys patrolling the perimeter of this building and two guys inside. Do you know how many entrances there are? Four. Just in this section of the compound. With those four guys roaming around all night I figured we'd have sufficient coverage. Apparently not."

Wolfe was beating himself up. Anything Alex or anyone else had to say to him on top of the self-flagellation would be gratuitous. Alex knew it wasn't his fault, but she wanted to blame somebody, if only to vent her anger.

"Okay, then. How the hell did this guy get in here—with a dead body—and then out again, with no one seeing or hearing him?" Alex said to herself, just loud enough for all to hear. She raised her voice slightly, "Anybody got any theories?" No one said a word. "Oh my god. Has someone checked on Roshi? Is he okay?"

"Roshi's fine. I checked first thing when I made my rounds," Kluny said. "Before we even discovered the body. And the guys on patrol had nothing to report, everything was peaceful last night—except for the obvious," indicating Zenji's body with a nod of his head.

Silence fell once again on the group as they absorbed the truth that no one would utter. If this madman could move around unheard and unseen, he could probably get to Roshi, even with them there. And would, eventually, if Roshi was his target. *"Though each move is ahead of the next, there is still a transcendent secret."*

This mystery killer was always a step ahead. Trying to figure out who was doing it was beginning to feel as impossible as figuring out a koan. It couldn't be done.

"It's time we moved everyone out of here," Wolfe said, saying what was on everyone's mind. "I'll make arrangements today."

Roshi would still be resistant to leaving, Alex knew that, but she agreed with Wolfe—they had to do something before Roshi was harmed and someone else showed up toes pointing skyward.

"Wolfe, I agree with you, but don't you think that if we move everyone out of here we'll never find this guy? Isn't our best chance of finding him staying put?"

"Maybe. But it's abundantly clear that everyone's life here is in jeopardy now. It's my job to protect those lives, and so far I'm not doing such a good job. The only way I can protect Roshi and his crew is to get them the hell out of here, tout-de-suite."

Alex's mind was racing. She wanted to protect everyone, but knew that if everyone left the monastery grounds they would never catch this guy, whoever the hell he was.

"Okay, okay. I hear you. And I agree. But I have an idea. Will you at least listen to it before you do anything?" Alex had absolutely no idea what she was about to say. Something was brewing inside her, a germ of an idea. If Wolfe would agree to listen then she'd hear it at the same time.

"What is it?" Wolfe was at the end of his rope, yet still flexible enough to entertain a suggestion that might help them apprehend this maniac. His pledge was to serve and protect. Running away might be helping to protect, but it wasn't serving to capture the killer. He needed a way to do both, even if a plan to accomplish it came from her, the uninvited pain in his ass.

Just then Kluny walked up to them from the zendo. Alex hadn't even noticed he'd left the group.

"Thing about this place with the no shoes rule is that when shoes are worn inside it's very obvious." Everyone turned and stared at Kluny. "Looks like he came in the door on the west side of the zendo. There's a trail into the woods just outside that door that he must have used. He probably timed the movements of the two guys on patrol and slipped in while they were around the corner and then slipped out the same way. Come here, look at the dirt he tracked in. I could be wrong about this, of course, so tell me what you think."

Alex knew that he wasn't wrong. She'd learned the day before from one of the CSIs that Kluny was an expert tracker, from hunting in the woods since he was a kid. He saw things that no one else saw until he revealed it, and then it was so obvious that no one could understand how they missed so blatant a clue in the first place.

They followed Kluny into the zendo, being careful to avoid the areas that he pointed out to them. Alex was grateful for the diversion. It gave her time to formulate a plan. One message she was getting loud and clear, they couldn't leave the monastery yet. Not only would they not catch this guy, but the monastery would be off limits indefinitely. That could not happen. Roshi wouldn't allow it, she knew that much about him. Time would pass, the killer would return, and the killing would start all over again. Alex was sure this guy would wait. No, it had to be finished now. They had to stay. She had to come up with a plan.

***

When they walked back into the dharma hall, Roshi was at the altar staring down at Zenji. Roshi's white kimono looked to be neither a meditation robe nor a bathrobe. Alex had never seen him dressed, or undressed, this way. It was some other foreign-looking garb that would have made any other man she knew look ridiculous.

Roshi's feet were wrapped in tabi—white, glove-like socks that separated his big toe from the rest. Roshi did not appear absurd in this costume. Instead, he looked imperial. Even Wolfe and the other cops looked impressed and gave him his time with Zenji.

Muin, the ever-respectful attendant monk, was standing a few feet behind Roshi. Everyone else was on the periphery waiting for Roshi to finish the soft incantation he was chanting over Zenji's body. No one wanted to interfere, even though they were all anxious to get Zenji away from there and down the mountain to the morgue. It would probably be the same cause of death as the others, but they had to confirm it.

Roshi finished his chanting, turned around, and scanned the group till his eyes locked on Alex.

"Please see me in the meeting room when you're done here," he said.

Before Alex could respond Muin leaned over and said something to Roshi that no one else could hear.

"Okay, after breakfast then," Roshi said.

He walked down the hall, head bowed, hands clasped behind his back, Muin trailing behind. They could hear Muin muttering under his breath. "Shame about Zenji. What a shame. All of it."

Their retreating bodies encapsulated grief, defeat, and helplessness. It was hard not to stare and feel their suffering.

Or is this an act? Put on for the benefit of others, to deflect suspicion? Alex was the only one with this thought cutting in, though it wouldn't take much to draw the others into this mode of thinking.

27

Breakfast was a solemn affair. Conversation was allowed, but no one had the heart. Each mourner was wrapped in a personal maze of silent reflection. No one ate much. Even the visiting cops and forensic technicians who were accustomed to dealing with unnatural deaths were caught in the larger web of grief.

The isolation of the monastery and the close community deepened the impact of the three murders. All the chanting and sitting by hundreds of spiritual seekers over the past twenty years had permeated the very walls and floors of the monastery to open the hearts of even the most cynical. Three lives had been ruthlessly and barbarically put to an end. An innocent feline creature had been split in half without the luxury of drugs. The person responsible was nowhere in sight.

There was neither rhyme nor reason that they could fathom yet. And few clues. Mortality stared them all in the face. The precious and precarious nature of life was foremost in Alex's mind. No crossword puzzle, no Sherlock Holmes or Nancy Drew mystery, no Zen koan was going to help her solve this mystery—nothing of the usual sort, not even her brain.

It was eight o'clock by the time breakfast was over, 5:00 A.M. in California. Way too early to start phoning the West Coast students. In the meanwhile, background checks could be run on the names to see if any criminals, other than the known ones, popped up. In three hours they'd make some good progress on that.

Wolfe and Kluny were agreeable to Alex's idea of focusing on the students who hadn't left Roshi, splitting up the names four ways and making calls. They figured the devoted students were more apt to talk if they knew something, even if it was just a rumor, especially if it could help Roshi. But until the list came back and time passed she couldn't do much. She was betting there'd be a good number of names with records. She wasn't convinced their guy would be one of them, but was sure the effort would produce something.

She was itching to get into Zenji's room, look through his stuff, see what she could dig up, but the CSIs would be in there so she'd have to bide her time on that one. They allowed her involvement in the investigation, but only to a point. This was their territory.

Alex took a break to check in with Roshi as he'd requested. Muin wasn't in attendance. Once again, being alone with her teacher without the ritual form of koan dialogue to contain it made her nervous. She sat down. With palms together they bowed to each other. This custom helped to calm her.

"The detectives do not understand the significance of Buddha's birthday and will again want us to leave. You must try to convince them that running is not our way. Everyone who is coming will want even more to be here on Sunday to pay respects to their dharma sister and dharma brothers who are now dead. Please tell them it is not a party in the American sense, it is a religious matter—perhaps this will help them to see with more clarity. This is not only our home, it is our church.

"Those students who are here now and want to leave are free to do so. But whoever does leave will be back on Sunday with the rest of the sangha. They will not miss this precious occasion."

"I will pass this message along Roshi. I understand."

"Good, very good."

Neither of them had anything more to say. Alex left feeling slightly worse. She wanted to promise him an end to it all. It wasn't even in sight.

When she walked back into the library, Wolfe and Kluny were sitting quietly at their respective work stations lost in the sad and murderous state of affairs. It was a simple matter to get their attention.

She conveyed Roshi's message about not leaving and then handed each a piece of paper with a new koan written out.

The Sound of One Hand Clapping

A very young monk wanted to work on koans with his master. The master said he was too young, the young monk insisted. The teacher said: "You can hear the sound of two hands clapping, now show me the sound of one hand." This young monk, Toyo, came back to his teacher time after time for a year with various sounds— music, water dripping, wind sighing, animals crying etc.—but was always refused. Then he entered true meditation and transcended all sounds. He reached "soundless sound," realized the sound of one hand clapping and passed his koan.

"I don't think there was any reason for our killer to cut off Zenji's hand, except to refer to another koan, communicating who knows what through it. I think it's this one. Maybe Zenji was in on the killings with someone else, and maybe that someone else had no more use for Zenji's hand, so to speak, and got rid of him too. Or maybe that's too easy an explanation, because I never got it that he could have killed Sonja or been involved with that."

Wolfe was hardly listening and barely looked at the koan.

"This is all religious mumbo-jumbo. All I care about is real evidence and finding this creep. Kluny, get the cousin back up here—he definitely knows more than he's saying, and at this point he's our best lead," Wolfe said. "And when's that public defender getting here? We gotta get Clark talking, too."

"Should be sometime today, tomorrow at the latest," Kluny said.

"Shit," was all Wolfe said.

He said nothing about evacuating so maybe that idea was off the table for now. As much as Alex wanted to protect the sangha from further carnage, she believed that they had to stay put to find their killer. She also thought that if Roshi were the ultimate target, Sunday would be his day. So they had till then, less than three days, to nab the guy. They desperately needed a break. She hoped whatever it was it wouldn't lead them to Muin. Or to Roshi. She didn't know which would be worse.

***

"Hey, Uncle C."
"Hey, what's news up there?"
"Not good."
"Zenji?"
"Yeah. Now it's three."
"Jeezus! It's out of control."
"No kidding."
"Where and how?"

Alex brought Charlie up to date on Zenji's hand and his dead body. She faxed him a copy of the newest koan and told him her theory.

"The messy altar scene, the severed hand, it all sounds a little untidy for our killer—even considering the koan reference. This didn't seem as neatly thought out. Maybe the hand was an afterthought. Maybe Zenji was. Maybe this guy's beginning to lose it."

"I doubt that. He was able to come and go without being seen or heard, carrying a dead body around. There were at least four cops awake and patrolling the grounds all night. He knows his way around up here, there's no doubt about that. Being in the middle of a forest definitely puts us at a disadvantage. I always thought the worst place to hunt for someone was the city. I was wrong. This is."

"One of the reasons Vietnam was un-winnable. We couldn't find the enemy."

"It feels like a war up here. And we're the sitting ducks. Wolfe wants everyone to leave. I'm afraid that if we do we'll never get this guy. And Roshi refuses to go anywhere. I hate to keep him in harm's way but I think he's right. Our only chance will be staying put and outsmarting whoever's doing this. Get him at his own game. Because he will strike again. I'd bet on it."

"You're probably right, about that and about staying."

"I hope Wolfe agrees and decides to see this through up here for a few more days. Two at least. By my figuring, we've got that much time before another body, if our killer conforms to his habit of killing every two days. And something big is liable to happen on Sunday if we don't get this guy by then. The cops are getting antsy. The sangha's in a panic ... any luck yet with the list of names I sent you?"

"Matter of fact there is something ... and it's not a coincidence."
Uncle Charlie took a long pause.

Alex waited. He'd get to it.

"Robert's aunt and uncle, Lawrence's parents, were Roshi's
students once upon a time—they're on the list. That is, before they
both died—perhaps of suicide as the record states, perhaps not.
Drugs were the cause in one case, same as now. Is Wolfe looking at
the cousin?"

"He's the prime suspect at this point, now that Zenji's dead.
He'll be up here again today if he hasn't flown the coop. I'll give
Wolfe and Kluny this news soon as we hang up. ... Does the cousin
have a record?"

"Nah. He's squeaky clean," Charlie said. "Thing is, though, he
seemed to vanish into thin air, dropped off the face of the earth over
thirty years ago, when he left home at fifteen. Maybe he changed his
name. As Lawrence Bowden there's no sign of him anywhere, till
about five years ago when he moved up to the Catskills, right about
the same time Robert got there. He never filed a tax return, was
never fingerprinted under the name Lawrence Bowden, far as I can
tell.

"Plus, even though his parents and his cousin Robert were
followers of Roshi, there's no indication that he was ever a student—
I didn't find him on any of the lists I have. So unless he studied on
his own or with someone else, he wouldn't know about koans."

"But he did spend time with Robert so he probably heard
mention of them at least. And I think that the branch, the hand and
the cat are too literal an interpretation for someone who's studied
koans, so it could be someone who hasn't really worked with a
teacher. I don't profess to understand all of this stuff by any means.
Who knows? Maybe he was Enji's student.

"This guy Lawrence and Zenji both made reference to a head monk at Enji's temple that no one liked," Alex added. "Maybe Lawrence was referring to himself, maybe he was that monk. But that doesn't make any real sense cause Lawrence has hair down his back, would've had a shaved head if he were ever a monk, although if he left when Kosen did, I suppose it could have grown that much. I can't figure it out."

"Has anyone looked through Zenji's stuff yet? His personal papers, any written correspondence he might have kept, or journals?" Charlie asked.

"I'm gonna do that later with Kluny after the forensic guys finish up." Alex stared out the window as she said this and saw a red truck and a police cruiser drive up and park just outside the back door. "Uncle C, I gotta go ... looks like the cousin and the Feeb are both here."

***

Alex rushed to intercept the agent but was too late. He disappeared into Roshi's room and the door closed behind him just as she got there. She saw Lawrence down the hallway as he turned the corner toward the library, escorted by two uniforms. Muin stood outside Roshi's room along with the officer assigned to guard Roshi.

"You're not invited into the meeting?" Alex asked.

"Got to get them some tea first. Then, maybe ..." Muin said. The stress of the week showed in the dark, puffy circles under his eyes. He needed a shave. The light in his blue eyes had burnt out. "But I'm not sure I want to be in there, don't think I can handle more bad news."

"Do you know something? Has anything happened since breakfast?"

"Roshi got another letter. That's all I know."

"Damn. Who the hell is this guy?"

"I wish I knew. I wish I knew." Muin walked off to make tea—
the formalities and niceties of Zen Japanese culture could not be
ignored even as a blackmail/killing spree was being waged.

Alex joined Wolfe and Kluny in the library, just as Lawrence
was sitting down.

28

"There's really no need for the handcuffs, and I could have driven myself up here if you wanted to talk to me. Fuck man, what the hell's going on?" Lawrence was not a happy camper and looked like hell. The predominant color in his eyes was red. If wrinkled was in fashion, he'd be on the cover of *GQ*. And he kept squirming in his seat as if he had hemorrhoids.

"Look at it this way, you got your own personal chauffeur up here, you'll save on gas, and if we don't arrest you, we'll see that you get back home safe and sound," Wolfe said. "If we find cause to arrest you, then we won't have to deal with your truck. So, just sit down, Lawrence ... or LT ... or whatever the hell your name is."

"It's Lawrence, I told you that already, twice now. What do you want from me? What are you talking about? Arrest me? I haven't done anything. Why aren't you out tracking down Robert and Sonja's killer?"

"Here," Kluny said, "let me undo those bracelets for you. It was just a necessary precaution. You tell us what we need to know and you'll be on your way in no time."

"I've already told you what I know. What the hell do you want from me, man?"

"We want you to stop lying for one thing ... and if you didn't kill Zenji, we want you to tell us who did," Wolfe said.

"What do you mean Zenji? I didn't kill Zenji. Now you're playing with me, aren't you? He's not dead, Robert's dead. What the hell's going on?"

"Do you know what the sound of one hand clapping is?" Alex asked.

"What're you talkin' about?" He squinted at Alex as if to see her better. "Is Zenji dead now, too?"

"Yes, he's dead." Kluny said.

"Oh, man ..." Lawrence covered his face with his hands and rubbed his forehead briskly.

"And he didn't kill himself. Where were you last night?" Wolfe asked.

Lawrence held his head in his hands and said nothing.

"Where were you?" A softer tone from Kluny.

"I heard him the first time ..." His eyes darted to Wolfe and then back to Kluny. "And it depends on what time you're talking about. I was in an AA meeting till about ten and then I was home ... where I usually am at that time ... alone."

"Tell us about LT. Is that you? Is it someone else?" Wolfe asked. He and Kluny were taking turns with this one.

"I don't see what that has to do with anything ..."

"This will all work out a lot easier for you if you cooperate. Tell us what we want to know and you'll be home for lunch," Kluny said.

"Okay, okay. When I left home as a teenager I was pretty mixed up. I hated my parents, hated their drug addiction, their religion, all of it. I didn't want to have anything more to do with them. I started going by the name Lance Tracy, people started calling me LT. I got into booze and lost a few years of my life. When my parents died I drank at them even more, blamed Roshi for their drug use and deaths. Didn't clean up my act till quite a few years after."

"Where were you living?"

"I moved around ... North Carolina and Tennessee mostly in the early days—that's where I first met Jason ... um, Zenji ... and then I moved back to California. Stayed away from Roshi and his crowd but hooked up with Robert and Jason who'd moved to California about then." Lawrence stopped squirming.

"Were you ever a Zen student?" Alex asked.

"Nah, I just hung around with those types, never got into it myself. Booze was my spiritual practice. After seeing what Zen did to my parents I wanted nothing to do with it. 'Course now that I'm clean I see that it was the drugs and not the Zen that made them crazy and killed them, but I didn't know that back then. ... So, Jay, I mean, Zenji's dead now, too?" He was settling down, getting stiller, relieved to be unburdening himself.

"'Fraid so," Wolfe said, his tone following Lawrence's lead, becoming softer, slower, less angry.

"What else can you tell us about the people that Zenji and Robert knew out there in California? Know anyone who'd want them dead? Enji, for instance?" Wolfe asked.

"Crazy as Enji was, he loved his students. But he did fuel the beef between Robert and Jason, said it reminded him of old monk stories. But he never let it get dangerous. There was always some Zen lesson in it that he'd pontificate about, or so I heard. And they adored Enji. They got along with everyone but each other ... and the head monk."

"Who's that and where is he now?" Kluny asked.

"Name is, or was, Kevin Bawlder, now goes by his Zen name Gigen—I think he even officially changed it, like all those one-name celebrities—and I suppose he's still out in LA with Enji. He was a lifer, devoted to Enji. Did whatever Enji wanted him to do. Gigen was screwed up. Haven't met anyone who wasn't though, so ..."

"Screwed up, how? And how well did you know him? Was there anyone else there who hated Kosen and Zenji enough to kill them?" Kluny asked.

"I don't know anyone crazy enough to kill, man ... shit ... except maybe Gigen's father, or so Gigen said."

"He still around?" Wolfe asked.

"Nah, he died in prison. I never met him. He'd been taken under Roshi's wing when he was out on parole, but never got the Zen stuff, was always up to no good to hear Gigen tell it." Lawrence's eyes looked to be clearing up with all this sharing.

"What was the father's name?" Alex asked.

"Tommy. I never met him, but Gigen told me that his father insisted that he call him Tommy, not Dad, or Pop, like most kids, even when he was a little boy. I felt for him, having a mean son-of-a-bitch for a father myself. Least he let me call him Dad." He fidgeted in his seat, pulled at his pant leg, stretched his back.

"So you knew Gigen pretty well then?" Wolfe asked.

"We used to hang out, dropped acid and shit like that together ... till I stopped. He had no real friends but me. And no one at the Zen center liked him except Enji, who felt responsible for him, sorta like a big brother. I felt sorry for him. He was okay, harmless, I guess ..."

"What do you mean, you guess? Was he harmless or what?" Wolfe asked, the bark back.

"When I knew him, yeah, he was harmless, just a little off. But when I started to clean up my act, 'bout ten years ago now, he drifted away ... or I did ... whatever, we stopped seeing so much of each other. And then I moved here five years ago, 'round the time that Robert came here, and I haven't seen or talked to him since."

"So he's still in California?"

"Far as I know."

"Did he ever visit you here?"

"Nope. We weren't close in that way. I changed my name back to Lawrence and I'm sure he never knew that—or maybe he did, I don't know—anyway he'd probably have trouble finding me."

"So then, if Gigen's father was with Roshi, where was Gigen at that time?" Alex asked.

"With Roshi, too, I guess ... but he was just a kid then. When he got a little older he became Roshi's student—Roshi was sort of a father figure to him, since his own father was in and out of prison. Then he left Roshi, left home you could say, and went to LA when Enji did. And like I said, Enji was like a big brother to him ...

"But if you're thinking he had anything to do with this, you're all crazy. He wouldn't kill anyone—that would make him too much like his father and that was what he was running from his whole life. He'd be about as likely to kill these guys as me. And I didn't do it," Lawrence said as he crossed his arms and leaned back in his chair till it almost tipped over.

"Did you know Muin?" Alex asked.

"I knew of him, never met him till I came here to visit Robert. Gigen would write to him once in a while, he was another sort of brother to Gigen. Muin looked after him when he was a kid and his father was on a tear. Seemed like a nice guy from what I could tell."

That he is ... but what else? She could see that Kluny and Wolfe were asking themselves that very same question.

***

By the time they were done with Lawrence, it was nearly lunchtime. Wolfe told Alex to be back at 2:00, he wanted to have a little chat with her before he grilled Muin. She was not looking forward to either session, but couldn't blame Wolfe for the attitude.

All she wanted to do was take her body out on the open road and run about twenty miles. That would have to wait. Instead, she paid a visit to Kido's grave for a little chat of her own, to sort out the details swimming in her head and talk to someone who knew and loved Muin.

"Why'd you have to go and die on me, Kido? I need you here with everything that's going on. I feel like I can't trust anyone."

"Hmmm ... I—I—I—me—me—me ... do you even know who 'I' is? Who 'you' are?"

This was Kido's voice in her head, but she could have sworn that Roshi was the one that had said this to her once. She went with it.

"I'm not sure what you mean."

"Don't take everything so personal. I didn't die 'on you.' I just died."

"Okay, okay ... but I'm worried about Muin. I think he's been lying—or at least holding something back from me ... that is, from the investigation. If Lawrence can be trusted, and I believe all of what he just told us, it doesn't look good for Muin."

"Lay it out for me."

"Zenji had said that Muin and Kosen had been arguing about the cat, then Kosen shows up dead. It was Muin's cat. He must have known about Zenji and Kosen before they got here, but he never let on that he did. Plus he was in contact with Enji's head monk, Gigen ... and that seems totally weird. Why wouldn't he have brought up this guy's name when the blackmail was revealed?"

"Are you sure that he didn't? Are others keeping secrets from you?"

"I ... that is I, me, myself, Alex Sullivan ... I don't know. Maybe everyone's holding a secret. Like I said, I feel like I can't trust anyone. And maybe Muin's the blackmailer, maybe Roshi pissed him off—he hasn't been himself this week, says he's been acting weird toward me because he still loves me, but that could be a lie."

"But if he were the blackmailer, why would he bring Enji into it?"

"To implicate Enji and turn Roshi against him. Even though he says not, perhaps Muin wants to be Roshi's dharma heir. Maybe when Enji and Roshi started corresponding again, he felt threatened.

"Or maybe Kosen and Zenji were blackmailing Roshi for Enji's sake. Maybe Muin discovered this. Maybe that's what he and Kosen were fighting about ... maybe he killed both of them because they wouldn't stop."

"Maybe. And Sonja?"

"As I've always thought about her death—she got in the way."

"But didn't a letter arrive just today, after all three were dead?"

"It could have been sent before Zenji died. Maybe Muin wrote it to throw us off his track. Or maybe he's in cahoots with Enji and he sent it."

"This all sounds very logical and rational ... and might be true. But you know Muin on a deeper level than all that. What you must do is sit with all of this and listen to that place deep within you. Don't just notice the external clues. Pay more attention! Listen! Be still and let the solution appear in the space between your thoughts."

"But there's no time for that. People are dropping like flies. I think the cops are going to be looking closer at Muin and I can't protect him. I'm not sure I want to. I don't have time to just sit!"

"What other choice do you have right now?"

"None, I suppose. But I have to say ... all that talk just now about rotten fathers really got to me. Lawrence had a drug addict father who killed himself, that guy Gigen's father was a criminal who died in prison, Zenji never even knew his father, and I know—if I can trust anything Muin told me—that Muin and his father never got along. It doesn't make me happy that Daddy died, but I wonder how we would have gotten along had he lived. Shit, I'm even questioning my own father and the feelings I have for him."

Alex lit the incense she'd brought with her and placed it in the incense burner on Kido's grave. She sat a moment longer and listened to the sounds of the mountain, her own breathing. She missed Kido and her father desperately. Her eyes welled up but no tear fell. She did not want to lose Muin and Roshi as well. She needed to get back to work and find the true killer. She hoped like hell that it wasn't Muin.

29

Alex was on time for her 2:00 with Wolfe and Kluny. When she reached the library door, the officer who'd been assigned to protect Roshi was guarding it.

"Roshi's in there with the detectives?" Alex asked.

"Yes, ma'am."

Damn, again without me. As she moved to open the door the cop held out his arm and barred her way.

"Sorry, strict orders to let no one in."

"They didn't mean me, officer" —Alex looked at his name badge —"Johnson."

"They didn't tell me 'bout no exceptions."

"Look, just let me peek in and ask."

"Can't let you do that."

"Well then, you do it."

"Sorry ma'am, can't do that either."

"You mean you won't."

"Whatever you say."

"How long have they been in there?"

Johnson looked at his watch. "'Bout a half hour."

Shit.

"They'll be done soon I 'spect," Johnson said.

Two minutes later Roshi came out absorbed in thought and walked right past her without saying a word. Johnson followed on his heels. Alex pushed open the door and faced Wolfe and Kluny.

"So, did you intentionally exclude me from that meeting with Roshi or was it just an oversight?"

"Sit down detective, we need to ask you some questions," Wolfe said.

Alex noticed a few things at once. One, he called her detective, so things weren't so bad for her. Two, he and Kluny both looked worn out and depressed—like every other guy up there they needed a shave, a fresh set of clothes, and some sleep. And three, the Marlboros in Wolfe's shirt pocket had been opened. She couldn't tell if he'd smoked one, there was no stale tobacco odor emanating from him, but he was certainly getting closer to lighting up. Had something happened in the past half hour to put him over the nicotine edge?

"Roshi still wants you involved here, but I'm having some reservations about you, and, Zen Master or not, it's not his call ... I get to say if you can be here," Wolfe said. Kluny was just watching. She figured he was on her side or at least neutral. She said nothing.

"Now that we're looking seriously at Muin as a suspect, we need to know if you can be objective."

"Absolutely, without question." She didn't know if she trusted this, but she had to make Wolfe believe. There was no way she was going to be excluded from Muin's interrogation.

"Good, and if I get even a whiff you're taking his side, you'll be outta here so fast ..."

"Don't worry, it won't happen. What did Roshi have to say?"

Wolfe was done talking to her for the moment. Kluny answered. "He corroborated Lawrence's view of history, but he doesn't really know Lawrence, just *of* him. He remembered his parents when we reminded him how they died. Said he had no idea Kosen was their nephew. I believed him.

"And, no surprise, he cannot fathom Muin being involved—refuses to even consider it."

"When I saw Muin this morning he said Roshi had received another note—did he show it to you?" Alex asked.

"He gave us a copy." Kluny picked up a slip of paper on the top of the pile on his desk. "What do you think?"

> *Your BBB—in other words, your ass, if you haven't been paying attention—is grass if you don't agree to my terms. You have till Sunday. The 3 blind mice are gone—ha! That's on you. I mean it. Just do as I say and no one else will get hurt. This will be our secret—and I know you know about those.*

"Tiny handwriting ... looks like someone forced to stay within the lines all his life," Alex said. "Psycho of some sort."

"Yeah, and that's enlarged on the copier," Kluny said. "Sounds like a kid, though, doesn't it?"

"Yeah. Could be intentional, of course ... Roshi say what BBB means?"

"Said he had no idea."

"And of course he also had no idea about the reference to secrets, right?" Alex said.

"Right," Kluny said.

"I s'pose you've already got handwriting samples from everyone here?"

"In the process ..."

"When is Muin coming?"

"He should be on his way ... I've got something else I want you to look at," Kluny said as he picked up a stack of spiral-bound notebooks and handed them to her.

"These came from Zenji's room, they were all under his mattress, so I figure he had something to hide. Mostly it looks like notes related to being a monk, but a few times he digresses. I can't make any sense of his scribbling, he used some kind of shorthand, with initials for names and other things. I'm betting he knew more than he 'fessed to when he was still with us. Maybe you'll be able to decipher some of the shorthand quicker than me or Wolfe."

"I'll take a look," Alex said. "I love this sort of shit, like figuring out a puzzle."

"Well, this case is surely that, a puzzle," Kluny said

Muin walked in, sheepish and drained of color. Alex felt sorry for him. In her gut she knew he was innocent of any wrongdoing, even if her head told her otherwise. She had to keep her wits about her or Wolfe would throw her out of the room. She vowed to zip her lip, or as Kido whispered to her:

"Keep noble silence and just listen."

***

Kluny warmed up Muin, told him most of what Lawrence had told them. Muin's demeanor and quiet acceptance of everything indicated to all three cops that he wasn't surprised. They deduced that Roshi had squawked, which they'd asked him not to do. Wolfe was pissed.

"So you and Gigen were penpals? Who else were you writing to? Did you invite Robert and Zenji here to help you with your coup to take over Roshi's throne?" Wolfe asked.

Muin just sat there, said nothing.

"And then get rid of them when you had no more use for them?"

"That's ridiculous," Muin said.

"I'll tell you what's ridiculous ... monks killing each other vying to be the favorite son. You want to be a Zen Master, is that it? You want to be Roshi's dharma heir? Take over when he's gone? You plan to kill him soon, too?"

"That is also ridiculous. I have no interest in being Roshi's dharma heir. All I am and ever cared to be is a monk."

Alex wanted to voice her agreement with this, but kept quiet. Even as he said it, Wolfe and Kluny heard the ring of truth in his voice.

"I wrote to Gigen, yes. I never said anything about our correspondence because it did not seem important till now. Even now I'm not sure what it has to do with anything, but I'll tell you how I know Gigen and why I stayed in touch with him," Muin took a deep breath, closed his eyes for a moment, shifted in his seat and then continued. He sat up straight with his hands cupped in his lap. He slowly looked straight in the eyes of each of the three cops in front of him.

"I met Gigen when he was just a kid—he was Kevin then—he was about ten-years-old, around the time I first started going to Roshi's zendo. I was about nineteen. His father, Tommy, was a rough character—one of those wayward men that Roshi took in and tried to guide away from prison life. He often left Kevin alone to fend for himself. I felt sorry for the kid, so I started showing up early, throwing the ball around with him, taking care of him when his father was off someplace. He grew up around the zendo but it was rough on him, his father in and out of jail. I thought I could be a positive influence ... and Roshi of course ... and other Zen students doted on the kid. He was like the zendo mascot.

"He grew up, started practicing under Roshi, became a Buddhist and was given the name Gigen. By then his father was dead—killed in prison, I don't remember exactly how or when—and Roshi became his surrogate father. At some point, Gigen got mad at Roshi and attached himself to Enji. When Enji left, so did he. He and I had a falling out over that, but then made it up and kept in some contact. He would send me letters every now and then, tell me about life in LA with Enji, but I haven't seen him since ... must be almost thirty years now. I felt sorry for him—he was like a little brother to me."

"What was your quarrel with Gigen?" Wolfe asked.

"I wanted him to stay, thought he'd be better off with Roshi. He needed taking care of and I didn't think Enji was up to it. I worried about him the way any older brother would. But then I realized he had his own life, had to leave home at some point, and so I let it go."

"So you knew Zenji and Robert before they arrived here," Wolfe said. It wasn't a question he was posing, just a statement of fact.

"I didn't actually know them. Gigen would write rambling letters about all the students there. It seems he didn't get along with any of them—I figured it was a result of his mixed up childhood. Like I said, I felt sorry for him. And Zenji and Kosen are common Buddhist names and they were only a couple of the people Gigen would complain about, so they didn't stand out ... and when they came here, I never made the connection."

"You expect us to believe that?" asked Wolfe.

"It's the truth."

"When was the last time you heard from Gigen?" Kluny asked.

"It's been a while. But he was never very consistent in keeping in contact. There were often long stretches when I wouldn't hear from him, and when he did finally write he'd tell me how mad he was at me for something I'd written—would never say what—but that as a good Buddhist he had forgiven me. I never asked for an explanation. As you can imagine, he had some untreated psychological issues."

"Any idea what B-B-B means?" Kluny said.

"B-B-B?"

"Yeah." Kluny handed Muin the copy of the recent blackmail note. "And do you recognize the handwriting?"

Muin read the note with a puzzled brow. The character lines etched in his face looked deeper than a week ago. "I've never seen the handwriting." He handed the note back to Kluny. "BBB is an acronym for Buddha Bumpkin Body."

Alex understood the words, but even she had no idea what this could mean. Wolfe paced and Kluny sat patiently, both anxious for Muin to enlighten them.

"It's Zen jargon for a person ... though I'm not sure how widespread it is... might only be used by Roshi's acolytes. You could Google it, I suppose, but I'm sure you've done that already."

"Anyway, it's just sort of a funny reference to how we're both enlightened and not enlightened at the same time, and how we are all in a physical body and can't forget that ... it means we need to use our body to reach enlightenment but at the same time it imprisons us. It's being in samsara and nirvana simultaneously, but that might be too esoteric. ... Anyway, I haven't heard anyone use the term in years."

If Muin were speaking the truth, all three cops in the room knew this could be a significant clue to the blackmailer's identity and maybe even the killer's. It certainly confirmed that the perp was in the Buddhist community, and probably one of Roshi's students, present or former. That was something. But was it enough to find him before Sunday?

"Did Roshi use this term or know of it?" Alex asked. She knew that there was a certain language used among students that Roshi was not privy to—it was often irreverent and base, and because the language barrier between Roshi and his American students often created misunderstandings—humor didn't always cross that gap so easily—Roshi was sometimes not included in the fun. But Alex also knew that he had a way of knowing everything, especially having Muin as his assistant.

"I'm not sure. Probably. I never used it in front of him and never heard him say it, but he always seemed to know what everyone was talking about even when he wasn't in the room. You'll have to ask him."

30

"Call me naive," Kluny said, "but I really thought we wouldn't have to question the veracity of religious monks. I think at this point we even have to take with a grain of salt everything Roshi has told us. We can't hold him above suspicion anymore."

This hit Alex in her solar plexus. She knew he was right. Her silence expressed her agreement.

"That's for damn sure," Wolfe said. "I am tired of treating him with kid gloves. At this point, he and Muin both are questionable characters as far as I'm concerned. And neither gets any special treatment from here on in. Understood, detective?" He was looking straight at Alex with this question. She just nodded, knowing if she opened her mouth she'd for sure say something she'd regret. She felt like the monk in the koan, hanging from a tree branch.

"Okay, so let's review what we've got and see where we're at," Kluny said.

For the next two hours the three of them talked through the facts of the case. No new insights came. The list of known suspects had only grown by one. They were all painfully frustrated. Alex was surprised that Wolfe hadn't yet lit up a smoke.

A break of sorts came when a member of the forensic team reported finding a fingerprint on the altar near Zenji's body, a print that wasn't in the system and belonged to no one on site. And another one that came from Clark, which definitely kept him on the suspect list since he stayed mostly in the kitchen, hardly participating in the daily activities of the monastery except when forced. He rarely made an appearance in the two rooms where the meditation and chanting took place, so his print on the altar was suspicious. No one could give Wolfe a good reason why Roshi condoned Clark's absence from monastery functions when everyone else had to be there.

Clark's lawyer came and went. The fingerprint wasn't enough to hold him even if he was high on Wolfe's list as possible monk killer. Although his lawyer advised him to say nothing during the interview, Clark couldn't help himself. "My prints are all over this monastery. It doesn't make me a murderer. You cops are all alike— blame the ex-con first and ignore the real evidence." This time, Kluny and Alex agreed with him.

At about six o'clock the three of them took a break from making phone calls to Roshi's old students and ate some dinner that Jito had brought up to them. When in the city and on the job Alex ate at her desk all the time. She never thought she'd be doing such a thing at the monastery. Eating was always a mindful activity on the mountain, not something to do while doing something else. This day she had no choice. There was no time for the normal rituals. When Jito left, she followed him out.

"Jito, hold up a minute," called Alex, rushing to catch up with him in the stairwell.

Jito stopped, turned and waited.

"How're you holding up?" Alex asked, as she stroked his arm.

"Lousy. It sucks. And I hear some of us are leaving today—those that have family nearby at least. I wish I could go, but I have no one to go to. It sucks."

"I know, it does suck. At least there are locks on all the doors now. That's something."

"Yeah, like that's gonna keep this maniac out?" Jito said. He was close to hysterical. Alex couldn't blame him.

"Well, cops are everywhere now—so it's probably safer here than anywhere else right now. Anytime, no matter what or when, you need something, you come find me. Okay?"

"Thanks. I'll be fine, but thanks."

"I'll even get a futon and sleep in your room with you if you'd like."

"Thanks, but I'll be okay."

"You ever hear the term B-B-B?"

"Haven't in a while, but yeah. Means Buddha Bumpkin Body or Bumpkin Buddha, I forget the order, s'pose it doesn't matter... For a while some of the guys used it to refer to the women who'd come up here to do yoga in the guest house. Called them BBB's, but instead of body, they meant Babes. Horny, straight guy humor. ... Why do you want to know?"

"Someone made reference to it earlier today and I had never heard it. Just wondered who uses it."

"It's not used so much anymore, but when it was, some years ago, everyone used it just for fun."

"Do you know if Roshi used it, or what he thought of it?"

"He knew about the Babes one—I heard him use it once. I don't think he realized that those 'yoga babes' might not take too kindly to a Zen Master referring to them as babes."

"Yeah, he's funny that way. Sometimes he seems to understand many nuances of English, other times not ... I'm never really clear about what he understands and what he doesn't."

"Oh, he understands more than he lets on sometimes. Don't kid yourself. I think he knows more than we do," Jito said. "Don't forget, he's been here a long time. English might be a difficult second language to learn, but he's a smart guy ... he is a Zen Master after all."

"True, true. Thanks Jito. Remember, find me anytime if you need me. Don't even hesitate," said Alex as she hugged him goodbye. She did not like this news about Roshi.

"Okay, Alex," said Jito as he hugged her back.

"Promise?"

"I promise. Scout's honor." Jito crossed his heart and raised his palm to her.

"You were a boy scout? I thought their signal was a three-finger salute."

"I don't know what it is ... I was only a scout for about a day, dahling. That was more than enough for me ... and them, I'm afraid." Jito laughed. Alex enjoyed the sound of it. She returned to the gloom of the library and her food, for which she had little appetite.

For the rest of the day Alex read through some of Zenji's notebooks and made lists. Kluny made phone calls to some ex-students in California and kept trying to reach Enji. And Wolfe coordinated the search teams—they were combing the woods for clues.

Wolfe had every known entrance and exit to the monastery covered. So if the perp tried another stunt, they'd have him. They were stopping all cars that headed up that way. They were ready for him. Kluny had called in more state troopers. Wolfe pulled some guys from two neighboring counties, which he hated doing, but at this point with the bodies piling up and hundreds of people expected on Saturday and Sunday, if Roshi continued to insist on the gathering, small things like territory didn't mean a thing.

***

Shortly after ten, Alex took a break to call Uncle Charlie. She moved out of the library and down to the public phone near the office. She felt like she needed some privacy and the phone was in a small room, the size of an old-fashioned phone booth, and it had a door. She sat on the stool and collected herself before she dialed. The tiny, soundless cubicle was a comforting relief from the fray.

Alex quickly brought Uncle Charlie up to speed on the blackmail note, the cousin, Gigen, BBB, and what all the cops were doing.

"And forensics found a print at Zenji's scene that doesn't belong to anyone here. Seems our perp got sloppy. No idea who belongs to it yet but they're working on it," Alex said. "I'm reading through Zenji's notebooks. They're a bit hard to read and I don't understand some of the language. He was using a code of some sort ... plus he had them hidden under his mattress. I don't know who he was hiding them from, but it must have been someone here, otherwise why would he choose to conceal them?"

"Maybe it was just an old habit from living in foster homes. You know how those places can be," said Uncle Charlie.

"Could be ... both Muin and Roshi aren't being completely honest. It makes me mad for more than one reason."

"I understand that, but reserve judgment, honey, trust yourself, trust that you weren't wrong about them before this week started. Murder makes everyone hide things, say things they don't really mean, act weird ... you know that ... give them the benefit of the doubt, but don't trust them completely yet. Be open to the unexpected."

"You're beginning to sound like Kido. You been reading those books I gave you?"

"Matter of fact, every night before I go to sleep I read a passage from the one you gave me for Christmas last year, *Tao te Ching* ..."

"Yeah, I love that book. Simple, yet every time I read it I get something different, even from the same passage," said Alex.

"I'm beginning to know what you mean," said Uncle Charlie. "Last night I read something ... let's see, I remember the last two lines. They might apply here: *Do your work, then step back. The only path to serenity.*"

"Yeah, I know that one. I can't get there today I'm afraid. Even in the city, I had a hard time with that whole concept when it came to the job ... anyway, there's no serenity to be had at the moment."

"I'm thinking I might come up there tomorrow ... I imagine you guys can use all the help you can get."

"That's true." Alex wasn't sure how she felt about this until her breath reached her belly. It was the first deep breath she'd taken in days. "It'll be great to have you here, Uncle C."

"Good. I thought I might first check out the town before I head up to the monastery, you know, snoop around, ask some questions of the local folk. I've already googled it and have directions. I never realized, all this time you've been going up there, how isolated and deep in the woods that place is."

"Yeah, and it's been great till now. ... I just had a thought. Unless something weird happens overnight here, I'll meet you in town tomorrow. There's a coffee shop on the main street, you can't miss it, why don't we meet there about noon?"

"Sounds perfect."

"Cell phones should work down mountain so if anything happens and one of us is late we should be able to communicate. Worst case, we could call the monastery and communicate through them—the town actually has pay phones on the street that work."

"Sounds like a plan. Try to get some rest, Alex."

"I will, I'm exhausted, I think I'll be able to get a coupla hours … we'll see."

Alex returned to the library and Zenji's notebooks. The halls were eerily quiet. The students who had a home to go to or friends to stay with had left before dark. They all planned to come back on Sunday, but now the place felt empty. Only those who called the monastery home stayed on: Clark, Jito, Hokan, Gyozan, Hoja, Muin, and, of course, Roshi. They were all behind their newly locked doors.

31

Friday, April 6, 5:00 AM

Charlie woke early in the end of a dream. He always dreamed with what seemed to him to be wakeful participation. Perhaps this tendency was what contributed to his five hours of sleep feeling like eight. He didn't jump right out of bed as the dream lingered and he tried to take hold and bring it to its completion or move it in a new direction during this not-yet-fully-awake state.

He had done some reading about lucid dreaming and despite his skepticism, found himself practicing the technique of becoming aware that he was dreaming while he was dreaming and then becoming the director of his dream. This Friday morning the dream that he chased flickered behind his eyes a few times before disappearing. He could call up feelings from the dream more than images once his eyes opened for the day. Panic, tenderness, and uncertainty. He didn't tarry. Rested and ready he began his chores and was in his car two hours later heading northwest. He had a plan ... not a solution, but at least a plan.

***

Alex slept from two till about five, sat an hour with the remaining residents—that seemed to refresh her more than sleep had—and then worked with Wolfe and Kluny for a couple of hours.

There were too many unanswered questions. Wolfe demanded another meeting with Roshi, on Wolfe's terms—that meant in the library where he'd taken up residence, and sitting in chairs like normal people. He'd had enough of the no-shoes-squatting-on-the-floor-bent-like-a-pretzel bullshit. He sent Kluny off to corral Roshi. Kluny finally went to Hokan after Muin was nowhere to be found. Hokan went directly to Roshi, who was happy to oblige the detectives.

Roshi sat in Alex's chair with an imperial air as if it were his office and he'd asked the detectives there for his meeting.

"Roshi, if we're going to track down whoever is doing this, you're going to have to be honest with us. Even if you think it has no relevance, we need to know about the 'transgressions' and 'secrets' mentioned in the blackmail notes. We don't mean to disrespect your position here, but people are being killed and it's our job to end it," Wolfe said.

"Of course, of course, it is a delicate matter. I allowed certain things in past to happen that I am not proud of. They have now returned to cause more problems," Roshi began.

"As you know, the blackmailer wants me to appoint Enji, an old monk of mine, as my dharma heir, my successor. Whoever is writing these letters threatens to expose some things and blame me if I do not agree to do this. Years ago, I selected Enji as someone who could carry on my work, who was ready to be official teacher. But he disappointed me and I was forced to sever all ties with him."

"Disappointed? Enough to sever all ties?" Wolfe asked, his exasperation and impatience held in check only by his clenched knuckles and gritted teeth. "Something more than disappointment must have caused you to kick him out and then be blackmailed thirty years later. With all due respect, Roshi, please, just get on with it."

Roshi glanced at Wolfe and then set his eyes on Alex, who was sitting in Kluny's chair. Kluny was leaning against a bookshelf in the background. Wolfe finally sat down, leaned his elbows on the table in front of him and stared at Roshi.

Roshi continued telling his story to Alex, as if it were confession. His voice was sad and slow. His hands rested in his lap. His body was rock solid still.

"Two years ago, Enji wrote to me. We have been in communication since. He has cleared up his bad ways. Agent Hawkes, the FBI man on blackmail case, and I do not think he is behind blackmailing. Enji will be here Sunday. It will be our first meeting since we separated."

"What happened back then that was so bad you expelled a monk and now you're being blackmailed and people are dying?" Wolfe reiterated, trying to keep the telling on track.

"A few years after I came to America, there was much free love and drugs and music and many young people searching for spiritual connection. Many of them passed through my temple. Enji helped me to bridge cultural gap.

"But a young woman, while in the company of Enji, while in my temple, died of drug overdose. It was quite upsetting, but many young people were lost then and many found solace and then death in drugs. It was confusing time for them. I never knew exactly what happened to that girl—maybe I did not want to know—and I decided to believe Enji's story. And with my help it was all kept very quiet."

"Did Robert and Zenji have anything to do with that?" Wolfe wanted to get on with it.

"They weren't even born yet. Please, let me tell what happened." Roshi still didn't look at Wolfe.

"And there was LSD," Roshi continued. "At the time, LSD seemed to help people open up spiritually. Many, many students would pass koan after koan. It was very exciting. Enji was making and selling LSD. I did not think it so bad. The money helped us to grow."

Alex hated hearing all this. It meant the rumors were true. It meant Roshi did some bad things. She hated that he was looking at her, telling her. She wanted him to look somewhere else. She could hardly breathe or swallow.

"But then it turned. I asked Enji to stop. The LSD became hindrance rather then aid to enlightenment. He said he would end production and focus all his attention on being a monk and preparing for his place as my dharma heir.

"He lied and I found out he was still involved in drugs and in frivolous sexual parties ... so we parted ways. I could no longer turn a blind eye."

"So, if you did nothing yourself Roshi, then what could this blackmailer expose?" Wolfe asked. He banged his fist on the table. Alex jumped. Roshi did not flinch.

"Early on I did some things I am not proud of, like I said. I too succumbed to sexual revolution. There are photos. I also experimented once with LSD. I regret that, but I was not alone when I did it. I am led to believe that there is proof of this. I made mistakes. It will not be pleasant to have this made public now. But I cannot hold this secret any longer. And no more lives should be sacrificed for this ancient transgression."

"What does all this have to do with the killing? Has Agent Hawkes figured out who this blackmailer is?" Wolfe asked.

"No, and this has been my personal koan to figure through since the first letter. I have no idea who would do such horrible things. I am sorry that I cannot be of more assistance in this matter. Agent Hawkes will be coming up today, very soon. Perhaps you can engage with him and work together to solve this mystery."

The sadness that washed over Roshi as he said this affected the rest of them. No more questions were necessary. Roshi's burden seemed greater than anyone's and it was clear that he was blaming himself.

***

8:57 AM

Alex really needed to move her body, get out on the open road and take a run. Plus she had to meet Charlie at 11:30. There was no time to stay for the meeting with the FBI agent. Wolfe and Kluny would fill her in when she returned. Running and meeting Uncle C was her priority right now. She threw Zenji's notebooks onto the back seat, maybe they'd have time to look through them together.

On her way out, she passed the red truck that held the FBI agent she had yet to meet. Along a narrow, curvy stretch where they both had to slow down. It had to be him, it certainly wasn't the cousin in his red truck, and the agent was expected. When she got a close look at his face she saw that it was him. He still hadn't shaved, his beard was longer, softer looking than when she'd seen him a few days ago, with his hair now wavy and unkempt.

As they passed each other, they locked eyes, green hazel on her side, hazel brown on his, for as long as it was safe to take their eyeballs off the road. He was stern looking, and scruffily handsome. She thought to turn around and follow him, go to that meeting. Thinking better of it, she stuck to her plan. She needed to move her bones.

A few miles down the mountain, she found a running spot off the beaten track. She figured she had time to run ten miles no problem and maybe even work on her speed. Her lungs had adjusted to the altitude—it was only two thousand feet, but still, it had its effect. And the weather was cooperating at a cool and crisp sixty degrees or so—unusually warm for this time of year, but she wasn't complaining.

The mountain seduced her into the rhythm of running and in no time at all she was in the zone, her body and breath in charge. Endorphins swimming in her brain took away all body pain and thoughts of monks killing monks.

The idea that no death is tragic, it's just death, came to her unbidden. She didn't really believe that, but there it was. Her legs just kept pumping. She wondered why everyone didn't run. There was nothing in the world like it. The hell with shrinks. This was her therapy.

Most of the vehicles on the roads were trucks and vans. Sturdy transport. So when she saw the red truck in the distance coming toward her she thought nothing special about it. Until it got closer and sped by without participating in the local custom of waving. *Was that Lawrence's truck or the one I saw in the woods? Couldn't possibly be the Feeb guy, could it? Not unless he followed me.*

She turned to catch sight of the license plate, but it was well away, around a curve and out of range. She abandoned the idea of running back in that direction. On foot she was at a serious disadvantage and her car was too far away.

Today, Alex's koan was: "Who the hell is killing all these Buddhists?" She didn't end her run with a solution but she felt a little closer to it.

32

Before she finished stretching, Alex was behind the wheel of her Subaru heading away from town in pursuit of three vehicles. The first was Lawrence's red truck. He hadn't waved as he passed, but had slowed down to ogle her. He was focused on her ass and legs and clearly didn't notice that she was the cop from the monastery. As he crawled by her, a dark green truck with a friendly local behind the wheel passed Lawrence's truck and sped away.

To add to the veritable stream of traffic and the morass, Feeb guy in his red truck raced into view taking up the rear of the convoy with a passenger that she swore was Muin.

She had a half-hour before she absolutely had to head to town, Uncle Charlie would give her some grace period. It would afford her time to learn something, perhaps the relationship of the two red trucks to each other and where the hell Muin was going. And maybe she'd get lucky and get a phone signal to call Uncle C.

***

Alex followed at a distance safe enough to deflect suspicion. The green truck was long gone and she was having some trouble keeping the other two in sight, what with all the curves and not wanting to get too close. She was glad for the red of the trucks. She was getting farther and farther away from town, heading in the opposite direction. She'd have to turn back soon. Uncle Charlie would surely worry. The red trucks disappeared. Around each bend she expected to see them, but was met with disappointment.

And then, a flash of red up ahead, off to the left, somewhere in the woods. Through the early springwoods she could see a fair distance. A month from now nothing would show through the dense foliage. Again, she was glad for the red. And glad she had opted for the blue on her new wheels. It wasn't camouflage, but it wasn't as easy to spot as red.

Why would anyone trying to keep a low profile choose red? She began to doubt that either of these characters were up to no good. Red vehicles were notorious for getting more speeding tickets than any other color, because they stood out. The killer owning a red vehicle just didn't fit. Camouflage green would have been a better choice and more in fitting with the rest of his MO.

She slowed down, now it was just a game, not a search for a killer. All she wanted to know was whose red truck took the turn and where Feeb guy and Muin had disappeared to.

The cousin not waving back at her signaled something. Maybe he was just a garden-variety psycho, a casualty of bad parenting spending his damaged life alone in the middle of the woods.

She watched for an opening in the woods—a private road or a path wide enough for a truck. She crept along scanning the left side of the road for a break. At once grateful and worried that there were so few passing cars—not one since she started tailing red trucks—it dawned on her how isolated this area was.

There it was. That had to be it. A narrow dirt road leading into the woods. It was now close to noon. She should turn back. Instead she took a left. She continued at a slow crawl. If she didn't come to a clearing soon she'd have to back out, the road was too narrow to turn around.

Claustrophobia settled into the seat next to her. She was glad the forest was lean—it gave her a tiny space to breathe. Suddenly she felt chilled.

A quarter of a mile in and no sign of a clearing or a red truck. This road seemed to lead nowhere. She must have missed a turn or not gone far enough. She had to stop to collect herself, decide the next thing. The sun slipped behind a cloud. The slivers of sky she could see turned gray and forbidding. *Back up. Go home.* That message was loud and clear.

She could use her side mirrors to guide herself out, but old habits die hard, so she shifted into reverse and twisted in her seat to look over her right shoulder before backing up. If her seat belt hadn't been engaged she would've jumped out of her seat.

Feeb guy was standing directly behind her. If she moved she'd run right over him. And he wasn't budging. He stood in a firing-range stance with a non-expressive face. He wasn't moving, neither was she.

He might not be their killer, but he was menacing. *Where is Muin? Has he done something to Muin?* Alex's eyes darted to the dashboard clock. Twelve-thirteen. She had to go. Stalemate over. She gave in, rolled down her window and stuck her head out.

"I'll back out of here if you move to the side. I'm sorry to be in your way. Come around I'll explain everything," Alex said.

Feeb guy didn't move, he said nothing. *Did he hear me?* She stared at him through the rear view. Then she saw it. His gun. She rolled up her window, shifted into drive and moved forward, struggling to unlock the glove compartment where she'd put her gun as she maneuvered over the rough surface. *Maybe there's another outlet.*

Feeb guy followed behind her on foot, forcing her deeper into the woods. If she could just turn the car around she'd feel more in charge, able to look him in the eyes, challenge him through the windshield. She wasn't ready to get out of the car yet and didn't like him behind her with a firearm.

A short way in, there it all was, a cabin, a small clearing, one clean red truck—Lawrence's truck nowhere in sight. *Shit, what have I done? What sort of cop are you? I got to get out of here.* She maneuvered her car around, but Feeb guy was standing firm, blocking the only visible exit.

Again she rolled down her window and leaned out. She did not want to step out and play brave cop, she didn't want to end her career with a bullet through her skull. *Maybe he's Roshi's hitman. Jesus, am I out of my mind?*

"Look, I'm real sorry about being here. There's no need for the gun. Really. I'll be on my way now if you could just move over and let me pass." Face-to-face she knew he heard her. And she knew that he knew who she was.

Stone-faced nada. No reaction. Not even a twitch. At least his gun was clasped harmlessly in one hand, dangling by his side, pointed at nothing. It looked as though he didn't have his finger on the trigger. Small comfort. She finally had her gun on her lap. *That feels better.*

33

"**H**owdy," Charlie said as he walked through the door of Lucky's Hardware, the tinkling of the bell over his head announcing his entrance.

Charlie was greeted with a friendly "Hi-ya," from the only other person in the store, a sixty-something gentleman high up on a ladder fussing with some inventory. He was wearing the de rigueur country outfit of work boots, jeans, plaid flannel shirt and baseball cap.

"A little dangerous 'round here isn't it?" Charlie asked as he watched the man make his way down the ladder.

"Well, I'm not as young as I used to be, that's for sure, but I get up and down okay."

"I meant your cap," Charlie said, indicating it with a twitch of his head and eyes toward the top of Lucky's head. "Being a Boston fan in these parts could mean your life, or at least a limb. No?"

"You'd be surprised how many we are. Makes for some lively conversations. I've seen some feathers ruffled but nobody's ever pulled a gun," he chuckled.

"My name's Lucky," he said extending his hand to Charlie. "Can I help ya find somethin'?"

"Nah, thanks, I'll just have a look around ... I'm Charlie," he said, shaking Lucky's hand. "I've a bit of an addiction to hardware stores and bookstores. I love browsing both. Hope you don't mind."

"'Course not, be my guest. As addictions go it's not a bad one to have."

"Yeah, I'm rather fond of it. Is there a bookstore in town?"

"Just a block away," Lucky indicated with a slight nod of his head. "She doesn't open till eleven ... but she'll stay open late if there's customers."

"Not a Barnes and Noble, I bet."

"Nope, this one's been here far as I can remember. But rumor has it that there's a new mall comin' on Route Seventeen. That'll kill lot a business in this town. Hope for Dottie's sake she survives me. I'm 'bout ready to lock the door and kick back. Though I can't say I won't miss this place. And chattin' with folks."

"You get mostly local trade I imagine?"

"Yeah, homeowners, contractors and such ... but I won't be able to compete with the new Home Depot that's comin', even with the new housewares section I added last year. Just as well ... soon as that's built I can plant my butt up at the diner and catch up on the local happenings." Lucky leaned on the counter, rolling a toothpick between his teeth.

"You get many out-of-towners like me in here?"

"A few ... any strangers I get are usually lookin' for batteries, campin' equipment, not nuts and bolts like the locals. Sometimes people on their way up to the Zennie place come in for a flashlight or some other small light for their room."

"They tell you they're on their way up there?"

"Yeah, most people like to talk ... they're okay, most of them. Are you with them?"

"Sort of. My niece is up there now, I came up to help."

"We all heard some of what's been going on. Some in town figured it was only a matter of time but ... I don't hold to that view. It's awful but I guess there are crazies everywhere."

"You ever been to the monastery, Lucky?"

"Yeah, once. A good number of years ago they had an open house sort of thing. They do it every once in a while, but I only been the one time. They invite the locals up for a meal and a talk—for us to get to know them I guess. Bunch of us went up just for the hell of it—wanted to check it out, thought there was some outrageous cult thing going on, which made all of us a little nervous, 'specially for our kids—and who would've figured? We had a good time. The whole thing was foreign and screwball, but not dangerous. That head guy was a hoot. Had us all laughin', made us feel comfortable. Since then the town's been happy to have them as neighbors. No one can figure who would want to kill them."

"You never went back?"

"You mean to the monastery?"

"Yeah."

"Nah. Wasn't my thing. One trip satisfied my curiosity. Don't think anyone from town has been up there more than once. Most of the people who go there come from other parts. Lots of foreigners and people from the city. You from the city, Charlie?"

"Not anymore. Was once."

The doorbell chimed, a customer came in. Charlie strolled around the store with Lucky's gentle chatter as background music and the shelves of hardware a balm to his mind. He loved seeing and touching all the various small shiny metal shapes used to anchor down and paste together the mosaic of human industry. Charlie walked the aisles for forty-five minutes, picking up shiny objects, feeling the texture and shape of hard metal in his palm, then putting each one back down, moving on, slowly, thinking with his hands, his eyes, his feet. He picked up a flashlight for his car and a new spade for his garden. He didn't need either but Charlie always paid for the privilege of spending time in a church of hardware.

As Lucky was ringing him up, Charlie said, "Have you noticed anybody over the past week or two, probably a stranger, but maybe not, in here buying an odd assortment of things? Anything out of the ordinary spring to mind?"

"Hmmm, let me think on that a minute. Any clues of what the odd assortment might've been?"

"How about a saw? You sell any of those this week?"

"Now that you mention it—though I can't imagine it has anything to do with anything— there was a fellow in here early this week who bought a saw ... and four plastic drop cloths, a turkey baster, a roasting pan, a Colman stove, a saucepan and a few other odds and ends. I remember what everyone buys. It was weird only because he was definitely not the camping type—and I'd never seen him before so I don't think he lives 'round here. I tried chattin' him up but he wasn't interested. I thought he might be a Zennie and that sorta fit, but then again it didn't."

"How do you mean?"

"Well, most of those types are friendly sorts, 'specially if they come by after spendin' some time up there. But this guy didn't look happy, looked like he hadn't talked to anyone in a while, he was sorta spaced out. And people who go up the mountain aren't space cadets. They're an odd bunch, that's for sure, quirky and eccentric, but not spacey. Believe you me, I know spaced out when it's in front of me."

"I know what you mean. Have you seen this guy before or since?"

"Nope, just the once. Only thing he asked was what material the saw would cut through—wouldn't say what he wanted to cut, just wanted the strongest hand saw I had. Didn't think much about it then, still don't, but that's about it," Lucky said as he put a fresh toothpick into his mouth.

Lucky gave Charlie a decent description of this customer. Charlie used the store phone to call up to the monastery. He spoke with Kluny, who immediately sent a sketch artist over to Lucky's. But Charlie had no high hopes about how useful that would be. According to Lucky this character hid behind dark glasses and long hair that appeared to be a wig. Most likely he was the guy they hunted but maybe he wasn't as spaced out as Lucky had thought and maybe he had other disguises as well. About all that would be useful from the description was he was in his forties, average height, average build, with a bit of a potbelly.

Charlie exchanged cards and handshakes with Lucky and continued nosing around town.

***

Wolfe, Kluny and a handful of state and local cops were spending the day calling Roshi's ex-students, especially those who were around in San Francisco when the sangha split asunder. There were no clear records of who followed Enji and who renounced Roshi altogether. They had two days before the denouement on Sunday. It was going to take a miraculous stroke of luck to get to the right person, who knew the perfect amount of information that would lead them to the true suspect. Luck sometimes figured into police work but miracles were rare and maybe didn't even exist in Buddhist lore. So Kluny prayed, Wolfe worried, and they both dialed and asked questions.

34

Just as Feeb guy started walking toward her side of the car—*at least his weapon isn't pointed at me*—Muin popped his head out of the door of the cabin.

Shit. Are they in this together? Is the Feeb actually Enji? Did anyone ever ask for his ID? Is he FBI? Wolfe said he met him, but Kluny never did. Wolfe wouldn't let such a thing slip past him, would he?... maybe he never asked for an ID, maybe Roshi saying it was enough.

"You can come out now," the Feeb guy said.

"Alex, what the hell are you doing here?" Muin said, as he walked rapidly towards her.

"You don't need that thing," Feeb guy said, indicating her gun. He holstered his. "I wasn't sure who you were at first. Can't be too careful."

Alex held on to her gun. She was freezing.

"Muin, what the hell is going on? Why are you here? Did something happen? What did I miss?"

"It's okay, Alex, let's go inside, we'll tell you all about it," Muin said.

"I have to make a phone call. Is there cell service here?"

"Nah, you can use the land line inside," Feeb guy said.

"Whose house is this?"

"Mine."

"And who are you?"

"Agent Hawkes, FBI." He extended his hand to Alex. "I've been working with Roshi ..."

"Yeah, yeah, the Feeb guy. You got an ID?"

"Well, aren't you thorough, Miss—"

"Detective Sullivan."

"No kidding?" he said, his eyes smiling, the lines at the edges showing that he did that a lot.

"Yeah, no kidding. And if you really were the Feeb guy you'd already know that, wouldn't you?" *And if I were a guy, that comment would never pass his lips. Damn.*

"Yes, well, I wasn't focusing on you. Here" —Agent Hawkes reached into his back pocket, pulled out his ID and held it out to her —"you got the Guy part of my name right."

Agent Guy Hawkes. It looked legit. She was freezing and starting to quiver.

"What sort of name is Guy?"

"Maybe I'll tell you about it some day."

Did he just wink at me? Is he flirting or patronizing me?

Alex ignored him and walked to the back of her car for her sweats. Her body was covered in goose bumps and she was shivering, from the cold, from hunger or anger or the subtle flirtation that just happened. Or from all of it.

Guy and Muin turned their backs to her and moved toward the house as she stepped into her warm clothing. She took a few moments to collect herself, took a deep breath and ran her hands swiftly over her arms and legs to warm up and control the trembling. Then she followed them inside, gun in tow.

***

After trying Uncle Charlie's cell phone to no avail, Alex finally reached him on the coffee shop phone.

"I'm with Muin and the FBI guy I told you about, in a cabin about five miles out of town," Alex said. "Okay if we meet up a bit later? I want to talk to Muin for a bit and see what I missed, why he's here."

"Sure thing. Folks round here seem happy to talk to me, so I'll keep at it. Spoke to a fella in a hardware store about a suspicious character who'd bought a bunch of weird stuff including a saw. Sketch artist is with him now, so maybe something will come of that."

"Good news! Let's talk again in a few hours, okay?"

"Yup, till then ..."

Alex was starving and hoped the guy named Guy had some food in the house. *What sort of name is Guy, anyway? Why do I even care?* She dialed the monastery and got Kluny on the phone.

After telling him about where she was, she said, "And I've got Zenji's notebooks with me. I'll spend some time looking through them down here this afternoon. Maybe something will reveal itself."

When she hung up, she turned to Muin and Guy. "Okay, now fill me in, what happened?"

Guy started to speak.

"I'd like to hear Muin's version first if that's okay with you."

"Suit yourself, but he doesn't know much."

"Muin?"

"All's I know is that Roshi got a letter today that threatened my life, and they all wanted me as far away from the monastery as possible since they figured I was next if it comes to that," Muin said.

"Shit, is this true?" Alex said to Guy.

"'Fraid so."

"So, what, Alex, you don't believe me? You got to ask this guy who you don't even know just because he has a badge and gun?"

"No, of course I believe you, sorry Muin. He just said you don't know much so I guess I knee-jerked trusted the badge. I'm sorry."

"S'okay. We're all on edge. Anyway, Agent Hawkes offered to let me stay here in his cabin till whoever it is that's on a rampage is stopped."

"Muin, when did you learn about all the blackmailing?"

"This week. Seems it's been going on for some time now, but I only found out this week. I can't believe Roshi kept it from me."

"I insisted on that," Guy said. "The fewer who knew, the better. That's my philosophy. Which is why we didn't tell you guys" — indicating Alex —"right away."

"Still, I see everything that goes on up there. I can't believe I missed this," Muin said. "Why didn't he tell me before he called you, Agent Hawkes? I don't get it. Are you sure the letters are legitimate? I always open Roshi's mail, and never saw anything close to threatening, let alone blackmail."

Alex heard hurt, disappointment and anger in Muin's voice. Her Zen brain wanted to comfort him, her inner cop wouldn't allow it just yet.

"It seems they weren't posted," Hawkes said. "They were slipped under Roshi's door during the night. Either someone snuck in and delivered them, or someone already inside the joint is responsible."

"I don't get it. I just don't get it. Who the hell could be doing this?" Muin sat with his head in his hands.

"Tell me about Enji," Alex said. She wanted to give Muin some space, but knew it was necessary to press on. "What's he like? Why didn't you like him?"

"He was such an egomaniac. A real character. Women loved him and guys, too, once they got over their envy. He oozed charm. I don't know, maybe it was my Bronx upbringing, but I never trusted him— he was too slick for my taste—so I kept my distance. Maybe I didn't like his closeness to Roshi."

"Why would Roshi start up with him again?"

"From all accounts—I did some calling around when Enji resurfaced—he has really cleaned up his act. And Roshi is big on forgiving past sins if there is true atonement, so he let him back in. But I don't trust him. Not yet anyway."

"Do you think he could be behind all of this?"

"I wouldn't doubt it." Muin closed his eyes and paused. Alex was getting more and more irritated. If he'd been a stranger she'd be all over him. She gave Muin a moment more. Guy was letting her take the lead. *Big of him.*

"Who else would want Enji to succeed Roshi?" Alex pressed on.

"He could've put Zenji and Kosen up to something—maybe they slipped those letters under Roshi's door ... maybe they were from Enji ... maybe Enji got rid of both of them after he had no more use for them. That would be just like him."

"What do you mean by that?" Alex asked. "I want you to try to be objective here, Muin. I know it's hard being so close, but we need to know about Enji, not how you felt or feel, but what was he really like? Is he capable of killing?"

"Before this week I never thought a monk would kill. Truth be told, I was privately glad when Enji and Roshi split up and he was out of our lives. He could get anyone to do anything, he was that persuasive. He even had Roshi conned for a while."

"That's all good information, Muin, but is he capable of killing his students? Would he want Roshi dead?"

"Oh my god!" Muin sat bolt upright. "I just realized that there's a meeting set up with Roshi and Enji on Saturday ... that's tomorrow! He's planning on arriving early. We can't let that happen now, can we?" Muin's devotion to Roshi resurfaced, his sense of betrayal gone.

Agent Hawkes and Alex locked eyes and silently communicated their agreement. They understood each other with barely a look. She was no longer a praying girl, but she prayed that they'd get to the answer before anyone else was killed.

"I'll call Wolfe, have him intercept and isolate Enji soon as he arrives up there. Make sure he gets nowhere near Roshi," Alex said.

"Maybe Enji's arrival will bring our guy out into the open if it's not Enji himself doing all the bad," Hawkes said. "If blackmailer and killer are one and the same, and that scenario seems more and more likely ... okay, maybe I was wrong about the connection, so shoot me," he said looking directly at Alex. "But whoever our blackmailer is, he's desperate to have Enji succeed Roshi—so he has some connection to Enji, past, present or future."

"Kluny hasn't been able to reach Enji. Maybe he's already in the area. This is not getting any better. We're not any closer to an answer than we were four days ago," Alex said. "You got a copy of the latest note?"

"Yeah, give me a minute." Guy went in the back of the house to another room. Alex and Muin waited in silence. There was nothing to say. They were both stunned and depressed. Alex's body ached, she needed to stretch her muscles. She needed to eat something.

"Here it is." Guy handed her a copy of the note.

> *You have two days. More time than you deserve.*
> *Maybe I'll take your precious little James*
> *away—maybe that will convince you that I'm*

serious. And maybe I'll keep him around—he's the only other one who knows about your b b b— maybe if he turns on you, you'll do the right thing. Tick tock. Tick tock. I'm not kidding. This is not a joke. This is not a test. This is not a koan. This is YOUR LIFE!

***

With Alex and Muin down mountain, it fell to Wolfe to brief Roshi on what was and wasn't going on. Roshi dropped by the library, said he'd check in every couple of hours. "If something happens please feel free to knock on my door, Detective, to keep me informed," Roshi said.

"You must consider leaving here," Wolfe said. "I'm doing my best to keep you all safe but it will be easier for all of us if we move everyone out."

"I appreciate your position on this as officer of law, Detective. And you are all welcome to leave. I give permission for my students to go. But I will stay. I cannot leave. I must see this through. Whoever is doing this, I must face. I can only think of him as an avatar of Buddha. If his actions have anything at all to do with something I have said or done in the past, I cannot escape that."

Wolfe had no idea what the fuck avatar of Buddha meant. He didn't want to get into that. "You do know that whoever is doing this could be after you. They might want to kill you."

Roshi looked at Wolfe with a soft, gentle smile and said nothing.

Wolfe broke the uncomfortable silence. "Sorry to be so blunt Roshi but the facts are the facts." Wolfe didn't think Roshi looked upset but he figured he must be. Anyone would be scared at the prospect of his own demise by the hand of a cold-blooded killer.

"If I am meant to die on Sunday, so be it. That would be my karma, I am prepared for that. But I don't think my time is quite yet." Roshi spoke as if to himself.

Wolfe didn't get it. But there was no doubting Roshi's sincerity.

"So many people are coming from so far away," Roshi added. "I would like not to cancel our event, the sangha will want to process and honor the three who have died. Perhaps, with so many people here it will be more difficult for our troubled killer to succeed further. As policeman do you agree?"

"It's possible. And perhaps letting things go as planned will draw this person out into the open, whoever he is. We'll have people undercover, dressed as your students, and many uniforms patrolling."

"Thank you, Detective Wolfe, for all you've done. Now I must go. There is much to do before Sunday. With Muin gone I am very busy." Roshi got up and bowed to Wolfe, who was tongue-tied. As much as Wolfe liked being in charge, telling others what to do and when, this gesture from Roshi had him feeling awkward and unsure of himself.

Roshi left. Wolfe was glad to be alone for a few minutes. As a cop, Wolfe faced the prospect of his death sometimes on a daily basis, but he knew he wasn't even close to being at peace with the idea. He wondered if he ever would be and then batted that thought away and got down to work.

Wolfe took precautions and arranged to have some undercover cops there on Saturday and Sunday to mingle with the invited guests. He didn't like this scenario, but he was as prepared as any officer of the peace could be. Now they waited.

35

Waiting, waiting, waiting ... thrillers and TV cop shows never show this part of the life of catching bad guys. Fuck! And I suck at it. Why I started sitting, but even that is about waiting. For fucking what? The answer? Resolution? Happiness? Ha! To die, maybe. Maybe we're all just biding our time waiting to die. Plus, I always do something stupid when I'm waiting.

Alex sat on the couch looking through Zenji's notebooks, trying not to look at Guy's back as he stood at the sink cleaning up after lunch. Trying not to notice his muscles through the white of his T-shirt and the shape of his ass in his tight black jeans. She adjusted her position so that he was off to her left and she'd have to make a special effort to look at him. Muin was on the floor behind the couch doing zazen. They were all waiting.

Up mountain Wolfe and his gang were waiting for tomorrow when Enji and others would begin to arrive, along with more cops from across the state. Other than Agent Hawkes, the FBI wasn't involved yet. Seemed more like a family matter than a serial killer or terrorist on the loose. And there was no safe house safe enough to keep family members away from family members who wanted to kill. Eventually they'd find them. And no one could force Roshi to leave his home. So they were staying and serving and protecting as best they knew how.

Roshi was a Buddhist and Buddhists would just as soon immolate themselves if it would put an end to violence. If Roshi were the target, he was choosing to stay put and face his enemy. And wait. *Roshi is about the only one I know who's the master of waiting. And maybe Muin. Who the fuck knows? Maybe all monks. Maybe everyone but me is good at this. Everyone but most cops I know, that is, who are such adrenaline junkies that they all suck at it too. And put me in the same waiting room with a sexy adrenaline junkie, I lose all sense of what is reasonable. Thank god Muin is here to keep me from making a fool of myself.*

Alex's attention was drawn to Guy as he moved over to the door and let a cat in. *Shit, just what I need.*

People either loved cats or they didn't. If it hadn't been for Uncle Charlie's love affair with them she'd definitely sit squarely on the 'didn't' side. Remaining neutral, she tolerated and was a magnet for them. Sure enough, when the cat finished eating, it immediately came over to Alex, rubbed against her leg, jumped up onto her lap and stuck its tail in her face. It made its point and then moved on.

She watched as the cat stretched and gracefully contorted its body before circling into a nap position on what looked like its normal resting place—a large Indian print cushion on the floor beside the couch.

The phone rang and startled her upright. A question immediately popped into her brain. *How did the killer—if he were from Enji's camp—know about Muin's cat in Kido's cabin? How did he know the cabin even existed?*

The call was for her.

"Any chance I can talk you into coming up here to help make phone calls?" Kluny asked. "We got our hands full and could sure use another body."

"Much as I'd like to help, I really don't want to leave Muin. I know Agent Hawkes is capable of protecting him, but two guns are always better than one and if I leave and something happens to Muin I'd never forgive myself."

She was convinced that the clue to the killer's identity lay inside Muin's brain, even if he didn't think so. It was time to ask him some tough questions. She took advantage of Muin in meditation to talk to Guy about their next step—she wanted him as an ally without putting Muin on the defensive. Without disturbing Muin she asked Guy to meet with her in the bedroom—she was all business.

***

"I think Muin knows who's doing this—I think it's locked up somewhere in his brain and his past." Alex didn't make nice and beat around the bush. "I want to know what you know." She wasn't beyond pleading. "Please. Look, this is just another case for you, but I know these people, they're like family. Tell me what you know. Maybe together we can get to the answer quicker. We haven't much time." Alex sat on the edge of the bed.

"You first," Guy said. He leaned casually against the doorframe as if they'd been friends for years, his muscular forearms crossed over his chest. He turned his copper-flecked, intense hazel eyes on her, momentarily distracting her. *I am sure glad Muin's in the other room.*

"Fine." Alex wanted to get up and pace so as not to have to just look up at him, but there wasn't enough space to walk around without getting too close to him. "The reference to Muin as James in the last note from the blackmailer makes me think that it goes way back to his pre-monk days. Maybe even to the Bronx. He never talks much about that time, but I know he was a tough street kid—maybe even involved in a gang, in drugs, I don't know. Maybe he did some things that are just now coming back to haunt him.

"I never thought much about the tattoo he's got on his left shoulder, but maybe with your resources you could check that out—see if it leads to someone. If it's not the Bronx, then it's San Francisco and his druggy college days. I only know the when, we need to get to the why and the who. We need to know more about the Roshi-Enji split, who else was involved, Muin's role in that. I don't think he was being totally forthcoming with us earlier. There are too many questions left unanswered. I know you're FBI and I have no authority here, but will you work with me on this?"

"Okay, I'll tell you what I know, but it may not help—all we've run into on this one is dead end after dead end. Roshi didn't want to involve Muin when the letters first started. And he only agreed to let Muin know the barest details once his name was brought into it. Roshi is protective of Muin and Muin is loyal to Roshi—maybe both to a fault.

"Anyway, we checked out Muin's New York past—there's nothing there. It was a strong lead for a while since Enji, aka Patrick Ryan, is related to one of the guys Muin used to run with. But that led nowhere—just a weird coincidence I guess."

"You believe in coincidences?"

"Not usually ... but we looked at that connection from every angle and got nowhere.

"Enji's drug dealing history was much juicier—but that was small time really and not such a big deal considering the counter culture back then. Roshi made more out of it than there was—I figured it was his religiousness getting in the way so I let it go.

"And Kosen and Zenji being students of Enji and then coming to Roshi ... at first, that too seemed like a coincidence."

"Hell, I don't believe in coincidences, and with them we now know it wasn't."

"What do you mean?"

"Roshi didn't tell you about Enji sending Zenji and then Kosen to spy on Roshi?"

"No, goddamn it ... what else ... I was convinced that it was normal Zen movement, musical chairs in a spiritual sense," said Guy with a grin, smile lines perking up all over his face.

"But they were both calculated moves and Roshi knew about them at some point at least," Alex said.

"Damn, it seems that people come and go from these communities all the time for no obvious reason ... no offense meant."

"No offense taken, it happens here with Roshi, too. People move on, get bored or tired or restless and stop their practice—it's not an easy thing to maintain and it certainly isn't for everyone. I'm actually surprised that I'm still involved—I'm so commitment phobic." Alex winced internally. *Do I really want him to know this about me? Is it even true anymore?*

"Without a sacred vow in your life, your life is worth shit." *Damn Kido.*

"Anyway, with most of the students who leave," Alex said, "there are usually no hard feelings on either side—it's just the natural flow of things—or so Roshi says. I can understand why you overlooked this 'coincidence.'" She made a gesture of quotes in the air. *That's not very nice, but fuck it ...*

"We gotta talk to Muin again. It's our only chance. Will you help?" she asked, having no clue how they'd get what they needed from her ex-lover-monk.

"We can try, but I'm doubtful we'll get what we need," Guy said, saying out loud what Alex feared but didn't want to say.

Good of him to let my jab go by without comment.

"The way I see it, we have no other options," Alex said. "Just tell me, are you game? Or should I do it without you?"

"I'm in, I guess."

"Do you want to be good cop or bad cop?"

"Bad, of course."

"Yeah, that would be my choice if I had one, but I don't think that would work here," Alex said as she slapped her thighs and rose to her feet off the edge of the bed. "Okay then, let's do it."

***

"Sorry we had to interrupt your zazen," Alex said, once they were all sitting around the table.

"It's all right, my head's such a mess I couldn't find any stillness anyway. I just keep going over it and can't make any sense out of anything," Muin said.

"I know you've thought and thought about this, but you have to keep trying. We're convinced you know who's doing this."

"But I don't, Al, I really don't."

"Maybe it's not at the front of your brain but it's in there somewhere, I'm sure of it. You've been with Roshi longer than anyone and you've been the closest to him for a long time. Whoever is doing this has probably crossed your path many times."

"Hell," interrupted Agent Hawkes, now the stern interrogator, all smile lines hidden, "he was probably your best friend once upon a time. Who are you protecting? You have to tell us now!"

"I don't know anything ... for all I know it could be Roshi," Muin said with exasperation.

"What do you mean, what's he done? Go with that idea, Muin. Don't shake it off," Alex said. "I'm beginning to wonder about him myself."

"I really don't mean it, but maybe he wrote those letters himself, maybe I don't know as much about him as I think I do. I can't believe he kept those letters secret from me."

"Oh, boo hoo. Get over that and move on," Hawkes said. "If you even think he might be capable of writing the letters you must know something. What is it?"

"Look, it was a long time ago and my memory is very vague. My mind wasn't too clear back then ... I smoked a lot of dope."

Agent Hawkes raised a judgmental eyebrow and caught Alex's eye, but said nothing.

"I can't believe I'm going to tell you this. I don't know if it has anything to do with anything, but it has haunted me this week, and with that latest note and the reference to b-b-b I'm more worried than ever. But please, you must promise, if it has nothing to do with current events you won't spread it around."

"Get on with it already," Hawkes said, keeping up the bad cop role.

"When I was nineteen, I was going to college in San Francisco, smoking lots of pot, dropping acid here and there. Like most people my age back then, I was a lost soul. I started going to Roshi's zendo on Thursday nights when he gave talks. One day—it was a Wednesday I think, it was late, maybe midnight—I walked by the zendo and saw Roshi and this tough guy, Tommy, doing something very suspicious. Like I said, I was stoned, it was dark, and it was a long time ago."

"We know, we know ... just spit it out." Hawkes took the words right out of Alex's mouth.

"They were stuffing a huge black bag into Tommy's Volkswagen bus." Muin stopped.

"And? What was in the bag?"

"I don't know."

"Shit. You're right, it's nothing. This is not helpful," Hawkes said.

"There's something else, isn't there, Muin?" Alex said softly.

"Yes."

"Please tell us."

"I think there was blood all over Roshi ..."

"You think?" Hawkes asked.

"Well, it looked like blood, it was red, I thought it was blood, but I was across the street and when I got closer I was only able to see Roshi's back. The next day everything was normal, so I just forgot about it," Muin cast his eyes to the floor and mumbled to himself. "All these years ... maybe Roshi isn't what he seems ... I can't believe this ..." He looked back up at Alex. "Do you think he's involved in all this? Do you think that could have been blood?"

"One way or the other he's involved," Hawkes said.

"Yes, but let's reserve judgment till we talk to Roshi again. There could be an innocent explanation," Alex said.

"With Tommy involved I doubt it was innocent," Muin said. "And Tommy's son, Kevin, who was just ten at the time, must have seen it, too. He used to refer to the bloody bodybag that his father and Roshi got rid of. I always told him he was seeing things, but maybe he saw me there that night and knew all along that I, too, had seen it."

"He's the one that left Roshi and went with Enji, right?"

"Yeah, Gigen's his dharma name. But I can't believe he'd do anything like what's been done. Do you have to tell Roshi who you heard this from?"

"Maybe not, we'll have to wing it. We'll try to keep your name out of it if we can," Alex knew that would be impossible, but reassuring him came automatically to her lips.

"Thanks. This whole thing sucks. I really wish it would all get back to normal. But things won't ever be the same, will they? Not after all the killing and mistrust."

"Maybe not ... maybe not," Alex said. She too wanted normalcy to return, but she feared that Roshi and the monastery—her haven—would forever be tainted.

Alex called Kluny to see if he'd been in touch with Enji yet. No such luck. And Gigen was probably with him. More than ever they needed to locate both of them.

36

"We best get our asses back up there first thing tomorrow to interview his highness and greet Enji when he arrives," Guy said, waving his fork around as he spoke. They were at dinner at one of Guy's favorite restaurants in the area. Charlie had met Alex, Guy, and Muin there and had been briefed on everything they knew and didn't know.

"Maybe they're in it together," Guy continued. "Maybe Roshi wanted Muin out of the way because he wanted Muin out of the way, pure and simple, and couldn't bring himself to kill him … maybe Roshi and Enji are squabbling over territory and who's the best Zen Master? Maybe we should have the two of them duke it out, winner take all."

Alex couldn't help herself, she laughed out loud. "That is ridiculous, you know."

"Yeah, well, it's just a theory."

Charlie steered the conversation off Roshi and back through time into Muin's memory. "I don't want to let Roshi off the hook just yet, but if he is involved he's not alone. So I'd like to try to tap into Muin's memory a bit and see if someone other than Roshi, Enji or Gigen shows up as a possible suspect."

So they went back into time, deeper and deeper into Muin's history, his Bronx upbringing, his hippie California days, his transformation into the monk world. Muin talked about those who followed Enji, and one-by-one they were eliminated as suspects for various reasons: Dead, married and living in Australia, corporate executive in Chicago, no longer practicing ... Muin seemed to know where all the bodies were, dead and alive, the entire Zen community in America being rather small, and the underground Zen gossip mill being what it was.

"If Tommy were still alive I'd think it was him, right away," Muin said. He was such a mean dude ... why, I thought that maybe it was a body all those years ago when I saw him and Roshi with the bag ... and the blood."

Everyone stopped chewing their food and thought about this.

Agent Hawkes broke the silence. "I can't wait to confront Roshi about this ..."

"Yeah, if Wolfe will even let you near him now," Alex's teasing tone slipped out. Muin and Charlie hadn't picked up on it, but a twitch at the corner of Guy's mouth told her he'd caught it and liked it. *Damn it!*

"Oh, he'll let me near him, you can bet on that," Guy said, directing his words and eyes across the table straight into Alex as if Muin and Uncle Charlie weren't there.

"I'm just saying," Alex said, back to her this-is-business-cop voice but holding Guy's gaze. "I've just spent a few short days with Wolfe, and he's like a dog with a bone here, doesn't like to share. His case and all. Still ... anyway ..." Alex shrugged and averted her eyes from Guy's penetrating stare. It was getting dangerously intimate. *Another time, another place, maybe. Not with Muin and Uncle C sitting here, no way.*

"And let's not forget about the stranger that showed up in town," Charlie said. "I brought a copy of the sketch that was made today." He passed it around. "Anyone recognize him?"

"Muin, what is it?" Alex said, as she reached over and took his hand. "Are you okay? Do you know this guy?"

"If I didn't know better, I'd say it was Tommy ... it sure looks like him, but he's dead and buried ... Oh my god!" Muin covered his mouth with his hand. "Maybe it's Gigen? He looked a lot like his father when he was a kid."

"When was the last time you saw him?" Charlie asked.

"I haven't seen or spoken to him in thirty years, since he left for LA with Enji."

"How old was he then?" Charlie asked.

"About seventeen, I think."

"Which would put him in his late forties today, which would match this guy." Charlie nodded to the police sketch.

"I can't believe it. He was so young and lost, his father a criminal, in and out of jail, his mother dead. Roshi took him under his wing, let him live with him when Tommy was incarcerated. His relationship with Roshi was sort of a love/hate one. And Roshi had no idea how to take care of a mixed-up, angry American boy, but he did his best."

No one wanted to interrupt Muin, he was talking as if he were in a trance, conjuring up the past.

"Kevin attached himself to Enji and left when he did. By then he had been given the dharma name of Gigen. The last I knew, he was Enji's assistant, doing for him what I do for Roshi ..."

"Look again at the sketch. Do you really think it's him?" Alex asked.

"Well, like I said, I haven't seen him in a long time, but this does resemble Tommy ..."

"Do you know if he and Roshi stayed in touch?"

"A week ago I would have said no. But today, I haven't a clue. Roshi sent him birthday cards and such, but I never saw a card or letter come back from him. Who knows, maybe Roshi sent him down with Enji as a spy and they were in secret contact. At this point I'd believe anything ..."

After a pained pause, Muin continued. "Gigen didn't come to his father's funeral, but he was informed about it. His anger was enormous and some of that transferred to Roshi. I would also say the love was just as strong, though. He was a very confused and angry kid. I identified a lot with him. I felt sorry for him."

***

There was cell phone reception at the restaurant, so when they got to dessert Alex took advantage of it to alert the gang at the monastery about their suspicions. Kluny took the call, Wolfe was out having a smoke.

Their plan was to stay down mountain for the night, go up first thing in the morning to interview Roshi and to be there when Enji arrived, hopefully with Gigen in tow. Kluny put Alex on hold while he retrieved the roster of expected guests with their estimated arrival times so they'd know how early to come up. They were in a relatively private alcove in the restaurant so she put the phone in the middle of the table on speaker so all could hear.

"Gigen's name isn't on the guest list," Kluny said.

"Are you sure? Who's coming with Enji ... Patrick Ryan?"

"Just a sec ... let's see ... Ro ...ku ... ju." Kluny stumbled over the foreign name. "Margaret Ryan."

"Enji's wife?"

"I have no idea. Maybe it's his sister."

"Yeah, right. From what Muin's told me about this guy, I doubt it," Alex said, smiling across the table at Muin. "And you're sure Kevin Bawlder or Gigen isn't on the list?"

"I'm sure."

"Oh my god," Alex said. "I just made the connection ... Gigen must be KGB."

"What? Who?"

"KGB ... the person, not the organization. In Zenji's notebooks there are many references to a KGB. I thought it was a nickname for some guy in Enji's zendo who drove people away—Zenji and Kosen included—because he would spy on people ... KGB, get it?"

"Yeah ... but spy how? Did Zenji spell that out?" Kluny said.

"It seems that KGB or Gigen would go through people's mail, snoop around their rooms, read their private notebooks, etc. He'd tell Enji if they had anything illicit in their possession, drugs, alcohol, that sort of thing. Guess he wanted to weed out those he didn't get along with, which if we can believe Zenji, was just about everyone."

"That's probably why Zenji kept his notebooks under his mattress ... old habit."

Alex looked at Muin with a 'did you know about this?' on her face. He raised his eyebrows and shook his head.

"Enji went along with the spying?" Charlie asked.

"Hard to say from Zenji's scribbling. But Zenji sure as hell hated this KGB guy—one reason he agreed to come to Roshi. It must be this Gigen character—it can't be a coincidence." Alex looked into Guy's hazel brown eyes. He met her gaze and silently agreed.

"It must be. ... Hey, Kluny, Charlie here, we spoke earlier."

"Right, hey Charlie."

"If he's the one the hardware guy saw and if he's planning to make an appearance tomorrow or Sunday with everyone else there, you can be sure he'll be disguised and is probably on the list under a different name ... if he's on the list at all."

"So, what're we gonna do, round up all the forty-plus-year-old guys with pot bellies and interrogate them?" asked Wolfe, who was back. Alex could almost smell the stink of tobacco on his breath.

"Right, that's likely to be most of the people coming." Alex laughed. "No, someone who knows Gigen will have to scan the crowd. We've got the sketch, but eyes who know him will be best as he's likely to be in some sort of disguise. With Kosen and Zenji dead that leaves Muin, Roshi and Enji, three people who will know what Gigen looks like, since they all knew Tommy."

"We can't trust Enji or even Roshi yet, not till we have a conversation with him ... so it'll have to fall to Muin," Alex said, staring across the table at Muin, wondering if he'd be up to pointing the finger at his old friend.

"I agree," Wolfe said. "I'll brief Roshi, but will wait for you to arrive to interrogate him. When will you guys be up here?"

"Bright and early." There was agreement on this around the table.

"What time is Enji expected?" Charlie piped in.

"Ten a.m. He has a meeting with Roshi at ten-thirty. He's first on the list. Many won't be arriving till late afternoon. Most are coming early Sunday morning," Kluny said.

"We'll call when we're on our way," Alex said.

"One other thing ..." They could hear Wolfe and Kluny talking to each other in the background but couldn't make out what they were saying. Kluny continued, "Our guys found a place deep in the woods, up past the northeast corner of the lake, it probably served as this guy's hideout, hangout, lair, whatever. Anyways, we found some of the stuff that was purchased at the hardware store. We decided not to touch anything, wait for him to show up. We've got a couple guys assigned to keep watch."

"Shit," Alex said, as soon as they hung up.

"What? What is it?" Guy asked.

"Muin hasn't seen Gigen in thirty years—this won't be easy."

"You're right, but there's no other choice at this point," Guy said. "Are you up for this Muin?"

"I guess so."

***

By the end of the day on Friday, Roshi and his students were carrying on much the same as the week before, embodying a twist on the old Zen aphorism: "When it's cold, shiver, when it's hot, sweat."

Wolfe was holding down the fort on the monastery mountaintop doing what he'd done hundreds of times in the past when a case refused to crack open—pacing, smoking, worrying, trying to figure out the next thing.

The three slain Zen students were being cremated, their families in various stages of claiming them. Kosen's parents were staying at the Roscoe Motor Inn and were to be Roshi's guests for lunch the next day. There was no relative to call about Zenji; he'd be buried on the hillside by the lake where many before him were settled. Sonja's brother was in the air, halfway to Kennedy Airport from his home in Switzerland; he would be taking Sonja's ashes back with him.

Roshi was planning a special service on Sunday to honor the dead, along with Buddha's birthday celebration, which would be a very subdued affair, considering. Human plans were just that, plans ... the law of the universe often laughed at such hubris and interceded with designs of its own.

***

By midnight, Alex was showered and in Guy's bed, in one of his T-shirts. Muin was in the spare bedroom and Guy was on the couch. Charlie had chosen to stay in town. Along with Zenji's notebooks that she'd brought with her that day, she also had a book of koans in bed. She read through the three koans and the commentaries once again, her instinct telling her that they held the clue that would lead them to the killer. Once she closed the book, she also wrote out the three koans from memory to see if anything new arose in her mind from that exercise.

All of this helped to keep her focus on the case and not on the fact that she was sleeping alone one room away from two gorgeous men. But never mind that, priorities being what they were, they had a killer to catch.

In the 'Nansen Cuts the Cat in Two' koan, the monks had to come up with a word to keep Nansen from killing the cat. *Maybe the message is come up with a word and Roshi, or the next victim, won't die. But what and who? And what about the one hand? How does that fit in?* Alex eventually fell into a deep sleep, no closer to a solution than she was four days ago.

37

Alex tossed around under the sheets and tried to dip back into her dream. She had been chasing someone or she was being chased, she couldn't be sure. She thought it was the man they were after. She wanted to see his face. She knew they were close. But was there enough time? It wasn't working. She was wide awake. And exhausted.

Ancient Zen Master Ummon got it all wrong when he said: "Every day is a good day."

This thought was in her head when she sat up. There wouldn't be anything good about this day until they eliminated Roshi as a suspect and found Gigen. It would get worse if he were not the monk killer. She wanted to sit zazen for a while, check out the brain in her belly, see if it agreed with the one above her neck that told her Gigen was their guy, but she knew she wouldn't be able to sit still.

Present circumstances called for action and no Zen Master would be able to convince her otherwise this morning. Even if Dogen or Hakuin or Rinzai could come back from the dead and stand before her, even if ... they wouldn't be able to sway her. No, this morning she was all cop.

She wasted no time getting ready—it wasn't as if she had a wardrobe choice. Chilly enough to don Guy's sweater again (she'd borrowed it to go out to dinner last night) after she removed his T-shirt that she'd slept in, she shivered with the thought that this man was all over her. Bare feet on the cold floor drove this feeling away.

She made haste out to the main room where Muin and Guy were sitting quietly, each clutching a mug of coffee. Alex hurried them along and they were in their cars by 6:30 on their way to rendezvous with Uncle Charlie for breakfast at the Batman Diner on the fringe of town. They took all three cars since the plan was to head straight up to the monastery after eating—it seemed like a terrible waste of energy to Alex, but she looked forward to the drive up alone.

***

Charlie had arrived long before and was sitting in a booth observing the local denizens, a favorite pastime of his. Being that it was Saturday, many of the weekday regulars were still home in bed, but a handful of craggy men sat at the counter, engaged in their daily ritual of drinking coffee and catching up on whatever had happened in the past twenty-four hours. They covered the same territory each day and watched each other grow older.

Charlie guessed that the talk was livelier than usual this Saturday, given the monastery murders and the search for the mysterious hardware store customer. He also knew that these men would be sitting there with each other no matter what was going on around them. Every town had its version of this group.

Charlie was on his second cup of coffee when Alex and her men walked in. They ate quickly and heartily.

Conversation was minimal while they ate, there wasn't much to say, they were all itching to get up mountain and have it over with.

When their plates were cleared, Alex pulled out some papers she had tucked under her sweater. A page with the koans written out, copies of the two blackmail notes, and two pages with her handwriting. She spread them on the table.

"Okay guys, I've been going over and over this and I think I've come up with a viable theory. Are you ready?"

Everyone nodded. The sound of plates being put down and taken away, the tinkle of silverware, and the hum of voices became their background music. Still, they kept their voices low to keep from being heard by any curious eavesdropper. Surely there were a few among them straining to hear whatever this motley crew of strangers—three of whom had a cop vibe, all of whom were connected to the monastery murders—were discussing.

"Okay, first, there was the rakusu left behind when Kosen disappeared. We all thought it was Kosen sending a message that he'd given up the practice and was out of there. But when he showed up dead, that didn't seem right and then when it came up murder we knew that it wasn't.

"I'm sure it was left by the perp, who at this point I'm assuming is Gigen, saying: 'Your Zen means nothing, this is just the beginning.'" She took a big gulp of coffee. The three men waited.

"Then there was the tree branch in Kosen's mouth. At first I thought it meant that whoever killed him was sending a message that he did it to keep Kosen from talking, that maybe Kosen saw Gigen up there and was going to let Roshi know. After reading through the commentaries on the koan last night, I thought of three things—depending on how crazy Gigen really is.

"One, he could have been saying 'let's see who can bring him back to life—if anyone can, he would be the true dharma heir.' Or two, in killing Kosen, Gigen felt that he gave Kosen freedom, saved him from the pain of losing Sonja—I think he knew that she and Zenji were getting together or that he was going to kill her ..."

"Because she saw Gigen, or Kosen told her about him and Gigen knew that?" Charlie asked.

"Something like that, yeah."

"Or three," Alex continued, "maybe it's simpler than all that. Maybe Gigen asked Kosen for help and he said no, which made him fall from the tree, so to speak, and had to die."

Muin chimed in. "Maybe Gigen knew that Roshi had denied Kosen monkhood, maybe he knew how much it meant to him—I'm still not exactly sure what their relationship was—and he wanted to save Kosen from the pain of living with that. It's a little far-fetched, maybe, but koans can be interpreted in so many ways ... "

"... and this perp is crazy." Alex took a deep breath. Charlie and Guy studied the koans on the table as she spoke. Muin knew them by heart.

"Then there was Sonja and 'Nansen's Cat.'" Alex took another deep breath. "At first I, like most of us, thought it was about the East-West business. You know, Roshi and Enji, California, Japan, here ... and their discord. But here, too, I think it's simpler than that—although some of the East-West stuff could be in there, too. I think it's just that Sonja got in the way and Gigen had no choice at that point but to get rid of her, too. And there was no one there to 'give a word of Zen' to stop him."

She looked at Muin, who nodded in agreement.

"Then there's what I hope will be the last one, Zenji and 'One Hand Clapping.' At first I thought Zenji had been the one responsible for Kosen's and Sonja's death and then someone else killed Zenji ... but now I think that Gigen, or whoever it turns out to be, is saying with this one that Zenji would easily figure out who killed Kosen and Sonja, would tell Roshi, and Roshi would believe him, in other words, Zenji would be listened to. Whoever killed him feels that someone hasn't been listening to him. That someone is most likely Roshi."

"That all sounds pretty good," Guy said, "of course I don't get how you got all that from the koans, but hey, it works for me. Muin, what do you think, being a monk and all, about Alex's theories?"

"Well, I think it's all plausible, especially as I remember Gigen and how mixed up he was. Maybe the years have made him worse. From a Zen perspective it all could make sense, too."

"Not bad, Alex my dear, not bad," Kido whispered in her ear. She wondered where he'd gone to, figuring he visited her only while she was on top of the mountain. Here he was again.

"And remember, as you so clearly elucidated ... Zen is first of all practical. And ta-da ..."

Alex imagined him in his black robes, arms spread wide, exclaiming: *"Zen is life."*

Just then, Alex's cell phone vibrated on the tabletop. It was Kluny. She didn't dare put it on speaker for the whole town to hear. She spoke in a whisper, mostly just listening. The rest of the table waited with bated breath.

"Enji called this morning," Kluny said. "He had no idea we were trying to reach him. Just called to ask if the monastery needed anything that he could pick up on his way. We asked if Gigen was with him and he's not. If Gigen was planning on coming he didn't know. Turns out he hasn't seen Gigen for about nine months now. Claims he had to send him away. Tried to get him some help but he refused."

"Help for what?"

"Psychological help. Apparently he was getting stranger by the day and he would hassle and torment other students—so maybe Enji didn't know about the KGB spying. At first, Enji protected and defended him, but then it became clear that he needed help other than what he could offer through Zen. Gigen refused to get help, Enji couldn't force him, so he was asked to leave."

"Where'd he go?"

"Enji claimed not to know. He'll be here soon enough. We'll question him more face-to-face. He could still be a part of this mess."

"I agree," Alex said.

When she hung up, she briefed the boys on the news and then Alex, Muin and Guy left quickly one after the other. Charlie decided not to rush. Maybe there was something more to learn here.

He moved over to the counter and ordered more coffee that he didn't need, but for his pride he would have ordered decaf or tea. He was familiar with this scene, knew to say nothing before being invited to, and simply nodded a greeting to those who looked his way as he took his seat.

He knew that they knew that he was involved in the investigation, as he was keeping company with Agent Hawkes, who'd been unsuccessful in keeping his connection to the FBI a secret from his neighbors.

Charlie also knew that it would only be a matter of time before they engaged him. Had he been a stranger just passing through there would be no exchange of words. But his business there impacted on their routine lives, he was a part of them now whether they liked it or not. They couldn't and wouldn't ignore him. And Charlie's most enduring quality was his patience.

***

Wolfe, Kluny, Hawkes and Alex were waiting in the library for Roshi to arrive. Muin was in the protective hands of one of the cops until the interview with Roshi was done. Wolfe was the designated interrogator. No one else wanted the job, least of all Alex.

Roshi came in escorted by Hokan, who left as soon as Roshi sat down. Officer Johnson stood guard outside the door.

"It seems that a few things have come to light over the past twenty-four hours that raise some questions only you can answer," Wolfe said as he sat on the edge of a table directly in front of Roshi.

"I will be happy to help however I can—as I've said many times." Roshi tried to slide his chair back further away from Wolfe but was stopped by the table behind him. For the first time all week he looked physically uncomfortable. He crossed his legs and hugged his knee, hunching over ever so slightly.

"First, let's get straight to the point. Why did you ask Agent Hawkes here to keep everyone, including Muin, including us, in the dark about the letters you were getting?"

"I did not want to worry Muin—it was my business to deal with alone. And I did not want to distract you from your business here. I am sorry if it caused concern. It was an innocent, mistaken judgment on my part."

"We'll decide about that soon enough ..."

Alex hated watching Roshi being put through this.

"Second, what was your relationship with Tommy and Kevin Bawlder?"

Roshi straightened his posture and relaxed the grip he had on his knee. He uncrossed his legs. He didn't appear the least bit fazed by this question, which meant either that he was expecting it or he was being his usual enigmatic, straight-faced self.

"Ah, poor Gigen. You are referring to Gigen?" He looked at Alex, she nodded. "Is he involved in all of this?" Roshi exhaled loudly and plaintively.

He continued. "Gigen, that is Kevin, is Tommy's son. Tommy is buried up on the hillside here. He got himself into much trouble when I first met him. I tried to help. I thought Gigen would be okay for a while. But after he left with Enji we lost touch. I think he blamed me for some of his father's misdeeds. Is he okay?"

"We'll get to him later. Third thing we need to know about is the bloody bag you helped Tommy get rid of almost forty years ago. Thirty-eight to be exact. In San Francisco. Back of the Volkswagen bus. Ring any bells?"

"Bloody bag? I'm not sure what you mean." Roshi once again crossed his legs. Alex had never seen him so twitchy.

"You and Tommy were seen stuffing something into a Volkswagen bus late at night. You were covered in blood. The bag was big enough for a body. That's what I mean. Now does it ring a bell? What were you up to? Don't say you can't remember. Unless this was common practice for you back then and you were in the habit of stuffing suspicious, bloody bags into the backs of cars ... I'll give you a minute to think."

Roshi sat with his eyes closed, his temple and face knitted in thought. Alex crossed her fingers that he'd come up with an explanation that would take him off the hook he'd been hung on. Even if he didn't seem to know he was a suspect, everyone else in the room was on that page together.

"What went on that night?" Wolfe asked.

Roshi sat another few moments in silence and then opened his eyes.

"The only thing I can think of is bad in its own way, but not so terrible really. Certainly there was no body in the bag.

"I was helping Tommy get rid of some marijuana he was hiding in the apartment. Some friends of his had grown it outside the city, cut it down, stuffed it in some bags and delivered it to him to dry and sell. He couldn't keep it at home—he was on parole—so he tried to hide it in my apartment. I refused to allow it once it was discovered. I helped him, perhaps that decision was not so brilliant on my part, but he told me he would give it back or destroy it. This is the only event I can think of. I don't recall any blood. Only once I helped Tommy with such a chore. I'm sorry. Who did you say saw us doing this? Maybe if I could talk to this person to jog my memory."

Alex didn't know what to think of this answer. *It had been dark, Muin had been stoned, could've imagined the blood, maybe the shirt was just wet or dirty, and from a distance ...*

"It doesn't matter who saw it. You can go now Roshi. And until you hear from us please stay in your rooms."

"Of course, but what does this have to do with what is going on now? I don't understand."

"Just let us do our job. Stay out of the way for now. We'll call you again when we need you." Alex hated the way Wolfe was speaking to Roshi. She was glad he was in charge and not her.

"What about my meeting with Enji? He should be arriving any time—we're to meet at ten-thirty. And I have a lunch scheduled with Kosen's parents." Roshi stood up and took command of the room. "I will not keep them waiting."

"We'll let you know about lunch. But we can't let you see Enji yet. That will have to wait till the right time," Wolfe said.

Roshi gracefully listened. "Ah yes, till time is ready ... that is fine ... but I will dine with Kosen's parents. Unless you plan to arrest me. Is that what is going on here?"

"No Roshi," Alex said. "There's no plan like that. We just had to ask these questions. Thank you for being so forthright."

Wolfe did not like her butting in, but Alex didn't care.

She still didn't know what to think about Roshi's involvement in the goings-on, but she would continue to give him the benefit of the doubt until Enji and then hopefully Gigen showed up. Maybe then things would become clearer. Enji was due to arrive at any moment. *But where the hell is Gigen? And if he's not our perp then who the fuck is it?*

38

"Roshi's lying about something," Wolfe said. "I can feel it."

After Roshi left the library, Wolfe, Kluny, Hawkes and Alex were not much wiser and their collective frustration was palpable. Wolfe was grasping at straws.

"I don't know who he's protecting or if it has anything to do with present circumstances, but there's something he's not saying. And I don't like it."

"I agree," Kluny said, "but let's wait and see if we need to really grill him—we're all allowed a secret or two, and if it doesn't interfere with justice, what's the harm? I don't believe he's involved in killing people, then or now. Does anyone here think he is?"

Everyone answered in the negative, Wolfe reluctantly.

"Okay, so where does that put us?" Wolfe ran down the suspect list. "Tell me if you don't agree ... Lawrence, the cousin, I see as just a harmless, burned-out ex-hippie, whose only concern had been his cousin's welfare. I think he blamed himself for Robert's death—he called yesterday and was real weepy, said: 'I shoulda seen it coming, I failed him, I don't know what I'll tell his parents, they were counting on me.' He plans on being here for the lunch with Roshi, his aunt and uncle in tow. So he's not our guy."

Heads nodded around the room in agreement.

"And then there's Clark, who was my number one candidate after Zenji died, but I think he's just a mixed-up, angry guy who's up here trying to stay out of trouble." Again, everyone agreed. Alex could see that Wolfe was kicking himself for his obstinacy and getting stuck on Lawrence and the fingerless Clark—maybe why he broke into the pack of Marlboros yesterday.

"And the other monks and residents?" Alex just wanted to be sure that Jito, Muin and the rest of the sangha were also out of the land of suspicion.

"Living with these people this week, seeing how they live, think, carry on day-to-day, the devotion they have to Roshi, to the practice here, Kluny and I agree that none of them could've done anything like what's been done here," Wolfe said.

Alex breathed a sigh of relief.

"So that leaves this guy Enji, who'll be here momentarily. And this character Gigen. It's got to be one of them or both. If it's not, we're in deep shit.

"Kluny, you and Sullivan go greet Enji, bring him here. I've got some phone calls to make."

"Me, too," Hawkes said. "I'll catch up with you all later."

**

Alex, Kluny, Muin and Rich—Muin's assigned bodyguard (Muin thought this was unnecessary but couldn't find anyone with a badge to agree with him)—walked down to the parking area to await Enji's imminent arrival. When he did make his entrance, only Rokuju Ryan, his recent bride, accompanied him.

Enji's six-foot-four frame rose up out of his silver Honda and walked around to open the passenger door for his petite, five-foot-two wife. Alex knew by this gesture, by his obvious grace, and by her honed instinct that he was no killer. But they had to go through the motions of the dot-every-i-and-cross-every-t cop procedure. So they did.

"Are you Enji Patrick Ryan?" Kluny asked as he walked over to meet and greet their murder suspect, or Roshi's possible successor, or both.

"Yes sir, I am," Enji said, smiling broadly and extending his hand.

"I am Detective Tom Kluny." Kluny rebuffed the handshake. Alex noticed that Enji wasn't the slightest bit ruffled by this rejection.

"And you must be ..." Kluny looked at the beautiful bald woman who stood regally beside her monk husband, filling the difference in their heights with her graceful carriage.

"Rokuju Ryan, Enji's wife. Very nice to meet you." She offered her hand.

Kluny took it and smiled. He was drawn into their field of serenity despite himself.

Alex wasn't worried, she intuitively knew there was no threat there. Enji had an indescribable, *je ne sais quoi* aura about him that had her tongue-tied for thirty seconds—way too long for her liking.

"Hello Enji ... Rokuju." Alex put her palms together in front of her chest and bowed. Both Enji and Rokuju bowed back. "I'm Alex ... welcome ... Enji, you remember Muin ..."

"My god, Muin! How good to see you." He bowed and then rushed over to Muin and gave him a big hug. "How is Roshi with all that's happened up here? What a tragedy."

"He's fine, considering. It's good to see you too. But—"

Alex could see that Enji was horrified that two of his former students had been murdered. The sadness in his eyes was deep and authentic.

"Do you have any idea where Gigen is?" she asked.

"I've been thinking about this since I spoke to Detective Wolfe last night," Enji said, his eyes piercing hers. "Is this detective here?"

"He's waiting for you up in the library, I'll take you there," Kluny said.

"I have no idea where Gigen might be, I wish I knew ... I feel awful letting him out into the world when I knew something was wrong. But I couldn't help him, he wouldn't let me. If it turns out that he's the one killing people, I'll never forgive myself." Enji looked over at his wife, his entire body expressing remorse. It was clear that they had talked about this for many miles. His body also expressed love, concern and compassion. Alex didn't know quite how he did it, but she felt it.

She showed Enji the sketch. "Is this him?"

Enji put on his reading glasses to study the drawing. They made him even more handsome, something Alex didn't think possible. "I suppose it could be him, but he's not so full in the cheeks and his mouth is smaller—but there's a resemblance. He doesn't have long hair. The last I saw him he was shaved bald."

"Thanks."

"May I see Roshi now?"

"Sorry, but we have to postpone your reunion for a while," Kluny said.

"That's fine. I understand. Is there anything I can do?"

"Maybe, once we find Gigen. Officer Berg over there needs to go through your bags—sorry about that but it's a security precaution at this point."

"No problem."

"Then I'll take you up to see Detective Wolfe. After that, Berg here will be with you at all times until we can be sure that you're not a potential target."

"That's fine, that's fine. I just can't believe this." He shook his head and wrapped his arms around his wife. Clearly his days of drug use and womanizing were at an end. *Maybe he is ready to take his place alongside Setsu Roshi.*

Alex walked off and left them with Kluny and Berg. "Muin, come with me, I'll need you around when Gigen shows up."

Muin and his shadow, Rich, moved toward Alex. "How can you be so sure he'll be here?"

"I can't say really, but he will be here. Plus" —Alex winked and patted her gun—"I'll be able to protect you when he does get here."

"You're my hero. Did I ever tell you that? This week more than ever before," Muin said.

Alex swatted playfully at his arm. And then they began the wait, employing the non-action that they were practiced at but tired of at this point.

***

Roshi's lunch with Kosen's parents and his cousin Lawrence went off without a hitch, but the reunion with Enji was still on hold. Nothing of consequence happened the rest of the morning and by 2:00 P.M. more guests began to arrive. Most of the students had heard about the murders but never considered not showing up for Roshi. They took the police presence and the search of their cars, bags and persons in stride and offered to help however they could. No one suspicious resembling Gigen or the hardware customer appeared at the gate.

Muin had taken a break to help with Roshi's lunch guests. Alex was beginning to worry about Uncle Charlie and wondered what the hell he was doing all this time in town. She was determined to go find him if he didn't turn up soon. Just as she resolved to do this, he came driving up the road.

"Sorry I didn't call Alex, things got a little busy and you know how cell phones are in these parts and I wasn't near a landline." Uncle Charlie quickly walked toward Alex and wrapped his arms around her.

"I was about to go hunt you down," Alex said as she hugged him close.

"I know honey, I'm sorry."

"Don't ever do it again," Alex said with a laugh.

"I promise." Charlie laughed. "Any sign of our boy?"

"None."

"Enji?"

"Yeah, he arrived with wife in tow. Gut tells me he's not involved in the least. And whatever his problem was all those years ago, he seems to have become a model monk. Maybe it's wisdom they say comes with age."

"So, what now? We wait?"

"Yup, we wait. And I for one am getting pretty damn tired of that."

"Well, I'm going to head up to see Wolfe, try to make myself useful."

"Wolfe's got cops from all over the state up here, some being obvious, some blending in. Plenty of eyes and gunpower, so I don't think there'll be much for you to do at this point."

"Doesn't hurt to ask. Phone calls, maybe. Surely they didn't get through all those names yet."

Waste of time if you ask me. Alex bit her lip on that one.

"Think I'll go for a walk around the lake, see if I can spot Wolfe's sentries," Alex said as she hugged Charlie and kissed his cheek.

"Mind if I come along?" Guy asked, popping up behind Charlie's right shoulder. He smiled directly into Alex's face.

Her whole body shuddered at his sudden appearance and deep gaze. She moved quickly away from Uncle Charlie's embrace so he wouldn't feel her reaction.

Before Alex could respond, Charlie said, "That's a great idea, why don't you two do that and I'll see you both later." He turned, waved and started walking toward the monastery.

Alex felt like a teenager on her way to a prom, nervous and excited to be alone with her date. *He looks perfectly at ease, damn it.*

"Which way? Clockwise or counter?" Guy asked.

It took her a breath to get what he meant, but then said, "Counter, of course. Walking that way will get us close to Gigen's lair quicker. Or, whosever hideout that is in the woods, one the uniforms found. I'd like to check that out."

"Wolfe says it's off limits, he's got a couple guys nearby keeping an eye out, doesn't want to risk scaring away the perp if he decides to visit."

"You always obey the boss man?" Alex teased with a sideways glance and half smile.

"Unless I can be tempted otherwise." Guy didn't look at her, but she saw his smile lines light up.

"I'll come up with something by the time we get there." *I have to gather my wits here.*

They walked for a ways in silence until they approached the cop standing guard at the southeast curve of the lake, parked there to keep visitors from walking the lake path, a favorite activity of the monastery sangha, especially upon first arrival. It was practically a de rigueur ritual for all returning students.

Guy leaned into Alex, cupped his hand gently around her bicep and whispered, "I'll take care of this."

"Be my guest," Alex whispered back. Her arm was warm from his touch.

"Hey, Officer ... McNulty," Guy said, squinting to read his nametag. "I'm Special Agent Hawkes and this here is Detective Sullivan." He flashed his badge. "Wolfe wants us to go check out the guys guarding the perp's hideout, see what's going on, if they need anything."

"Sure thing," McNulty said as he moved aside to let them pass.

"Smooth," Alex said.

"Just part of the job," Guy said in mock seriousness. "They train us in smooth at the FBI."

"Your teacher would be proud."

The path quickly got too narrow and overgrown to walk side-by-side. Before he could suggest she go first, Alex said, "Why don't you lead?" *I'd rather look at his ass than have him looking at mine.*

"No problem. Took a course in that, too."

"I'll bet you did."

They walked to the sound of their footsteps and the lapping of the lake. A few voices from the other side floated over to them every so often. Normal life, normal mountain sounds, normal activity. Except they were all in a state of not-so-normal expectation. It felt to Alex as if the woods surrounding them were also in that state, on their side, the good guys' side, waiting, listening and ready for the evil one to arrive and be swiftly taken out of commission. *If only*.

Ten minutes later they were directly across from the monastery. They stopped and looked around.

"This place is quite beautiful," Guy said.

"Yeah, it is."

"You see any of Wolfe's guys yet?"

"No, you?"

"Nope, guess they're well trained in hiding behind trees."

Alex nodded. "Do you mind if I take a minute here before we move on?"

"No problem, I'll just go check out that gigantic Buddha over there. Just let me know when you're ready."

"Okay."

Alex did her turning-in-place ritual. By the end of it she turned her back to the lake and stared into the woods. Something was off. She felt it in every bone in her body. And it wasn't about Guy. She kept staring and inching slowly into the woods. She knew she should alert Guy, but didn't want to break her concentration. *He's a smart cop, he'll notice and follow me.*

She drew her gun and kept moving.

39

All Alex could hear as she made her way deeper into the woods was her own footsteps on the floor of dry leaves. She stopped to listen about two hundred yards in. Either Guy halted when she did or he wasn't following her. Or he was playing a game with her. *Doubt that, but fuck, where is he?*

All the usual noises prevailed. She stood still and held her breath. Let her gun arm drop to her side. *Okay, this is silly now. There's no one in here.*

Then she heard a soft moan coming from her left a short distance ahead of her. She couldn't see any movement, but as she made her way the moan got clearer. Someone was on the ground leaning against a tree. All she saw was a leg outstretched. She approached carefully.

"He went that way." An arm and finger pointed off to her right. She looked and saw an orange blur way off in the distance. *What the fuck? Why didn't I hear that?*

She checked on the body by the tree. One of Wolfe's men.

"Are you okay?"

"I'll be fine. The bastard jumped me. Was waiting up in a tree. Whacked me with a sharp blade of some sort. Go, before he gets away."

"You sure you're all right?"

"Yes, go! He's got my gun so be careful."

"I think there's someone coming up behind me. He'll be able to get you help."

Alex darted into the woods, praying that Guy wasn't far behind and that the officer down would be okay. Looked to be an awful lot of blood lost. Not caring how much sound she made now, she ran toward the orange blur she'd seen and hoped no one else was perched in a tree waiting to pounce.

***

Guy had waited the appropriate amount of time before he came out from behind the Buddha statue. He thought Alex was making a nature call in the woods and had been too polite to say so.

"Alex? Okay to come out now?"

No answer.

Even if there'd been a line of women waiting for the bathroom, as was usual for most places with lots of females, he'd given her plenty of time.

Guy looked up and down the path and didn't see her. Looked into the woods and didn't see her. She'd be easy to spot with that neon orange sweatshirt she had on. He dug into his pocket for his driving glasses. They weren't there, damn it.

"Alex? Where the hell are you? It's not funny anymore. Please make your presence known."

He had a bad feeling. He looked again into the woods and thought he saw orange. He made his way deeper in, gun drawn.

By the time he got to the injured officer, fashioned a tourniquet for his leg, and was off in search of Alex and whoever she was chasing, way too much time had passed. And he was pissed at Alex for taking off on her own without a word.

***

Alex continued to follow what now looked like an orange hat bobbing through the trees. She ditched her orange sweatshirt and shivered in her short-sleeve T-shirt. *Better cold than dead.*

Fast as this guy moves, whoever the hell it is, he's definitely at home in these woods, knows his way around. I wonder where the fuck he's taking me. I know he's got a gun and probably that saw he used on the cat and Zenji. Wonder what else he's got out here?

Not what she wanted to be thinking right now, but she was not in control of her thoughts, just of her body, and that would serve her well, that she could depend on. *I sure hope Guy is behind me.*

The trees were bare. It helped her see the perp's head with its neon orange hat. Despite this disadvantage he kept putting more and more distance between them. He knew the topography, no doubt about it. That was his advantage. She had a gun and experience chasing bad guys. That was hers.

She had to put a name to him. If it wasn't Gigen, she'd apologize if she ever met him. Gigen, had to be Gigen.

And his weakness was bound to be his deep and abiding anger—he would trip up, bad guys always did. She wouldn't take her eyes off his orange head—it was the only indication of his whereabouts—whatever he was wearing beneath his neck blended in with the trees, which were getting denser. She neither saw nor heard anyone behind her. She was making a ruckus and she was sure her prey was, too. *This place should be crawling with cops by now. Where the hell are they all? Someone that Wolfe had stationed out here has to be within earshot of one of us. Fuck!*

The ground was uneven, sloping, hard in spots, soft in others, rocky and rough going, but she dared not look down to secure her footing and risk losing the orange beacon. Her progress was slow, her feet kept sinking into ruts and dips and depressions. She picked up her pace, her eyes glued to the carrot top. She slipped into a ditch, turned her ankle. *Fuck!* She got up, kept going, the pain excruciating.

She hobbled along, her sprained ankle getting bigger by the second. She couldn't put much weight on it. The orange beam was still in front of her, then it stopped moving, then it was gone.

Her eyes focused on the tree she thought he'd slid behind and then they all looked alike. *Where the hell did he go?* She crept along, in her condition it was impossible not to make noise.

Behind her she heard rustling—someone was getting closer. Thank god for that. Waiting for them was not an option.

She inched closer, pushing through the pain, the throbbing in her right foot now just a minor distraction. Her focus was pure and directed at a four-foot-high structure that had been erected between two trees. A primitive man-made lean-to constructed from tree parts, large and small. One of Gigen's bases that Wolfe's guys hadn't found. She had to scope it out before presenting herself. *Damn foot.*

She slinked through the trees in an arc around the shelter to gain a view from the side. As soon as she caught a glimpse around the edge of this sorry refuge, she knew she didn't have to worry about making noise or being attacked.

It was Gigen, she was sure now. He sat there in full-lotus zazen, eyes closed, tools and paraphernalia all around him, a saw balanced across his knees. The officer's gun nowhere in sight. He had removed the hat, his freshly shaved head glowed white and shiny.

As Alex edged closer she could hear him chanting the heart sutra. She wondered what had happened inside his brain or his heart or wherever it was that held his essence, to turn this once-upon-a-time monk into a murderer and now, in this moment, back into a docile, meek man whom she was sure would offer no resistance to being captured.

She heard someone close behind her. She took a quick look, saw that it was Guy and turned her attention back to Gigen.

"You okay?" Guy breathed softly into her hair.

She nodded and stared straight ahead at Gigen.

"That him?"

She nodded again.

Guy was up like a flash and moving toward Gigen before Alex could warn him away. "It's time we brought this fucker in ..."

She knew this was a mistake. She had no time to protest. Her foot kept her on the ground.

It took about ten seconds, but it seemed to play out in front of her in slow motion. Guy approached Gigen, gun drawn. Gigen whipped the saw off his lap, wielded it like a sword to knock Guy's gun out of his hand and into the woods. Then he stood up and faced Guy, saw in one hand, gun in the other, pulsing with rage.

He sure stirred up that hornet's nest, damn it.

Alex crawled behind a tree. *Damn ankle, damn Guy charging in like a bull. Where the hell are the other cops?* Her only hope was that they were local and knew how to move without sound in the woods, maybe they were closer than she thought.

She knew how years of repressed anger in Gigen could combine with adrenaline in the moment to create unnatural strength and stupidity. *I won't be any help restraining this guy.* Together, she with a sprained ankle and Guy without his weapon, they were no match for Gigen. *I'm not in the mood for this goddamn it!*

"Gigen, I know you can hear me. It's over now," Alex said. "Agent Hawkes is not alone and there are others on the way. And I have a gun pointed at you, so don't try anything funny." She had her gun aimed at his heart. She could take him out easily. He couldn't see her, she was sure of that. Not yet. And she couldn't shoot him. It would be like shooting someone in the back.

She had to try talking him down first. She crawled into the open, her gun still perfectly aimed despite the blinding pain in her foot.

"Put the saw and gun down, Gigen. Do the smart thing and give up. There are cops all over these woods. You don't have a chance."

"Why the fuck are you down there? Why don't you get up and face the music?" Gigen shouted.

"I will if you put one of your weapons down."

Gigen kept the gun pointed at Guy and he held onto the saw like it was an extension of his arm.

"Gun's not loaded," Guy said.

"What the fuck are you talking about? Course it's loaded. Took it off that idiot calls himself a cop. What self-respecting cop would carry an unloaded gun while in search of a killer?" Gigen asked.

"Try it, you don't believe me," Guy said. He was betting that the safety was on and that Gigen didn't know the first thing about guns. He'd never get off a shot by the time he figured it out.

Alex tried to stand. Pain shot up through her leg. She thought she'd black out. It wouldn't hold her weight. She had to fake it. She stood on one foot.

"Okay, I'm up." Could he see his advantage? Could he smell her weakness? Could he hear her pain? Her gun was still pointed at his chest.

"Now, put the gun down."

"And what about your gun? I'm not stupid, don't think I'm stupid."

"On the contrary. I think you're one of the smartest killers I've ever known."

"Yeah?" Gigen said, glancing over at her, and keeping Guy in focus.

"Yeah. And a smart killer would know when it's time to give up."

"I'll never give up. Giving up is for losers."

"Who taught you that, your father?"

"Leave my father out of this."

"Enji then? Or Roshi?"

"Fuck them—both of them. They're two-faced liars."

"So, what now Gigen? What will you do? Where will you go?"

"I'll finish what I came here to do and I don't care what happens after that."

Alex moved ever so slowly forward. She could see that Guy was ready to pounce on Gigen when she gave the signal. She only hoped he wasn't bluffing about that gun in Gigen's hand.

Gigen turned his gun toward Alex and tried to shoot. Nothing happened. He threw the gun at Guy, hurled the saw into the air toward her. She ducked out of the way and fell to the ground. Gigen took off into the woods, Guy right behind him. She shouted for help. The woods around came alive with cops. They took off after Gigen and Guy.

As she waited for her police brethren to find and capture Gigen—she knew it would only be a matter of minutes—she sat as comfortably as she could and fell almost instantly into an alert meditative state, the pain in her foot an aid to concentration.

She listened to the sound of the woods. She heard a gunshot. *Damn, I fucking hate being sidelined.*

Soon after, Gigen came into view, in handcuffs surrounded by six cops. Guy trailed behind.

They stopped to check on Alex. Two of the cops lifted her up to help walk her back to the monastery. She hated not being in control.

Soon as Alex was upright and saw that Gigen was contained, she said, "What happened to you, Gigen? How could you kill people? Don't the vows you took mean anything?"

"What do you know? Are you one of Roshi's bitches? You think he's so pure? Well, he's not. He went back on his word—he needs to check his own vows."

"Who made you judge and jury?" Alex felt a bit ridiculous leaning on two men and trying to sound tough.

"It's not your business—it's dharma business," Gigen said. To his guards he said, "Let's get the hell out of here already."

Alex stalled them with a gentle hand gesture.

She turned to Gigen and said, "You'll get your chance real soon to talk to Roshi. And Enji."

"Enji? Enji's here?" This seemed to confuse him. "I'm warning you, stay out of this." Gigen tried to lift his hand, his face was red with rage. "Or else—"

"Or else what? You'll drug me, kill me, burn me like you did the others? Maybe cut my foot off?" she spat.

"Hand, you dope, it was a hand. You don't know a fucking thing."

"Tell me then, please, enlighten me."

"It's not worth my breath. Can't you guys control her?"

"Okay, let's go," Guy said, "Start walking and shut up. You said you understood your rights. Anything that comes out of your mouth now will be held against you, you got that? So you'd better just keep quiet and move."

"Oh, so, what then ... you're the new boyfriend? What happened to Muin?" Gigen said.

How the fuck does he know about that?

"Let's get this jerk out of here," Guy said to the cops holding on to Gigen.

The adrenaline that had been pumping through Alex seeped out of her body as they all made their way back to the monastery. She lagged way behind the group with Guy and Gigen, and could hear Gigen chatting away. She didn't even care anymore what he was saying. It was as if she'd been filled with air and someone had pin-pricked her. She was relieved that it was over, but exhaustion rushed in to take the place of the false energy. She felt like a crippled, deflated bag of bones by the time she got to her room.

40

"We're going to start recording you, if you don't be quiet," Guy said.

"Fine with me," Gigen replied. "You'll do whatever the fuck you want to do anyway, no matter what I say."

"You guys all heard that, right?" Slight nods from the other cops in the posse. Guy took out his phone and opened the recorder app. This wasn't the most ideal interrogation room, but if this guy wanted to utter these spontaneous remarks he might as well try to capture what he could. Wolfe would appreciate the help. Gigen's probably off his rocker and might not even be mentally fit to stand trial, but Guy figured what the hell. He pushed record.

"Do not kill, ha! What about, if you see the Buddha on the road, kill him? What about Roshi's vow to not kill? Promising Enji one thing and then reneging. What's that if not killing his chances to become dharma heir? I had a duty to set things right. And don't talk to me about karma. I'm not one of their ass-kissers anymore, willing to accept everything they say.

"If karma really means anything, then getting killed was their karma, I was only helping it along." It was plain to all those listening that Gigen had no remorse for his actions.

"I did what I had to do. They all deserved what they got," he rambled on.

They came to a narrow section of path where they had to walk single file. Gigen stopped talking till he knew he had an audience again. They were nearing the bottom of the lake where the path turned to the dirt road that curved and led up to the monastery.

"Kido's cabin's right up there," Gigen said, casting his eyes and chin to his left into the woods. "I found Kosen and Sonja there one night. Tried to talk sense into Kosen, get him on my side. He was ignorant, I had no choice but to get rid of him. He would have ratted on me. And Sonja was collateral damage. Girls always are, aren't they?

"Hey Officer, why aren't you back there with your girlfriend?" Gigen asked Guy. He looked over his shoulder to Alex and her human crutches, who were lagging way behind and out of earshot.

"Just keep moving and mind your own business," Guy said.

"That was Zenji's problem, stuck his nose where it didn't belong. I had to set things right. It was up to me to turn around everyone's upside-down-topsy-turvy-skewed-way-out-of-proportion point of view. I just wanted to get Roshi to listen to reason. I didn't plan all of this."

Gigen's voice was getting softer and softer and Guy wasn't sure his phone would pick it all up.

"All I wanted was to be back with Enji," Gigen was almost whispering now. He slowed his pace down and no one rushed him along. "To have Roshi make Enji his dharma heir, and go back to the way things were. Do you think that would ever be possible now?"

No one answered him.

As they approached the monastery, a cruiser sitting in front with door open ready for him, Wolfe and Kluny standing by, Gigen pointed up into the woods behind the large gong that sat up high on a small knoll. "You'll find all of Gigen's things up there a ways in black garbage bags."

Gigen was folded into the back seat of a cruiser that led the police caravan down the mountain.

Wolfe stopped and rolled down his window when he reached Alex.

"You hurt yourself?" Wolfe asked.

"Yeah, just a little sprained ankle. I'll be okay."

"Thanks for your help here, Detective."

"I would say anytime, but wouldn't really mean it."

"I get that."

"Hey Wolfe, what happened to that pack of cigarettes you been toting all week?"

"Crushed them, decided that's no way to die."

"Smart man." Alex smiled.

"Write to me," Wolfe said. "You know what I mean ... write down what happened out there, send it to me soon as you can."

"Will do. And I'll stop by to say hi whenever I head back to the city."

"Okey-dokey. See you then." Wolfe waved and sped off down the hill, trailed by Kluny, who blew her a kiss out his window.

***

Alex iced and then taped up her ankle—these ministrations had it feeling better and she was able to get around on her own. It wasn't quite as bad as she'd feared, but she wouldn't be running anytime soon. Now that Gigen was in the hands of the cops, she could get back to why she'd made this trip to the monastery in the first place. She'd extend her stay a few days to chill out, get serene and decide what to do with the rest of her life.

Jito came to her room with a snack tray and some top-shelf tea.

"You're a doll, this is heavenly, thank you, thank you," Alex said. "You look like you're dying to tell me something, Jito, what is it?" She laughed.

"Oh nothing, you're the patient here, I'll be fine," Jito said, pouring her tea and nervously arranging a napkin.

"Come on, spill it."

"Oh, okay, if you insist ... Roshi confronted me about the drugs."

"Oh yeah, the drugs, I almost forgot. What did he say?"

"He said I could stay, he'd give me another chance."

"That's fantastic."

"But only if I promise to attend an NA meeting in town, or AA since there aren't many NA meetings up here, at least once a week."

"How do you feel about that?"

"After all that's happened this week, I think I'm finally ready. I definitely don't want to leave here, so that's the deal. I'm a little relieved, to be honest about it."

"I'm glad."

"Well, if those twelve steps turn me into a moonie or something worse, you won't be so glad."

"Oh, don't be silly, the Jito we all know and love won't be changed by a little dose of sobriety."

"Let's hope you're right, dahling ... and now I've got to get back to the kitchen." He leaned over, kissed her cheek and said, "You're going to love what's cooking."

"Mmmm, I can't wait. Do me a favor, would you?"

Jito stood back up and towered over her. "If it's in my power, dahling, you know I'd do anything for you."

"This one's simple. Since I can't get around too good with this ankle, and dinner will be buffet-style I imagine?"

Jito nodded.

"Will you fix me a plate and bring it to my table so I won't have to make a fool of myself?"

"That's an easy one. Consider it done. And now I really do have to go." At the door, he bowed, waved his fingers, and said, "Toodles."

A minute later there was a soft knock on her door.

"Come on in," she yelled.

"Hi, you got a minute?" Muin said, poking his head in.

"As you can see, I'm not going anywhere at the moment. I've got all the time in the world now, especially for you."

He came in, gave her a kiss on the forehead and sat cross-legged on the floor. Alex was stretched out on her futon.

"I wish I had known how bad off Gigen was, maybe I could've done something. Maybe I could've prevented some of what happened. I feel awful."

"It's not your fault, you need to know that." Alex wanted to hold and comfort him. Her ankle and the tea tray on her legs kept her in place. *Probably a good thing.* Muin just stared at her.

"Do you think instead of putting him in jail they'll get him psychiatric help?"

"There's a good chance, especially if Roshi and Enji agree to testify."

"And what about us?"

"We probably won't have to get involved with his case unless we want to."

"That's not what I meant. What about us, you know, together ... as a couple ... you and me ..."

This she didn't expect. She was struck speechless for a few breaths. *Didn't we settle this just a few days ago? Maybe he's changed his mind?* She couldn't turn her mind around to the romance page just yet. There was no rush to get into it with him.

"Jeez ... I don't know if I can even think about that right now. I'll be staying a few more days. Can it wait? Can we talk about this another time?"

"Of course, another time." Muin got up and bent over to kiss her. She offered him her cheek. He kissed it gently, then turned and left without another word.

***

Uncle Charlie was spending the night in the room next to hers. When he checked up on her he said, "If you'd only told me how magically beautiful this place was I'd have visited years ago. Why'd you keep it such a secret?" As usual he made her laugh. They planned to hook up after dinner and chat the night away. She looked forward to that. His mere presence helped elevate her mood.

Dinner was planned for 6:30 so Alex had an hour to rest and ruminate alone in her room. She knew that the theory she'd presented at breakfast that morning about Gigen and his koans was pretty close to the truth, especially after what Muin had told her, but she also knew that it went deeper than all of that.

Gigen was clearly off his rocker, but what drove him were complex feelings toward, and relationships with, his criminal father Tommy, with Roshi, Enji, and the whole Zen community. He created his own reality when he was just a kid and confused all the father figures in his life with one another.

The image of his father and Roshi getting rid of what he thought was a bloody body bag was always with him. His father went to prison and Roshi went free, how could that seem fair to a little boy?

She knew it was devastating to lose a father at a young age. How much worse it would be if that father were lost in prison.

Something must have snapped in Gigen when Enji expelled him. So he came to Roshi's temple to settle the score, finally get revenge and justice. The blackmail was most likely another confused attempt to reconcile his world. He felt rejected by all of his father figures, and thought that if he could secure the dharma heir for Enji, he could resume his role as favorite son.

Alex felt sorry for him. Maybe the feeling was compassion.

"Compassion actually means 'to suffer with,'" Kido said. It freaked her out that he knew her every thought. She decided to be still and just listen, see what pearls of wisdom he'd offer her in the aftermath. *"Do you think you are capable of doing what Gigen did?"*

"Of course not."

"Well, until you can dig deep down into your heart and understand that he and you are not so separate as you think and that until you forgive him ..."

She waited. Kido was silent. "What? Tell me, please, go on. I need to hear this."

"I can see by your expression that you are not quite ready. But do not worry, when you are ready to hear it, I will be here to say it. Or better still, it will come from your own heart. Then it will be yours to keep. Practice more, suffer more, sit more, my dear Alex. That is what there is for me to say and for you to do right now. Take good care of yourself. Don't forget to sing." Kido faded out singing: *"Love is all there is, love is all there is, love is all there is ..."*

***

By 6:30 the monastery felt close to normal. All of the cops had gone for now, though a few would be back again in the morning to finish with evidence gathering. But for now it was quiet. The incense burning throughout the building set a calm tone, and everyone she ran into seemed especially tranquil.

'Monastery slayer in custody' added to the serene atmosphere. Everyone was breathing easier now that Gigen was off the mountain. Alex's gun was back in her closet, locked and secured, and she was glad to finally put it down and morph from cop to student.

She hopped her way down the corridor and was the first to arrive for dinner so she wouldn't have to ask for anyone's help in getting there. She arranged herself at one of the tables in the dining room, sitting on the floor with her leg stretched out in front of her and waited for the others. Being that it was an informal dinner, she could sit like this on the floor and at least appear to look like everyone else. But until her ankle healed, sitting meditation would have to be done in a chair. She hated the thought of that, and could hear Roshi saying, "It will be good for your ego."

With that in her mind, and cogitating on what might transpire during dinner—she knew Roshi would say a few words to his students—a swell of anger inside her that had been waiting for a reason to express itself overtook her, caught in her throat, and settled on Roshi.

41

The realization that she was pissed at Roshi struck her like a bolt of lightning. It was as if someone were behind her with the kesaku 'encouragement' stick, whacking at her shoulders: Wake up! Wake up!

What the hell happened all those years ago? Why did Roshi allow himself and his students to get involved in shady activities involving sex, drugs and money? What about this business of a successor? If it were so important to keep the lineage going, why hadn't he chosen someone? Why had he lied? What other secrets was he keeping?

With all this swimming in her head, feeding the anger in her stomach, she wasn't sure if she could continue as his student. For that matter, she wasn't even sure she wanted to sit through dinner with him in the same room. She could use the excuse of her foot to eat in her room. She was about to get up, when everyone but Roshi filed into the room. She stayed put. *Might as well see this through. Besides, I'm starving.*

Roshi came in, stood by his seat, put his palms together and bowed to the group. Everyone returned the bow. He looked like Buddha, an enigmatic smile at the corners of his mouth, his eyes full of life and glee. *How can he be so serene in the face of everything that's transpired?*

Maybe it is true, as he's so often said: "This is it. Now is the only thing there is. Be here for it. What other choice do you have?" Maybe she'd indulge her angry passion later. For now she decided to just sit there and let whatever was about to happen, happen.

Roshi looked around the room and made eye contact with everyone. They all sat without a word for what seemed like ten minutes, but was only two, according to the clock ticking on the wall behind Roshi.

"Before we eat, I'd like to say a few words about our dharma brother, Gigen. I'm sure many of you are angry and hurt about all that happened here this week. It will take time to heal from the trauma we've all been through. But we must not hate Gigen. He is a very confused and probably very ill young man. I am sorry I did not do more to help him. I am sorry I did not see how far he had strayed.

"Special Agent Hawkes over there told me that Gigen talked about karma, that it was Kosen, Zenji and Sonja's karma to be dead. This is not true. He is mixed up. He does not realize yet he had a choice to kill or not to kill. He broke the first vow in a very terrible manner. He will suffer for this. We will all suffer for this. That is his karma. And ours."

Roshi closed his eyes and paused.

Alex had seen many versions of Gigen over the years. All she ever cared about once they were arrested and charged was whether they'd spend enough time behind bars to satisfy the victims and their families that justice had been served.

In this case she felt a victim. Roshi was a victim. Muin and all his other students were victims. She didn't have a clue right now how she wanted Gigen to pay for what he did. Her experience couldn't help her. She paid close attention to Roshi. Despite her cloud of anger, she was struck by Roshi's composure and aura of compassion.

The soft, gentle way Roshi said Gigen's name carried love and forgiveness. When he started speaking again, his tone had settled deeper into its compassionate gear. "Is okay. Many Americans do not yet understand this karma thing. Is okay, do not worry. I will give explanation."

"Karmic law is not about reward and punishment—man's law will decide that about what Gigen has done—it is only that good creates good and bad causes bad. In Gigen's case, I want you to see how his hate caused him to behave with hate—killing people because of this hate. He created the hate, he is responsible. I hope he will soon come to see this. It is the only way to end it. Nothing can undo what he did, but he can change. And I will do everything in my power to help him.

"Karma is not fate, is not determinism. This is what so many think. What Gigen thought. But karma is only law of cause and effect. Every action—good or bad—creates result. So, with Gigen, his bad actions created bad results, results that cannot be undone.

"But in Enji's case, and his attachment to some bad ways, the karmic principle here is that he made his choices, he had to suffer the consequences, as Gigen will suffer the consequences of his actions. Enji understood this and does now. At any time he could have tried other path. One moment to the next moment all new and different. We can all change our karma anytime.

"Enji made his bed and slept in it. Now he is willing maybe to change the sheets. It seems so. We will have to see."

Roshi's words, his bearing, his huge capacity for compassion and forgiveness, captured the essence of this Zen monk. It held the secret of his charismatic pull and his deep understanding of some universal truth. Any doubts Alex had had about Roshi began to dissipate. As he spoke, she automatically straightened her spine. So did the rest of his students. He was no charlatan. He was the real thing. He was a true Zen Master.

As she watched and listened to Roshi she reflected on her own hatred. Ever since the day she had been robbed of her father when she was ten, a seed of hate had been planted. It was meant for her father's killer, but since she had no knowledge of who that was, the hate had festered and found other targets. It needed to be expressed and mostly it was directed back onto herself.

It had interfered with love and commitment to anyone or anything except her job, and, of course, Uncle Charlie. Now, under Roshi's roof, thinking of Gigen, someone she could choose to hate, she wasn't persuaded that releasing her anger onto him would expunge it from her heart. In fact, she knew this to be true. Yet there it sat still inside her. Love and compassion was the solution, but she hadn't a clue how to activate them.

As she listened to Roshi talk about karma and hate, she felt as if his words were meant especially for her. How different was she from Gigen? She hadn't killed three people, but even now she wanted to find and kill her father's murderer. She saw then how hate could lead to hateful acts, and that the only way to prevent them was simply not to engage in them.

Easier said than done, even if the Zen adage that Kido whispered in her ear, *"The occurrence of an evil thought is a malady, not to continue it is the remedy,"* boasted otherwise.

So, stop nurturing the hate and maybe it will go away? That I can try to do, because frankly, I'm tired of it.

She knew that both the *Tao te Ching* and the teachings of Buddhism say: "When there is no desire, all things are at peace."

Same with hatred she supposed, for what was that, really, except another way to express desire? All she really wanted was peace. She had a desire for that. If this teaching were true, she'd even have to let go of peace in order to get it. Little by little she was beginning to understand.

She was grateful to be reminded of this today. The anger she held in her belly that belonged to Roshi settled like chalk dust at her feet and blew out the open window.

She wasn't yet ready to forgive Gigen, or the person who took her father from her, but she might be ready to give up some of the hatred.

Roshi spoke more, but the essence of his message resided mostly in the long pauses when no one said a word and only the ticking of the clock penetrated the silence. This was where the healing began. By the end of Roshi's speech Alex could think of Gigen and of the lives he stole without having her heart clench. It was a beginning.

***

Dinner was informal and exquisitely delicious. Jito had outdone himself: Baked tofu with an orange glaze, beets and red onions simmered in herbs, kasha with garlic and mushrooms, broccoli, snow peas and zucchini sautéed with a light lemon and soy sauce. For dessert, apple crunch pie topped with creamy vanilla soy ice cream. Alex couldn't imagine how the feast that was planned for Buddha's birthday the next day could be any more delectable.

Informal meal or not, they chanted before anyone took their first bite. And then Roshi said a few more words, a sort of Zen prayer. He expressed gratitude for all the help from the law-enforcers, especially "Alex Sullivan, our very own dharma detective," and for the patience and resilience of all his students. Then they got down to the serious business of enjoying Jito's fare. They were all in elevated moods despite the grief they all shared.

Being around the same age as Roshi and "the uncle of their very special dharma detective," Roshi had invited Uncle Charlie to sit with him at his table. Enji too was there, back in Roshi's good graces, with his wife by his side. Alex kept glancing over at their table throughout the evening. Uncle Charlie was perfectly at ease, as if he'd been sitting on a floor, eating with chopsticks and hobnobbing with Zen Masters his whole life. Roshi was in rare form, she could see from across the room. He'd never looked so on a par with any dinner companion.

Alex wondered to whom powerful people like Roshi and Uncle Charlie went to ask advice and share personal confidences. Perhaps Roshi and Uncle Charlie had found in each other such a friend. Alex loved this idea, these two men being buddies. She lost her father at an early age, but gaining two Zen Masters as surrogate fathers somewhat mitigated that loss. Maybe this was her karma. With that thought she wondered what she'd done 'good' to create such a gift. All she knew was that she was one lucky girl.

The men who were sitting at her table with her confirmed it. Guy, Muin, and Jito (once he finished in the kitchen and after everyone else was served) for starters. Gyozan and Hoja, the two very funny Japanese monks, also joined them and kept them all laughing throughout the evening. Laughter that was much needed by everyone. And it kept her from having to decide who to pay most attention to, Guy or Muin. She put all romantic notions on the shelf for the evening and had a good time.

When everyone got up to get dessert, Muin offered to get some for Alex.

"That would be great, thanks," Alex said.

Guy waited for Muin to leave and then leaned over to whisper to Alex, "How about coming to my place for dinner tomorrow night? I'll cook you a meal and serve a dessert you'll never forget."

His breath on her neck gave her goose bumps. She hoped he didn't notice the shiver that shot through her and settled between her legs.

"Can I let you know tomorrow? Not sure yet about this ankle business and Uncle Charlie and—"

"How about I go ask Charlie if it's okay?" He started to get up.

Alex grabbed his arm. "Don't be silly. We don't have to get his permission. I was just—"

"I know, only kidding. You let me know tomorrow then, okay?"

"Okay."

"Great. And I probably won't take no for an answer, so keep that in mind." Guy stood up. "Can I get you a cup of tea?"

"Sure, that would be nice, thanks."

As he walked off she couldn't help but stare at his ass. And she didn't care who noticed.

42

Sunday, April 8, Buddha's Birthday, 7:00 AM

There was a late wake-up on Sunday with a buffet continental breakfast available at 8:00. A memorial service was planned for 9:00, followed by a formal ceremony and an informal feast, to celebrate Buddha's birthday.

Alex was in touch with a lingering melancholy, and on the yang side a buoyant bliss. She decided to follow Roshi's dictum and let the sadness just be sadness without trying to change it. With that came an understanding for the very first time how sadness and happiness were not mutually exclusive. She stretched lazily after her solid eight-hour slumber, sat up, hugged her knees to her chest, and, without wanting to, smiled.

These few moments gave her a chance to think about Guy's invitation to have dinner with him that night. She knew she would go and felt a bit giddy about it. She dreaded the talk she had to have with Muin, but quickly put that thought aside. Nothing was going to get in her way of finally having a little fun.

Meditation practice had taught her to become the detached observer of her own mind. Even in the midst of all her complex feelings during dinner last night that is what she had done. She saw the hate that rose up in her toward Roshi and then toward Gigen, and how this hate in her had nothing to do with them. It was just there. Perhaps the seed of it was planted when her father died, perhaps she'd been born with it.

It didn't matter. Because of it she understood Gigen's singleness of purpose, his need to punish and maybe even kill Roshi in order not to feel his deep feelings of loss and anger, his desire to quash whatever he did feel, and his need to redirect his emotions and funnel them into hateful acts.

She knew that nothing but time could assuage suffering and that everyone suffered with something. She also knew that in order to let time do its job, she had to express some love and compassion toward Gigen and people of his ilk. This was a tall order. She could try. Time and practice would help.

This effort might make her a better Zen student and maybe even a better person, it might even make her more open to romantic commitment, but what would it do to her as a cop? Maybe this lesson was the universe telling her it was time to move on to another livelihood. Maybe it was offering another way to be a cop. She didn't know. She didn't have to know anything this morning. She simply had to be.

KILLING SACRED

An Alex Sullivan Zen Mystery

Nancy O'Hara

Prologue

Albuquerque, Tuesday, September 11

Marco's back was on fire. It felt like he'd fallen asleep for hours under a hot sun and burned to blisters. He also wasn't helping himself by not covering his shaved skull and wearing a black shirt in the desert heat. But there was a job to finish, so he pushed away the pain-pleasure as his training clicked in. Having the horns and eyes etched into his back was a brazen flouting of the rules. He didn't care. After today they'd have no choice but to honor him and put him on the fast track to warrior.

Be prepared. It was the first vow. Still, he'd have to keep the tat his secret for now. Tattoo Jack had enough dough in his pocket to keep his trap shut, the almighty buck working better than trust or a man's word. The time was near for him to take his rightful place in the circle with all the others. He'd paid his dues, plus some.

One more stop and then dinner, a quick fuck if he was lucky, a few hours' shut-eye, then head north in the morning.

He strolled up to the front entrance of San Felipe Church, camera dangling from his neck, feigning tourist. The curved, flesh-toned adobe walls looked more like soft skin than hard clay. White wooden crosses jutted skyward from every large and small spire atop the rosy rooftop. The church was a tourist stop, so his visit would hardly be noticed. He'd just slip in and then back out with booty in hand. He'd scoped it out the day before, saving the easiest for last. Sort of like dessert, the main course tucked away in his backpack. He'd make them proud and then they could all move on to the Big Prize of Eternal Power.

"I'm sorry, sir," said the security guard with the baby face and belly spilling over his belt, blocking the doorway. "I'll have to search your bag or you can leave it with me while you're visiting."

Marco wondered where the hell rent-a-cop had come from as he tried to push past him. He hadn't been there yesterday.

"Sir, you cannot go in with that bag!"

"Since when?"

"Since now. Today is only 9/11! Duh! And I'm sure you've heard about the Spiritual Looters, quote-unquote, stealing valuable statues and such from churches. Well, steps are being taken and no one gets by me without getting searched."

This guy doesn't even have a gun. How pathetic. Don't make a scene. Don't make an impression. Don't be noticed. Vow number three: Be vigilant.

"No problem," he said, even though it was a big one, a major problem. "I'll just drop this off at home and come back. Whole life's in here you know, can't be leaving it lying around." He gave the guard his back and hugged his backpack to his chest.

"Sure thing," the guard said.

Damn, now I'll have to skip the booze and come back late. I'll need my wits. Fuck.

He walked across the street to the plaza, past the gazebo smack in the center and headed toward a bench on the far side that faced away from the church. It was the only unoccupied seat in the small park. As soon as he sat down he knew why. It was blistering hot. But he needed to sit and think about what to do without calling attention to himself, so he stayed put and endured the pain.

The final object of this self-assigned mission was in that church. He had to make a plan to get inside. Or did he? He had plenty enough already, but his heart was set on the small, golden statue of St. John. It would please the others.

Next time ... he could wait till next time. But here he was now. No waiting. No putting it off. He would get it—somehow he would.

But where to stash his bag? The other loot? No way could he leave it alone in a room with a flimsy lock. No way could he trust anyone to guard it. No way could he let rent-a-cop put his lazy bug eyes inside. So now what?

His warrior sixth sense was aroused. Told him he was being watched. He felt this same way when he was a teenager and his stepfather would creep around outside his room while he jerked off under the covers. But he did nothing wrong then or now, even if priests, cops and self-righteous assholes would say different. So why did he feel so dirty? Maybe it was just the sun beating down. He needed a shower. His back reminded him of his assignment. He drew his breath in and steeled himself against the pleasure of the pain. *Stay focused! Vow number four: Wake up.*

He would wait. It felt like a hundred eyes were boring into his back. He turned and saw no one.

Dark wasn't coming quickly enough. He needed shadow light to walk back into the church. Patience finally settled into his bones. The night was long. He would return to his room, shower, eat, meditate, maybe sleep a bit. Fortify and prepare himself. Engage his warrior training regimen. Now that he was on this thought train, his body felt grounded, his mind weightless. No regret that carnal pleasure had to be forsaken.

Walking back to the hotel, even with laser-sharp focus, he couldn't shake the feeling that he was being followed. He ducked and detoured his way back to his hotel, which was only two blocks north. The circuitous route took him to another small park, the Natural History Museum, and some shopping areas. The streets were hot, his back burned, he had no water, and he got all turned around. At one point he found himself in a residential neighborhood that made him very nervous. He was often the only one on foot and he got lost in a maze of private, earth-colored houses surrounded by high-desert flora. He wouldn't have looked more out of place if he'd been wearing his meditation robes. Finally, he found his way back to Mountain Road and got his bearings. He saw no one that seemed to be following him, but whatever had been lurking on the periphery of his energy field for the past hour was still there when his key released the lock to his hotel room and he reached inside for the light switch.

He was in. He was alone. He laughed off his paranoia. He convinced himself that he was all but invisible in this town. And he'd be gone before the morning sun woke another soul. The smell of him would remain only till his sheets were flapping clean in the wind, the desert breeze replacing any hint of him.

When he turned around to lock himself in, the door was thrust open into his face. It slammed him backward onto the musty, chenille bedspread and took with it all sense of relief and safety he had just breathed in.

Splayed on his back on top of his backpack he stared into the eyes of his enemy. How did he let this happen? He looked over at the second enemy by the door to assess the situation, all in half a heartbeat.

You?

No one, not even he, heard this last question of his life. The utterance of it was drowned in the crack of his neck breaking. Then he felt nothing. He did not have to suffer the shame of being robbed, of being off his warrior guard, of failing the cause. In fact, he suffered no more.

If he'd been able to watch from the edges when the police found him the next morning, he would have taken some satisfaction with him to his grave. There was no ID. There was no bag of sacred treasures. There was no one to mourn his death.

But he had no after-death insight.

He was just dead. John Doe dead.

About the Author

Nancy O'Hara is a meditation coach in real life who kills people in her fiction. She is the author of six books on the subject of mindfulness and meditation, including the bestselling ***Find a Quiet Corner***. Along with her writing, Nancy shares her experience through her Mindful Life Coaching practice, meditation classes, workshops, and retreats. This is her first work of fiction in the Alex Sullivan Zen Mystery series. She lives in New York City with her perfectly imperfect husband, trees outside her windows and noisy upstairs neighbors.

Connect with Nancy online at www.nancyohara.com

www.ingramcontent.com/pod-product-compliance
Lightning Source LLC
Chambersburg PA
CBHW030402180626
46812CB00005B/1900